Don't Pretend I'm Yours

NATASHA ANDERS

Also By Natasha Anders

The Unwanted Series

The Unwanted Wife

A Husband's Regret

His Unlikely Lover

Alpha Men Series

The Wingman

The Best Man

The Wrong Man

The Broken Pieces Duet

More Than Anything

Nothing But This

(Un)professionally Yours Series

The Best Next Thing

Protect Me Not

Standalones

A Ruthless Proposition

All I'll Ever Need

Fornever Yours

This is a work of fiction. Names, places, characters and incidents are either the product of the author's imagination or are used fictitiously, and any resemblance to any actual persons, living or dead, organizations, events or locales is entirely coincidental.

Editor – Tamsyn Bester

Formatting – Ashleigh Giannoccaro

Cover Design – The Dirty Tease

Cover Image – Xram Ragde/Marx Edgar Chavez

ONE

I give you this ring...

Benjamin Templeton had always dreaded the inevitability of his wedding day to Lilah Beckett. He'd hoped to somehow delay it, even avoid it. But here it was—sooner than he'd anticipated—his own personal doomsday.

There he stood, wearing the most ridiculous clothing, tails and a cravat—Ben had balked at the suggestion of a matching top hat —hands clasped in front of him, watching the woman who would soon be his wife make her way down the aisle toward him.

She was moving excruciatingly slowly, keeping pace with the eighty-two-year-old man beside her. It gave Ben ample time to turn tail and run for the hills.

"Last chance to do a runner, mate," his best man, Rhys Harper, leaned toward him and said in a low voice. The words were joking but there was an undertone of seriousness to them. Rhys knew exactly how loath Ben was to do this.

He didn't want to marry this woman. God, he didn't want to marry anyone. He liked his life. Enjoyed his freedom. And—the worst of it? — Lilah was not his type. He'd never been the slightest bit interested in her. But he'd always known that one day he'd have to bite the bullet and marry her and attempt to make some kind of passable life with this bit of fluff who didn't appear to have serious thought in her head.

So why the fuck are you marrying her, Ben? his dickish inner voice asked with a sneer and Ben sighed quietly, his eyes drifting to the old man beside his soon-to-be bride. He had legitimate reasons for doing this.

The best reasons.

But he honestly hadn't expected Lilah to get so caught up in the wedding planning. And now this… this… *ballgown*. Jesus, she looked like a little girl playing dress up.

Honestly, he didn't know why he'd expected anything else. The woman was twenty-seven but right now she reminded him of the twelve-year-old he'd first met more than a decade and a half ago. The girl with braces and pigtails, in a catholic girl's school uniform that had lost an inch in the hemline every year as she matured.

Ben had been seventeen when Cyrus Beckett had first brought him to live with them and Lilah had obviously had a crush on him, which he'd done his damnedest to discourage.

He'd been so certain, when they started this engagement thing, that Lilah had outgrown her infatuation with him. She'd certainly given the appearance of maturity. Even-tempered, usually affable, she was as sweet and bland as rice pudding. He was sure they had an understanding. They both knew why they were doing this.

But then she'd started planning this thrice damned wedding. So much fucking secrecy and coyness around the wedding dress. It had been ridiculous. He'd expected… well, he wasn't sure what he had expected but this cupcake-shaped gown—with a strapless lace bodice and massive poofy tulle skirt—was certainly not it. The dress had likely cost an obscene amount of money—with Lilah flying from Cape Town to London for the final fitting—but Cyrus, Ben's mentor and Lilah's grandfather, would deny his precious granddaughter nothing.

She was wearing a long veil and he could barely see her face. It was an antiquated custom, this veil wearing business. It had been the one detail of her bridal attire that Lilah had shown him upfront. She'd been excited to wear it. Some sentimental drivel about it being her mother's veil. Now, watching her painstaking progress down the aisle, Ben felt like he was watching an innocent lamb being led to the slaughter.

And he was the damned butcher.

They *finally* reached his side and her grandfather lifted her veil to plant a kiss on her cheek. She was smiling. That ridiculous, wide, happy smile of hers.

Typical.

Ben had never felt further from smiling than he did at this moment, but his bride-to-be was grinning mistily up at her grandfather who'd bent down to whisper something in her ear. She nodded, blinking back tears, and the smile—which had slipped ever so slightly—widened again when she met Ben's gaze. There was something shining in her eyes that made him uncomfortable and he felt his brows lower.

Cyrus shook his hand.

"Take care of my girl, Ben," the old man said on a note of affectionate warning.

"You know I will, Cyrus," Ben promised with a curt nod. His mentor beamed approvingly, before lifting Lilah's hand and placing it in Ben's grip.

He shuffled over to the—thankfully close—family pew, but Ben barely noticed. He was too focused on the small, slender hand he now had clasped in his own. He hadn't touched Lilah much in the past. The obligatory kisses in front of Cyrus, an occasional hand to her back, but rarely skin-to-skin contact like this. He was surprised by how fragile her hand felt in his. How vulnerable that made her seem.

He ran a troubled gaze over her face. She looked too fucking happy. He wasn't sure why. They'd both put up an appearance of happiness for Cyrus, but—despite those dumb drama classes she'd taken, during her late teen emo self-expressive phase—he hadn't thought she was this good an actress.

The officiant was speaking. Her tone warm and indulgent and grating. Ben figured he'd better tune the fuck in before he missed something. He now wished he'd taken Rhys up on that offer for some hard liquor this morning while they'd been dressing. It would have taken the edge off.

"Lilah and Benjamin have opted to write their own vows." The officiant nodded at Ben, who still held Lilah's left hand in his right. The hand that looked way too small and delicate in his larger, rougher palm.

Fuck! The vows.

For some reason, Lilah had insisted they write their own vows. He couldn't for the life of him figure out why she wanted it so badly, but when Cyrus—whom they'd been having lunch when she'd suggested it—had nodded approvingly and said that it sounded like a wonderful idea, it had been hard to refuse. Ben wanted to keep the old man happy. She did too. And this was something that would make him happy.

Ben had thrown together something last night at the hotel bar. He'd typed it in the Notes app on his phone, memorized it, and called it a day. Now he struggled to recall how it started and he was tempted to tug his phone out of his breast pocket to…

Shit, had he switched off his phone for this? He thought he had. But he couldn't be sure. He expected a call from Tokyo later, but what if they called early? It would be bad form to—

"Ben?" the officiant prompted. "Nervous? I get it, public speaking can be daunting."

The guests tittered politely from the pews and Ben forced a smile, knowing it wouldn't do to level his infamous face-melting glare on the woman. She was just doing her job.

"Uh, no, I…" He bared his teeth in another semblance of a smile again and cleared his throat. "I'm good."

The officiant gestured toward Lilah with a smile. "Whenever you're ready."

"Right."

Lilah was watching him expectantly. Her cute-as-a-button dimples flashing as she smiled up at him. His grip on her hand tightened slightly. Shit, he honestly couldn't believe they were really going through with this.

He inhaled deeply before speaking.

"Lilah Iris Beckett, the course of my life forever altered when I first met you." Yeah, that was an honest enough start. Ben knew that he'd always been heading to this moment like a train hurtling toward a concrete wall. He heard her soft sigh and the sound was so dreamy it gave him pause for a second. Her smile never wavered, but her eyes were doing that weird melty thing they did when she saw puppies.

He was too distracted. It wasn't like him. This was just another task. He could do it.

He continued, "I, Benjamin Elijah Templeton, take you, Lilah, as my wife. I promise that you will never want for anything. I will care for you to the best of my ability. I will honor you and remain faithful and true to you throughout our marriage."

Did her smile fade just the slightest bit? Some of the sparkle seemed to leave her eyes, and—mercifully—she no longer had that swoony expression on face.

He glanced over at Rhys who handed over the ring. A diamond encrusted platinum hoop that looked ridiculously small in Ben's grasp.

"Lilah, I offer this ring to you as a token of my respect and my commitment to this marriage. With this ring I marry you and pledge to live a life entwined with yours." He slid the beautiful slim diamond encrusted wedding band into place behind the perfect diamond solitaire that he'd put on her finger two months ago.

He looked down at the top of Lilah's downcast head as she splayed her fingers and stared at the rings. When she lifted her head, he inhaled sharply at the tears he saw gleaming in her pretty amber eyes. For a second, he thought maybe she was regretting this as much as he was. But he couldn't be certain.

The officiant prompted Lilah into beginning her vows and she smiled up at Ben through the tears gleaming in her eyes. She didn't look sad, so he wasn't sure what the tears meant.

Until she spoke.

"Benjamin Elijah Templeton, I have loved you from the very first moment I saw you. You are—and always have been—the owner of my heart."

Jesus Christ!

What the fuck? This was *not* the plan. Ben felt immediately ambushed. Why was she talking about love? This was not about love and she knew it!

Surely this was part of the act? It had to be. She couldn't be serious. But he didn't think she was the type of person who would lie in her vows. He'd expected the same generic bullshit he had spewed. Every word he'd uttered had been the God's honest truth. But none of his vows had contained sentimental lies about loving and cherishing and whatever the hell else it was that people said at these things. Sure, it hadn't been romantic but it had been honest.

But this... what the hell was this? He felt his jaw drop. He had absolutely no control over it. He knew his mouth was gaping but there was nothing he could do to disguise his utter shock at her opening lines. She was beaming up at him again. That joyful smile, her eyes alight with happiness.

She started speaking again, and he braced himself for another body blow. And he was right to do so because...

"I vow to love you every day, in sickness and in health, with my every breath till the end of my days. I promise to honor and cherish you. And I will remain faithful to you for as long as we both shall live."

Damn it.

She was supposed to be over this. She was supposed to have outgrown it. She'd had boyfriends since her ill-advised crush on Ben so many years ago. She was no longer the innocent little girl he'd known back then. She was a grown woman and she knew the stakes.

He felt trapped. Like he had been conned. Love didn't factor into this arrangement. It shouldn't. Why the hell would she do this? He was punch drunk, confused, resentful.

This was not what he wanted. Not what he'd signed up for.

Lilah lifted his left hand and her maid of honor—her best friend Blake Landry—handed her a ring. Which she slid onto his left ring finger. A brushed platinum band, similar to hers but broader, with a strip of black diamonds running down the center. The diamond points gleamed in the warm light spilling in through the stained-glass windows of the Beckett family chapel.

"Ben, I give you this ring as a symbol of my absolute love and trust. With it, I pledge to be your loving wife and accept you as my beloved husband from this day forward into all of eternity and beyond."

Ben couldn't remember any other time when he'd felt this incandescent with rage. He tried his damnedest to keep a lid on all of that negative emotion. But he could barely think straight he was so fucking furious right now. She met his eyes, that soft loving smile still lingering in those amber depths, and he stared back intently, unable to hide his absolute fury from her.

Finally, *finally*, he saw reality intrude into the deluded depths of whatever fucking fantasy she had spun around this marriage. Her smile flickered, the light in her eyes faded… and she looked bewildered. Uncertain. Even a little fearful.

Good, he thought, with a curl of his lip. *Fear me, little girl! I am* not *your knight in shining armor.*

The woman seemed have been operating under some massive misapprehension about this marriage. He wasn't doing this for her. He barely even liked her.

This was for someone to whom Ben owed his life. It was the only way Ben knew how

to repay that debt.

The officiant spoke, bringing Ben crashing back to their present reality. The one in which he'd just married this woman he did not love, whom he would *never* love.

"Lilah and Benjamin, I now pronounce you man and wife. You may kiss."

TWO

Six Months Ago

"So did this one break your heart?"

The question startled Lilah out of her contemplation of the glass of *Vilafonté, Series C 2014* cabernet sauvignon she'd been nursing throughout dinner.

It had been Gramps, Lilah, and the ubiquitous Benjamin Templeton as usual for dinner tonight. She couldn't remember the last "family" dinner they'd had without Ben present. She wouldn't have been surprised to find that he'd moved in during her much-needed three-month hiatus in Paris. Gramps already considered him family—the grandson he'd never had—and he would love to have Ben living at the family estate. The old man had frequently said that Ben—like Lilah—could have his very own wing.

"What did you say?" Lilah asked, suddenly becoming aware of the fact that Gramps had left the table without her noticing. It was just Ben and Lilah seated at the massive dining table. Thankfully, Gramps had long ago dispensed with formal seating and she and Ben were sitting directly across from each other. Gramps usually sat at the head of the table with Ben directly on his right and Lilah on his left.

"I asked if this one broke your heart," Ben repeated. He set aside his fork and lifted his napkin to his mouth.

So refined.

What Ben had known about table etiquette, when she'd first met him fifteen years ago, wouldn't even have filled one side of that napkin.

"Nobody broke my heart."

Except you.

"You randomly closed up shop on your precious little photo business thing—nice work if you can get it, right?—and fucked off to Paris. Where you paid for your lover's vacation and he repaid you by dumping you to run off some a cute French mademoiselle." How very like Ben to remind Lilah of that still fresh humiliation with an easy shrug of his broad shoulders.

"I left *him*." Only after she'd caught the snake in bed with the aforementioned *mademoiselle*. "We were together for less than a month. And he wasn't..."

"Wasn't what?" His eyes narrowed on her face intently.

"I wasn't in love with him. Where did Gramps go?"

"Seriously?" His expression was incredulous. "You nodded when he said he was tired and going to bed."

"Oh, yeah." She vaguely recalled Gramps pressing a kiss to her cheek. She was doing this too often. Zoning out, barely aware of what was going on around her. Her new prescription for her chronic asthma was making her spacey. She felt confused, anxious, and found it hard to concentrate for too long. This weird fugue state was new though. She really needed to see her allergist about it soon.

"You okay?"

"I'm fine." She didn't elaborate, having learned long ago that Ben wasn't interested in her *drama* — as he'd once called it.

"So, if you're really not nursing a broken heart…" Why was he still on about that? "Then I think we should go out."

"Go out where?" she asked, drawing a total blank.

"Together. Us. On a date."

"What? Why?"

"You know why, Lilah."

She did?

"I'm not sure I do."

"Cyrus."

"Gramps? You want to go out with me because of Gramps? Why would I do that? Why would *you*?"

He gave her a hard, searching stare before saying, "This was inevitable, Lilah. It works. We work. And you know we're out of time and out of options now."

"But I didn't think you liked me enough to want to spend time with me."

"My feelings for you are… complicated." He shifted, looking uncomfortable. She'd never seen him this discomfited before and stared at him in fascination.

"Complicated? How?"

"You're full of questions today," he said irritably.

"Because I'm confused. I don't know where this is coming from."

"Of course you do," he snapped. "Stop being so disingenuous. I think we should go out."

"I don't agree."

"What will make this happen? A grand confession of love? Is that what you want?"

Wait, what?

Why was he talking about love? What was going on here?

He looked so *tormented*. That was the only word she could think of to describe the range of emotions that flickered across his austere face in such rapid succession.

The one thing she knew about Ben was that he didn't handle strong emotions very well. She'd realized that a few years ago when Gramps had had a mild heart attack. Ben had closed up, gone silent. He'd looked so grim and emotionless; a casual observer would have thought he felt nothing.

Lilah might have thought the same, if she hadn't later discovered him sitting in the hospital chapel, head bowed, clearly praying. She'd left before he'd known she was there, reluctant to intrude on a private moment, while also understanding that Ben would lash out if he knew that she'd been witness to his vulnerability.

Still, seeing his stark fear and concern had made her feel less alone. Even though he'd never shown her even a glimmer of that same emotion. He'd remained closed off, but his strength and his commanding presence had been a comfort to her.

"What if I *want* a grand confession of love?" she asked, tilting her head consideringly, watching him closely.

"You wouldn't get one. It's just a date. Not even the most idealistic romantic expects claims of love *before* a first date."

"This isn't even remotely romantic, though," she pointed out, finally taking a sip of her wine.

"I don't do romance. You know that."

She did know that. Watching his interactions with the opposite sex over the years had been like watching a National Geographic wildlife documentary.

And now the alpha male sees the female he wants, he doesn't hesitate. His courtship ritual is brutal and brief. He easily dispenses with the compe-

tition, winning the female's attention and favor. She is interested and presents herself to him for mating. Their union is perfunctory. He dominates the submissive and meek female and then, satisfied, he moves on, searching for the next potential mate.

This was probably as romantic as it got for a man like Ben.

"I'm not one of your fuck-and-flee floozies, Ben."

He blanched at her words, looking both horrified and nauseated by her words.

"*Jesus*, Lilah. Firstly, that's a reprehensible turn of phrase and such language doesn't suit you."

"Alliteration, though," she inserted with a grin but he wasn't amused at all.

He continued as if she hadn't interrupted. "*Also*, it's insulting to my former female companions, all of whom were *accomplished*, independent, and strong women who knew exactly what the stakes were."

"My point stands," she maintained, even though she hadn't liked his emphasis on the word 'accomplished'. He made no secret of the fact that he thought her career was frivolous.

To a rigid, type A personality like Ben, any creatively oriented career like photography was on par with pissing your life down the toilet. Unless you were in a boardroom, curing cancer, or litigating multi-million-dollar law suits, you were a slacker.

And he definitely thought Lilah was a slacker. Never mind that she'd built a respectable, lucrative business as a highly sought-after and in-demand pet photographer. So *in-demand* that she'd run herself ragged over the last few years trying to accommodate too many clients in too little time, leaving no room for rest. After a few too many stress-related mild asthma attacks last year, her doctor had urged her to take a break, warning her that her health was taking a knock and her condition—

currently stable—could worsen if she didn't rethink her business model.

Ben would never understand how someone could spread themselves too thin taking "silly little dog pictures" as he'd once called it. Which was the reason she hadn't told him *why* she was taking that three-month break. She knew he'd thought the absolute worst of her just upping and leaving like that, as was evidenced by his mocking comments earlier, but she'd desperately needed the break.

"Look, you're obviously different from my previous companions," he said, in that annoyingly reasonable tone of voice. She barely refrained from rolling her eyes at his choice of word for his former lovers.

Companions... please. As if any of them had been around long enough to provide any kind of companionship.

"How am I different?"

"Because I have to be serious about you. About cultivating a relationship between us. It can't be casual."

"Ben, you don't need to *cultivate* anything with me. There is no doubt that you're going to be Gramps's successor at Beckett Maritime Express."

"It's not about that. Come on, Lilah. I know it's a shock but you can't walk around feigning ignorance like this. It's not healthy. You've been sitting here like someone in a daze all evening. I know this all must have come as a shock. It hit me like a ton of bricks as well. And I don't admit that easily. The only way forward for us is to at least try this. See where it leads us."

She shook her head.

She felt foggy, unsure. Her medication dulling her senses and her instincts. But she wasn't sure what Ben was confessing here.

Was he saying that he had feelings for her? That those feelings had hit him like a ton of bricks?

Her own, long dormant emotions for this man bubbled to the surface. Emotions that she thought she had—if not overcome—successfully suppressed. What if there truly was a chance that they could finally find a way to each other?

It was true, this conversation was confusing and not very romantic. But why not agree to go out with him? Just to see where it would lead?

"Fine. One date, Ben. Just one."

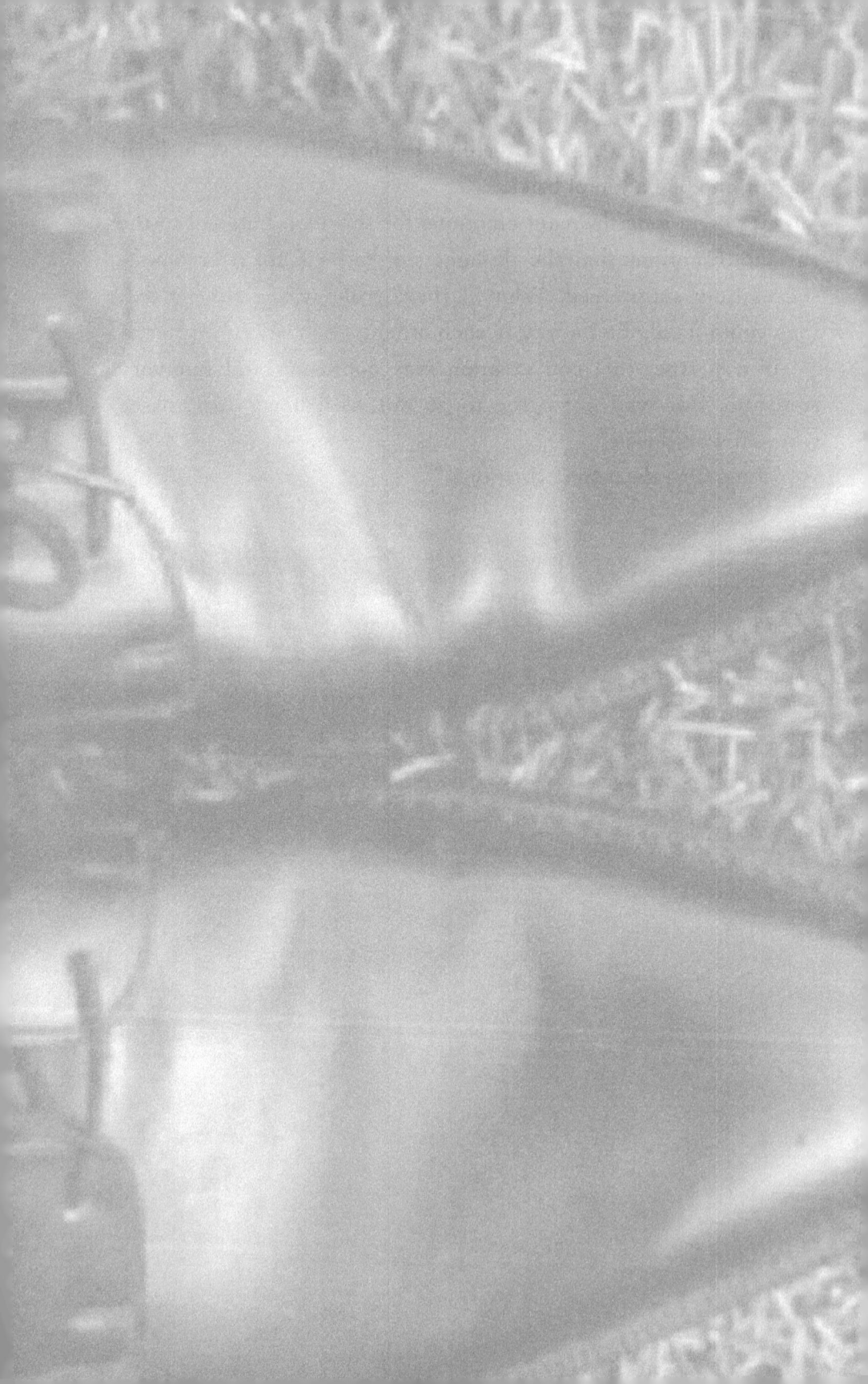

THREE

The Groom's Cold Kiss

L ilah tensed when her brand-new husband—upon the instruction of the beaming officiant—bent his head to kiss her. She'd been dreaming about this moment for so long, it was hard to fathom that all of her naive hope for a happily ever after, had come crashing down around her feet in mere seconds.

He didn't love her. How could he love her when his eyes were filled with such loathing and animosity? He despised her and he resented every moment of this. And up until just a minute ago—when he'd stared at her as if she were a two-headed venomous snake—Lilah hadn't even known it.

How could she have been so stupid? So blinded by her rose-colored glasses that she hadn't seen this for what it was? For what it had always been? Yet another way for Benjamin Templeton to ingratiate himself to Cyrus Beckett. Ben didn't love her, but he loved and admired her grandfather. He would do anything for the old man. And now Lilah wondered if her grandfather had orchestrated this union.

Her eyes flickered to the happily smiling man in the front pew. He was wiping tears from his eyes and was clearly unconcerned that Ben had just been blindsided by Lilah's admission of love. Her grandfather loved her. And he loved Ben. This was a dream come true for him.

Why hadn't Lilah realized this sooner? How could she ever have believed that Ben loved her?

Because you wanted him to. Because he's all you've wanted for years.

Ben's hard, unrelenting mouth pressed against hers, and she gasped. Hating how clinical the gesture was. How utterly lacking in passion.

He didn't love her and—humiliatingly—this frigid kiss made it clear that he didn't even want her.

Yes, he had blown hot and cold during the entirety of their short engagement, but she'd thought it was because he respected her grandfather too much to sleep with Lilah before the wedding.

Oh, God, she was such an idiot. If Ben Templeton wanted a woman, he wouldn't be deterred by old-fashioned values. She knew that, but her ego wouldn't let her see it.

Of course he wants you, she'd often appeased herself after yet another "date" night without so much as a brush of his fingers against hers. *He just respects you and Gramps too much to act on his desire.*

His hand closed around her elbow and she jolted back to the present. She pasted a sickly smile on her face as people applauded while they walked hand-in-hand down the aisle. Well, Ben walked, Lilah half-stumbled in his wake, remaining upright thanks only to the firm grip he had on her arm.

Guests had lined up outside, armed with tiny bottles of suds, and there was a flotilla of shiny bubbles to greet them as they exited the chapel. Ben kept his head down, barreling toward the waiting white limo, while Lilah managed a dazed smile for the clapping and cheering crowd. Not wanting any of them, especially her grandfather, to realize anything was amiss.

It soon became clear that he had no intention of stopping until they reached the car, and Lilah was forced to dig her heels in. She finally created enough drag to bring his unrelenting forward momentum to a stop, causing him to whip around and level a fierce glare at her.

"Th-they're expecting pictures," she managed to croak out despite her dry throat.

"The very last thing I want to do is stand here pretending to be happy," Ben said, the low growl meant only for her ears.

The words served as brutal confirmation of everything that she'd merely suspected before.

"Ben..." she whispered. She hated the whining note of pleading she heard in her voice, but—while she wasn't in any mood to stand here forcing smiles for the camera—she also wanted to delay the inevitable conversation they were bound to have the second they were alone.

Ben's eyes scanned the crowd, before coming to a halt.

"*Fuck.*"

Following his line of sight, Lilah spotted her grandfather at the top of the stairs, looking a bit confused as he watched them.

"Fine, but only a few. I want to get this farce over with as quickly as possible."

Farce.

The word hit her hard. That's what he thought this was. All along, while Lilah had been planning every special detail of a wedding to the man whom she had adored for more than half of her life, he'd thought of it as nothing but a farce. An absurdity to be endured.

Why?

Surely this couldn't be what Gramps wanted for her? Surely, he couldn't have coerced Ben into this?

"A little eager to get her all to yourself are you, Ben?" someone from the crowd called. The laughter that followed was ribald and more comments in a similar vein were bandied about.

Lilah could barely force a smile for the cajoling photographer, and when she snuck a peek up at Ben, his face remained expressionless. Jaw rigid, eyes burning.

The photographer was trying to convince Ben to swing Lilah up into his arms, while her husband — it gave her a jolt to think of him as such — glared at the man. It was the first emotion she had seen from him since she had spoken her vows nearly half an hour ago.

"*Enough,*" he snapped through tightly clenched teeth. "We're leaving."

More teasing from the crowd, but Ben barely seemed to notice. Instead he grabbed Lilah's arm in the same tight hold as before. He pushed through the crowd — making his way to the car — while impatiently swatting at the bubbles floating all around them.

The driver had the door open and waiting. It would be a twenty-minute drive from the chapel — which was built on the expansive grounds of their home in the affluent suburb of Constantia, located in the heart of the Cape Winelands of South Africa — to the hotel where they were having the reception. The prospect of that drive now felt like torture to Lilah, who longed to dash across the grounds toward her home, where she could lock herself in her bedroom, and hide from this man who confused and frightened her with his inexplicable fury.

Ben ushered Lilah into the spacious back seat, before sliding in beside her. Her organza and tulle skirt took on a life of its own, filling the space, seemingly everywhere at once. It wrapped around Ben's long legs, despite the distance between them.

As soon as the driver shut the door, Ben pushed the button to raise the privacy screen. Lilah immediately felt claustrophobic, hating how silent the car had become. The interior of the Rolls Royce Phantom was completely soundproof and they couldn't hear the crowd outside at all anymore.

Ben was staring at Lilah, making her feel like an insect pinned on a display board.

"Drink?" he asked abruptly and Lilah jumped at his voice.

"No, thank you."

He made a noncommittal sound. She loved his voice. It was a deep and velvety rasp, more suited to a rock singer who had been belting out epic ballads for twenty years, while subsisting on a diet of straight whiskey and cigarettes. It wasn't the voice one expected the future CEO of the fourth largest shipping company on the planet to possess.

She watched as he poured a couple of fingers of brandy into a crystal tumbler and tossed it back. He grimaced as he swallowed, but all too soon the tumbler was empty and Lilah was once again the focus of all that formidable attention.

"So what the fuck was all that about?"

Right.

"I'm not sure what you mean," she hedged and he levelled an unimpressed glare on her.

"It was part of the act, right?" he prompted and she swallowed painfully.

What act?

"Yes?" She didn't want him to know she had no idea what the hell he was talking about. But sensed that it was an out. A way to save face. A way to get out of this conversation with her dignity intact.

He looked relieved, even though something in his eyes, something behind those layers of impassivity and disinterest, told her that he didn't believe her uncertain response at all.

"I don't want Cyrus to know this is fake. And I know you wouldn't want that either. It would upset him. So far, I think we've done a pretty decent job of convincing him that this is a legitimate union. He thinks we want this. That we love—" *Did he have to sneer the word?* "—each other. We're in this for the long haul. Clear?"

As mud.

She inclined her head—not wanting to commit with words—when she had no idea what was going on. But it did now seem clear that at least Gramps wasn't a part of this deception.

"Lilah," he prompted, impatience layered through the two syllables of her name. "Are we clear?"

"Explain it to me one more time?" she asked, barely able to raise her voice above a whisper.

The look he gave her was filled with active dislike, mixed in with a massive dose of contempt. It ripped her breath away and left her reeling.

"You're playing dangerous games, little Lilah. I'm not amused."

Who *was* this man? How could she ever have thought he loved her? Perhaps the warning signs had been there all along?

Only Lilah had been too stupid and too naïve to see it.

But she was seeing it now. The veil had been ripped from her eyes—metaphorically and literally—and she now understood that she had walked straight into a spider's web with no way out. She was trapped and helpless and unsure of how she got here.

"You don't love me," he informed her, leaning toward her almost threateningly. "*Do* you, Lilah?"

"Ben…"

"Oh *come* on," he interrupted her with an impatient slash of his hand. "This is bullshit and you know it. Tell me why *you* think we're doing this."

Lilah blinked, not sure how to reply to that. Not knowing what to say to make this better. Only knowing that admitting to loving him would make it far, far worse.

"I think…" she floundered beneath the weight of that icy, brooding gaze and blurted out the first thing that came to mind. "The-the… board?"

His mouth tightened and, if anything, that remote gaze went even more frigid.

But once the words had escaped her lips, they made so much sense and she picked them up from where they'd landed heavily in the space between her and Ben, and ran with them.

"Gramps seemed to be pushing for it. I assumed it had something to do with the business. That maybe you both needed the family connection to make your succession to CEO more palatable for shareholders and board members." She had no clue if any of what she'd just said was at all plausible. She barely paid attention when Ben and her grandfather were discussing business, but her words had sounded convincing to her. It seemed like that could be a thing.

His brow lowered and he was pale and—if anything—he looked even more terrifyingly grim. Had they discussed this? Lilah couldn't recall. Before changing her asthma medication back to the old prescription, she'd had several scary dissociative episodes, which she'd kept from Gramps and Ben—they could be stiflingly over-protective at times. She'd had entire conversations with people she couldn't quite recall afterwards. Maybe Ben had spoken to her about his real reason for wanting to marry her during one of those?

She was grasping at straws here. They'd discussed no such thing, but she'd just married this man and she needed to give him some benefit of the doubt. Even though she knew that whatever relationship she'd hoped for with him as her husband was now doomed.

"The board," he repeated flatly. He broke eye contact and his gaze flickered to the passing scenery, which he stared at for a long moment, his jaw tight, mouth still drawn into a thin line, before he nodded abruptly.

"Okay." His voice was even raspier than usual and he sounded as though he were humoring her rather than agreeing with her. "The board. But if that's true then what the fuck was the song and dance about at the wedding? With the love stuff?" he asked with a formidable frown.

"Well, I assumed we had to make the whole thing look convincing, right? Since most of the senior board members were there."

"So... you don't love me? That was all bullshit?"

"Yes." *Dear God, please don't strike me down where I sit.*

He didn't look convinced but he seemed keen to believe her. She could see the moment he decided to take her at her word. The tension seeped from his body in increments, until the only remnant of it left was in his white-knuckled grip on the glass. Then even that hold relaxed. He gave her a long, *long* look but she could see the relief edge into his wary gaze.

When he spoke again it was to issue a grim warning in an unemotional voice.

"Lilah, let's be crystal clear about this... I don't love you, okay? Hell, I barely even *like* you. I will never love you. Since I *had* to marry at some point, I thought why not marry you if it'll make Cyrus happy?" He paused before continuing between gritted teeth. "And it makes good business sense. We can play happy families. Maybe have a kid or two. It can be a good life. But I don't want you going into this thing believing a lie. If we both understand each other, I don't see why we can't make this work."

He didn't want her to *go into this thing believing a lie*? She was already *in* this thing.

"And Gramps doesn't know why you married me?"

His nostrils flared and he poured another drink. The delay tactic was revealing.

"No."

Lilah wasn't sure she believed him. "Are you lying to me?"

"I'm not. Cyrus doesn't have a clue. And even if he suspects something isn't quite right, he'll convince himself that it's fine. Because he wants this. He's always wanted this. So we'll damned well pretend we're madly in love if we have to. For his sake."

"So... in your mind, this is a permanent arrangement?"

"Yes, of course." He looked surprised that she would ask.

How absolutely horrifying. To be trapped in a union with a man who'd just claimed he would never love her. With a man she'd once believed cared for her. Someone she had thought she loved, but now realized she'd never really known.

Such a prospect was untenable. Impossible.

And it was not at all what Lilah wanted.

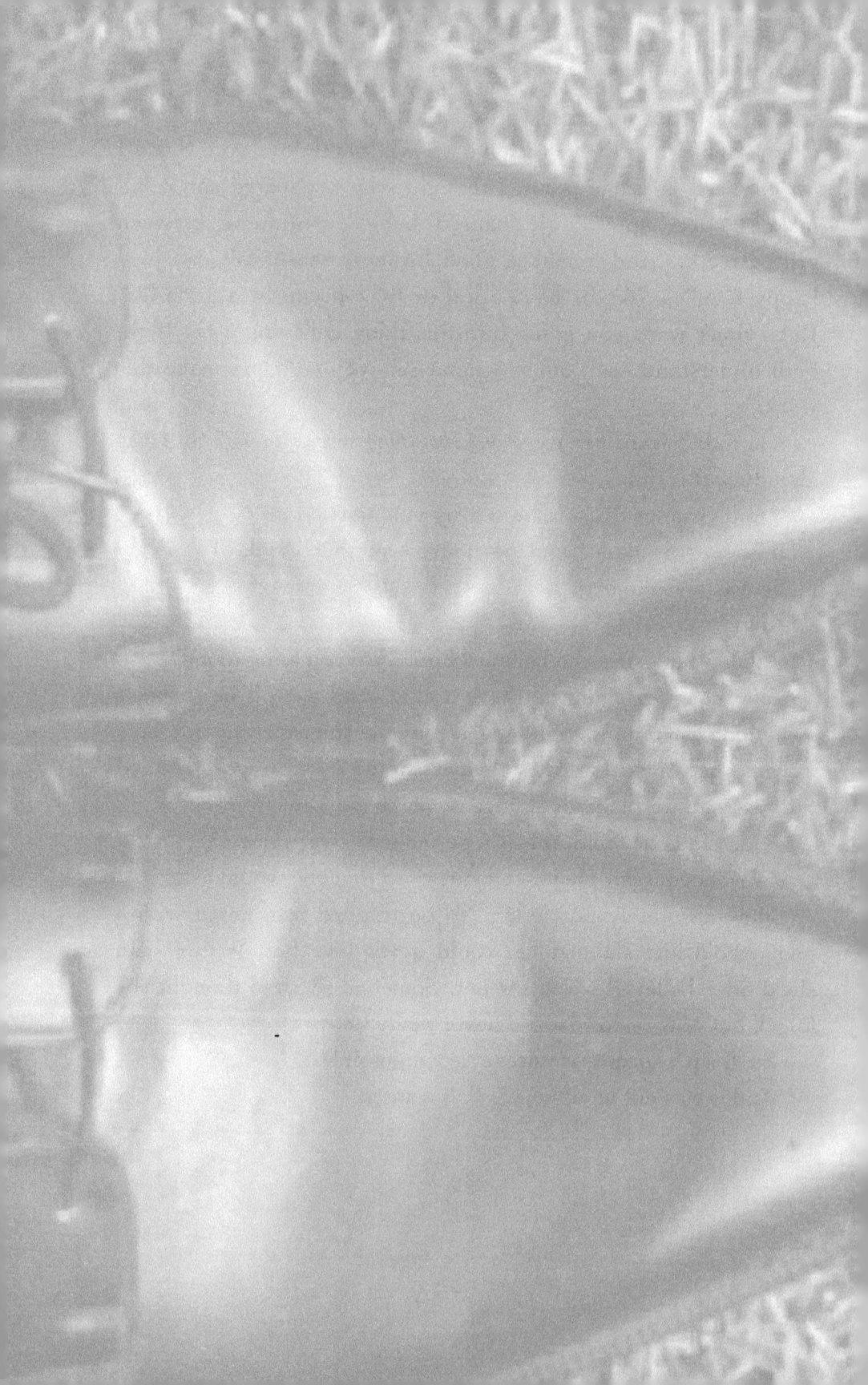

FOUR

Four Months Ago

One date had become two, then three, at which point Lilah had stopped counting, tentatively hopeful that this thing blooming between them was real, and not just a bizarre whim on Ben's part.

"I don't want you to see other men anymore," Ben informed her one night, while they were out to dinner at a trendy restaurant on Camp's Bay beachfront. He'd surprised her with the venue. Lilah had made a passing comment about wanting to eat here when he'd driven past it on the way home from one of their dates a few weeks back. Getting a reservation at the swanky eatery was nearly impossible on short notice and Lilah had never been one to use her name or her grandfather's influence to get what she wanted.

It had been an idle remark, and the conversation had moved on to something else after that. She certainly hadn't been hinting at anything, or wanting Ben to arrange an evening at the restaurant, so she'd been genuinely delighted and surprised when he'd brought her here this evening.

Now, on their dessert course, after an evening of the usual idle chitchat—he dropped this bombshell on her.

She choked on her wine and, after a brief but violent coughing fit, stared at him in stunned silence.

He had that usual furrow on his handsome brow, making him look pissed off. He always looked mad about something, but Lilah had long ago learned that it was his resting brood face. She knew how much it terrified his minions at the office, but it did not frighten her.

He used this default expression to keep people at bay, usually to devastating effect. Back when she'd first met him, the expression had terrified her. And his silence had unnerved her. Lilah didn't enjoy being around such reticent people, but Ben had been the one exception to that rule. She'd often gravitated to his quiet company, content just to be with him, even if it meant not speaking for hours at a time.

During Lilah's years at the private all-girls Catholic school, and later at college, her protective grandfather had always preferred to have her driven to the massive, gleaming Beckett Maritime Express company headquarters on the Foreshore in Cape Town after school. Before Ben had started working for him, Lilah had often chosen hidden corners in empty offices, or random storage closets in which to study.

But when seventeen-year-old Ben had come seemingly from out of nowhere to start living with them—first finishing high school in Cape Town before starting college and interning at the company under Gramps's mentorship—Lilah had shadowed him everywhere. After graduating from college Ben quickly worked his way up the ranks to marketing executive, VP of transportation, and higher still to the youngest ever vice chair on the board. All while studying for his MBA.

He'd already moved out of the house by then but Lilah had literally trailed after him like a lost little puppy. First, because she'd had a ridiculous schoolgirl crush on him, and later because she'd never been more at peace, or more focused, than when she was around him. Instead of seeking out those hidden corners, she'd been happy to sit with Ben.

Initially he'd tried to deter her but she had persisted, until one day—when she was about fifteen—she'd ventured into his small office to find a tiny desk set up in the corner. He had glowered at her when she'd paused in the doorway and pointed to the desk with a curt *sit there and shut up. I have work to do.*

Lilah had been even more smitten. After that, for the next seven years until she finished college, as his star rose and he shot up the corporate ladder, he'd always had a desk set up for her in every new—bigger—office he was moved to.

"What did you just say?" Lilah now asked after controlling the coughing with water, quite certain she'd misheard his previous remark.

His only attempt at helping her during her coughing fit had been to hand her the glass of water, after which he'd sat back to wait.

"We should be exclusive. We've fucked around with this pretense long enough, don't you think?"

"What pretense?"

"This play dating. It's time for us to just get to the point. We're running out of time. I want this, you want this... so let's just get it over and done with, okay?"

"Ben, we've been on roughly ten dates... and I'm being generous in calling them dates. We eat and exchange very little meaningful conversation. We haven't even kissed…" It embarrassed her to bring that up. Ben shied away from her every attempt to be close to him. In fact, she'd intended to tell him tonight that she wouldn't be seeing him anymore. A girl could only take so much rejection. She had her pride and she was sick of constantly trying to make the first move with barely any encouragement from him. He must think she was thirsty as hell and gagging for his attention. Okay, maybe he'd be mostly right, but long-standing crush or not, she was over it, and ready to finally give up.

She glared at him, happy to be airing this. "So what exactly do you want from me?"

"I'm trying to treat you with respect, Lilah. I want you to know that this will be different from my past relationships and that I'm serious about making it work."

"Where is this leading?"

"We're getting married."

She gaped at him, her mouth opening and closing without a sound emerging. Eventually, she managed to squeak out the briefest of questions, "We are?"

"You know we are. What the fuck do you think this has all been about?"

Lilah had no words. None at all. How did marriage fit into this? If anything, these dates had proved how totally incompatible they were. She'd known it for a while now. But she'd still jumped at the chance to go out with him. She'd felt like she owed it to herself—after so many years of one-sided mooning over the man —to see if maybe there could be something there. Some spark between them that could bloom into something deeper. And while Lilah had felt that tug of attraction, she was almost certain it was one-sided.

It had always been one-sided.

So *this* was unexpected.

And confusing.

"Ben, do you have feelings for me?"

He stared at her, eyes burning with frustration that didn't make it to his annoyingly expressionless face.

His mouth thinned. Those beautiful, sensuous lips pressed close together, while his nostrils flared.

Finally some emotion. Even if it was only exasperation.

He flagged their waitress, and the young woman—who'd been swooning over him all evening—came tripping over with a bright smile.

"I'd like the bill."

"Please," Lilah tacked on weakly, with a conciliatory smile at the woman to make up for his rudeness.

"I don't fucking need you to speak for me," Ben growled at her after the woman had left.

"Well, maybe if you weren't such a rude prick to the poor girl, I wouldn't have to," Lilah retorted, keeping her voice mild, even while her heart raced in her chest. She wasn't sure what was happening here. But Ben had certainly been triggered by her quiet question.

They didn't exchange another word until he stopped his sleek metallic gray Jaguar F-Type in front of Lilah's private entrance to the family home in Constantia. Once there, he turned in his seat to stare at her.

Well... no. He wasn't staring, he was glaring. And Lilah threw her eyes heavenward. Sometimes, Ben could be so needlessly dramatic. She'd asked him a fair question and he—

Oh.

He hooked his palm around the back of her neck and tugged

her toward him without a word, and within seconds his lips were on hers. She made a muffled sound of surprise, but it faded into a quiet sigh when Ben's mouth tasted hers in soft, nibbling kisses that made her knees turn to mush and her stomach melt into a pool of hot liquid. The kiss intensified, heated, and that liquid warmth seeped into her bones, her blood, and finally pooled heavily at the juncture of her thighs. She opened her mouth and he didn't wait for a second invitation, his tongue boldly swooping in to lick, explore, taste, and tantalize…

His palms cradled her face, their only other point of contact, thumbs leisurely stroking the sensitive skin next to her lips.

Lilah made a soft sound of acquiescence beneath that hard, relentless mouth and her own hands came up to cover his. As soon as she touched him, he stiffened and withdrew. First mentally, then physically. Hands retreating, lips lifting, and then he shifted his body until he was staring out of the windscreen into the cold, wet night.

His chest heaved as he strove to gain control of his breathing, and only once he managed to regulate that, did he attempt to speak.

"You're an attractive woman, Lilah," he said, his voice rough but level. "Most men would want you."

Still giddy, and not thinking clearly, Lilah lifted a wondering hand to her lips, unable to believe what had just happened.

"I had no idea you felt this way."

"Is this what you need to hear?" He practically sneered the question and she recoiled at the anger she heard in his voice. "To make the prospect of a life with me more palatable? Despite everything at stake, you want to play these games?"

Games?

Hazy, and a little confused, Lilah blinked up at him uncertainly. It was too dark in the car to see him clearly, but his head was turned toward her and he was staring at her.

He sighed, seeming to see something in *her* expression that answered his question.

He reached over to stroke her jaw tenderly.

"If it helps, I can tell you I care about what happens to you, Lilah." His voice throbbed with tenderness and stole the last of her breath. "Hell, what if I told you I loved you? I could even do that. If it's what you need to hear."

He loved her?

Lilah's heart stuttered in her chest, before restarting with renewed vigor. As if all she had ever needed was to hear those words from this man. Yes, this was the weirdest courtship—for lack of a better word—ever. But this was Ben, and Ben had never been one to do things the conventional way.

"And you want to marry me?" she asked, her voice whisper soft.

"I *have* to marry you. Stop doing this, for fuck's sake. Stop pretending. You have to face reality at some point. And I don't…" His voice floundered and for once he seemed as confused as Lilah often felt around him. "Look, I know Cyrus likes to treat you with kid gloves because of your asthma. And, *Jesus*, I'm trying to be patient and trying to give you that same consideration… but I'm concerned about you, okay? This isn't… it can't be healthy."

"You don't have to be concerned about me," she told him quietly, inserting as much dignity as she could into her voice. Is this why he had been behaving so strangely? Had Gramps warned him to go slow because of her asthma? Was Ben afraid of overwhelming her and triggering an attack?

Suddenly it all made so much sense. How he'd kept her at a distance, the formality in the way he treated her and spoke with her… his reluctance to respond to even her most blatant attempts to instigate more intimacy between them.

Oh, God, how could she have been so blind?

"Ben, I've faced reality, as you put it, a long time ago." Another frown from him as he stared at her intently, not removing his gaze from her face for even an instant, while she spoke. "I can cope. I *have* been coping. I don't need you or Gramps to pussyfoot around me. It is what it is… and I'm making do in my own way."

He mulled over her words, looking somewhat relieved, and nodded.

"*When* you ask me to marry you," Lilah continued and then glared at him when he raised a brow. "I said *when* and I meant it… whatever that was earlier, it wasn't a proposal. It was a statement of intent, sure, but not a proposal."

His lips twitched and he nodded, looking a little more relaxed now.

"As I was saying, when you ask me to marry you, I probably won't succumb to shock and start gasping for breath and die on the spot." He looked a little wild-eyed and queasy at the notion and Lilah grinned wickedly, before emphasizing, "*Probably*…"

"That's not funny at all, Lilah! It raises a concern I've never really considered before. About —*uh*— intimacy and your asthma."

She laughed and shook her head. "Don't worry, Ben, experience has taught me that my lungs can withstand the occasional kiss… and so much *more*." Her grin widened when his expression darkened at the last two words.

Was he *jealous*? How thrilling.

"If we're doing this thing, Ben, we're going to do it right."

"Kisses only for now," he ground out from between clenched teeth.

"I solemnly swear not to jump your bones," she said, pressing one hand over her heart and holding the other up. She fought back her laughter at his disgruntled expression. She felt stupidly lighthearted now that she knew Ben *did* want her but was probably keeping his desire in check out of respect for her grandfather. She felt lighthearted and daring enough to poke this adorable stuffy bear of a man.

"And I also," she continued, "reserve the right to ask you whatever personal questions I want to about your past."

"You can ask."

She could totally hear the unspoken *but I won't answer*, in his tone of voice. But decided that it would do for now.

She continued to grin broadly at him and was gratified when she received the tiniest of smiles in return.

FIVE

The Wedding Reception

"Jesus, what a fucking dog and pony show," Ben muttered when the DJ announced their arrival into the extravagantly decorated ballroom at the five-star Mount Nelson hotel in Cape Town an hour later.

They'd spent the last hour fake smiling for wedding photos in the beautiful hotel gardens, with the pale pink walls of the grand old building as a backdrop, while their waiting guests had been served light refreshments in the conservatory. Lilah had hired the best photographer for the wedding photos and Stefano Giannini had bullied her and Ben into smiling, touching, hugging, even kissing...

It had been painful to pretend, when all Lilah had wanted to do was escape, tear off this wedding dress, and process what she'd learned in the last few hours.

Blake, her best friend, had sensed that something was off, and had tried to catch Lilah's gaze a few times. But Lilah had diverted her friend's attempts at communication, and focused instead on smiling, smiling, *smiling*…

Even Ben's usually remote and moody best man, Rhys, looked concerned, but refrained from saying anything. Luckily, the bridal party was small, and Lilah didn't have to contend with any other worried glances. Gramps had stood for a couple of pictures, looking proud as punch as he'd posed between them. And then a picture with only Lilah. Followed by one with Ben, who had no family. Gramps had always been like a grandfather to Ben.

Lilah's world had tilted on its axis. The man she'd believed she loved above all else had lied to her and betrayed her in a most unforgivable way.

No… that was wrong.

Her vision blurred as she forced herself to acknowledge that Ben hadn't lied to her.

Not once.

He hadn't even told her he loved her. She had *chosen* to interpret his words as such. He had mentioned love once only and *that* had been as a hypothetical. He'd never said the word again, but Lilah had foolishly believed that it was because Ben wasn't one to wear his heart on his sleeve. That an aloof man like Ben wouldn't find it very easy to say words like *I love you*.

And she'd hugged the memory of that one time close to her heart, telling herself it was all she needed.

This pain was her own doing. She'd been blind to the obvious truth and the veil had been ripped from her eyes just moments too late.

Now, as smiling friends and colleagues surrounded them, Lilah felt like she was swathed in masses of cotton wool. She could barely breathe and she automatically clutched for her inhaler, only to remember that she'd opted not to carry one today.

So stupid. She knew better than this. Regardless of what she expected, she should always carry her damned inhaler. Or at least have given it to Blake to carry for her.

But she'd been anticipating a happy, stress-free day surrounded by loved ones.

This reality was the exact opposite of that expectation. Her loved ones felt like strangers to her and Lilah had never felt more lonely or more grief-stricken.

The pain was immeasurable. And like Ben, Lilah wanted this farce of a wedding over with.

His sharp blue eyes had narrowed on her. Ben never missed anything and he'd seen her hand flail uselessly toward a non-existent pocket. His grip on her arm tightened and he lowered his head to ear.

"What's wrong?" The urgency in the question belied the calmness in his expression.

"Noth—" She heard the high-pitched wheeze in her chest when she attempted to speak and his gaze sharpened.

"Where's your inhaler?"

She shook her head mutely and his brow lowered in concern. The first time she'd seen an emotion, other than indifference or impatience, on his face all day.

"You don't have one?"

Another panicked head shake from her and he swore beneath his breath.

"It's okay, it's alright," he murmured, his voice calm and soothing. "Breathe, Lilah."

He'd turned fully toward her, his bulk shielding her from their guests.

"Ca... can't."

Her chest had closed up and her throat was swelling shut, her eyes watered as panic set in.

He quickly lifted her into his arms and elbowed his way through the now concerned and silent crowd.

"I've got you, you're okay."

She was so *not* okay, and despite her fear, she found herself annoyed with him for saying that she was.

She didn't know where he was taking her, but could hear the panic in her grandfather's voice as he asked what was wrong.

Ben ignored the old man and eventually dropped Lilah on a padded chair, before he squatted in front of her and gently smoothed her hair from her face. He lifted an inhaler to her lips and she clutched at it urgently—not sure where it had come from, but grateful that it was there. When one metered dose didn't immediately work for her, she followed it up with another, which thankfully did the trick. Her head dropped and he cupped her jaw in his palms, lifting her chin to maintain eye contact, while he continued to quietly urge her to breathe and assuring her that she was okay.

When the fear and discomfort receded, she stiffened and sat upright, pulling her face away from his tender touch.

"Where'd you find the inhaler?" she croaked.

"In my pocket," he said, shocking the hell out of her. He wavered for a second, seeming on the verge of saying something else, before clearing his throat uncomfortably and pushing himself to his full six foot even height. He stared down at her while she nervously tucked the wavy strands of her hair behind her ears, hating how uncomfortable she felt in his presence.

"Why?" she finally asked, raising her eyes to meet his. He looked discomfited. His shoulders shifted and he raked a hand through his thick, dark hair.

"Just in case."

"Just in case? In case of what? Why?"

"In case of this."

She flushed and fidgeted with the inhaler, twirling it aimlessly between thumb and forefinger. Did he do that often? Pocket one of her inhalers "just in case"? And how the hell did he have access to any of her spares in the first place?

She had so many questions, but no real desire to ask them in that moment. She was exhausted, her brain too sluggish to even attempt to grapple with the question.

"I just thought today would be fun and stress free." She left it at that.

"Weddings are notoriously stressful," he said awkwardly, avoiding her eyes.

"They are," Lilah agreed. Especially when you discovered that your groom didn't love you and barely liked you. "I should have ensured I had an inhaler close by. I don't know what I was thinking."

"Lilah... earlier. In the car. I was a little harsh. The shock of your vows stripped me of my filter. I shouldn't have said that thing about not liking you. It was needlessly harsh. I—*uh*—I apologize."

Lilah didn't respond. Frankly, a little shocked he had apologized. Before this she didn't think she'd ever heard anything close to an apology cross Benjamin Templeton's lips. It was a little disconcerting. He was always so certain of his absolute rightness in any given situation.

"Where are we?" she asked, glancing around the small room for the first time since he'd brought her in here.

"Not sure, it was empty, private, had a chair, and was close to the ballroom."

"I think it's a changing room."

"Whatever," he dismissed, his eyes boring holes into hers. "Are you feeling better?"

"Much. Thank you."

"Look, Lilah, I know this has all been a lot. But we're in this together, okay? A team of sorts."

She almost laughed at that. Ben Templeton was not a team player. Never had been. Everything he did was solitary. He was an extremely active man. He ran, kayaked, swam, occasionally climbed, and cycled. While those were not necessarily solitary pursuits, he preferred to do them alone. Rhys Harper was his only real friend… and the only thing the two men appeared to have in common was a love of fly fishing and tennis. They occasionally went on fishing camping trips together, and Lilah had often wondered if they spent their days just grunting at each other, drinking beer, and rhapsodizing over the size of the last trout each had caught.

Now Ben, the quintessential loner, was telling her that they would be a team. Going into this marriage, Lilah had fondly imagined that it would be her and her loving husband against the world. The ultimate team. A union forged in love and mutual respect. Now it would be a mockery of everything she'd hoped it could be.

A team based on lies and deception. The two of them lying to Gramps in particular and the world in general.

She swallowed down a sob, and blinked the blur of tears from her eyes.

"We should be getting back. Gramps will be concerned."

She pushed to her feet, and he steadied her with a gentle hand to her elbow when she wobbled slightly. She instinctively shrank from his touch and he immediately withdrew his hand. But his eyes were still laden with concern.

"Don't you usually need rest after an attack? Are you sure you're up for this?"

"Do I have any other choice?"

His silence spoke volumes.

"Well, then, lead the way… husband."

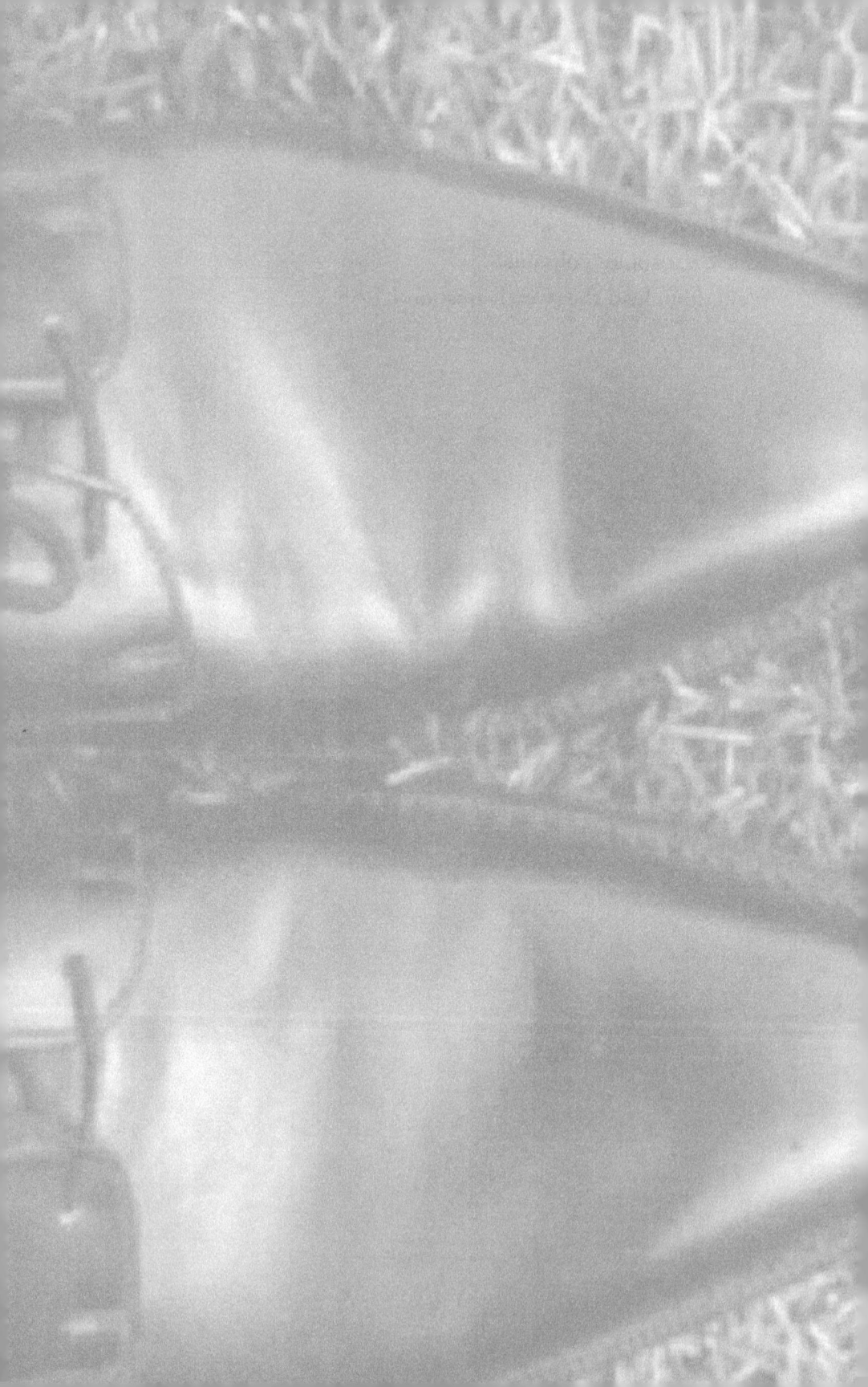

SIX

Two Months Ago

"We should have done something momentous to mark this occasion," Lilah said for at least the hundredth time since she, Gramps, and Ben had sat down to dinner.

"Nonsense," Gramps placated happily and swallowed down a spoonful of malva pudding. "This is all I wanted. An evening with my two favorite people."

"But it's your birthday, Gramps," Lilah grumbled as if he needed reminding.

"Eighty-two is nothing special," he said with a broad smile. "We had that big to-do with my eightieth, what more could a man ask for? This is perfect."

"I agree," Ben inserted quietly, slanting Lilah a speaking look. She hated it when he did that, silenced her with a look as if he were her minder, or her teacher, or a very stern librarian. And she loathed that she immediately lapsed into silence, as she always did when he looked at her like that.

Ugh. So annoying. She was trying to be more assertive around him, but still had about as much defense against his disapproval as a sand castle did against gale force wind.

They were spending the weekend at the beach house in Bantry Bay for Gramps's birthday. A modern seven-bedroom, multilevel house built into the face of the mountain, with a panoramic view of the ocean, and a huge infinity pool that blended seamlessly with the horizon.

Gramps loved this house. It wasn't very far from their home in Constantia, but Gramps spent a lot of time here. Often staying by himself for weeks on end. It had come as no surprise that he'd wanted to spend his birthday here as well. It was his retreat. The place he came to relax.

"I'm glad it's just us," Ben volunteered with a tight smile and Lilah stared at him, wondering why he looked so odd. If she didn't know better, she'd swear he was nervous.

But Ben didn't get nervous, or scared, or agitated, or very excitable. She'd discovered over the years that Ben had three moods.

Impassive, disinterested, and mildly intrigued.

And three months of dating hadn't changed her opinion. He was attentive toward her, listened when she spoke, offered ideas to help her expand her business. He was happy to do whatever interested her, and showered her with flowers and gifts. He smiled—even laughed—on occasion, and touched her more freely.

But Lilah still felt as if she was standing outside of the impenetrable protective bubble that he'd constructed around himself.

She kept chipping away, considering it a victory if he offered any intriguing glimpse into his inner sanctum… but it was an uphill battle.

Still, he was wonderful to her, despite that. He seemed to *want* to be around her. Once even tagging along to one of the volunteer photoshoots she did at animal shelters to showcase their adoptees. Lilah—already more than halfway there—had fallen completely in love with him that day. Watching him happily pet and play with those animals, and comfort the scared and anti-social ones, had been eye opening. He clearly enjoyed animals—dogs especially—even when they peed or shed on him, he'd handled each situation with aplomb.

So to see him fidget nervously with his napkin, his cheekbones flushed with color, was unsettling to say the least.

He set aside his napkin and reached for her hand, which was resting, palm down on the table beside her bowl of dessert. She pulled back in shock—this was not a man who was into public displays of affection at all—but he tightened his grip around hers, almost crushing it. His beautiful dark blue eyes pinned hers and she froze beneath that icy, meaningful stare.

"Lilah, sweetheart—" *sweetheart?* He had never used a single endearment in reference to her before now. "—these last few months have proved to me just how much I need you in my life. I don't want us to ever be apart…"

He pushed out of his chair and shocked her by sinking to one knee in front of her seat.

Oh, God, he was actually doing this!

Right in front of Gramps.

How could he be proposing? It was too soon. She had so much more to learn about him. She didn't understand why he would do this now.

"Ben, I don't—"

"I don't want to waste another moment," he declared, interrupting her in a slightly raised voice. Another thing that shocked her because she'd never heard him speak at this volume before. Also, was that a note of warning she heard in his voice?

Nothing about this made sense. Yet there he was—the man she had been falling more and more in love with by the day—on bended knee.

Proposing.

Why was she even questioning this? It was everything she'd ever wanted.

And yet it felt… *off* somehow.

She glanced over at Gramps, wondering if he would look as baffled as she felt, but he was watching the unfolding scene with a huge, sentimental smile on his face. His faded blue eyes were misty and, while she watched, a tear overflowed onto his wrinkled cheek before disappearing into his beard line.

There was no doubt that he was ecstatic about this proposal.

Ben, who must have noticed her gaze slide to her grandfather, spoke again. "Cyrus, I wanted you here for this special moment, because—while I asked for your blessing months ago—" That was news to Lilah. "—I felt that this moment would be incomplete without you. You're important to both of us. And I wanted you to know how much I care for *and* respect Lilah. When you gave me your blessing, I promised you that I would always take care of her. And right now, in front of you, I want Lilah to know that she can count on me."

He diverted his burning gaze back on Lilah, and the absolute sincerity she saw in his expression, quite literally stole her breath away. "I'll make you happy, sweetheart. I can't wait to share my life with you. Have children with you. Grow old with you. Please, say yes."

At the mention of their life and their future together, of the children he wanted to have with her, Lilah's reservations melted away like butter sizzling beneath the scalding summer sun.

Her eyes flooded and she wriggled a hand free to cup his jaw, loving the scratchiness of his afternoon stubble as it abraded the sensitive skin of her palm.

"Yes. Of course, *yes*, Ben. I lo—" The rest of her words were smothered beneath his hot and demanding mouth and she sighed and leaned into the kiss. She opened her mouth, hungry for the sweep of his tongue, but he withdrew a second later. Before she knew it, he was back in his seat and she was staring down at the massive rock he had placed on her ring finger.

Still a little disoriented by how fast it had all happened, she was vaguely aware of her grandfather calling for champagne. She was still staring fixedly at the ring, while only hazily aware of the two men discussing possible wedding dates.

By the time the champagne arrived, and Lilah was finally emerging from her befuddled fog, Gramps and Ben had already chosen a wedding date.

Stunned, she stared at the two men, feeling utterly railroaded, but not at all sure how to apply brakes to the speeding, out-of-control train her life had just become.

She now had a fiancé. And it seemed that she was getting married.

In two months' time.

SEVEN

At Last...

It was hard to smile when your heart was breaking and your world was crumbling beneath your feet. And yet, that was what Lilah valiantly attempted to do all evening.

She laughed at the appropriate times through the endless speeches, choked down the dinner which tasted like sawdust, smiled brightly when they cut into the elegant five tier wedding cake with its cascade of pale pink peonies and roses. She feigned joviality at the bouquet toss, aiming the sweet posy of peonies and roses at Blake who caught it with a triumphant squawk.

But she was running out of steam now and just wanted this torture to end. She longingly thought of the garden cottage suite to which she and Ben would be retreating after this, even though her mind scurried away from the fact that it would be set up for newlyweds.

"Could you at least *try* to look happy," Ben muttered on a growl when he gathered her into his arms for their first dance.

The criticism in his voice—when she'd been trying so damned

hard—was the last straw. Lilah's eyes flooded and her lips quivered as her feet froze. She stopped swaying in time to the slow beat of the heartbreakingly beautiful *At Last* by Etta James. A song which she'd been certain reflected the deep and abiding love that she and Ben felt for each other. The love that she'd *always* felt for Ben.

Now the song rang hollow and she was cringing on the inside that she had chosen the timeless ode to the eventual fulfillment of true love as their wedding song.

At the sight of her tears, Ben cursed beneath his breath and gathered her close, pushing her head into his shoulder.

"People are watching. Keep it together for fuck's sake," he whispered harshly into her hair, his hands sweeping up and down the column of her back as he urged her to dance again. They were barely moving, and the relatively short song felt interminable.

Lilah knew how they must look to their guests. Wrapped up in each other's arms, swaying slowing, his face buried in her neck while her cheek rested on his shoulder. They looked like lovers who were absolutely enthralled in each other even though it was nothing other than a face-saving lie. Yet when the song ended and they stepped apart—Lilah's emotions firmly under control again—the expression on her grandfather's face made the deception worth it.

Gramps claimed her for the father/daughter dance immediately after that. An old-fashioned waltz that Lilah had chosen because she knew how much her grandfather loved the dance.

But all she could think of during was how fragile his arm felt beneath her palm, the skin of his hand was parchment thin. She was only now realizing how truly frail her grandfather was getting. She was propping him up more than he was leading and it was a relief when Ben cut in less than halfway through the dance. Gramps made a show of protesting the move, but Lilah could see the fatigue on his face and in the sag of his stooped shoulders.

It strengthened Lilah's resolve to try and keep up this crazy pretense with Ben for a little while longer. For Gramps' sake. He needed a stress-free transition at the company. And he truly was so happy for them.

An hour later, while everyone was dancing and having a wonderful time, Lilah turned to Ben, her eyes pleading, "Do you think we can go now?"

Her grandfather had left shortly after the father/daughter dance, hugging them both and telling them on a reedy whisper how happy he was that they had found each other. With the old man gone, Lilah and Ben stopped pretending to be having fun and retreated to the bridal table to watch as their guests got more and more drunk. Friends and acquaintances stopped by the table occasionally to make raucous jokes about wedding nights and honeymoons, but everyone largely seemed to have forgotten that Ben and Lilah even existed.

Lilah had been concerned that Blake—normally so astute— would know that something was wrong. But her friend had been flirting with Rhys all night and now the two of them were snogging on the dance floor. Shocking really, since they had very little in common and Rhys was one of those damaged men Blake tried to steer clear from.

"You want to leave?" Ben asked, his eyes running over her face in concern.

"I'm tired. It's been a day and the asthma attack exhausted me. I just want it to be over."

He looked back at the teeming dancing floor. Nobody else had left yet, their guests were clearly making the most of the lavish setting and the open bar.

"I think we can make our escape. I doubt anyone would notice."

"Please." She hated the naked note of pleading in her voice, but she was desperate. He looked strained as well. Those wickedly curved lips had been drawn into a tight line for most of the night, deep lines of stress fanning out from the corners of his beautiful cobalt eyes. His resting brood face was showing some cracks.

His normally perfect thatch of wavy hair was mussed because of the restless fingers he had tugged through the short strands all evening. His hair was thick and luxurious and such a dark brown it could be mistaken for black. Ben always looked immaculate, but this evening he was a disheveled mess. His cravat had been tugged free long ago and carelessly dropped beside his dinner plate, the top three buttons of his shirt were undone and the beautiful charcoal grey coat had been tossed over the back of his chair. He wore a pale blue vest—the same color as Blake's bridesmaid dress—over his snow-white shirt. The sleeves of said shirt had been rolled up to his elbows, showing off his strong, ropey forearms.

At any other time, Lilah would have sighed dreamily at his messy sexiness. But tonight, she couldn't—he didn't belong to her. Not really. Not the way she'd believed he would. He was on loan, temporary, and once they were alone, she would make it clear that none of this was real and that they would move on from here eventually.

THEY MADE their escape without fanfare and walked purposefully toward their cottage. A normal couple would have meandered, enjoyed the tranquil, romantically lit gardens at night. The summer evening was alive with buzzing, chirping and trilling insects. Further in the distance they could hear frogs croak, the lively music from the wedding reception from which they'd just escaped faded into the background, until there was just their soft footfalls on the grass.

Lilah held her ridiculous skirt aloft, not wanting the hem to drag along the ground. In hindsight, this frothy confection of a dress had been a ludicrous choice. She'd always wanted to marry in a larger-than-life ballgown. Something a Disney princesses would envy. And she'd felt special and beautiful in it. Now she looked down at herself through jaded eyes and considered what Ben must have thought when he'd seen her in it.

Her expectation had been that he would be bowled over and breathless.

When in reality he had probably been gobsmacked and gasping in horror.

"Do you need help?" he asked, his voice quiet in the soft night. "With the skirt? The grass is wet and the hem could pick up mud and loose blades."

"I'm fine," Lilah muttered. She felt like such a fool and wished she could sink into the ground and disappear into a puddle of tulle and organza.

They reached the cottage in no time at all and as they walked through the beautiful, fragrant rose garden toward the front door, Lilah's skirt snagged on a thorn. She surreptitiously tried to tug it free but Ben noticed.

"Stop tugging at it. You'll tear the fabric," he warned, stooping to inspect the problem.

She ignored him and continued to wrench at the skirt, uncaring if she ripped the fragile, expensive fabric. As much as she'd started out the day loving this dreamy Vera Wang creation, she now loathed it and wanted it off as soon as possible. And that wasn't going to happen while she was caught on a rosebush.

His warm, dry palm curved around her calf and she froze and gasped in shock at the contact of his skin against hers. She was wearing silk stockings, but they were whisper thin and his hand might as well have been on her naked skin.

"Stop pulling it, come on, Lilah. It's a beautiful dress, you'll ruin it."

He gently disentangled her hem from the dress and squeezed her leg, sending a shudder of... *something*—Awareness? Desire? Revulsion? At this point it was anyone's guess—up her spine.

He rearranged her skirt around her feet, carefully scooping up a handful in the front and holding it up to her. She grabbed it from him, making certain to keep her fingers well away from his.

He straightened lithely and dug the keycard from his trouser pocket. He turned toward the front door and made short work of opening it.

There was a moment's awkwardness when he hesitated before stepping aside to allow her to enter the suite before him. And Lilah knew that they were both aware that under ordinary circumstances, this would be when a real groom would sweep his bride up into his arms and carry her into the quaint little structure.

Instead, Lilah scurried past him, making every effort not to brush against him in the process. Not that there was any chance of that at all—he stood so far back he reminded her of a little boy on a playground, terrified of catching cooties from the hideous girl.

Once inside the beautiful cottage, she found herself at a loss. The bed was strewn with rose petals of the same pale pink as her bridal bouquet—exquisite attention to detail from the hotel staff —there was a magnum of champagne in a silver ice bucket on the table, a congratulatory card stood up between a couple of flutes beside the bucket.

It was all so sickeningly romantic.

Lilah made a distressed sound in the back of her throat and moved toward the open door of the bathroom.

"Lilah, wait."

"I have to get out of this dress." She was aware of the urgency in her choked voice, but she couldn't bear to remain in the gown for a second longer. She tore at the pins in her hair—they'd started digging into her scalp, adding an extra layer of pain to her already pounding head—leaving them scattered in her wake.

"It'll keep for a while longer. I think we have to talk about this."

"A little too late for talking now, don't you think?" she asked bitterly, but nonetheless paused halfway across the room and reluctantly turned to face him.

He had his hands thrust into his trouser pockets, and his teeth worried his lower lip as he stared at her from beneath his fall of hair, his gaze brooding and intent.

"Earlier… in the car. The stuff you said about marrying me because of the board? I know that it was all bullshit."

"I don't know why you'd—"

"Lilah, cut the crap. I know you were lying. I can always tell when you're lying. You didn't marry me because of the board, you only said that because you thought it was what I wanted to hear. And, because we had that whole fucking circus of a wedding you organized to get through, I didn't challenge you on it then."

"I'm tired, I don't want to talk about this now," she said, feeling short of breath in a way that had nothing to do with her asthma and everything to do with the panic she could feel setting in.

Please, dear God, just let her salvage some pride from the shit-show her life had become. Just a little bit of dignity.

But it wasn't to be. Because her asshole of a husband was relentless and seemingly determined to strip her of the little pride and dignity she had left.

"Look," he murmured, gentling his voice, which was somehow worse because that gentle tone of voice screamed pity. And Lilah didn't want, or need, his damned pity. "I thought we were on the same page when I proposed. I assumed you knew *why* I—" He stopped abruptly, not completing the sentence and instead shook his head impatiently. "Lilah, if we *didn't* marry for the same reasons, then it stands to reason that your motivation was fueled by something else. Something more emotional. And while I was staggered by your vows and didn't react in the best way, I think that maybe it would be more convenient—*better*—if you *do* have those feelings for me."

Lilah gasped at those words and stared at him in horrified disbelief.

"Are you saying it would be better if I loved you even though you don't love me? Convenient and better for whom, Ben? You? Because it certainly wouldn't be for *me*."

"But why? You'd be getting what you want, right? You'd be getting me." That he said it without a trace of irony or arrogance was somehow more offensive than if he'd been smug about it. He truly didn't grasp how casually cruel he was being right now. "I meant it when I promised you today that I'd be faithful to you. We could have a good marriage, Lilah. I could be content and *you* could be happy. And when we start a family, you'd have someone else on whom to focus your love. We're *in* this now, we might as well make the best of it. You and I wouldn't be so..." His voice tapered off and he sighed heavily. "I just think we should give it a fair shot. And if you feel that you're in love with me, this could work. We would *make* it work and start a family."

She swallowed down a surge of nausea and concentrated on keeping her breathing steady. She wanted there to be no misunderstandings between them anymore. He needed to hear her next words loud and clear, without any room for error.

"You're wrong, Ben. It won't work, because I'm actively focused on loathing you right now. And every word coming out of your mouth is reinforcing that revulsion. So maybe you'd better concentrate on shutting the hell up."

He stared at her mutely, his eyes burning with some emotion she didn't care to interpret. She didn't give one damn about his feelings right now. Ben had taken up too much of her time, energy, and focus since he'd come into her life. And now — after she'd made the dumbest mistake of her life — she finally recognized that he'd never been worthy of her attention.

"You can't make me happy, Ben. You *won't* make me happy. Any man who thinks that what you're offering me is enough, is incapable of comprehending what constitutes a happy, healthy relationship. I'd spend every single day of our married life miserable with you. I don't want that. I can't stomach the thought of a passionless, unhappy marriage with you. With anyone. I deserve better than that. Hell, even *you* deserve better than that."

"You're such a fucking child, Lilah. This is real life... it's *our* life. It's best for you to come to terms with that fact really soon. You can decide to be miserable, but it would be so much easier on both of us if you'd just grow the hell up and start taking responsibility for your actions. You *married* me this morning. You stood up in that church and promised to 'love' me for all eternity or whatever the fuck." The fact that staid, uptight Ben had lowered himself to use air quotes with the word *love* further added to Lilah's mortification and she felt the burn of tears in the back of her throat. "You don't just get a do-over from that. You made a commitment. I plan to honor the promises I made. Why don't you show some strength of character and work on keeping yours as well?"

The smile she mustered felt small and frigid on her lips and that suited Lilah fine. It matched the way she felt right now.

"Thank you, Ben. That's exactly what I needed to hear to make me despise you even more. Now if you don't mind, I need to get out of this *fucking* dress."

The profanity was uncharacteristic for her and she could tell it shook him but she didn't stick around long enough to savor his shock. Instead she retreated to the bathroom in a flurry of tulle and organza.

FORTUNATELY THE BATHROOM was huge and could easily accommodate Lilah's full skirt. She slammed the door and reached behind her to frantically tug at the fitted bodice of her dress in an attempt to access the fifty satin buttons that marched down her back in a neat straight line.

Blake had been the one to fasten them for her. And her friend had teased her about how impatient Ben would be to unfasten them.

"I hope he doesn't rip them off," Blake joked.

"He'd better not," Lilah replied with a blush. *"How will I explain that to my daughter when it's time for her to wear this dress one day?"*

"Daddy was so hot for Mommy; he couldn't wait to get her naked?" Blake suggested saucily. *"And* that, *my child, was when you were conceived."*

Lilah's blush deepened, but she couldn't stop her heart racing at the thought of Ben being so overwhelmed by desire for her that he'd tear the buttons off her dress. Even though it was difficult for her to imagine him wanting her that badly.

Misgivings like that should have sent her running from this union months ago. How the hell did she think it was okay to marry a man when she wasn't even sure if he found her hot enough to be impatient to see her naked?

Stupid, she chastised herself contemptuously. *Because you're stupid!*

Now Lilah was the one desperate to tear the buttons off her dress. Only she couldn't reach them and after several futile, frantic attempts, she sank to the floor, her skirt poofing up around her.

She buried her face in her hands and sobbed.

She didn't want to be here. She wanted to go to sleep and wake up in her own bed back home, relieved that this day had been nothing but a terrible nightmare.

There was a soft, tentative knock on the door.

"Lilah?" She could hear the concern in Ben's voice.

"Leave me alone," she called, her voice thick and nasally with tears.

"I think..." he hesitated. Ben rarely hesitated, he was a man of action. Lilah didn't like that uncharacteristic glimmer of vulnerability. She wanted him to be his usual arrogant self, so that she could continue targeting her rage at him. "I think maybe you need some help? With the dress?"

"I'm fine," she insisted. She was being silly. She knew that. She *did* need help with the dress and he was the only one around to aid her. She couldn't very well call Blake. How would that look?

Oh, God... she couldn't remember the last time she'd felt so *lonely*. She had no-one to talk to about this. No-one to ask for advice. It was too humiliating.

The knob turned and, before she could utter a word of protest, the door swung inward.

She'd been so keen to get the dress off, she hadn't thought of locking the door behind her. Dumb mistake. Then again, she never would've believed that Ben would follow her in here.

He stood framed in the doorway for a moment, looking ridiculously beautiful in that hopelessly wrinkled shirt and suit pants. He was a tall, solidly built man, with broad shoulders and chest, narrow hips, and killer thighs and butt. The advantages of being an active, sporty man.

His well-defined jaw was shadowed with stubble, his mouth pressed into a straight tense line as he took in her huddled form on the floor. His eyes—normally so enigmatic—revealed his strain and concern. A sure sign of how tired and stressed he was.

It was that small indication of emotion from him, combined with how uncharacteristically messy he looked, that reminded Lilah that he was trapped in this shitshow as well. Sure, he'd gone into it with his eyes wide open but it made her feel a little better to know that he currently appeared as miserable and uncomfortable about this as she was.

"Lilah, let me help." His already raspy voice was even hoarser, the burr of his barely perceptible Scottish accent more evident than usual. He stepped toward her, careful to avoid treading on her dress, and stretched out a hand to her.

Lilah stared at the strong, veined hand where the ring she'd placed on his finger gleamed in silent accusation beneath the bright light of the bathroom.

She looked beyond that hand into his eyes. The concern in his gaze contradicted his stern, expressionless face.

She swallowed and hesitantly lifted her hand to his. His palm closed around hers and he tugged her to her feet. He used more strength than her slight figure needed and she collided with his chest before she could stop herself. They stood like that for a moment, plastered together, her skirt wrapped around them. He loosely looped his arms around her back and stared at her, his eyes intent and probing.

"You look exhausted."

She ducked her head to avoid his eyes but he wasn't having that and caught her chin between the thumb and forefinger of his right hand to tilt her face upward.

"Let's get you out of this dress so that you can have a bath or shower and get more comfortable, okay?"

"I don't want you to be nice to me," she told him knowing she sounded a little petulant.

"Why not?"

"Because I'm angry with you and I want to stay angry with you."

He sighed, his chest shifting against hers, making her aware of his heat and hardness.

"You can go back to being mad at me after I've unfastened your dress," he said in a perfectly reasonable tone of voice.

"Well, you'd better get to it then." She turned in his arms and swept her long, wavy nutmeg colored hair over one shoulder to allow him access to the buttons.

"My God, how many of them are there?" he asked incredulously.

"Fifty."

He smothered a curse under his breath, before inhaling deeply and tackling the first one.

It took him longer than she expected. His strong, long-fingered, capable hands were surprisingly clumsy and judging from the amount of swearing from him, he was finding it hard to grip the buttons.

"Finicky fuckin' things," he growled, sounding heartily annoyed. And Lilah felt like laughing for the first time since they'd left the chapel that afternoon. Ben usually excelled at everything, which made his reaction to the tiny buttons unexpectedly funny.

Then again, maybe she was just bordering on hysteria, and laughter was the only outlet for her roiling emotions.

Finally, he got the first one unfastened.

"Only forty-nine more to go," he muttered, his voice thick and shaky.

He seemed to get the hang of it after that and he slowly, methodically, undid each button with a measure of care that Lilah would not have expected from him. As the bodice loosened, she clutched the front of the dress to her chest.

The corseted dress had fit her so snugly that she'd actually forgotten that she wore nothing but a pair of delicate, lacy white panties and silk stockings held up by hand-stitched lace garters. Lilah had floated the idea of a garter toss while planning the wedding and Ben had shot it down almost instantly. Knowing what she now knew, she was grateful that she'd not had to go through that humiliation as well. But she'd chosen to wear a pair of pretty, frilly garters because she'd imagined him sexily peeling them off her tonight and —

She groaned and shook her head, trying to rid herself of the image. But as the air hit her naked flesh, she couldn't help but be aware of the brush of his fingers against the sensitive skin of her back.

And because she was so hyperaware of his touch, she definitely noticed that his fingers were starting to linger between each button. She shuddered when, after the next button, one long finger delicately stroked the line from one vertebra and to the next.

He stepped closer and her eyes lifted to their reflection in the mirror above the vanity. His head was bowed, hair falling forward over his brow, face taut with concentration, eyes half-mast as he remained focused on his task. His breathing was heavy and fast and she could feel it disturbing the strands of her hair.

He glanced up and caught her staring and she inhaled sharply at the expression in his beautiful eyes. There was no disguising the astonished look of stark desire she saw there.

He swallowed, and his palm flattened against her naked back, his hand so big it almost spanned the entire length of her spine. She moaned at his touch and he groaned in response to the sound. His hand slid under her bodice and around the front of her torso to cup one of her breasts. Her nipples had been hard since the moment he'd released the first button, but when his hand closed over one sensitive peak, they grew even more painfully engorged.

The sound that escaped from the depths of Lilah's throat embarrassed her. It was somewhere between a squeak and a mewl and her knees buckled. His other arm clamped around her waist and he supported her between his body and the marble vanity.

Her hands fell from her bodice, and her palms flattened on the countertop of the vanity as she sought to maintain her balance. Without her support, the bodice gaped and revealed the tops of her breasts to his voracious gaze. The ruched borders of her areolas peeked over the top of the fabric.

He made an animalistic sound when he saw them. His supportive arm left her waist, and he lifted his hand to yank the bodice down, until her breasts were revealed to him in their entirety. Well, one of her breasts, the other was still covered by his cupped palm.

His hand looked big and strong against her delicate curves and soft contours and Lilah's stomach fluttered at the contrast. His palm was rough and it abraded against the puckered peak of her breast. A deep guttural sound growled from his throat when her nipple swelled even more.

He buried his face in the curve of her neck and swept his lips up over the cord of her neck to her jawline.

"Lilah, turn around," he urged, his hands dropped to the curve of her waist and applied gentle pressure in an attempt to turn her to face him.

Oh, God, what was she doing?

EIGHT

In Name Only

Lilah tensed and, before she could change her mind, she surprised Ben by shimmying out of his hold. She put a couple of feet's distance between them before tugging her bodice back into place, and turning around to face him.

"I don't want this," she told him, hating the edge of hysteria she heard in her voice.

"What do you mean?" he asked, his eyes icing over and his voice going frosty almost instantly.

Still, despite the insta-chill, he couldn't disguise the rapid rise and fall of his chest, or the impressive erection still surging against his zipper. An erection she was valiantly attempting to ignore.

"We're never going to sleep together, Ben."

"Lilah..." He used that insultingly reasonable tone of voice. Insulting, because it always made her feel like he was treating her like an irrational, hysterical child. "I acknowledge that maybe you went into this union under some kind of misapprehension but it doesn't change the fact that we just got married. And there are certain expectations attached to that commitment. Expectations from *both* of us. Maybe you need some time to—I don't know—process things... but *never* is a strong and overly-dramatic word, don't you think?"

"I said what I said," she insisted, turning her back on him again. "Now undo the rest of these and keep your hands to yourself this time."

He hesitated for a moment, before stepping forward and making quick work of the rest of the buttons.

"Thank you," she said over her shoulder and then dismissed him with, "Please shut the door behind you."

"Not until we've cleared this up."

She whirled to face him again, her brows lowered in a glare. "I don't know how I can make it any clearer. This marriage won't be consummated."

He remained silent, staring at her through narrowed, angry eyes.

"It can be a marriage in name only," she continued, hearing desperation and hysteria edge into her voice. "And after a decent amount of time has passed, we could quietly end it. I think that would work."

He glowered at her and she quailed inwardly, striving to maintain an impassive expression. She'd never seen him look so pissed off before.

"Why would you think that?" His voice was dangerously even, despite the fury in his eyes.

"Because I thought it would be temporary. For the board only and all that."

He gave her a *look*. One teeming with disgusted disbelief. She knew she wasn't fooling him, but she would cling to the lie as if it were the very last life preserver from an already sunken ship. It was the only way she could think of to save face.

"No, you married me because you think you're *in love* with me." She hated the snide inflection in his voice. Surely, he understood that saying it like that made her less likely to sleep with him?

"As I said before, if I felt that way at any point—and I'm not saying I did—rest assured I'm re-evaluating my feelings with every passing second, thanks to these thought-provoking exchanges." She was proud that she managed to keep the wobble out of her voice.

"This was always meant to be a real marriage, Lilah."

"Oh? Your idea of a *real* marriage seems to be sorely lacking in the love, honor, and cherish departments, Ben. And *I* don't want whatever soulless, icy substitute you imagined we would have. We can stay married for a year and then separate. That should be long enough for Gramps to think we made a proper go of it. And by then you should have settled into your role as CEO."

Something flashed in his eyes, something unreadable, but oddly vulnerable. Lilah wasn't sure what to make of it, but before she could properly assess the look, it was gone and his eyes had frosted over again.

"Like you said, we can play happy families for Gramps and the board," she continued, satisfied that she seemed to have hit some kind of nerve. "We can pretend to be blissful and content. But that's all it'll ever be. Pretend."

"That's *not* what I want."

"I don't care what you want," she told him, still clutching her bodice tightly to her chest. She was happy that she sounded braver than she was feeling.

"Of course you don't," he sneered. "Because you're a selfish, pampered little brat. You always have been."

"So why go to the extreme lengths of marrying me? Why saddle yourself with such a *selfish, pampered brat*?"

"I married you because I had to..." he paused and then swallowed, looking a little sick before continuing, "This marriage was always going to happen, and I — *we* — might as well fucking try to make it work. Cyrus wants it. It makes him happy and I promised him that I'd take care of you. Remember? I mean to keep that promise. For the rest of my fucking life if need be."

"How noble and self-sacrificing of you. But I don't need you, or anyone, to take care of me."

"Your grandfather obviously thinks differently, or we wouldn't be here."

"Why would you say that?"

"Because you're a fuck up, Lilah! You always have been. You've had so many opportunities just handed to you on a silver platter. And you've squandered them all. Then again, why do anything useful with your life when you don't have to, right? You're Cyrus Beckett's only living family but unlike the old man, you have no work ethic." The unfairness of that accusation ripped her breath away. This man really didn't know her at all. She'd literally worked herself nearly to death to maintain her highly successful business, and he had the nerve to look down on her for taking *one* goddamned holiday in the last five years!

"Then again, why should you have any work ethic?" he continued to rant. "When you can sit at home eating chocolates all day if you wanted to and get even richer doing that? You're spoiled. You've always been spoiled because Cyrus loves you, and he would let you get away with murder. Everything you ever wanted, you got. I was the one thing you couldn't have. But you even got *me* in the end, didn't you?"

"I don't want you."

"You can keep lying to yourself all you like, Lilah, but we both know the truth, don't we?"

"I had a *crush* on you back when I was a dumb kid who didn't know any better and was swayed by good looks instead of good character."

"There's nothing wrong with my character."

"You're a jerk."

"And you're immature."

"Get out! I've had about all I can stand of you today. Just get out of here and let me have my shower in peace."

"I'm leaving, but we're not done with this discussion. Whether you like it or not, this is a real marriage."

"It's not. I want a divorce!"

"Well, you can't have one. Not without breaking Cyrus's heart. And you've damned well disappointed him enough in his lifetime."

That shut her up and she stared at him with wide eyes, not sure why he'd said that. Or if it were true. Was Gramps disappointed in her? She'd always been certain of the fact that her grandfather wanted her to be happy and wanted her to chase her dreams. She'd assumed he was proud of her for building a lucrative business doing what she loved. He'd always encouraged her, wanted to know what she was working on, and beamed proudly when she showed him her portfolio.

But was Ben right? Had she broken Gramps's heart by never showing the slightest interest in his business? He'd seemed happy to take Ben under his wing, delighted to have someone he loved and trusted to take over from him eventually. But had that been his dream for Lilah that he'd transferred to Ben due to her lack of interest?

"I-I..." Words failed her as the possibility of having disappointed her grandfather—whom she adored—hit her like a ton of bricks.

"Lilah, I shouldn't have said that," Ben said, his accent thickening.

"Is it true?"

"Cyrus loves you deeply..." *Not* an answer.

"But I can't remember the last time I saw him as happy as he was today."

He said nothing in response to that and she sucked her top lip between her teeth to nibble on the center of it pensively.

"Please, just leave me alone, Ben." Weariness lent weight to her words.

"Would you like me to order some room service? You scarcely touched your dinner."

It surprised her that he'd noticed that. It was true, she'd taken only a few disinterested bites of the wedding dinner she'd selected so carefully just a couple of months ago. And she'd barely tasted any of it.

But the mere thought of eating right now nauseated her.

"I'm not hungry."

"You should eat, you'll make yourself ill. It's been a long, exhausting day."

"Don't worry about me, I'll be fine."

"I don't think—"

"*Look*, just trust me to know my own mind and body. I cannot eat a thing right now. I'll probably throw up all over this pretty cottage if I did. So just back off, okay? I know you believe that you've signed up to be my minder or something, but I *can* take care of myself. No matter what you and Gramps may think of me."

"I'll be just out there if you need me."

"I won't need you," she bit off impatiently, keen for him to just leave.

His luscious lips thinned and she saw the muscles bunch along his jaw as it tightened.

"Right."

He didn't linger a second longer, exiting the bathroom abruptly.

Grateful that he'd finally left, Lilah loosened her arms around the bodice of her dress and allowed it to fall and pool around her feet in a froth of icy white fabric. She stepped over the marshmallowy skirt and kicked it carelessly aside. She would have to place it into a garment bag later. She'd arranged for the hotel to courier the dress and Ben's suit to his apartment tomorrow after they checked out. But right now, she wasn't overly concerned about that. Instead she rushed to the door to click the lock in place.

She sagged against the wood once she knew it was securely locked and allowed herself to finally give in to her all-consuming rage and heartbreak.

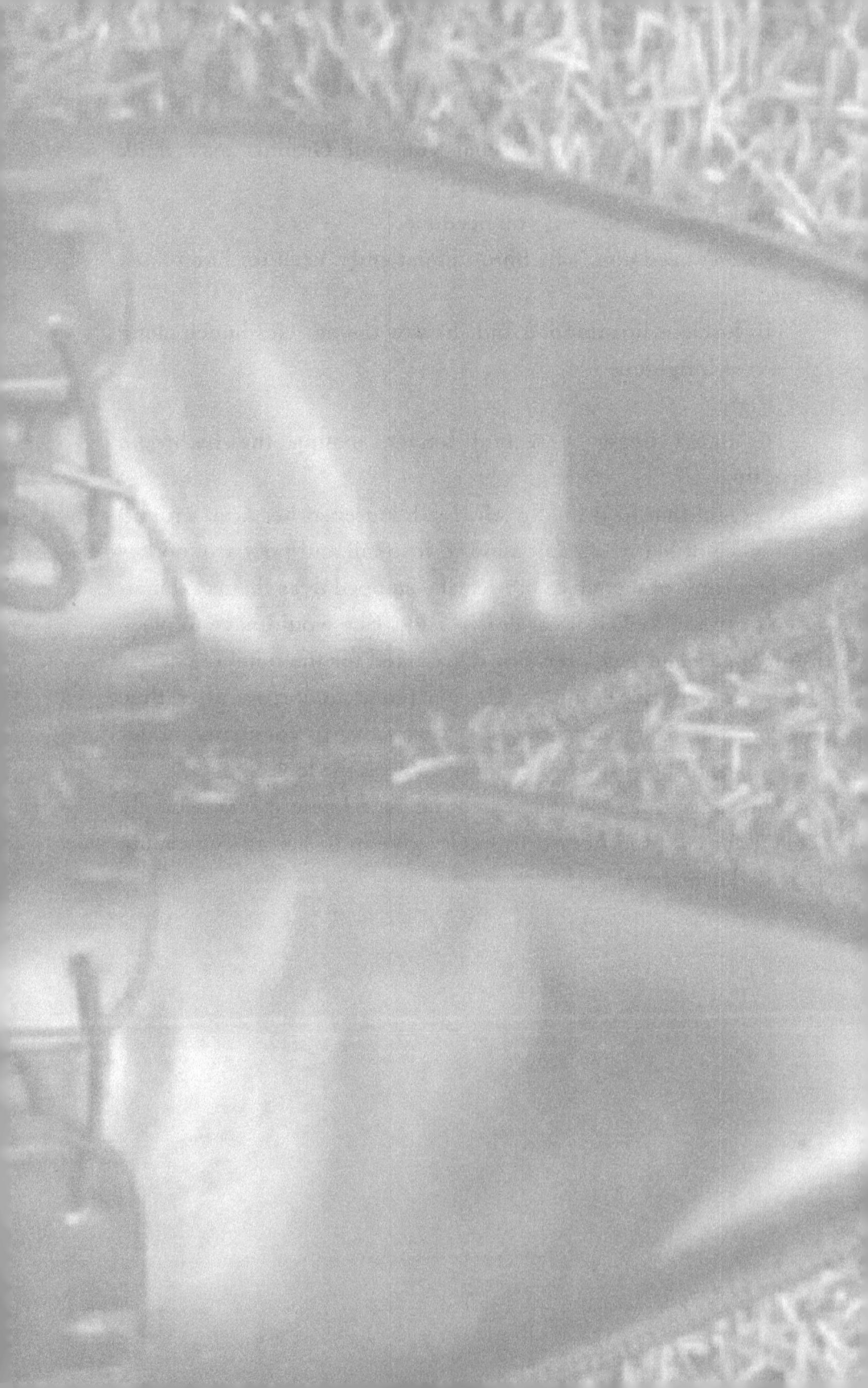

NINE

Honeymoons Are For Lovers

"I told you I wasn't hungry," Lilah muttered when she emerged from the bathroom forty-five minutes later to find a veritable feast set up on the round table.

She was snugly swathed in one of the fluffy, white hotel robes —having forgotten to take a change of clothing into the bathroom with her—with her wet hair wrapped in a towel.

She glared at the food resentfully, hating that Ben had simply gone ahead and done what *he* thought was best for her.

As usual.

"You should eat."

"Go to hell, Ben."

"What is your problem? I'm trying to make the best of this fucked up situation right now."

"I don't know, maybe I'm just resentful my grandfather and my so-called husband both seem to think I'm a child who needs taking care of. And now you expect me to remain trapped in this ridiculous, loveless marriage permanently?"

"How about you take ownership of some of your own decisions, Lilah? That would be the adult thing to do, right? You didn't find the idea of marrying me so ridiculous this morning. You trotted down that aisle eagerly enough. Full of promises of love and happily ever afters. And now you're trying to tell me that it was all a lie? Either you were lying then or you're lying now, so you have some fucking nerve to bleat on to me about dishonesty.

"*I* didn't make one vow I could call a lie today, Lilah. Every word I uttered was the God's honest truth. Can you say the same?"

Of course she could and he knew it… but she would never ever speak words of love or affection to him again. Not after seeing his reaction to the very vows he now wanted her to uphold. No matter where they went from here, or what he said and did, Lilah would never forget the grim parade of expressions that had flashed across Ben's usually unreadable face that morning. That quick succession of horror, disgust, and panic. It was seared into her brain and she saw it every time she closed her eyes.

She ignored his sneering question and avoided his eyes as she rifled through the overnight bag that he'd thoughtfully removed from the closet and placed on the bed for her.

She winced at the sight of the ridiculously sheer nightgown she'd packed for her wedding night. She couldn't possibly wear this tonight. Or any other night.

Ever.

She shoved the garment back into the bag and frantically considered her options. She refused to let him see this nightgown; it would only confirm his arrogant—*accurate*—belief that Lilah had married him because she loved him. To spare her pride, she'd wait for him to go to the bathroom and grab a t-shirt from her bigger suitcase, the one she'd packed for the—

DON'T PRETEND I'M YOURS

She groaned and his hand immediately hooked around her elbow, swinging her to face him.

"What's wrong?" he asked, his eyes searching her face intently.

"I don't want to go on honeymoon," she admitted.

"We have to."

They were leaving for the Maldives in the morning.

"Right now, I can't think of anything less appealing than spending two interminable weeks in your company."

"We're *going* on this honeymoon. It's expected."

"I don't want to go on honeymoon with you. Honeymoons are for lovers and we're never going to be lovers."

"There you go denying ownership of your decisions again, Lilah. *You* chose the destination, the hotel, everything. And you had no qualms about doing so. So stop being ridiculous and grow the hell up. What would Cyrus think if we didn't go on our honeymoon?"

That tripped her up and she clamped her lips shut.

"I just don't want to go," she said, sounding as miserable and confused as she felt and he heaved an impatient sigh.

"Yeah? Well, that's life, *sweetheart,* and I know it'll come as shock to you, but we don't always get what we fucking want."

His words made her wince—he rarely used profanity, and only did so when he was extremely angry or stressed—which, judging from the language he'd been using since they'd left the chapel that morning, seemed to be his constant state around Lilah today.

"Gramps would *never* expect us to sacrifice our own happiness for his sake," she whispered.

"That's not what we'd be doing." He shrugged nonchalantly, but the antipathy she saw in the depths of his frost-encrusted glare belied the casual gesture. "We'd be building something together. A life. An understanding. It could work."

"This is absurd," Lilah said with a bitter laugh. "Judging from the words that have been exchanged today, the only things we could ever build between us are resentment and anger. You don't even like me." The last emerged on a forlorn whisper and she wished the words back the instant they left her lips.

"We both love Cyrus and have a mutual desire to make him happy." It killed her a little when he didn't even bother to make a token denial of her last five words.

"That's a weak reason to marry someone you don't like and you *know* it."

"Cyrus is..." He paused and appeared to consider his words carefully before continuing. "Well, he's not getting any younger and a while ago he mentioned how concerned he was about what would happen to you after he was—uh—gone..." Like Lilah was a ten-year-old child instead of a twenty-seven-year-old woman. God, that stung so badly. "I saw the opportunity to ease his mind on that score. And I really *do* believe we can have a good life together."

"Are you telling me this is all because Gramps made a passing comment expressing concern about what would happen to me after he died?" she scoffed, not quite believing what she was hearing. "And you... what? Saw a chance to score some brownie points with your mentor? That's the most ridiculous thing I've ever heard. You didn't try to ease his mind? Didn't point out that I owned a prosperous business and have been doing very well for myself these past few years? You just thought, 'hey, I'll marry the brat and make the old man happy'?"

"I married you for several reasons." His voice was filled with caution and she sensed he was treading very carefully and immediately wondered what he was hiding from her. Because she still didn't believe she was getting the full story here. Not when he was watching his words so carefully. "Cyrus, business, and because I thought it was a good time to start a family."

"But what about love? What happens when you fall in love someday? Or *I* do?"

"Romantic love is a fairytale." His voice was so dismissive it was practically a shrug. "I don't believe it exists. Not the way *you* think it does. I believe we could have a mutually beneficial marriage, based on common goals. I've never understood the ridiculous need people have to muddy the waters with irrelevant emotions that never last past the honeymoon anyway. We could find common ground, *learn* to like and respect each other. Those are real and lasting emotions."

Unlike love. The silence that followed his passionless little speech screamed with those unspoken words and Lilah allowed them to hover awkwardly for a few, long moments before replying.

"How the hell are we going to do that? When you've made it clear that you think I'm selfish and spoiled? And you've made no secret of the fact that you think my career is a joke and the business I've built is a waste of time. It has become more than apparent to me that you don't respect me."

"You have some growing up to do," he acknowledged, infuriating her even further. "And, I concede, I could be less—"

"—of a prick?" she interrupted. "Bastardish?"

His brows lowered and his lips tightened. "Uncompromising."

"Less of a stubborn dickhead then," she said with an agreeable nod. She hoped to get some kind of reaction from him but he did nothing more than stare at her impassively.

Maddening man and his steely control.

His jaw moved, and Lilah smugly realized that he was gnashing his teeth.

Good. Why should she be the only one aggravated by this frustrating conversation?

"Look, Ben, the crux of the matter here is that you and I have entered into this union with very different expectations." And *how.* "I don't want what you want. I'll give this a year for appearances sake. After that, I want a divorce."

"We'll revisit this conversation, Lilah. I'm not in the mood to spar with you. It's been a trying day and attempting to speak with you about anything *adult* right now is proving to be a fucking impossibility."

"Just what every bride wants to hear from her groom on their wedding night." Her voice was dripping with scathing disdain.

"You're exhausting." He speared his fingers through his hair, making even more of a mess of it. "I'm done with this. We have an early start tomorrow. I suggest you get to bed. If you're still awake when I get out of the shower, I'll take it as an invitation for *more.*"

"More wh—" The heat in his eyes silenced her—let's face it—dumb question.

She remained mute as she watched him snatch up his toiletry bag and slam his way into the bathroom.

She sprang into action the second the door shut, knowing that she had limited time. She decided not to attempt wrestling her massive suitcase and leaped for Ben's overnight bag instead. After a few seconds of rummaging, she found an enormous white t-shirt. This would do nicely.

She tossed aside the robe and dragged the shirt over her head. The large garment immediately enveloped her. The sleeves drooped halfway down her arms, but because she was tall—five-ten—the hem hit her at mid-thigh, revealing the length of her slender, toned legs. She intended to be buried under the covers before he emerged from the bathroom, so he wouldn't get to see them. Not that he hadn't seen her legs before—Lilah had a fondness for tiny shorts and mini-skirts. But this was different… more intimate.

And—frankly—she didn't want him to see any part of her body tonight. Not when she felt as angry and betrayed as she did.

She grabbed a couple of pillows from the king-sized bed and tossed it onto the loveseat. The sofa was too short and narrow for Ben, and Lilah knew he would balk at spending the night on the uncomfortable piece of furniture. Which left her no recourse but to claim it for herself. She snatched up the light throw draped over the foot of the bed and dove for the sofa, where she buried herself up to her nose, under the covers.

She'd been so quick—the shower wasn't even running yet. Instead, she heard the low hum of a razor, or perhaps his electric toothbrush. She remained tense, vibrating with anticipation, as she listened to him move around the bathroom.

By the time she heard the shower go on, the day was catching up with her. No matter how hard she tried, she could feel herself start to drift. She fought to remain awake, but consciousness became increasingly elusive, trailing away like wispy tendrils of smoke whenever she made a grab for it.

In the end she succumbed, feeling herself sink into vulnerable oblivion as sleep finally claimed her.

TEN

A Web of Lies

Lilah awoke with a start. It was dark and she felt utterly disoriented.

Where was she? Why was she so hot? Her covers felt heavy and it was hard for her to move with the blankets so tightly wound around her.

"Stop wriggling," Ben's familiar whiskey rasp muttered sleepily into her ear.

And that's when the events of the last twenty-four hours came flooding back in a rush.

Ben.

He was her husband and he didn't love her.

A sob clawed its way up from her chest and out of her mouth.

She was in bed with Ben. He was the one wrapped around her—his legs and arms entangled with hers, weighing her down.

Imprisoning her.

She had a vague recollection of him returning from the bathroom and picking her up from the sofa, but she'd been so bushed, it had felt like a dream.

Now she became acutely aware of the fact that her purloined t-shirt had ridden up over her butt and that the lacy thong she'd bought especially for her wedding night offered scant protection against the insistent hardness she felt pressing up against her.

He was naked. There was no denying that fact. And there was not a single layer of clothing between her naked skin and the rock-hard shaft pressed up against the curve of her behind.

"Don't panic, okay," he ground out, his voice intimate in the darkness.

"Hard not to panic with that *thing* pressed up against me," she retorted, her own voice still husky with sleep. "I told you I don't want this."

"There's no *this* happening. It's just a natural physical reaction to your closeness."

"I was asleep on the sofa. And considering the situation, you *could* have worn clothes, for God's sake."

He moved away from her until there was cool air where before had been scorching heat. Gooseflesh skittered along her skin and she shivered involuntarily.

"I sleep nude."

"Then you should have left me on the sofa."

"You looked uncomfortable. It's a king-sized bed, I didn't see the harm in sharing."

"You didn't see the *harm in sharing*?" she repeated, mimicking his deep voice. "You groped me the first chance you got."

"I wasnae fuckin' gropin' you." She couldn't remember the last time she'd heard his accent so thick and she understood that she'd hit a nerve. The room flooded with warm light to reveal her beautiful bare-chested husband, propped up against the headboard on his side of the bed, a sheet loosely draped over his still hard penis.

"You were all over me like a…a cheap suit."

"You were having a nightmare. I tried to comfort you and I fell asleep holding you. The hard-on is merely a reaction to the way you were grinding your arse against my cock."

She went bright red. Not sure if she *had* been grinding up against him. But since he looked simultaneously outraged and smug, it was a distinct possibility.

She climbed out of bed, and his eyes honed in on the shirt she was wearing.

"That's my t-shirt."

"Is it?" Yes, it was a dumb response, but her brain had shut down.

"You know it is. You would've had to go through my bag to get it."

"Would I?"

"For fuck's sake, Lilah." There was a world of exasperation in his voice. "Are you going to tell me why you're wearing my shirt or not?"

"No?"

"What?"

"I, uh…" Gah, she was terrible at coming up with on-the-spot lies. She was the world's worst liar. "I forgot to pack a nightgown."

Those cobalt eyes sharpened.

"Seems like an odd thing to forget, no?"

"I mean I do have sleepwear, of course. But they're all in the suitcase. I just forgot to add a nightie to the overnight bag."

"Isn't that the entire purpose of an overnight bag? To pack the things you would need for the night and the following morning?"

"I forgot it, alright? It's not a big deal."

"Hmm…" Well, that sexy rumbling sound told her nothing. "I'll need that shirt back. I'm wearing it on the flight."

The thought of Ben wearing the shirt she'd slept in just the night before left Lilah feeling hot and itchy and uncomfortable. It would carry her scent, maybe still be warm from her body. The intimacy of it unnerved her greatly.

"I meant to get it laundered before you wore it again."

"Well, that's not going to happen. I'm not going through that bastard of a suitcase just to find a fresh t-shirt. That one will do me fine."

"What's the time?" Lilah asked, feeling it prudent to change the subject.

Ben lifted his phone. "Nearly five. The alarm will be going off in the next half hour or so anyway, best to just get dressed and order some breakfast."

Last night's untouched food was still spread all over the table and Lilah grimaced at the wastage. She didn't think she'd fare much better with breakfast.

"You're sure I can't change your mind about the honeymoon? We can just skip it and avoid people until the two weeks are up."

His expression remained hard as granite but a moment later he sighed and gave her a curt nod as if making his mind up about something.

"We could cut the trip short. Go for one week instead of two. I'm sure we could come up with a more plausible excuse for shortening the honeymoon than we would for cancelling it entirely. It's a shite time for me to leave work anyway. I only agreed to this godforsaken trip because Cyrus would have found it odd if we skipped it."

It was a fair compromise and Lilah pondered over it for a beat even though she knew he wasn't going to give her a better deal than that.

"Were you scared that Gramps would disinherit you or something if you didn't marry me?" It was the first time the thought had occurred to her and the question was out of her mouth before she could stop it.

He went utterly still and her breath snagged. Had she finally stumbled upon his real motivation for this marriage? His face remained expressionless but something in the way he held himself told her that her question had struck a nerve.

"Gramps loves you." She broke the silence with a whisper. "He would *never* place restrictions on that love. He trusts you with his company. With me."

Ben's mouth twisted bitterly and he uttered a cynical little laugh before shaking his head impatiently.

"You don't have a fucking clue about anything, cupcake."

"Enlighten me then! Clue me the hell in so that I can be on the same page as you for once."

Ben's expression remained unreadable for a few more seconds, before something close to regret flickered in his eyes and he sighed. "I can't."

The cryptic response confirmed that he had secrets. Secrets he refused to share with her.

What a perfectly brilliant start to a marriage this was.

"I'll get dressed," she said, knowing it would be futile to press him any further on the matter. She turned away from the bed and yanked up her overnight bag on the way to the bathroom.

"What do you want for breakfast?" Ben asked.

"I don't care," she replied, shutting the door before he could say anything more.

NEARLY TWENTY HOURS LATER, Lilah and Ben wearily trudged into their deluxe pool villa, set right on top of the crystal-clear waters at a private island resort in the Maldives. Gramps and Ben had insisted they use the corporate jet for travel and Lilah—who considered herself environmentally conscious—had cringed, but had been unable to deny that it was the most practical choice for the trip.

It had been an emotionally fraught journey. She and Ben hadn't spoken much at all. He'd retreated behind his laptop, conducting meetings, making urgent phone calls, barking out last minute instructions to his executive assistant. While Lilah had spent most of the trip pretending to be asleep, occasionally texting her friends, and avoiding eye contact with Ben as much as possible.

He was wearing that damned t-shirt and he looked amazing in the faded jeans and plain white t-shirt combo. But all the while Lilah had been excruciatingly aware of the fact that she'd been sleeping in that same shirt just last night. That it probably still smelled of her expensive after-shower lotion. That he'd had her scent intimately close all day long. She could not say why that thought disturbed her, but it did.

So much.

They landed quite late at night and Lilah was relieved to finally step off the plane and into the hot humid night after the interminable and exhausting flight.

Stepping into their luxurious villa—after another long, silent drive from the airport—Lilah was too tired to notice anything other than the king-sized bed dominating the space. She kicked off her shoes and threw herself facedown across the mattress.

She must have dozed off for a few minutes, because she startled awake when Ben opened the patio door.

"I'm exhausted," Lilah complained, flipping over onto her back and covering her face with her hands.

"Why don't you grab a shower and get some sleep?" Ben suggested.

"Aren't you tired?" she asked, parting her fingers to peer at him between the slits. He looked annoyingly refreshed. His clothes weren't wrinkled, not a hair out of place. While Lilah knew she must look like she'd crept out of the laundry basket that morning. When she had dared a glance into the mirror after arriving at the airport, she'd seen that her hair had begun to frizz in the humidity, and she had bags the size of her suitcases under her eyes.

"Traveling always leaves me too wired to sleep, I need to unwind first."

"How do you usually unwind?"

"I can think of several ways to unwind right now," he told her with a smoldering look and she flushed to the roots of her hair. "But I guess I'll settle for a swim."

"Swim?" She sat up in alarm. "In the ocean? It's too dangerous in the dark."

"I didn't think you cared, cupcake," he said with a cynical twist of his lips. "If I drowned, you'd be rid of your inconvenient groom far quicker than you expected to be."

"A divorce will do me fine, Ben. No need to martyr yourself," she retorted, pushing herself up from the bed and heading toward her bags.

"The villa pool is small, but I'll try to make do. I wouldn't want you to worry about me or anything."

"Don't let me stop you from throwing yourself in the ocean," she countered sweetly. "I don't care what you do."

She flipped her hair over her shoulder and turned her back on him to wrestle her heavy suitcase into submission, flipping it onto the side on the floor next to the bed, and rifling through it for a t-shirt and some loose running shorts to sleep in.

She was aware of him still watching her from his position by the patio door, but refused to look at him as she picked up her toiletry bag and retreated to the massive en-suite.

She paused for a moment to take in the sheer magnificence of the bathroom. Lilah was used to luxury and beauty in her surroundings, but this place was next level. The massive soaker tub, set right in front of the wall-to-wall, floor-to-ceiling window overlooking the patio and ocean, tempted her. But if she could see Ben's shadowy figure out on the patio, outlined in the blue light from the pool, then he could definitely see her, as evidenced by the smug wave he sent her. There wasn't a lot of room to hide in the brightly-lit bathroom, but the shower stall offered some privacy.

She sent him a glare, before dropping a regretful look at the tub, and trudging to the shower. A quick glance over her shoulder confirmed that he'd turned his back on her and as she watched, he disappeared from view, probably to climb into the pool.

Feeling a little more comfortable with stripping down now that he wasn't watching, she dragged off her wrinkled slip dress and underwear and tossed it into the hamper, before adjusting the water temperature and climbing beneath the spray.

Despite wanting to linger, she made quick work of her

shower, concerned that Ben would finish his swim—or whatever he was doing—before she was done.

Despite the brevity of the shower, she still felt refreshed afterward. When a sneak peek from the stall didn't reveal her husband's unwanted presence in the bathroom, she quickly wrapped a thick fluffy towel around her body and then another, turban-style, around her hair, before stepping into the bathroom.

She picked her toiletry bag up from where she'd left it on the wooden bench next to the bath and neatly lined her cosmetics and toiletries up on the marble vanity top. She smoothed her luxurious almond-scented lotion all over her body, and then moved on to cleansing and moisturizing her face.

The soothing routine settled her nerves and she felt almost relaxed by the time she slid the door between bathroom and bedroom open.

"Why are you wearing another t-shirt when you have a metric fuckton of lacy, frilly things in your suitcase?" Ben's deep voice immediately demanded to know.

Her eyes flew to the patio door, where he stood—a silhouette backlit by blue light—dripping on the tiled patio floor. She couldn't see his face, but his big looming body was outlined in exquisite detail. He had a towel clutched in one hand.

"Did you go through my bag?" she asked, outraged.

He snorted in response to that and the sound was infuriatingly dismissive.

"No. You're the one who rifles through other people's bags. You stole my shirt, remember? *Your* bag, however, was left open with half of the contents strewn across the floor. There are no maids to magically pick up after you here, Lilah. So if you leave your shite on the floor, that's where it's staying."

Her eyes flew to her open suitcase. In her rush she had

rummaged through her bag and—after finding what she'd been searching for—she'd abandoned everything else and hauled butt to the bathroom.

But she'd been careless in her haste and, sure enough, several filmy nighties were dotted around the floor like white, crumpled tissue paper.

"I was in a hurry," she muttered, hoping he would let it go at that.

She ambled over to her bag, not wanting to seem too eager to get it all tucked away out of sight again, and knelt on the rug to shove everything back in the back.

"You're going to wrinkle everything," he warned her and she shrugged.

"I'm too tired to unpack the bag tonight. I'll do it in the morning."

"So why do you have those sexy, frothy bits of nothing packed anyway? Planning to seduce me?"

"B-Blake packed them." God, so much deception. Lilah was concerned she wouldn't be able to keep this twisted web of lies straight. "She doesn't know the real reason behind this wedding."

"Bullshit." The rasp in his voice roughened even more as his voice deepened and Lilah's throat went dry at the sexiness of it. His face was in shadow, but she could see every inch of the hard, perfectly proportioned body that he was so lazily toweling. Her breathing quickened as she watched the towel sweep up the hard plane of his stomach toward the perfectly proportioned six pack above it and then down again.

He was still speaking and she stifled a moan of frustration when his words registered. "You bought those pretty, filmy things for me, didn't you, Lilah? For *us*."

"No. Blake bought them." It was an embarrassingly weak lie delivered in a voice that lacked anything resembling conviction.

The movement of his hand paused and he stepped out of the darkness and into the brightly lit room.

"You're such a little liar."

"You're a liar too," she retorted furiously and his eyes hooded.

"What do you mean by that?" His voice was guarded, his entire body had tensed—easy to tell when he was practically nude —and every muscle had bunched and tightened in response to her reckless and unthinking accusation.

His reaction further strengthened her belief that he was keeping something from her.

"I know that there's something you're not telling me," she accused and his eyes narrowed.

"This again? There are a lot of things I'm not telling you, Lilah. You don't need to know my every passing thought."

"Something specific to us. To this marriage. Something important."

"Even if that were true, it could hardly be classified as a lie."

"Oh, come on, Ben. Why not come clean? Why play this stupid game?"

"Whatever you think I'm keeping from you, Lilah… you're mistaken. I have nothing to tell you. So leave it the fuck alone."

He tossed the towel aside impatiently and strode into the room toward where she was kneeling by her suitcase.

She shrank away from him when he loomed above her and his eyes flared at her reaction. He took a small and deliberate step back, no longer crowding her, giving her the room to uncurl from her embarrassingly defensive huddle and straighten to her full height.

"I'll leave your secrets alone, when you leave mine alone," she told him hoarsely, tilting her head up to meet his intense, furious stare head on.

"*Your* secrets?" He scoffed. "Like the thinly disguised one where you're infatuated—oh, sorry...*in love*—with me but pretending not to be?"

ELEVEN

Mr. and Mrs. Fake As Fuck

"I don't love you," she maintained stubbornly, forcing back her searing pain at his blatant mockery, and trying hard to keep the hurt tremor out of her voice.

His snort of laughter was even more insulting than the sneer in his voice had been.

"You believe that romantic love is this deep, meaningful, sacred thing," he said, ignoring her denial. "Surely something so powerful and mystical can't just be switched on and off like a faucet. So if you loved me yesterday, it stands to reason that you probably still love me now."

She searched for the right response, hating how damned smug he always was in the absolute certainty of his convictions.

"Love is like an exotic plant." His eyes sparked with something that looked like laughter at her words and Lilah would give anything for the ground to swallow her up where she stood right now. Even to her own ears, her words sounded ridiculous. Still, she doubled down. "It needs to be nurtured, fed, watered. Without the proper care and attention it'll wither and die."

"I can keep a plant alive and thriving without feeling any kind of affection for it, cupcake. It's not exactly brain surgery."

"All I'm saying is that, like a *plant*"—Ugh, she really should let the damned plant thing go—"love can't flourish in an arid wasteland."

"Guess you've never heard of succulents," he rejoined calmly and she glowered at him and shook her head, disgusted with herself for even trying.

"It doesn't matter," she said softly. "I don't know why I'm arguing with you about this. Love has nothing to do with our union. It's an arctic tundra. Not even a fucking succulent can grow there."

He opened his mouth as if to correct her once again, but she held up an index finger to silence him. Surprisingly, he clamped his lips together and shut the hell up, maybe sensing that he'd pushed her to her limits.

Overwhelmed, exhausted, and horribly distraught by the devastating turn her life had taken, Lilah was unable to tamp down the hot surge of grief she felt at the loss of what she'd hoped would be a blissfully happy marriage.

She was running out of ways to berate herself for her extreme foolishness and naiveté. How had she not understood what she was getting herself into? She'd gone over it and over it during the long flight. Hindsight highlighting the many instances where she should have recognized how little Ben felt for her.

Most of his caresses and kisses had been a performance, played to an audience of one—well two, if Lilah counted herself—designed to fool Gramps into believing that Ben truly loved and wanted her. But when they'd been alone, on one of their many "dates", Ben had been glued to his phone, cursory in his comments. He'd barely looked at her, much less touched her. And Lilah, hopelessly clinging to the fairytale, had made excuses for him. He was busy, the transition at work was taking up all of his free time. She had to be patient and understanding. It wouldn't last forever.

What an idiot she'd been.

She stepped away from him, miserably aware of her welling tears. She turned her back on him mere moments before they overflowed, hot at first, and then chilling against her flesh when the night air hit the moisture. She wiped the tears away with the heels of her hands, but they were quickly replaced with fresh ones.

She sensed him moving until he was close, she could almost feel the chill coming off his wet skin.

"Lilah?" His voice was uncharacteristically hesitant and she flinched when his big hands dropped to her slender shoulders. "Are you crying?"

"No."

"Turn around."

"No."

"Lilah, c'mon, turn around." His hands cupped the balls of her shoulders and exerted gentle pressure in an attempt to coax her into turning around.

She resisted at first—but he was insistent. Bowing to the inevitable, Lilah swiped at the humiliating tears with the backs of her hands, and turned to face him. She folded her arms defiantly over her chest and lifted her chin to glare at him mutely.

He sighed, the sound soft and long-suffering, and lifted a hand to thumb away the residual moisture on her cheeks.

"I'm tired." An excuse? A plea? A prayer?

Lilah wasn't sure what she hoped to achieve with those two words, but they sounded small and weak and she hated that she'd felt coerced into offering them.

She continued speaking, the words tumbling from her lips in a humiliated rush as she confessed, "I don't think I've ever felt so alone in my life before."

"You don't have to be alone, Lilah. This is what I've been trying to tell you. You have me. We're in this together. We could be, *should* be, a team."

His eyes bore into hers, his face was etched with strain, jaw clenched and lips pressed into a grim line.

She watched him through a shimmer of tears, taking in those beautiful, taut features, before her gaze dropped all the way to his long, sun browned bare feet, which were planted shoulder length apart. Her eyes trailed up over the tanned columns of his muscular shins and calves, lightly dusted with dark hair, even further up over those beautiful, hard, well-muscled thighs. He wore light gray swim trunks that ended mid-thigh, which—though it must have been quite loose when dry—clung to him like a second skin and her eyes snagged at exactly the wrong spot.

But who could blame her? The shorts lovingly molded the substantial bulge at his groin, leaving very little to the imagination. Her face went hot and her breathing sped up, as her eyes refused to obey her brain's frantic demands that they move on.

He shifted, his thumbs hooking into the waistband of his shorts and dragging the wet fabric down a fraction.

"If you're that interested in the goodies, all you have to do is say so, Lilah. I'm happy to show you mine if you'll show me yours." The line was smooth as silk and, delivered as it was in that raspy voice, it immediately beaded her nipples and sent a flood of warmth to pool in her groin.

As the distraction they were clearly meant to be, his words proved effective, and her eyes jerked upward, but they didn't miss a single detail on their hurried journey up toward his face. The deep V of his Adonis belt, those rock-hard abs, the trail of hair on his flat stomach leading up to—and sprinkling over—his well-defined pecs. The water beading on that beautiful chest and his tight nipples. Those big, elegantly-fingered hands, veined and capable at the end of long, strong gorgeous arms, leading up to broad shoulders.

The grimness had fled from his face to be replaced by the smug confidence of a man who knew exactly how appealing he was to look at. Those stern features, so perfectly sculpted, had always possessed the power to leave her breathless. His beard was coming in. Stubble darkening his chiseled, indented jaw.

She was a shaky mass of nerves by the time she met his brooding stare.

"K-keep your pants on, Romeo. I'm not interested in your goodies," she said, grateful for the subject change, but hating how the quiver in her voice made a liar of her.

His lip curled—a smirking imitation of a smile—and he made a snorting sound of disbelief.

"*Suuure* you're not, cupcake."

Since their engagement, he'd taken to calling called her *sweet-heart*—or *leannan* which meant sweetheart or darling in Gaelic—on the odd occasion, but never *cupcake*. She had no idea where this new nickname—which he had been using on and off since the wedding—stemmed from. And she didn't know if she liked it. She wasn't sure if he meant it fondly or if it was deprecating. Something told her it was the latter.

She refused to respond to his words and turned away from him to glare down at her suitcase.

He chuckled—the sound deep and mocking—and headed to the bathroom. He turned toward the showers—out of sight from the bedroom—and left the sliding door between the two rooms open. Moments later his wet swim shorts came sailing into view, landing on the tiled bathroom floor with a splat. She heard the shower go on a second later, but her stare remained transfixed on the wet mound of fabric sitting in a puddle on the bathroom floor.

He was naked.

Of course he was naked, he was in the shower, for God's sake!

It was dumb to be so diverted by the mere thought of his nudity. He had been unclothed last night in bed with her after all.

This was nothing.

But still he was *naked*. And wet. Right there, in the bathroom… mere meters away from her.

Oh, God. Lilah shook her head, disgusted with herself for being so silly about this situation. She pushed to her feet and dashed to the en-suite door to quickly drag it shut. It was only after she heard the lock catch that she realized her eyes had been closed. Like a child afraid of the bogeyman.

Lilah knew that she *had* to be more adult about this unfortunate affair. She was trying to present an unaffected front to this man. She had to make him believe that she truly meant it when she said she wanted a divorce after a year, that she would not be tied down in this loveless marriage. She absolutely refused to spend the rest of her life futilely loving a man who barely tolerated her. Who'd married her only to please his mentor, who felt some kind of misguided obligation toward her. *Ben* might think that that was the recipe for an ideal marriage, but Lilah would be damned if she remained trapped in such a sterile arrangement for the rest of her life.

That meant she would have to stop being such a ninny about

his nudity. She had to be a stronger and better woman. She should shrug off his bewildering advances, excoriate him with her scathing responses, and swat him away like a pesky mosquito.

But, right now, Lilah was the exact opposite of the woman she wanted to be. She was vulnerable, hurt, and frightened. And too affected by his sheer physicality.

With nowhere to hide from herself. Or from him.

She carelessly stuffed her clothing back into the suitcase, closed it, and rolled it into the closet. She hurried to the huge bed and crawled in on the left side. Once there, she curled up and dragged the covers to her ear. She switched off her bedside lamp and lay with her back to the bathroom, stiff as a board, while she waited for his inevitable return.

She listened, growing even more tense when the shower stopped. There was a long silence as he probably toweled himself dry. The same hum of toothbrush or razor that she'd heard on their wedding night.

Finally, after what felt like hours, the door slid open. She sensed him pausing and felt his eyes on her like a spotlight. She'd claimed the side of the bed furthest from the bathroom. And she was facing away from him.

"No wedding night tonight either, I'm guessing," he murmured. His voice was so quiet, she wondered if the words were meant for her at all.

He sighed and the overhead and pool lights switched off, leaving only his bedside light to illuminate the room. Crisp, freshly laundered fabric rustled as he tugged back the covers and crawled in beside her. The bed was massive, but she still felt the mattress dip as his substantial bulk settled in beside her. More disturbingly, even though he wasn't touching her, she could feel his heat invading the space between them.

"Sleep tight, cupcake," he murmured seconds before his lamp clicked off, cloaking the room in darkness.

Silence followed his words. But—in stark contrast to the even rise and fall of his breathing and the gentle susurration of waves lapping against the stilts of their villa—Lilah's breathing sounded harsh and panicked in that silence.

It spoke louder than any words ever could and she fought to control the pace of her breaths, wanting to rid herself of the desperate edge of anxiety she could hear creeping into every inhalation.

"Relax." His voice was gentle, no louder than the whispering waves. "C'mon Lilah, breathe with me, okay?"

She tried. She really did, but when the telltale wheeze crept in, she tensed in dread.

"Shh, come on now, sweetheart. You're okay. Don't panic, I'm going to touch you. No funny business. I promise…"

Despite the promise, she still flinched when his palm flattened against her back. Warm and reassuring through the thin cotton of her t-shirt. His stroked her back in slow, circular motions. And she found herself relaxing and leaning into his touch.

He'd always been able to talk her down like this.

Always…

Before Ben, any whisper of an asthma attack would be full blown in moments and occasionally resulted in hospitalizations. But whenever he was present, more often than not, he'd ease her out of it.

"Do you need your inhaler?" he asked. He'd moved closer, and she felt his breath stir her hair as he asked the question.

"Yes, please," she gasped, and he reached across her body to switch on her bedside light. He picked up her inhaler, which was within easy reach on the nightstand and handed it to her.

"Thank you," she whispered. She sat up and took a couple of puffs which helped her feel immediately better. She avoided his eyes by putting her inhaler back on the nightstand and clicking off the lamp again, taking refuge in the dark.

"Okay?" Ben asked as she settled under the covers with her back to him.

"I'm fine. Sorry."

She felt him shift and lay down as well. His hand came to rest on her waist and squeezed reassuringly. "No need to be sorry. We do find ourselves in a bit of a ridiculous situation here, don't we?"

"Do you think so?"

"Hmm. I mean look at us…Mr. and Mrs. Fake as Fuck. On honeymoon in paradise. How the hell did this even happen, right?"

Despite herself, that elicited a giggle from her. She sensed his satisfaction at the sound and he gave her waist an approving pat, before he withdrew his touch.

She mourned the loss but told herself it was for the best.

There was a long moment of silence before Lilah sighed and turned. It was dark and she couldn't see him, but she knew they were facing each other.

"Thank you," she whispered.

"You don't have to thank me. I know that this has all been stressful for you. Not quite how either of us imagined this marriage starting."

He shifted, his big body settling more comfortably into the mattress. He didn't turn or move away from her, and he felt closer than before. She tensed and then flinched when she felt a finger brush against her cheek.

"Get some sleep, Lilah" he whispered. "You're exhausted. And, quite frankly, so am I. Switch off that lively brain and overactive imagination for a few hours. You can go back to resenting me tomorrow."

"I don't resent you," she said, and then immediately wished the ridiculous lie back.

He laughed, the deep rumbling—genuinely amused—sound coming up from his chest.

"Liar."

"Okay, maybe I do, but...*hmph*!" The last as he pressed his finger against her lips, effectively shushing her.

"Not tonight. I'm running on empty and I'm pretty sure you must be too."

Ben so rarely admitted to any vulnerability that his words gave her pause. He had to be pretty close to the end of his tether to even show her this small amount of weakness.

"Goodnight, Ben."

"Goodnight, Lilah."

They didn't speak again after that, and while Lilah sensed that Ben had drifted off almost immediately, it took a while for her to follow.

LILAH OPENED her eyes to paradise.

Ben hadn't drawn the blinds last night and the first thing Lilah became aware of was the bright natural light flooding into the room. When she opened her eyes, and looked out, all she could see was blue. So many shades of blue.

The azure of the sky blended seamlessly with the crystal clear cerulean of the ocean and the aqua infinity pool which was a shade or two lighter than the sea. She'd never seen anything so beautiful and for a moment she forgot all her concerns and simply enjoyed the pristine beauty of the tropical utopia within which she found herself.

"Wow," she breathed. She sat up in bed, folding her arms around her knees, and stared out.

"Wow is right," Ben's low rasp agreed as he imitated her actions and pushed himself up.

Mercifully, he'd dragged on a pair of loose shorts to sleep in last night and she silently thanked him for that consideration. Of course, it didn't prevent her from surreptitiously eyeing his beautiful body again. And it definitely didn't stop her from noticing the fact that he seemed to have an erection… oh wait, no. Not *seemed to*, he most definitely had an erection.

She couldn't fight the blush that followed that realization and when his eyes drifted from the view to her face they sharpened immediately.

"What's got you all worked up this morning, cupcake?" he purred, even though he likely knew damned well why she was blushing.

"Do you mind ordering breakfast? I think I'll go for a dip," she said, ignoring his question.

Truthfully, she didn't know what to make of this teasing and tempting man. The Ben she knew had always been brusque to the point of rudeness. He'd never had a playful side. He had come to them a moody teen who'd matured into a taciturn man. In anyone else she would call this behavior flirtation, but Ben—customarily abrupt in his dealings with everybody—did not flirt.

"What do you fancy?" he asked as he climbed out of bed with a lazy stretch and a yawn. Her throat and mouth went dry at the play of muscles in his shoulders and arms… he did nothing to hide his hard-on from her and she went even redder.

Yep, that swim was desperately needed.

"Pancakes," she said, heading for the closet to retrieve a swimsuit from the suitcase. Because of the way she'd shoved everything into the case the night before, it took some digging around to find the bikini she was searching for. She should probably unpack to prevent her clothes from wrinkling even further, but that was the last thing she felt like doing right now. "With bacon. And lots of coffee."

She moved to the bathroom to dress while Ben placed their breakfast order.

By the time she returned from the bathroom, he'd changed into a pair of black swim trunks and was stretched out on a lounger by the pool, clearly enjoying the morning sun. She inhaled deeply, wishing she'd brought a longer, more billowy cover-up than the skimpy, translucent little slip that dipped too low in the chest area. She tugged at the hem, but could do nothing to drag it any lower. It rode high on her thighs, offering the scantest nod to modesty where it hugged the curve of her butt and rested just below her crotch. It was the most modest of the three coveralls she had packed. Similarly, the ice white string bikini beneath the tunic offered the most coverage of the several bathing suits she'd brought along.

He lifted his head when she joined him, but he was wearing dark sunglasses and it was hard to read his mood. Still, she sensed that he was running his eyes up and down her body and she barely refrained from crossing her arms over her chest.

"Breakfast will be here in about five minutes," he told her, pushing himself up onto one elbow. "Want to wait until then before you take that swim?"

She sank down onto the other lounger and nodded.

They sat in silence for a moment.

"What do you want to do today?" he asked when it became clear that she wasn't going to speak first.

She shrugged listlessly, still sitting stiffly on the lounger. She hadn't made a move to lay down the way he'd done.

"I seem to recall you mentioning that you'd signed us up for a couple of sightseeing trips. And you were excited about a dolphin or turtle search? And something about a couple's cruise around the atoll?"

Lilah stared at him in open-mouthed shock. He'd seemed so disinterested and dismissive every time she had brought up their honeymoon.

That sounds fine.

Sure, dolphins. Great.

Whatever you choose will be okay, I'm sure.

He had barely glanced at the brochures when she'd brought them to him, merely saying it looked perfect and she should definitely book it.

Lilah, of course, had told herself he was busy. And had flattered and fooled herself into believing that he trusted her with their all-important honeymoon plans. To discover that he'd actually been listening, despite everything she'd subsequently learned about their marriage, was shocking to say the least.

"We don't have to do those things. I know you were just humoring me. Well, *barely* humoring me. You didn't even make a pretense of caring about this stupid trip."

His shoulders lifted and fell on a deep—bordering on exasperated—sigh.

"If you're incapable of enjoying this vacation right now, at least try to find some way to distract yourself. Sulking isn't the most productive of activities."

"And I suppose you have *suggestions*"—air quotes—"on how I should go about keeping myself distracted."

He moved his sunglasses to the top of his head and gave her body a lazy, appreciative appraisal, before his half-mast eyes came to rest on hers.

"I *was* going to suggest reading a book, exploring, and God help me, even the fucking turtle thing sounds appealing as hell right now, compared to sitting here and watching you pout all day."

And yet, even while he made that scathing comment, his eyes took another leisurely meander over her body, pausing at her shallow cleavage, before ambling downward to her long legs. Telling her louder than words could, the many other ways he could possibly find to distract her.

"*Stop* that," she snapped, and this time she did cross her arms over her chest. But only in an effort to hide her hardening nipples from him. "You've never looked at me like this before."

A borderline wicked grin ghosted over his lips. "Perhaps I wanted to. But you were off-limits before."

Lilah had thought she knew what desire looked like in Ben. Had thought that the cold, fleeting kisses and touches during their engagement had been as good as it got with him. And she'd convinced herself that it was enough, that if it was all he had to give then it was all she wanted and needed from him.

Was he now expecting her to believe that *this* had been simmering away beneath that aloof, controlled façade all along? And all that had prevented him from acting on it was his respect for her grandfather?

Lilah called BS on that. She knew Ben, she'd seen him go after what he wanted time and time again, regardless of Gramps's opinion on the matter. In fact, she had often seen him go against

Gramps's advice and wishes on both personal and professional matters. If he'd truly wanted Lilah, he would have made that clear long before now.

No, she definitely didn't believe his sly insinuation that he may have wanted her all along. The way he'd phrased it made her think of the one time he had mentioned love, it had been worded in a similar way. As a possibility rather than a certainty. But Lilah wasn't about to fall for the same trick again. She realized now, as she should have then, that Ben was a man who brokered in certainties. He was usually brutally honest about everything and Lilah had been a fool to not immediately see through his duplicity.

She was about to challenge him on his claims when a cheery knock sounded at the door, accompanied by an equally chirpy, "Room service."

Ben gave her one last look before heading indoors to let the server in. Lilah took the opportunity to take a shaky breath. She wasn't sure if she was relieved or disappointed by the interruption —either way, it had merely delayed an inevitable conversation.

TWELVE
Fifteen Years Ago

"Lilah, this is the young man I've been telling you about. Ben, this is my granddaughter, Lilah. I trust you two will get along well. Lilah, I expect you to help Ben acclimatize to the country and the house."

Ben stared down at the girl laying on her stomach on the huge, plush sofa in one of the biggest rooms he'd ever seen in his life. She was wearing a pair of shorts with a tank, and seemed to be all arms and legs, with overly long brown hair messily blanketing her narrow back.

She was staring down at her phone and lifted her gaze from the screen to give Ben a dismissive once over.

The look rubbed an already defensive Ben up the wrong way.

Jesus. What a brat.

It's not like he fucking wanted to be here. In this overly-hot country, and this stupidly big house, with these strangers. So he needed this kid's shite attitude about as much as he needed a third nipple.

He didn't even know this old geezer who claimed to be his granddad's best friend and Ben's apparent legal guardian. A legal guardian he'd never even heard of before three weeks ago when his whole world had imploded.

He shoved his hands into his front jean pockets and glared down at the floor, wishing he was back home in their tiny kitchen, watching his mam cook some trout Ben and his dad had caught fly-fishing.

He felt a pang of loss so sharp, his stomach cramped with it. The grief threatened to overwhelm him right then and there and he blinked rapidly, not wanting to humiliate himself by crying in front of this snobby girl and her strange, old granddad.

He was aware of the girl scrambling to her feet for some reason and sneaked a peek at her from beneath his hair. He was almost immediately overwhelmed by another spasm of grief combined with guilt. His mam had been nagging him to cut it every day for nearly two weeks before the bus accident that had taken both his parents from him. Now, three weeks after he'd lost them, he still hadn't done so. Why hadn't he just cut his fucking hair? It would've made her happy.

Suddenly Ben couldn't wait for a private moment, so that he could shave it all off. He couldn't stand the thought of it growing even another inch.

The girl was standing in front of him now. She couldn't have been more than twelve or thirteen. She seemed tall for her age. Not that Ben was an expert or anything. She just seemed to be lanky. Ben had shot up over the last few years, his mam had complained about the seams she'd had to let out of all his trousers. And if Ben's growth spurt was any indication, it only stood to reason that this girl would probably grow into those long, gangly arms and legs eventually.

She looked like a clumsy newborn colt in those denim shorts. And her t-shirt was too small and too tight over her flat chest.

She'd probably already started that growth spurt.

She folded her arms over her chest and peered up at him closely.

What the hell? Why was she staring at him?

Despite himself, Ben's eyes flickered down to hers. She had weird eyes. Light brown… almost gold. He didn't like them. They were eerie.

He wasn't sure he really liked anything about her. He wasn't used to being around kids her age anyway, but from what he knew about them—thanks to his friends' younger siblings—they were pests.

He was aware of the old man, Cyrus, watching them both expectantly and offered the girl—what did the man say her name was? Lily? Lilac? Something unusual—a nod and a grunted, "Hey."

"Hi," she replied, clearly trying emulate the boredom and disinterest in Ben's voice.

Ben watched—fascinated—as a range of emotions flickered across her freckled face. Wariness, resentment, fear, anger, and then—to his utter humiliation—pity.

Who the hell did this girl think she was? He didn't need her fucking pity. He hadn't asked to come here. He'd hoped Cyrus would cart him off to a boarding school and remain a benevolent, distant benefactor. But the old man seemed to be taking this whole guardianship thing seriously. He'd informed Ben that he would be moving from Inverness to Cape Town and living with Cyrus and his granddaughter. Ben had zero options. No money, no prospects, no family, not even a home. Their house had been a rental and Ben would have been left homeless if Cyrus hadn't shown up when he did.

"I'm sorry about your mom and dad," the girl offered. She was watching him closely, her uncanny eyes warm, an assessing tilt to her head. Her scrutiny made Ben uncomfortable. He started to feel like some kind of exhibition in a museum.

She looked away, her face going bright red, and Ben's eyebrows rose.

Aah. Well this was familiar territory at least. The girl seemed to be developing a crush on him.

Ben knew girls thought he was good looking. He'd been popular with them back home. And while he'd been mostly preoccupied with football, he'd started returning the attention the last couple of years or so.

This kid didn't interest him in the slightest, of course. He was nearly seventeen. He didn't have any interest in wee lasses with crushes. But at least now he understood why she was staring at him so intently.

"Thanks," he muttered belatedly in response to her condolences and a glance to the side revealed that the old man was beaming, seeming happy with their interaction so far.

"I'll leave you two to get acquainted. Lilah, why don't you show Ben to his room? You can ask one of the drivers to take you both out sightseeing later, and you can introduce Ben to your favorite places around town."

"Okay, Gramps." She bounced over to Cyrus and wrapped her arms around his waist. "I'm so glad you're home. I missed you."

It only then occurred to Ben that she hadn't seen her grandfather in three weeks because the old man had been in Inverness since the day after Ben's parents' accident. He watched Cyrus enfold Lilah in his arms and drop a kiss on top of her head.

"I've missed you too, sweet pea."

In that instant, Ben felt a crushing swell of gratitude toward the man, as he comprehended exactly how lost he would've been if this stranger—who was clearly an important and busy man—hadn't chosen to drop everything in an instant to come and help him.

His parents hadn't been rich people. They'd lived a hand-to-mouth existence, and while they hadn't left any debt behind, they also had not left any money for funeral costs. Cyrus had taken care of everything. There had been a lot of meetings with social services, with lawyers, lengthy calls to South Africa, all in an effort to make sure everyone was happy with the transfer of Ben's guardianship to Cyrus Beckett.

At the time, Ben had felt like a steamroller had come in and laid waste to his life. But now he understood that without the juggernaut that was Cyrus Beckett, Ben would have been left destitute and alone. It was a humbling, terrifying thought.

The old man left the room, dropping a hand on Ben's shoulder on his way out and giving it a comforting squeeze. And then he was left with just the girl... *Lilah*.

They stared at each other for a long, uncomfortable moment.

"Well? Are you gonna show me to my room or not?"

"I like your accent," she observed shyly, immediately getting his back up. He didn't need the reminder that he was a stranger in a strange land, where everyone *else* had the accents.

"Yeah? Shame your opinion means fuck all to me." *Not* his finest comeback, and he felt ridiculous for allowing this infant to draw the stupid, childish response from him.

"I want us to be friends," she told him after moment, and now it was his turn to glower.

"You're a kid. What would we even do together? Play dollies? Have tea parties?"

"I'm not a kid." He gave that response the snort it deserved and she seemed to bristle with fury and dislike. Her face went bright red. "Honestly? I didn't want you here. Because Gramps already has me to take care of. He doesn't need an extra person to worry about. And *I'm* his granddaughter. Family. I belong and you... don't. So I thought maybe you'd feel out of place and uncomfortable. I know how it feels to be an orphan, but at least I have Gramps to love me. You have no-one. You need a friend and I can be your friend."

Stung by the spiteful reminder that he had no-one left in the world to love him, Ben lost patience with this irritating little shit. He wanted to get out of here. Be alone. Cut his fucking hair. "I'll find the room myself."

He turned on his heel and strode toward the door.

"Ben—"

He lifted his arm in response to the sound of his name on her lips and raised his middle finger in a farewell salute as he left the room.

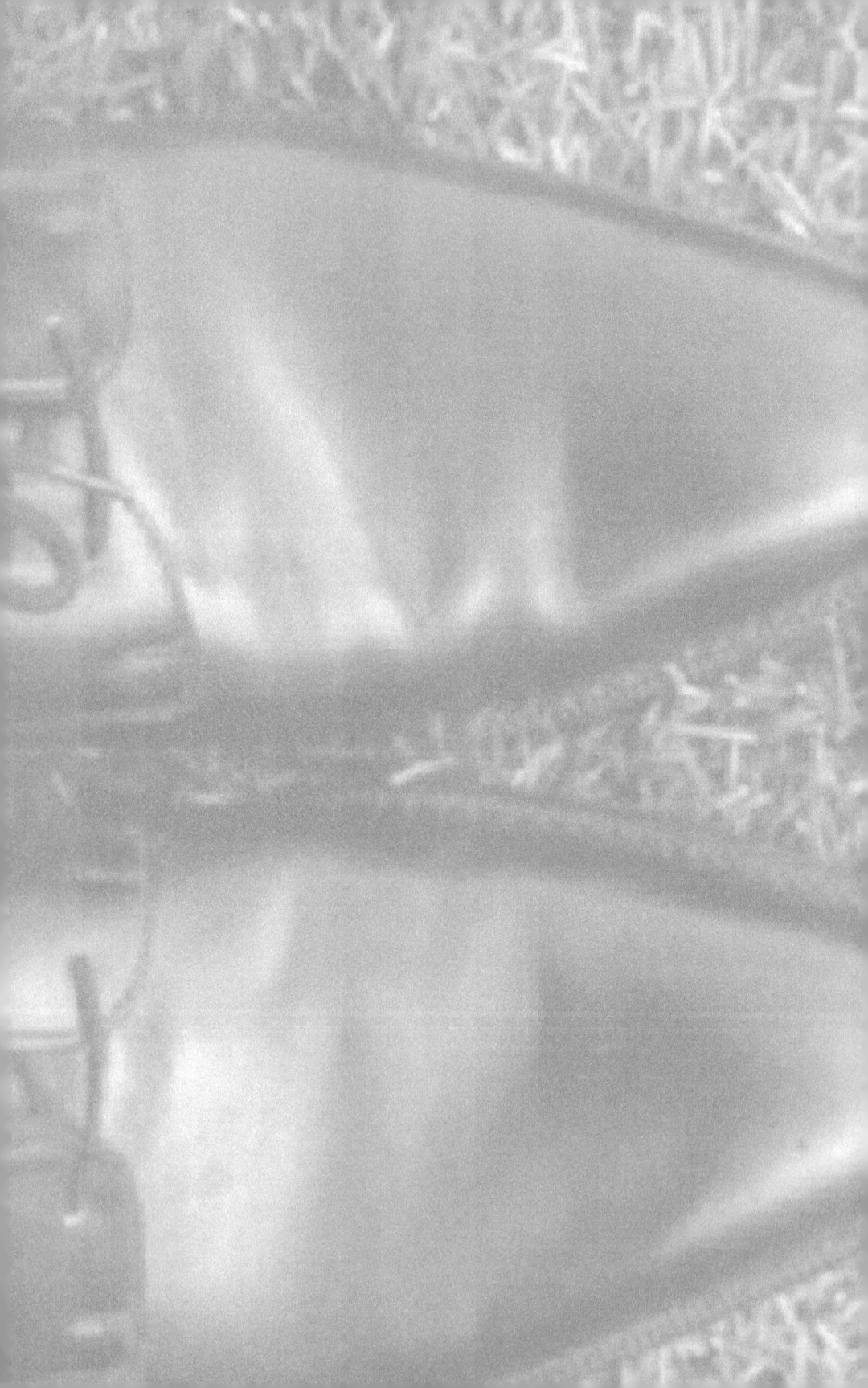

THIRTEEN

Her Tattered Heart

"So when have you signed us up for all the sightseeing stuff?" Ben asked Lilah after they'd finished their break- fast in absolute silence.

"I didn't sign us up for anything in the first two days, I thought—" Her cheeks flamed and she immediately bit back the revealing words she'd been about to utter.

"You thought we'd be too wrapped up in each other to want to leave our room, right?"

"Nope. Why would I think that, when I meant for our marriage to be nothing but a convenient arrangement?"

"You're so goddamned exasperating. I can't tell you how much I regret my honesty at our wedding. If I'd kept my mouth shut and played the happy, devoted husband, we'd probably be fucking right now. Instead, we're playing this dumb game of cat and mouse where you're punishing me for said honesty."

"I'm not punishing you."

"Of course you are. I don't love you and you're embarrassed

because you thought I did, and you think that somehow, you've been played for a fool."

She swallowed but refused to respond to that.

"Believe what you want, Ben. I don't care anymore." She lifted her phone from beside her plate, left the table, and made her way to one of the loungers, where she sank down onto her back and lifted the phone above her face to check her texts.

"So that's your plan? You're going to spend the morning on social media?"

"I'm catching up with my friends," she responded, not bothering to look at him.

"Your friends? Blake? And your emotional support... *uh*..."

"My emotional support *hoes*," she completed when his voice trailed off and he lapsed into silence. She tossed him a disdainful glance, astonished that he would be squeamish about the word. "From my gardening gal club, *The Horticultural Hoes*... spelled h.o.e. Y'know, like the gardening tool?"

He tossed aside his napkin and also got up, but he retreated into the villa, only to emerge seconds later, clutching his laptop.

"Since this day is a total fucking wash, I may as well get some work done."

"Whatever floats your boat," she murmured dismissively, her thumbs working furiously as she sent texts to her friends.

They spent the rest of the morning like that.

Together. Yet alone.

They barely exchanged half a dozen words in the hours that followed breakfast. A feat made easy through years of practice. All those afternoons Lilah had spent in his office, doing her own thing, while he did his, had prepared them for exactly this eventuality.

And Lilah wondered if this was the kind of frigid disinterest he expected from their day-to-day married life.

He had his laptop out, clearly working, while she swam and read and texted her *hoes* and Blake.

The ladies had initially been content with her pics of the villa and the view. But they were getting exasperated with Lilah's caginess.

> ### DARBI
>
> Seriously? We get it, it's pretty. And blue. So blue. Now show us what we really want to see. The newlyweds looking blissfully, shagtastically happy

GOD. Lilah pinched the bridge of her nose and fought back a groan. It had only been a matter of time.

> OLIVE
> Agreed! Show us the happy couple. You guys looked gorgeous at the wedding. Fairytale stuff. Ben couldn't keep his eyes off you. Siiiiiiigh. It was off the charts romantic 😻 😻 😘

Olive was the romantic in the group. The rest—Olive, Kes, and Ivy—all added to the demands and Lilah took a quick selfie, with the ocean as her backdrop, and sent it to them.

> **KES**
>
> Girl, you look smoking hot! And love the tan coming in. But you know that's not what we meant. Where's your man? 🤔

> **ME**
>
> He's taking a nap. I wore him out last night 😂

So many hearts and hot faces and a couple of squirting eggplants followed her blatant lie.

While that was going on, she took the opportunity to send the same selfie to Blake, with whom she was having a separate conversation. Blake cared little for gardening and even though she'd met most of the *Horti Hoes* at various outings and parties over the years, she wasn't really a part of their group.

BLAKE

Gorgeous 😍. That white bikini is a winner. Told you you'd rock that thing 👍

Blake had been the one who had gone shopping for honeymoon-wear with Lilah.

ME

You always give the best advice 😘

BLAKE

Where's Ben?

Lilah toyed with telling Blake the same lie, but her best friend wasn't as easily fooled or distracted.

> **ME**
> He's working. He had some stuff to finish up today.

> **BLAKE**
> Seriously?????
> YOU ARE ON YOUR HONEYMOON!

Blake wasn't Ben's biggest fan. She made no secret of the fact that she thought Ben should be more attentive and loving toward Lilah. Lilah had always defended him. Saying that was just the way he was. He wasn't affectionate or demonstrative. He loved her in his own way...

God, she felt like such an idiot right now. Blake had tried to warn her. But in the end, because it was clearly what Lilah had wanted, her friend had made the effort to be warmer toward Ben.

Lilah toyed with the idea of telling her friend the truth. But knew it was a conversation best had face-to-face. Instead, she dissembled.

> **ME**
>
> Tough time for him to be away from the office with his recent succession to CEO. Board is cagey.

She assumed there had to be *some* truth to that. Ben had effectively been at the helm of the company for several years, but his position hadn't been formalized. To all intents and purposes, the shareholders assumed that Gramps still made all the important decisions. But Gramps had been merely a figurehead for a while now.

> **BLAKE**
>
> Don't care 😠 How the hell can he be focused on work with his smokeshow of a bride within groping distance? The man has messed up priorities. You're the most important person in his life now. And he should damned well act like it 🤬🖕

Lilah's eyes flooded. Trust Blake to get to the heart of the matter immediately. She was a fierce champion of those she cared about.

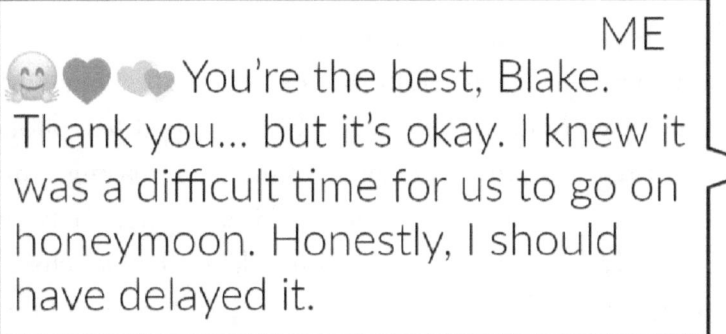

Talk about wishful thinking. But thankfully, Blake let it go and the conversation veered to who had been wearing what at the wedding.

There'd been insistent pings and WhatsApp notifications on her phone throughout her chat with Blake, the *hoes* were getting impatient.

"Can't you put that damned thing on silent?" Ben snapped from his seat at the patio table. "It's been going nonstop for the last half hour. You have it in your hand, no reason for it not to be on mute."

Lilah, who'd been stretched out on the lounger, pushed herself up and left the patio without a word.

"Now you're just being childish," he called after her and she flipped him off without looking back. She dropped her phone on the bed and tugged a pink slip dress from her increasingly messy, still wide-open suitcase—now that he'd seen her sexy night things, she really didn't have any reason to keep the bag closed.

She dragged the dress on over her head, before grabbing her phone and camera bag, along with her trusty Canon EOS 6D, on her way to the front door.

"Where are you going?" He sounded alarmed but she didn't care. She needed some breathing room.

"Out."

"Wait, I'll come with y—"

"No." She looked back to find him hovering above his chair, one hand flattened on the table and the other curled around the back of the chair.

"I've had about as much of your company as I can stand right now." She was proud of how assertive she sounded. "I think we could both use a break from each other. I'm going to do some exploring, take some photos. I don't need you for that. In fact, I don't need you for anything."

Lilah exited the room before he had a chance to respond. She took a huge, cleansing breath once she was outside. The air was tinged with salt and the smell of distant frangipani blooms.

Lilah felt like she was the only person on the planet as she walked along the wooden pathway above the turquoise waters that would lead her from the overwater villas to the green, lush island just ahead.

Despite the less-than-ideal circumstances within which Lilah found herself, she couldn't help but feel a little flutter of excitement in her stomach at the thought of exploring the tiny island. They hadn't seen much upon arrival last night, but this morning all she could see was a relaxing palette of blues and greens and whites. Lilah had travelled a fair bit over the course of her life but this was quite simply one of the most beautiful places she'd ever seen.

She stopped frequently to snap photos along the way, happy that she'd equipped the camera with a 16mm lens to get the best landscape shots. She wasn't taking any particularly original shots, but the camera had always been like an extension of herself and she felt naked without it. Besides, choosing the best angles and framing the shots kept her mind occupied. And that was exactly what she needed right now.

She roamed around aimlessly, taking pictures of people and of the ocean—enjoying the contrasts between the many shades of blues in the latter. The happy, honeymooning couples, were oblivious to her presence.

Lilah often felt a false sense of security behind the lens of her camera, invisible, untouchable, there but not. She always chronicled, but rarely participated. Her wedding, and her life with Ben after the wedding should have been her opportunity to finally be a part of something special. No longer the poor little rich girl, too fragile to play or partake, always forced to watch from the sidelines because of her asthma.

Lilah had had asthma for as long as she could remember, with only a brief respite during her mid-to-late teens. She'd hoped to outgrow it, and for a short time it had seemed as if she had, but it had returned with a vengeance during her first year of college.

As a result of her medical condition, Gramps had been extremely protective of her. It was only after Ben had appeared on the scene that Gramps had allowed Lilah some of the freedom she'd yearned for. Now, with the benefit of hindsight, Lilah understood that her freedom had been an illusion.

Ben had become her reluctant guardian. The one to watch over her when Gramps wasn't around to do so. And Ben had literally just committed to continue martyring himself in this unnecessary capacity for the rest of his life.

Lilah knew that Ben felt indebted and grateful to her grandfather, she just hadn't understood the extent to which he would go for the old man. Yes, part of this was probably for the business reasons, he certainly hadn't denied that, but Lilah recognized that Ben's greatest motivation by far was his need to please her grandfather.

She wondered if she'd hit the nail on the head with her wild theory about him fearing being left out of the will. But Ben had never struck her as a greedy man. He was proud and hardworking, and had accumulated his own wealth over the years as Gramps's right hand man. There was an expectation that he would be in the will, of course there was, it was inevitable... but the bulk of her grandfather's wealth would eventually pass to Lilah.

A tiny niggling voice in the back of her mind whispered that maybe he'd married her to eventually gain control of that wealth, but she ruthlessly suppressed it. Unable—even after the events of the last 48 hours—to believe Ben capable of such cold-blooded avariciousness.

Realizing that the world had gone blurry, Lilah swiped at the tears that had pooled in her eyes and forged determinedly ahead. Ben and — to a lesser extent — Gramps might have the rest of her life all mapped out, but Lilah wasn't even remotely on the same page as them. She would do what she had to do to convince Gramps that this marriage was real for now but she refused to commit herself to longer than a year of this hell. Once she got her divorce, she would sever all ties with Ben. They could tell Gramps that they'd tried but they were just too incompatible, nobody had been at fault, it was just one of those things.

It was the only way to salvage her pride and repair her tattered heart.

FOURTEEN

His casual cruelty

"Tell me again how you can take care of yourself," Ben's mocking voice invited from behind Lilah, seconds before an inhaler was tossed in her lap. He sat down on the warm, white sand beside her and plonked her hat onto her head in the same motion.

She didn't bother asking him how he'd found her. It was a small island, and he knew her well enough to recognize that she would have made a beeline for the closest, quietest beach.

Lilah wasn't going to let him disturb the peace she'd found while sitting on this tranquil strip of white sand. There weren't many people here—she'd seen a number of people hanging out at the activity center and the hotel pool—and Lilah had picked a spot a fair distance from the next closest, privacy-seeking couple.

"Thank you for bringing my hat," she said, and the blustery wind seemed to leave his billowing sails at her words. "It was silly of me to leave it behind."

"I'm less concerned about the hat than I am about the inhaler," he replied, his voice no longer as challenging. Instead, she heard a tinge of exhausted resignation in that rasp.

"I always carry a back-up in my camera bag," she said, nodding toward the canvas bag tucked beside her hip.

He sighed deeply and loosely folded his arms around his bent, spread knees. She kept her gaze directed toward the ethereally blue ocean, but was painfully aware of Ben's intense stare boring into her profile

"I do know how to manage my disease, Ben."

"I can think of several occasions when you didn't manage it so very well."

"Twice. That was it. The first time"—had been terrifying for both of them. She could still remember the look of panic and outright fear on Ben's face as he fought a losing battle to keep her conscious——"wasn't my fault. You know that."

"At the wedding—"

"I told you why I wasn't carrying one at the wedding," she interrupted him sharply. "It was stupid. I should have known better. But I thought..." She wiped the sand from her hands and met his gaze head on. "Well, I told you what I thought. No need to go over that again."

"I always—" He stopped talking abruptly, and shook his head dazedly, as if confused by whatever he'd been about to say.

"You always what?"

"It's nothing."

"I want to know."

"Nothing to know."

Frustrated, she glared at him mutely, before shaking her head and pushing to her feet. She tugged her dress up and over her head, dropped it—and the hat—onto the sand. Without another word to him she walked directly into the water. She knew that the white bikini bottom was designed to ride up ever so slightly on each side and was aware that he was getting a pert eyeful, but she no longer cared. While she'd felt too exposed earlier, she now felt a malicious swell of satisfaction in letting him see everything she would never allow him to touch.

She plunged into the cool waters, submerging her body entirely, before surfacing to face the beach, where Ben still sat with her stuff. He was too far away for Lilah to read his expression and he still wore his sunglasses, but she could see the tension in every line of his body.

She stared at him for a long moment, feeling his eyes on her, even though she could not see them.

What was he thinking? Did those glasses disguise a wealth of hatred, revulsion, and resentment toward her?

Did she care?

She considered the question for a moment, before deciding that yes, she did care. She cared a lot. She didn't want anyone hating her... and God help her, she *definitely* didn't want Ben hating her. No matter how ambivalent her feelings currently were toward him, she still didn't want him to hate her. Or resent her.

She was so damned pathetic.

Lilah made an impatient sound in the back of her throat and dove into the cool waters, swimming parallel to the shore for a few strokes until she was no longer in his direct line of sight. She flipped over onto her back and floated on top of the tranquil, rippling surface, feeling instantly calmer as she stared up into the cloudless azure sky. The surrounding world was muffled by the water, and she could hear the distant thrum of an engine and the rhythmic whooshing of gently lapping waves.

Her skin was pleasantly warmed by the tropical sun, while she remained cool thanks to the water all around her. The sound of her even, deep breathing was loud in her ears and it lulled her into an almost meditative state.

She moved her hands idly, happy to let the water carry her where it wanted. She didn't know how long she drifted, all she knew was that nothing could hurt her here, she was safe, protected by the ocean's cool and welcoming embrace.

"Lilah." She was so relaxed, that she didn't hear the muffled voice at first.

"Lilah?"

She blinked slowly, her focusing turning outward, as she became more aware of her surroundings. Was that Ben? His voice, distorted by the water, sounded close.

"Lilah!"

He came from seemingly out of nowhere, palms on her torso and back as he sandwiched her midriff in his big hands.

She gasped and swallowed a mouthful of water, and immediately panicked and floundered as she went from horizontal to vertical in a second. Her feet couldn't find the bottom and she went under for a brief moment. Ben's grip tightened, and he changed his hold to securely hook an arm around her waist and drag her up until her head was above water. Panicked, she wrapped her arms around his neck, while she gasped for air. They were both treading water.

"What the hell?" she spluttered once she had caught her breath. "Why did you do that?"

"I didn't mean to startle you," he growled the words directly into her ear, and Lilah abruptly became aware of the fact that she was wrapped around him like a vine. They were plastered together; their wet bathing suits the only things preserving even a modicum of modesty between them. She could feel every hard, perfect inch of his body rubbing up against hers, and she resisted the urge to burrow even closer.

"Well, if your intention wasn't to startle me, you failed miserably," she griped as she reluctantly removed her arms from around his neck and, instead, flattened her palms against his hard, naked chest, exerting enough pressure to get him to loosen his anchoring hold around her waist.

He released her completely and she kicked away from him, until there was about a meter of water between them.

"You were drifting out here for nearly ten minutes. The water is calm, but I was concerned about how far from shore you were."

A quick glance toward the distant shoreline confirmed his words and she tried to hide her shock from him. She hadn't realized she'd floated this far out. She was a good swimmer and there weren't any strong currents, but it had been foolhardy to not periodically check her surroundings.

Still, she didn't want to—once again—be lambasted about not being able to take care of herself... even though, admittedly, this time she'd been a complete idiot.

"I'm a strong swimmer. I didn't need you to come speeding to my rescue. I had the situation in hand."

She chose to ignore his skeptically raised brow and set out toward the shore in a slow determined crawl. He deliberately kept pace with her, which annoyed Lilah to no end because after a couple of minutes of dogged swimming, she needed to stop for a breather. God, how the hell far had she gone? The shore didn't seem that much closer. But if she stopped, he would know how winded she was.

His hand on her elbow brought her to a halt and they both tread water while they stared at each other.

"I need a break," he told her impassively. Even though he wasn't the slightest bit winded.

His blatant lie made her go a little fuzzy inside and she inhaled deeply... okay, more like gulped in a much-needed breath of air.

"You're such a liar," she said once she could breathe a little more normally. The wryness in her voice seemed to make his lips quirk. She squinted toward the shoreline, the salt starting to irritate her eyes, and begrudgingly admitted, "So maybe this *is* a little further out than I'd intended to go."

He didn't respond to that, merely quirked his brow in a "ya think" manner.

"I still didn't need you to come charging in on your white horse though. I would have been fine. I know this is getting old, when so much recent evidence points to the contrary, but I really *do* know how to take care of myself better than this."

He reached out and dragged a wet strand of hair from her cheek and tucked it behind her ear. His fingers lingered on the hollow behind her earlobe.

"Let's get back to shore," he said, choosing not to respond to her statement. "I don't know about you, but I'm starving."

"I THOUGHT you told her months ago, Cyrus. You *should* have."

Lilah awoke to those urgent words later that night. Something in Ben's whispered voice told her that this was a conversation he would rather she not hear, and so she instinctively kept her eyes shut and her breathing even, while straining to hear the rest of the muted one-sided conversation.

Ben wasn't in the room with her, the faintness of his voice

telling her that he was out on the patio, but sound carried in the hush of the late evening.

When they'd returned to their villa after dinner, Lilah had immediately showered and crawled into bed, pleading exhaustion. Ben had informed her that he had work to do and phone calls to make. It had been close to midnight local time, and Lilah hadn't thought anything of it. Even though South Africa was a mere three hours behind the Maldives, it wasn't inconceivable that he'd be calling her grandfather or other company executives at that time of night. Their time revolved around Ben. Not vice versa.

Lilah had slipped into a light doze. She wasn't sure how long she'd slept, but she didn't think it could have been more than an hour.

"I understand that you didn't want to ruin the wedding or our honeymoon, but you're going to have to tell her pretty soo—*of course you have to tell her!* What? No. Come on, Cy. Don't say shit like that. I *have* been facing reality. I feel like you're the one who hasn't. That's not my place…" There was a long, long pause as he listened to whatever it was Gramps was saying. "No. You can't abdicate that responsibility to me." Another pause followed by a heated, "And *you're* her grandfather! No. *No!* She's fine. Yes, she was a beautiful bride… you're trying to distract me with bullshit. It won't work." More silence, then, "Immediately after the honeymoon? Good. Take care of yourself, old man."

His voice roughened on the last six words and there was a long silence before he swore vehemently beneath his breath. Lilah opened her eyes and her gaze tracked to the patio, which was illuminated by only the blue light from the pool.

She could see his silhouette as he stood with his hands stuffed into his cargo shorts pockets, head bent as he appeared to stare down into the water.

He looked pensive and she wondered what his conversation with Gramps had been about. Well, it had obviously been about her, but what specifically? What nefarious scheme had they cooked up between them now? And how did it involve Lilah? She didn't like being the subject of discussion between two such bull-headed men. It never boded well for her. It meant they were making decisions on her behalf again. And she resented that. When the hell would they recognize that stripping Lilah of her agency in this manner was demeaning? An insult to her independence and intelligence.

She was about to sit up and ask him what the conversation had been about when something in his dejected posture stopped her. This didn't feel like Ben and Gramps's usual strong-arming bullshit, this felt terrifyingly weighty and Lilah wasn't sure she wanted to wade into this morass just yet.

She continued to watch him warily, not sure she ever wanted to know what this was about.

He turned back toward the villa, his broad shoulders slumped, and she couldn't remember ever seeing him look this defeated before. She didn't know what to make of it. She kept her breathing even and lowered her lids until her vision shrank to a sliver. He moved silently as he switched off the outside lights, and then retreated to the bathroom. She heard the muffled sounds of him brushing his teeth and a few minutes later, bathroom ritual complete, he re-entered the room. She once again lay facing away from the bathroom and felt the mattress dip as he climbed back into bed.

The sheets rustled as he settled in beside her and after a few moments, the movement stopped. He sighed. A long, sad sound, and then his breathing settled into a deep, even rhythm.

"Lilah?"

She tensed at the whisper of her name a few minutes later, not sure if she should reply or not.

The uncertainty kept her silent and he sighed again, this time the sound was shaded with frustration.

LILAH AWOKE to find herself wrapped in Ben's arms. She must have turned around during the night and snuggled against him — or he had tugged her into his arms — she couldn't be sure of which. All she knew was that she was pressed to his chest, her legs entangled with his, one arm draped over his waist and the other tucked between them with her hand flat against one hard pec.

Meanwhile, one of Ben's arms was buried under her neck, while the other was wrapped around her torso. His hand was beneath her t-shirt, his warm, dry palm pressed against her naked back. He was gently stroking her sensitive skin, the movement so subtle it took her a moment to realize what he was doing.

She tensed, opened her eyes and lifted her head, only to find herself staring directly into his cobalt blue gaze. His lids were half-mast, giving him a sleepy look, but there was nothing sleepy in those intense eyes.

Her heartbeat and breathing sped up as she found herself mesmerized by that seductive stare. He shifted his featherlight touch from her back, trailing his fingers to her waist, then walking them up over the shallow steps of her ribcage toward the underswell of one small breast. This time her breath stuttered to a halt as she waited to see where he would go next.

His hand remained where it was, palm cupped around her

narrow torso, while his thumb stroked back and forth over the tender flesh at the bottom curve of her breast. He was nowhere near her nipple, but the heat of his hand, combined with the almost absent stroking of her skin, sent a wave of gooseflesh over her body, while simultaneously beading her nipples, and knotting her clit to a painfully hard point.

The breath she was holding shuddered from her lips on a gasped, "*No.*"

"I'm not doing anything." The whiskey rasp of his voice scraped across her already sensitized nerve endings and she arched against him, not sure if she wanted to get away from, or push herself closer to, his big, hard body.

"You're thinking about it."

His lips stretched into a lazy grin. "So are you."

He looked like a pirate with his mussed hair, dark morning stubble, and wicked smile.

"I'm not thinking of anything," she squeaked unconvincingly and his piratical grin widened.

"Sure you are, Lilah," he said, his somber tone at odds with the glint in his eyes. "You're thinking about what would happen if I moved this hand just an inch to the north." His dropped to his hand and the laughter died from his gaze as his eyes went smokey with desire. His Adam's apple bobbed as he swallowed and when it emerged again, his voice was as fractured as crushed glass. "Or maybe you're wondering how it would feel if my hand moved south, to where you're scalding hot and soaking wet. Is that what you're thinking, cupcake? Hmm? I can make that happen. I can show you exactly how it would feel to have me touch you there, stroke your aching pussy. I can do that for you. I can make you come. You can make *me* come. We can do that for each other... with just our hands. Our mouths. Do you want that?"

She wavered, for just a second—she was only human after all—aching for him to touch her, wanting to run her own hands down his broad chest, stroking and exploring until she could close her palm around the rigid length she felt straining against her thigh.

God, she was so tempted. But even though rationality was fast losing the battle to the hypnotic rasp of his voice and the distracting stroke of his fingers, she knew enough to understand that if she caved now, if she allowed this, he would never respect her. She would never respect herself. He would win and she would forever carry the humiliating knowledge that she'd left her spine in the Maldives.

"I don't want that," she said, her voice faint and unconvincing. A sharp intake of breath when that long, agile thumb oh-so-lightly brushed over her hard nipple. Her voice gained strength, despite the full body throb his brief touch had resulted in. "Stop touching me, Ben."

His hand immediately retreated, and Lilah swallowed down her instant regret. This was for the best. Sex was the absolute last thing that Lilah wanted to happen between them right now.

Even though her clamoring body called her a filthy liar.

Ben's alert gaze scrutinized her face but his expression was hard to read. Despite the proximity of his body, the cold calculation in his beautiful eyes made it feel like there was a million miles between them and instantly reinforced Lilah's decision to call a halt to what she could now tell had been a cynical attempt at seduction on his part.

"Sex is just a tool to you, isn't it?" She spoke without thinking. "A means to an end."

He sighed, a long-suffering sound filled with frustration and impatience.

"It's a means to an orgasm," he corrected, shifting until there was no longer any contact between their bodies. It was a move that Lilah should have been grateful for, but instead she mourned the loss of his warmth and the deceptive sense of intimacy his closeness had created. He stretched, every muscle in his body tautening in an impressive display of sheer unbridled maleness, and then yawned while he pushed himself up until his back rested against the fan-shaped bamboo headboard.

She sat up as well, putting even more distance between them and he smirked at her pointed move.

He bent his knees, ignoring his still rampant hard-on, and watched her with a quizzical tilt to his head and that hateful little smirk still on his lips. "Let me guess, you want flowers and romance and violins whenever you fuck?"

"No. Just mutual affection. And if I can't have that, then at the very least, I deserve some respect." She wished the words had emerged with more confidence. Instead her voice was small and uncertain, which was exactly how she felt.

She needed to get better at shielding herself from his casual cruelty. She didn't even think he meant to be cruel, he likely thought he was being honest, straightforward, but everything he said and did left wounds ranging from shallow cuts to deep slashes on her heart.

But Lilah welcomed the pain, she needed it... every hateful barb, unintentional or not, hardened her against him. The wounds would heal and leave protective scars around her heart and when that happened, he would never be able to hurt her again.

He laughed, the sound genuinely amused, and shook his head, something akin to affection shining in his eyes.

"You've always been such a dramatic little thing," he said, his tone indulgent and warm. "It's early days yet, you'll see... this will work out between us. I promise you. And you know I always keep my promises, right?"

The supreme arrogance of the man. There was no point in arguing with someone who was so absolutely set in his opinions. There was only proving him wrong. And that meant staying the course and never wavering from her principles.

She swung her legs over the side of the bed and got up.

"Where are you going?" he asked.

"Shower."

"Should I order breakfast?"

"I'm heading out. I'll get something at one of the restaurants."

"Heading out where?"

"Who knows? Maybe I'll finally check out those turtles. Or the dolphins. I'll find something to do."

"I'll come with y—"

"No."

"Lilah, be—"

"If the next word out your mouth is *reasonable*, I won't be responsible for my actions," she interrupted him furiously.

His eyebrows shot to his hairline and his lips curled in that infuriatingly sardonic way. It was an expression that always made her feel about twelve years old. He held up both hands in a gesture of surrender and lifted his broad shoulders.

"Suit yourself, but take your inhaler. And keep your phone with you in case I need to reach you."

"I don't see why you'd need to reach me."

"Just indulge me, okay?"

She didn't respond, but when she left the room half an hour later, she had the phone tucked into her camera bag next to the inhaler she would've been carrying anyway. She used the phone to text her *hoes* and Blake. Occasionally she'd message Gramps whose replies were few and far between.

Ben messaged her twice. Once to ask if she would have lunch with him and then again to ask about dinner. She didn't join him for either, and after spending an evening taking long-exposure shots of the creamy, full moon above the black ocean, she reluctantly made her way back to the villa.

"Did you eat?" It was the first question he asked her when she stepped through the door. She carefully placed her camera bag on the floor next to the door, before kicking off her flip flops and walking barefoot to the minibar to retrieve a bottle of water.

"I ate."

"I hope you used enough sunscreen, it was a scorcher today."

"Will you *ever* stop treating me like a child?" she asked. There was no heat in her voice, just sadness and exhaustion.

His eyes flickered and he shoved his hands into the pockets of his blue cargo shorts.

"I'm just concerned."

"Stop it. I don't need a nursemaid."

His lips tightened and he nodded curtly.

"Fair enough."

Well, wasn't he being amenable as hell tonight?

"So what did you do all day?" he asked, approaching her cautiously, as if uncertain of her reaction to his encroaching closeness.

"Explored, took pictures."

"It's a small island, you must have walked the entire thing in just an afternoon."

"I explored. I don't rush when there are so many beautiful things to see and photograph. I think I covered maybe a quarter of the western part of the island."

"Seriously?"

"Not everyone is always rushing through life, Ben. Some of us like to take the time to enjoy the beauty around us."

He didn't look too impressed with her response and merely grunted in reply.

"And what do you want to do now?" His glance ambled up and down the length of her body. Lilah immediately became aware of the fact that she wore a pair of minute white cotton shorts, combined with just a blue bikini top. She was tempted to cross her arms over her chest, but refused to give him the satisfaction of knowing that his staring was making her feel all hot and bothered.

"Take a dip. Shower. Sleep."

"We could unwind in the hot tub," he suggested, his voice completely lacking in any inflection, and her gaze flew to his face, which matched his voice. Nothing to be gleaned from those handsome, impassive features at all.

The hot tub sounded tempting as hell though.

"Both of us?" she asked warily, and his eyebrows quirked.

"I did say *we*."

"I don't think that's a great idea. I think I'll just shower. Or maybe take a bath."

"You're clearly dying to get into the hot tub, Lilah," he said. "Don't be silly. It's massive. We would fit in it with room to spare."

"I don't want to share the tub with you, Ben. End of discussion. You knock yourself out. Maybe I'll try it tomorrow or the day after."

He made a rude sound in the back of his throat, but she ignored him, and in a fit of pique and an overwhelming desire to punish him, she unbuttoned her shorts and peeled them down over her hips before shimmying out of them. Revealing to his interested gaze, the length of her perfectly smooth legs and the minuscule bikini bottom that rode up between her butt cheeks.

She turned away from him, hyper-aware of his piercing gaze on her bum, and leisurely ambled to the patio, putting extra sway into her walk. She couldn't be certain, but she was almost sure she heard him groan, which brought a petty little grin of satisfaction to her lips.

Take that, asshole!

She submerged her overheated body into the cool waters of the pool and dunked her head under the water for a brief moment as well. When she resurfaced it was to find him standing at the edge of the pool and staring down at her. Hands in pockets, head bent, tension in every line of his body.

They stared at each other for a long, silent moment before he sighed impatiently and sank down onto one of the loungers.

"Aren't you going to ask me how *my* day was?" he asked.

"Why should I?"

"It's what a good wife would do."

"I think it's more than apparent that I will not be a good wife to you, Ben."

"Give it time, you may surprise both of us yet."

She laughed, the sound far from amused, and tread water, skimming her arms back and forth across the surface of the water as she contemplated his words.

"And do you think you'll be a good husband to me?"

"I think I already am."

She laughed again, and this time there was humor in the sound. "How do you figure that?"

"I want what's best for you. I care about what happens to you. I know I could make you *very* happy in bed."

She shook her head, a brief side-to-side motion, her lips still tilted upward.

"You're completely deluded, Ben. I'm so sick of having this same conversation. Why don't we both just agree that this is a subject we will never see eye-to-eye on and let it go for now? After this ridiculous excuse of a honeymoon is over, we can discuss next steps and living arrangements. But for now, why don't we just stay out of each other's way? Okay?"

This time he was the one who laughed, a harsh, acerbic sound that made her wince.

"And you call me deluded? Lilah, it's time you face up to the reality of your situation… we're married."

"Ugh. Stop. Please. I've had enough." She made her way to the steps and climbed out of the pool, picking up a clean towel from the other lounger, which she wrapped around her body. She wrung out her hair with her hands and tracked puddles of water into the villa. She went straight to the bathroom and closed the door firmly behind her.

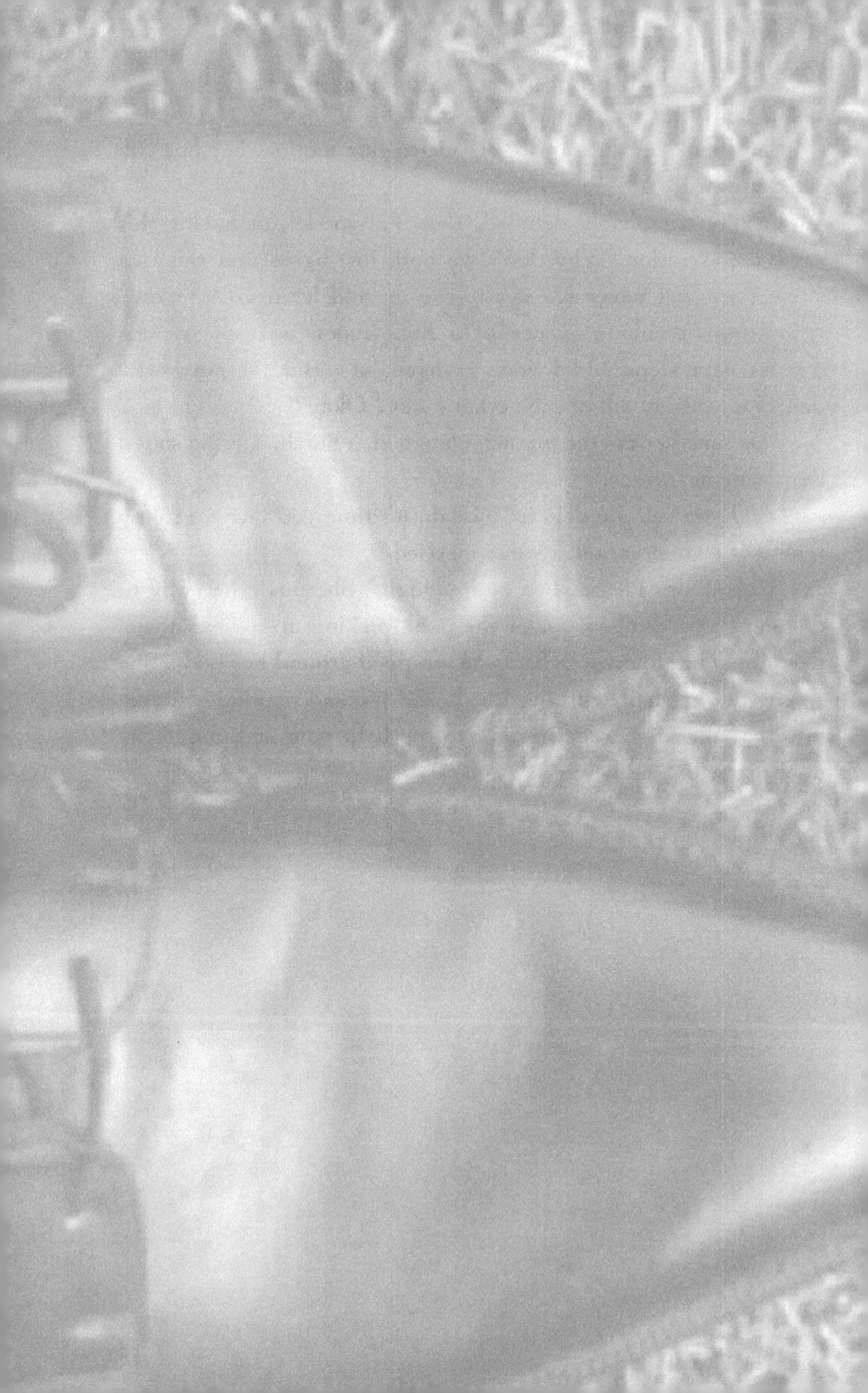

FIFTEEN

Purgatory in paradise

The next four days followed a similar pattern. They went to sleep on separate sides of the bed, and always woke up entwined in each other's arms. Lilah never lingered though, always pushing him away and escaping to the bathroom and then leaving the villa without exchanging any meaningful conversation with him.

She spent her days exploring, lounging on the beach, texting friends, taking pictures of the scenery, the wildlife, the resort, all the happy couples. She'd been massaged, waxed, primped, and preened. She'd gone snorkeling, kayaking, parasailing, dolphin spotting, turtle watching, everything she'd expected to do while on honeymoon, only — contrary to her expectations — she'd done it alone. She knew the staff, with whom she was becoming quite familiar, wondered why this honeymooning couple were never seen together, but they were discreet and never asked questions.

Lilah hated every moment of this purgatory in paradise. She longed to go home and wished Gramps — whom she missed and worried about—would respond to her texts with more frequency. When he did message her, he always seemed distant and not like himself at all. She would have expected him to have bugged her incessantly for pictures of herself and Ben by now. But nothing. If she hadn't been the one messaging him, she wouldn't have heard from him, since he hadn't instigated communications at all.

And trying to get him on Facetime? Or even for just a good old fashioned phone call? Forget about it. She'd even been desperate enough to ask Ben if he'd spoken to the old man. He'd been frustratingly vague in his response to her question, which made her feel completely out of the loop.

"Can we leave on Friday?" she asked Ben that Wednesday evening, after returning from yet another day of solitary sightseeing. "You said we could go home after a week."

He was sitting at the desk, laptop open, as he did what she assumed he'd been doing every day. Work. She'd never bothered to ask and suddenly she found herself curious.

"Have you been working every day?" She sank down on the bed, folding her legs under her butt as she watched him. He swiveled his chair around to face her.

"Why the sudden interest in how I'm spending my days?" His voice was laced with sarcasm and she immediately regretted her question

"Never mind."

He sighed and rubbed the back of his neck, then rolled his shoulders—exhaustion evident in his every movement. "No, I haven't been working every day. I've explored the island a fair bit myself. I've seen you around, taking pictures."

"You have?" That was an unexpected revelation. "I haven't seen you."

His lips tilted at the corners. "That doesn't surprise me. I never appreciated the amount of focus—no pun intended—you put into your photography. Once you've honed in on a subject, you're fixated. I watched you sitting cross legged in front of some shrubbery for nearly forty-five minutes a couple of days ago. You barely moved."

Lilah's lips spread into a delighted grin as she recalled the moment he had to be referring to.

"I spotted this adorable little oriental garden lizard. He was shy and reluctant to come out with me sat right there. So I stayed very, very still, hoping he'd realize I wasn't a threat and venture out."

"And did he?"

Her smiled widened and she nodded. "Oh yes. At first just his head, he was super cautious, but I could see him eyeballing me. He was absolutely beautiful. Bright orange, with this awesome little spiny crest at the back of his neck. I would have been happy with just those shots of his head as he side-eyed me. But he decided I was no threat and came out onto a little rock to sun himself completely. I got some amazing shots of him."

"I'd like to see them sometime." Ben's voice was quiet and startled her back to the present, where she realized she'd been yammering on about that lizard like an idiot. He was staring at her with a peculiar expression on his face, one she found herself unable to read. His eyes were narrowed, but there was a soft smile playing about the corners of his lips.

"See what?" she repeated blankly, and his lips stretched into a smile of genuine warmth.

"Your pictures. Of the lizard."

"Oh." A thought struck her and she tilted her head to regard him quizzically. "How do you know I sat there for nearly forty-five minutes?"

159

"Because while you sat watching a lizard for forty-five minutes, I sat watching my *wife* for the same length of time. You were luckier though... at least the lizard noticed you were there."

Well, hell. What was she supposed to make of that?

"At first, I thought it was deliberate. I thought that you were trying to prove a point, you didn't want to be here with me, you didn't want to spend time with me. But after that I soon recognized that for someone who's generally quite observant and clued in to the people around her, you just never saw me."

She wasn't sure how to respond to that. She always noticed Ben. If she hadn't seen him, it was because he didn't want to be seen.

"Were you following me?"

He laughed, a short, sharp sound. "Hardly. Like I said before, it's a small island."

"So no lurking in the bushes, watching me like a creeper then?"

"What the hell kind of question is that?"

"I would have seen you otherwise," she said with a shrug.

"I wasn't lurking, but I *was* keeping a low profile. Because I didn't want you to think I was lurking in the bushes watching you like some creeper." His smile invited her to join in on the joke, but she didn't crack a smile, instead watching him intently.

"Were you spying on me in the hopes that I'd do something stupid or childish that you could lord over me forever after?"

"No. But I tell you what, that *has* to go down as the most stupid and childish thing you've ever asked me... and there have been some doozies in the past."

She glared at him, hating that he was right about the question.

"And yet, it's a valid query."

"No, Lilah, I wasn't spying on you. I just happened to spot

you on the odd occasion. And I kept a low profile because I *didn't* want you to think I was intruding on your privacy."

She gnawed her lip pensively before nodding, deciding not the argue the point any longer.

"So back to my earlier question, can we leave on Friday?"

He sighed and nodded.

"If that's really what you want."

"Yes. Please."

"I'll make the arrangements tomorrow."

"Thank you." She toyed with the bedspread, her fingers tracing the pale blue pattern on the pristine white background. "Ben, I think we should probably spend the day together tomorrow. Take some pictures. People will be expecting to see honeymoon pics. My friends have already asked why there are no photos of us together."

"This is a dilemma of your own making, Lilah. If I'd had my way, we would have spent every day of this damned honeymoon together."

"Well, we still have a charade to maintain for at least a year, so if your intention is to keep Gramps and the board fooled, then we should probably have honeymoon pics."

"So you'll be doing this only for me?"

She gritted her teeth and glared at him, before honesty compelled her to say, "I don't really want my friends to know that this whole thing is a sham. I have some pride as well. I'd like them to believe that, at least in the beginning, we cared about each other."

"I care about you," he said, and she snorted rudely.

"Romantically."

His lips clamped shut and she laughed softly.

"Look, let's just get some pictures and get it over with. Okay?"

"And you'll be okay spending the day in my company? You sure you can manage that?"

She ignored the sarcasm in his voice and answered in a perfectly serious tone. "It'll be hard, but I'm sure I'll stomach it somehow. I'm tougher than I look."

"I hope so," he said, his expression somber and his voice deepening with some undefinable emotion.

"Why do you—"

"We should eat out tonight," he interrupted before she could complete her question and she frowned. The interruption had been deliberate. He didn't want her to pursue the subject and that infuriated her. "Get a jump on those photos you want to take."

She briefly contemplated pushing him further on the previous topic, but the mere thought of once again attempting to extract his jealously guarded secrets from him, was exhausting. Let him keep his precious secrets. She didn't care any longer.

She got up from the bed and stretched. His idea of eating out appealed to her. She hadn't had dinner yet, and the thought of sharing yet another strained meal with Ben within the confines of these four walls wasn't at all tempting.

"Give me half an hour to get ready," she said, and he nodded.

DINNER WAS an awkward and strained affair. Lilah felt conspicuous among the throngs of lovestruck honeymooners. They were surrounded by sickeningly happy couples, most of whom spent the entire meal exchanging long, loving stares, lingering touches, and feeding from each other's plates. It was quite sickening really...

Ben, meanwhile, had one arm hooked over the back of his chair, with his body angled slightly to the side—looking ready for flee at any second. He appeared to be a man who longed to be anywhere but here. They'd spoken in sporadic monosyllables since the entrée course had been served nearly half an hour ago, followed by excruciatingly long silences peppered with brief pleasantries about the weather, décor, food.

This had clearly been a mistake and Lilah yearned for the hellishly long meal to be over already.

Ben was idly twirling his wine glass between thumb and forefinger, while his restless eyes ran over everybody else in the restaurant, pausing only briefly on Lilah's face after each sojourn around the room. If she didn't know better, she'd swear he was nervous, but she inwardly scoffed at the notion. The supremely self-confident Benjamin Elijah Templeton did *not* get nervous.

"So why aren't you taking any pictures?" His question surprised her out of her own deep funk and she blinked up at him for an uncomprehending moment before the words registered.

"I have been."

"Of the food and décor, yes. None of us, or of me."

"Do you *want* me to take your picture?" She asked with a tilt of her head.

"I assumed that's what we were here for."

"Right." She lifted her camera, which was never far from her reach, happy to have its familiar weight back in her hands, and squeezed off a few quick shots of him. His expression remained remote and unreadable throughout the sequence of photographs, with only the deepening furrow between his brows indicating any kind of emotion.

She placed her camera to the side again, careful to keep it far away from any water or wine.

"That's it? They couldn't have been very interesting. Didn't you want me to do something? Smile or eat or stare lovingly into your eyes?"

"I'd never dream of asking you to smile, I wouldn't want you to break your face," she told him tartly, and amusement blazed in his eyes.

"I haven't had much reason to smile these last few days," he said, sounding a little defensive.

"Or even these last few years," she corrected him tartly, and his eyebrows rose.

"Yet you fell in love with me despite my apparent surliness," he pointed out, and she glared at him, hating that he was right about that. It was hard to remember why she'd fallen in love with him when he was such a difficult man to love. Now she wondered if the man she'd once believed herself in love with had ever existed, if he'd only ever been this cold and calculating man instead of the warm, giving, considerate man she'd thought him to be. The man she'd been convinced she caught glimpses of beneath all that reserve.

"Are you ready to order dessert?" Ryan, their handsome young waiter with the twangy Australian accent saved her from responding to Ben's last humiliating comment and she graced him with a warm smile.

Ryan flushed and Lilah sensed Ben's glare boring into her face, but she refused to acknowledge his look, keeping her focus on the waiter.

The last thing Lilah wanted was to drag this nightmare out even longer with dessert and she was about to refuse, when Ben surprised her by replying, "Definitely. My *wife* has a sweet tooth. She never passes on dessert. Isn't that right, cupcake?"

He released the stem of his wine glass and reached over to

cover one of her hands with his. It took everything in Lilah not to flinch at the unexpected contact and not to jerk back her hand immediately. His grip tightened over her hand, as if he sensed her reaction. His eyes were dark with warning.

Her own eyes widened speculatively and she swallowed back an irreverent giggle at the thought of ultra-powerful Ben feeling threatened by a friendly waiter. He must have seen the amusement in her eyes because his mouth thinned for a brief moment before his eyes sparked with purpose and he turned her hand over in his and lifted it to press a hot kiss in the middle of her sensitive palm.

Lilah's breath hitched in her chest when his lips lingered and she suppressed a squeak when his tongue darted out to scorch a brand onto her soft skin. His smoldering, intent gaze burned into hers the entire time, and Lilah was powerless to look away. Her eyes held captive by his.

She finally released her breath on a shuddering sigh when he lowered her hand, but his thumb continued to soothingly stroke the surface of her palm, as if he was aware of the burning imprint his mouth had left there and wanted to ease the discomfort. Only, his touch did nothing to set her at ease. Instead, it merely stoked the flames that he'd lit.

Ryan looked uncomfortable and shifted from foot to foot.

"I, uh… I could come back if you're not ready to order?"

"I'll have the mango and coconut pannacotta," Ben said. "My wife will have citrus and passionfruit cheesecake."

He'd never presumed to order for her before. It was a bold power move, which instantly raised her hackles, while simultaneously shocking her with his on-the-nose choice. She'd been thinking about that cheesecake since Ryan had handed them the menus and to protest or contradict the order would merely serve to cut off her nose to spite her face.

She gritted her teeth and held her silence, keeping a sweet, wholly fake smile plastered to her face while Ryan reconfirmed their order.

"Don't ever do that again," she said after the waiter had left and he gave her a bland smile, lifting his hand from hers to go back to twirling the stem of his wineglass.

"What?"

"All of that. The touching and kissing and speaking for me."

He made a noncommittal sound, quite unconcerned by her anger.

"I got the order right, though," he said.

"I wanted the chocolate fondant," she lied. "But I chose not to make a fuss."

He chuckled beneath his breath and shook his head almost indulgently. "No, you didn't. You can't resist a fruity cheesecake."

He had her there and again it startled her that he knew her so well.

She kept her mouth shut and avoided his eyes, restlessly perusing the crowd instead. Everybody looked so happy, and it merely served to highlight her own hollow misery. She blinked the uncomfortable sting from her eyes and willed back the threatening tears.

"Is it really so terrible?" His voice was gentle and she hated the sympathy she could hear in the undertone.

"Yes." She didn't pretend not to understand what he meant. "And it's going to get worse."

"Lilah... I don't wa—" He was interrupted by the soft chime of his phone. He frowned and fished the device out of one of the many pockets in his black cargo pants. "Sorry, I'd normally ignore it, but it's Lucille's ringtone."

Lucille was her grandfather's personal assistant, and the concern in Ben's voice immediately made Lilah sit up and pay attention as well. There was nothing odd about Lucille calling him at—she checked her watch—four p.m. South African time. Her grandfather was semi-retired but he still had his finger in quite a few pies. It wasn't entirely impossible that Lucille would be calling about business at this time on a Wednesday afternoon.

Yet, something about Ben's body language was troubling, and Lilah's alarm escalated when, after a curt greeting, he listened to whatever Lucille was telling him and paled dramatically.

His eyes flew to Lilah's and his throat bobbed as he swallowed before barking, "*When?*"

More silence while he listened, and his eyes closed for a moment. Lilah's heart lodged in her throat and her breathing came in short, harsh pants as she watched her husband reel from whatever he was being told. Ben fought hard to keep his expression under control, but she could tell he was shaken and Lilah's imagination shot into overdrive. Had Gramps fallen? Been in an accident? Was it his heart? As far as Lilah knew, Gramps was in excellent health, but anything could happen at his age.

"Yes, thank you," Ben said, his voice shaking. "We'll be ready. Right. Of course. Tell him…" His eyes found hers again. "Tell him we love him and we'll be home soon."

Lilah was already packing up her camera, and summoning Ryan over.

"We'll have to cancel dessert, I'm afraid," she whispered when the waiter came over.

"Is everything alright?" the young man asked, and Lilah's eyes flew to Ben's face. He'd lowered the phone, but now appeared to be texting someone.

"I-I'm not sure. Ben?" The last emerged on a panicked whisper and he lifted his distracted gaze to her.

"Wha—?" She watched him become aware of his surroundings again and he blinked slowly, before seeming to shake himself. "Uh… yeah, we won't be taking dessert. Bill the room as usual."

"Of course, sir," Ryan murmured, and tactfully retreated.

Ben nodded, and went back to his text, while Lilah watched him, feeling helpless, confused and not at all sure what to do next.

"It's Gramps, isn't it? What's wrong with him? I knew something was wrong when he didn't answer my texts and phone calls, it's not like him. Was it an accident? Did he fall? He's been so unsteady on his feet lately."

Ben set aside the phone and reached across the table to grab her agitatedly moving hands in his. His grip was strong and reassuring.

"We'll discuss it in the privacy of our room."

"Tell me now, Ben. How bad is it?"

His grip tightened to the point of pain but she barely felt it, keeping her eyes glued on his.

"It's bad, Lilah. Cyrus has collapsed. He's been admitted to the ICU. Lucille has arranged for the jet to pick us up first thing in the morning."

"Oh, my God, oh, my *God*, Ben." Her voice was a harsh whisper and her vision blurred as tears welled up.

"Come on, let's get back to the villa. I'll try reach his doctor and attempt to get more clarity on the matter, okay?"

She nodded and got up quickly. Ben held onto one of her hands and swooped up her camera bag with his free hand to sling it over his broad shoulder.

When they got back to the villa, they both—as if by unspoken agreement—swung into immediate action. Lilah to her suitcase to get everything packed and an outfit ready for the morning, and Ben back on his phone, trying to reach Gramps's doctor.

If the amount of muttered cursing coming from him was any indication, he wasn't having much luck with that.

After she finished packing, she sat down on the bed and watched Ben anxiously as he paced the floor while sending texts, scanning his phone, calling his market analysts, and members of the executive board. Lilah didn't care about any of that. She knew he was trying to do damage control, but her only concern was for her grandfather.

She grabbed her own phone and scrolled until she reached Gretchen's number. Gretchen was their live-in housekeeper. The sixty-five-year-old woman had been working for the family for close to forty years.

She chose FaceTime. People had the condescending propensity to try and downplay upsetting news from her, probably fearing that it would trigger an asthma attack. But she needed honesty right now. She didn't want to be pandered to or cushioned from potentially bad news.

Gretchen replied on the second ring. The tall, austere, woman with the steel gray hair, looked haggard and that told Lilah more than words ever could.

"How bad is it, Gretchen?" she asked without preamble, and the older woman—who usually handled everything with enviable calm—seemed to crumble right in front of her. Gretchen's shoulders hunched, and her eyes welled.

"It's not good, *liebchen*." Her German accent was even thicker than usual. "I found him in his office this afternoon. Not responsive. He was barely breathing. He did not regain consciousness when the paramedics worked on him. They tell me nothing, because I am not family. What is family? I ask you? I work for this man for forty years. I live in his house, I know his favorite food, the underwear he likes to wear. I know him better than I know my own *family*. But they tell me nothing."

"Which hospital? Do you know his doctor's name?"

"*Nein*, I do not know the doctor's name, but they took him to—"

"Thank you, Gretchen," Ben interjected, reaching over Lilah's shoulder to grab her phone. "I'll take it from here. We'll keep you informed of any further developments."

"Ben, I was still—" Lilah's outraged protest went unheeded as he hit the *end call* button and Gretchen's frazzled face disappeared from the screen.

Lilah rounded on him fiercely, and slammed the flat of her hand into his shoulder. It was meant to be a frustrated shove, but the blow landed harder than she'd expected and the impact stung her palm. He glowered at her, lowering his arm to toss her phone to the bed.

"I told you I was trying to reach Cyrus's doctor," he said from between clenched teeth. "Gretchen can't tell us more than he can."

"Well, I had to do something, since you seemed more concerned about share prices plummeting than ascertaining Gramps's condition."

"Until Cyrus's doctor is available to speak to me, I'll do my fucking job. The job your grandfather entrusted me to do."

"The job, the company, isn't more important than Gramps!"

"I never said it was, but it *is* his legacy and as such—"

"His *legacy*?" she spluttered in disbelief. "Why are you talking about legacies? You don't even know what's wrong with Gramps.

Why are you talking like he's dying? He's not dying! He's just had a bad turn. He'll be fine."

He stared at her unblinking for a long moment, before his brows lowered and his face softened a fraction.

"Of course, you're right... I don't know what his current condition is. But I *do* know how he would want me to proceed at this moment. Cyrus prepared me for exactly this type of eventuality. I absolutely care about how he is right now, it's all I can think of, but I don't have the luxury of being ruled by my emotions the way you do."

"Until I know what the hell is going on, you can't blame me for being *ruled by my emotions*... and I don't know why you're not making more of an attempt to find out exactly what happened to my grandfather!"

"Because everybody has the exact same information we do. He collapsed, he's in the ICU. We won't know any more than that until we talk to his doctor. I can't physically *do* anything more than I'm doing right now."

He turned back toward his precious laptop, effectively dismissing her.

Ben was wrong. He *could* do more than he was doing right now, Lilah reflected bitterly. He could take her into his arms and tell her everything was going to be okay. He could tell her that Gramps is tough, that he would be fine. Even though he couldn't possibly know that, Lilah would feel better, simply because he'd said it. Because he cared enough to make up the comforting lie. He could ease her fears and make her feel less alone. He could do *that*. But he wouldn't, because comforting her would never occur to him. Those were the actions of a loving husband, not... whatever he was.

She wrapped her arms around herself and inhaled deeply. The

sound was harsh and it dragged his attention away from the screen. He gave her a quick once over.

"You okay?"

"Don't worry Ben, I'm not on the verge of an attack or anything," she reassured him, and his eyes remained impassive as they bore into her face.

"Good." The word was curt. "Because that would be the absolute last thing we needed right now."

She gritted her teeth and turned her back on him. She picked her phone up from the bed and retreated to the poolside to call Blake.

Usually she would Facetime her friend, but wasn't in the mood to school her expressions right now. And seeing how much of a wreck Lilah currently was would only needlessly worry Blake.

The other woman answered immediately.

"Are you okay?"

Lilah's eyes flooded with tears at the concern she heard in her friend's voice.

"No." Her voice was small and emerged on a sob.

"What's the latest news on his condition?"

"We don't know anything. Ben's been trying to reach the doctor, but no luck so far. I just want to be back home by his side. I hate that Gramps is going through this without us."

"I'm so sorry, Lile," Blake murmured. "I know how tough this must be on you guys. How's Ben doing?"

Lilah's eyes drifted to the room where her husband was growling into his phone while glaring at his computer screen.

"Keeping busy," she prevaricated. "Doing damage control."

"Oh, God, of course, the stockholders must be in a panic."

"I think it would probably have been a lot worse if Ben

hadn't already been essentially running the ship for the better part of the last two years," Lilah said, lifting her thumb to her mouth to worry at a cuticle. She couldn't care less about anything company related right now and didn't want to talk about it.

"When will you be home?"

"We're leaving first thing in the morning."

"Do you need me to do anything?"

"I just need a distraction right now, Blake," Lilah whispered wearily. "I don't know what to do with myself. I'm a wreck and Ben..." Her eyes flickered over to him and she was startled to find him watching her, his eyes hooded, his face lined with exhaustion and concern. Probably petrified she'd start gasping for breath and add to his problems.

She only *just* refrained from rolling her eyes and turned her back on him instead, staring pensively out at the night sky.

Blake was saying something, talking about her pet grooming business, telling Lilah an anecdote about Moxy, one of her regular clients, a goofy giant Airedale terrier who seemed to fancy herself a lapdog. Usually, Lilah loved hearing stories about Blake's furry clients, a lot of them were her clients as well. Her and Blake's businesses tended to be reciprocal, with Lilah often referring doting dog parents to Blake and vice versa.

Right now, Lilah could barely focus on what Blake was saying but she was nonetheless happy for the attempted distraction.

Something on the water caught her eye and her breath snagged at the sight of the beautiful electric blue bioluminescence blooming among the calmly lapping waves. Lilah had hoped to see this phenomenon while here. She'd fondly imagined herself and Ben walking along a beach at night, holding hands and disturbing the glowing plankton as their footsteps agitated the water. She'd imagined them kissing with stars above their heads, as well as, carpeted at their feet.

Her eyes welled at the bittersweet reminder of how naïve and optimistic she'd been such a short while ago. Now the beautiful bioluminescence seemed to represent everything she'd lost. All she had left was a Ben-shaped hole in her heart and fear for her grandfather's life eating away at her stomach lining like acid.

She tried to blink away the moisture. But it proved to be an impossible task as the first fat tear overflowed and trailed down her cheek. She lifted a hand to her mouth and tried to stifle her sobs but the pause in Blake's slightly desperate chatter told her that she'd failed.

"Oh Lilah," Blake whispered, her voice throbbing with sympathy. "I'm so sorry."

"I'm fine… I just—"

"Lilah—" The raspy undertone of Ben's voice—much closer than she'd expected—made Lilah tense and she turned her head to find him standing directly behind her.

Once again, he plucked her phone from her grasp and lifted it to his ear. "Blake? Yes? Uh huh. Yeah, I'll take it from here."

Lilah didn't even care about the rude interruption this time. Not when he gently tugged her up, after shoving her phone into his back pocket, and enfolded her into his strong arms.

She shuddered, grateful to be in his anchoring hold.

"I know you're scared," he murmured into her hair. "I should have been more sensitive to that."

"Aren't you scared too?" she asked, her voice muffled against his chest. His arms tightened for a moment, before he loosened his hold slightly to lift a hand to her chin and tilt her head up.

"I'm trying not to think about it," he confessed when she met his eyes. Her lips trembled and she sobbed.

"I can't think of anything else."

"Shh, Lilah, whatever happens we'll face it together, okay?"

"Promise me he'll be okay, Ben," she begged, and his hand shifted from her chin to cup her face. He clumsily swiped at her tears with his thumb, but didn't speak. Refusing to say what she desperately needed to hear.

Her eyes searched his face for any sign of reassurance but all she found was weary resignation.

"Ben?"

"I can't make that promise, Lilah, you know I can't. We haven't even spoken with his doctor yet."

"How can you be so cold and detached?" she asked, her voice filled with confused despair.

"I'm being pragmatic, and you should know better than to expect me to make irrational promises that we both know would be difficult—if not impossible—for me to keep. Cyrus wouldn't be in the ICU if it wasn't serious. So how the hell will empty platitudes from me possibly help anything?"

"Are you even human?" she lamented, placing her hands on his chest to put some distance between their bodies. "Have you never just said something to make yourself or someone else feel better?"

He inhaled sharply and his other hand came up to cradle her cheek. He was now framing her face between his palms, her face tilted upward.

"I'm as human as the next person, only I prefer distraction as a coping mechanism," he murmured, dipping his head toward hers until his lips brushed against hers while he spoke. "This is the only way I know how to offer you comfort, Lilah."

SIXTEEN
The chaotic crescendo

The tip of his nose nuzzled along the side of hers, and she swayed toward him, helplessly drawn to his reassuring bulk and heat.

His mouth slotted over hers, smothering her soft moan. He exhaled and she welcomed the air into her mouth, in dire need of that life-affirming breath. She leaned into the kiss and opened her mouth to his demanding tongue. Right now she was so desperate for any warmth from this usually cold man that she would briefly set aside her pride and allow herself this temporary lapse in judgment and principles.

His kiss was controlled, confident, and—as was usual when it came to Ben—a little calculating. Lilah sensed his customary reserve—he always held a piece of himself back—and this time that reticence infuriated her.

Whenever he'd kissed her in the past, Lilah had remained a passive recipient. Never asking for more, always foolishly accepting whatever carefully portioned pieces of himself he was willing to share with her.

Well, to hell with that. She curled her arms around his neck and buried her fingers in the short hair at the back of his head, tugging at the silky strands to draw him even closer. She eagerly explored his mouth, relishing the heat and moisture she found there, enjoying the slide of his tongue against hers.

She moaned again, louder this time, the sound filled with need and frustration.

Her restless hands moved away from his head and down over his shoulders, kneading his hot skin and muscles through the expensive cotton fabric of his white dress shirt. She moved to his chest, impatiently tearing at his buttons, until she had a broad expanse of flesh exposed to her touch. She tore her lips from his and peppered open-mouthed kisses over the smooth, slightly sweat-dampened swathe of skin now available to her.

He didn't say or do anything, his hands still cradling the back of her head as she explored the muscular breadth of chest with her fingers, mouth, and tongue. She finally got the reaction she craved when her tongue trailed over the small, tight peak of his flat nipple.

A sharp inhalation of breath, followed by an involuntary jerk, and a startled grunt.

Sensitive there, was he? Her lips curled smugly at the corners as she kept her attention on that tiny bud of sensation. Another shuddering, reluctantly yielded groan, when the even line of her upper incisors scraped over his nipple. She licked and sucked away the sting, and he grabbed fistfuls of her hair in a tight hold. Lilah didn't mind the roughening hold, it told her she was finally breaking through that icy wall he kept between himself and the rest of the world.

She moved over to the other nipple, one of her slender thighs, meanwhile, pressing between his legs and up against the hardness straining at the fabric of his pants. She couldn't get her thigh as close as she wanted to, and opted instead to cup her palm over his pulsing cock. She purred happily when her fingers closed over that large, hot column of flesh through the thick cotton-blend fabric of his cargo pants. She gave him a leisurely stroke, before abandoning his turgid nipples in favor of his panting mouth. This time there was an urgency in his kiss that had been absent before. He was fighting to maintain control over his baser instincts, she could feel it in the way his body remained tense and rigid against hers, despite how his mouth devoured hers. Lips, teeth, and mouth ravaging hers with barely restrained violence.

Her free hand found the waistband of his pants, and she fumbled slightly with the button, before managing to get it undone and sliding her fingers down the front. He wasn't wearing any underwear, and she had immediate access to his naked flesh.

He hissed when she took hold of him and gave him an enthusiastic stroke. One of his hands came down to clamp around her slim wrist, exerting just enough pressure to keep her from exploring further.

"Easy, Lilah," he warned, the thick rasp of his voice sending a shudder of pleasure down her spine. God, she loved that whiskey rough voice of his.

"Let me touch you." She heard the frustrated demand in her words, and if his tightening fingers were any indication, so did he. Ben didn't like taking orders from anyone, especially not her.

He dragged her hand up and around to pin it in the small of her back, holding it firmly in place without causing her any pain. The move brought her breasts flush against his chest, and she whimpered helplessly at the contact against her aching nipples.

"Ben, let me *go*," she gritted out between clenched teeth, trying to pull her wrist free from his hold.

To no avail.

"Don't think so, Lilah," he drawled lazily. "I'll do the touching from here on out."

He walked her backward into the room until the backs of her knees hit the edge of the bed and, before she knew it, she was sprawled flat on her back in the middle of the mattress, with his hard body on top of hers and his hips cradled between her spread thighs.

His gaze scraped over her face and body, not missing a single detail. It was a look that left every nerve ending in her body feeling raw and exposed. She was achingly aware of the picture she presented to those ravenous eyes, with the short skirt of her cute white sundress bunched up around her waist, lacy bikini panties on full display. And she wasn't quite sure how it had happened but her aureoles were peeking over the top of the sweetheart neckline.

His eyes dropped to her breasts, narrowed intently, and lingered there.

Lilah's breath hitched in her chest at the predatory gleam she saw in those beautiful eyes. He licked his kiss swollen lips and swallowed thickly before making a helpless little sound of surrender in the back of his throat and swooping down to clamp his lips over one of tightly-knotted tips of her breasts through the thin fabric of her dress.

Lilah was helpless to stop the squeak of shocked delight from escaping her throat. His teeth, lips, and tongue plumped her eager nipple into shape before he moved over to the other one to lavish the same treatment upon it. When he finally lifted his head from her diamond hard, distended nipples, he brought up a hand to tug her bodice down and stare at his handiwork in smug satisfaction.

"Perfect," he growled, one corner of his lips kicking up. He took a moment to suck each naked nipple in turn, deeply into his hot mouth and she cried out in helpless response to the stimulation. He lifted his head again to stare into her eyes. "Want me to do the same for your sweet little clit, cupcake? Want me to suck and lick and nibble until it's plump and throbbing and needy? Until you're wet and juicy and desperate for my cock?"

She arched helplessly at his words, grinding herself against his hardness in an attempt to ease the ache between her legs.

He chuckled, the sound rusty as a can of nails, and slid a hand down her flat belly and beneath the flimsy scrap of lace and silk covering her femininity. His fingers found her immediately, and she frantically rubbed herself against them, overly stimulated and in dire need of release. He laughed again, and kept his touch frustratingly light.

"Hell, *mo leannan*, you're already wet and juicy and desperate, aren't you?"

"Please," she begged, tugging at the waist of his pants with her fingers in an attempt to help him slide them down his narrow hips. He gently pushed her hands aside and quickly and efficiently divested himself of both his pants and his already unbuttoned shirt. Lilah had only a brief moment to appreciate his perfect body before he pushed himself up to his knees — depriving her of his weight and warmth — to tug off her panties. She helped him eagerly, shimmying to get the superfluous scrap of fabric off.

He went for her dress next, dragging it up over her head and tossing it aside with a carelessness that showed little regard for the pricey Dolce and Gabbana cotton sundress.

The sudden wash of cool air on her overheated skin allowed a moment's sobering clarity to creep into Lilah's fuzzy brain. She wanted this. Needed it. But she couldn't allow it to confuse the situation between them or further complicate their already messed up relationship.

Then his deft fingers found her clitoris and she just about leaped out of her skin at the longed-for contact, reason taking a flying leap out of the nearby window.

"Oh, *God*," she mewled, and his eyes bored into hers, hair flopped over his forehead. The expression of intense concentration on his face gave him an evil genius kind of appeal that made her want him even more.

"Good?" As if he needed to ask. He expertly finessed her hard clit, stroking, circling, and occasionally dipping two and then three fingers into her tight, spasming channel, which greedily clutched at the intrusion, needing something longer, harder... *thicker*.

"Hmm," she agreed. "So good."

He smiled, a beautiful, perfect, open guileless smile but didn't let up on the sweet torture.

"You're so beautiful, Lilah," he told her, an appreciative gleam in his eyes. "I don't think I tell you that enough."

Or ever, Lilah thought with a cynical little twist of her lips, but she was immediately distracted when he twisted his fingers and sent her into a spasm of ecstasy.

"Want more?"

"*Yes.*"

He gave a satisfied little nod and hooked his palms under her butt to yank her roughly up over his hard thighs.

"Christ, you're so fucking wet," he muttered gruffly. "But I want you sopping. I want you fucking drenched."

Oh, God, what did that mean? Lilah wasn't sure she could

take much more of this... but he showed her exactly how much more she was capable of feeling when he lifted her up to his mouth. It was ridiculous, Lilah should have felt self-conscious when, instead of lowering himself to go down on her, he planted his palms on her ass cheeks and easily hoisted her lower body up to his mouth. But who had time to feel anything other than extreme pleasure when your extremely sexy husband draped your knees over his shoulders and with barely a tilt of his dark head, quite enthusiastically feasted on your already over-stimulated pussy and clit?

Sucking, nibbling, using his tongue, nose, teeth, even the stubble on his jaw, he drove her to the brink of insanity and beyond. She'd lost track of the orgasms, major and mini, when he finally lowered her back to the mattress and knelt between her spread thighs.

He stared down at her in smug approval as she lay naked and spreadeagled before him, her limbs jelly, and her brain mush.

"You already look well-fucked," he said, the thickened rasp of his voice barely comprehensible. He made a deep, rumbly sound of satisfaction and reached down to encircle his thickness with his hand. He was so hard by now, he had to peel his cock away from his abdomen and angle it downward. His other hand covered her mound, a thumb pressed against her swollen clit.

Lilah's breath came in pants as she watched him position himself at her entrance.

"Ready?" he asked.

"Yes."

He grunted in satisfaction at her breathless reply and pushed forward until the broad head of his penis pushed its way into her warm, very wet, and welcoming pussy.

Lilah gasped at the incomparable feel of him right there where she need him most, but she had something to say. Something that needed saying even though she feared her warning was coming way too late.

"Wait," she implored, flattening both palms against his hard chest in an attempt to halt his forward momentum. He stopped, just the tip of him wedged tightly inside of her, while his tense face lifted and his fevered eyes scorched into hers.

His entire body shook with strain, muscles bunched and tense.

"Wait for fucking *what*?" The question was less than gracious and delivered in a tone of seething resentment, but he'd stopped and that was what counted.

"This won't change how I feel about our marriage, Ben."

"I don't honestly give a fuck about that right now, Lilah," he ground out from between tightly-clenched teeth. "Now are we doing this or are there any other pressing matters you need to get off your chest right this very second?"

God, he was such a dick.

Lilah glared at him, tempted to prolong the moment just for the sheer perversity of it… but he moved his hips just the tiniest fraction of an inch and it sent a wave of sensation rippling through her.

"Oh *yes*," she sighed, and he grinned wickedly.

"Like that?" he asked, not even bothering to conceal the arrogance in his voice or on his face. "More?"

"Yes, damn you," she snapped, digging her feet into the mattress and lifting her hips in invitation.

"Then hang on because this is going to be rough and fast." He grabbed hold of her wrists, shackling them both in one large hand and pinning them above her head.

He surged all the way into her aching, clenching passage and she grunted in shock at the sheer size of him. He allowed her a moment—a very brief moment—to adjust before withdrawing all the way to the very tip of his cock and plunging back in again. God, the feel of him on top of her, inside of her, all around her, it was both foreign and familiar at the same time and she was overwhelmed by his complete hijacking of every one of her senses.

Lilah kept her eyes glued to Ben's beautiful face, wanting to know if this was affecting him in more than the obvious way. His eyes blazed down into hers, looking feverish and intense, but his strained face revealed no real depth of emotion. He was turned on, he was deriving pleasure from her body, but nothing more than that.

"My cock. Your pussy. That's all you need to be thinking of right now, Lilah," he commanded her with a growl and broke eye contact to stare fixedly down at her mouth. A second later he dipped his head to cover her lips with his. He still had the earthy, salty taste of her on his lips, while he practically ate her mouth alive, his lips hot, tongue demanding. An act of penetration equally as deep and intimate as the one his body was mounting on hers.

She bent her knees and used her feet for leverage to meet him thrust for thrust. He was as good as his promise—the sex was rough, fast, and lacking in any kind of tenderness or affection, but it was exactly what she needed right now. He still had her hands imprisoned above her head, and she resented that. Resented that he exerted this much control over her movements right now. She struggled against his hold wanting to touch him, wanting to drive him over the edge, needing to—

He freed her mouth and immediately latched onto a nipple instead and all thought fled from Lilah's mind at the harsh, almost painful tug of his mouth on her sensitive flesh.

At the same time, his thumb pressed down harder on her clit

and she cried out wordlessly and bucked violently beneath him as she came with the force of a tsunami slamming to shore.

He finally released her hands, grabbed hold of her hips to keep her steady, and continued to pound into her while she writhed beneath him. His mouth was still clamped tightly over her nipple and—finally left to their own devices—one of her hands curled around the back of his neck in attempt to keep his mouth in place and the fingernails of the other dug into the muscled flesh of his shoulder blade. As Lilah rode the turbulent wave of her orgasm, she was vaguely aware of Ben crying out against her breast, before he tensed and shuddered against her, his thrusts becoming jerky, shorter, as if he couldn't bear to leave the snug warm haven he'd found inside her.

They descended from the chaotic crescendo together, the peaceful glow that began to radiate between them only occasionally wracked by a violent shudder as their orgasms waned. Lilah felt as if every bone in her body had simply melted away and Ben, for the first time since she'd met him, appeared completely relaxed.

Ben was still slumped on top of her, a growing dead weight of hot, hard masculine flesh that blanketed her from chest to foot. His penis was still buried inside her, sporadically jerking and sending gentle ripples of sensation through her as it gradually lost its formidable hardness. His head was snuggled between her breasts, an ear pressed against her heart, and Lilah only then realized that she was stroking her fingers through his damp hair.

"I'm heavy," he mumbled against her breast, making no attempt to remove his weight from her.

"Hmm," she agreed, still stroking his hair, enjoying the novelty of being able to touch him so freely.

"I should move."

"Hmm."

"Later…"

"Hmm."

A soft snore was her only reply and she smiled and sighed quietly, her other hand exploring the contours of his broad back. He was magnificent and she could definitely appreciate that male beauty.

But, a tiny voice reminded her, *he's not yours to appreciate. And he's not yours to keep.*

She shifted slightly, and became aware of the spreading dampness beneath her.

Ugh, seriously?

"Hey!" She balled her hand into a fist and thumped his shoulder.

He jerked in shock and lifted his head to glare at her.

"What the fuck? What's wrong? I'm too heavy, sorry." He shifted his weight to the side and flopped down on his back. Lilah sucked in a deep—much-needed—breath, both relieved and regretful that he'd moved.

"You didn't use a condom," she told him, and pushed herself up onto her elbow to glare at him. He yawned in total unconcern, lifting one heavy arm to cover his face with his forearm, the other folded over his torso with his big hand spread over his abs. It was a pose of complete relaxation. His long, bare legs were crossed at the ankles, even his damned penis looked all smug and content and sleepy where it lay curled against his left thigh.

"Did you hear me? You didn't use a condom."

He shrugged and shifted his arm just enough to peek at her with one eye. "So?"

"So? I could get pregnant, you dick!"

"Well, I don't have any condoms because *you* said you wanted to try for a baby straight away."

"That was *before*."

"You're really destroying the whole post-sex buzz thing, y'know?"

"You know what my plans are, and those plans don't include single motherhood."

Any semblance of relaxation fled that big body and his arm came down as he pinned her with his piercing stare.

"Any child we have *will* be raised by both of us. Together. Understood?" His low, lethal tone brooked no argument, but Lilah refused to be cowed. She sat up, scooting up to lean against the headboard, and happily moving out of the huge wet spot. Seriously, it was impressive how much the man had come. But at the same time it was a little daunting, considering their current discussion.

"This conversation is probably moot. Thankfully the likelihood of pregnancy is very low for me right now. But if—and right now it's a very big *if*—we ever do this again, you're using condoms. Understood?"

"I tossed all my condoms before the wedding," was his moody response.

"Get more." She regretted the command as soon as she said it, and then regretted it even more when she saw the calculating gleam in his eyes.

"Sounds like that *if* is shrinking by the second," he pointed out, no small amount of smug in his voice.

Lilah frowned down at his rapidly lengthening and hardening penis, which seemed to be growing in direct proportion to that shrinking *if*.

His hand dropped to her thigh, just above her knee, and

kneaded her soft, sensitive flesh gently. "Up for a repeat performance?"

She stared at him in shock, unable to believe the staggering gall of that question. But he wasn't looking at her and so didn't see the expression on her face. Instead, his focus was on his hand, which was moving up her thigh with inexorable painstaking slowness.

For a brief, *infuriating*, moment she forgot herself and her thighs slackened and opened slightly, before she came to her senses and clamped them shut over his impertinent hand.

"No."

The word brought his head up sharply and he stared at her in blank confusion. "What do you mean *no*?"

"I literally just told you that we wouldn't be doing that again. Not without condoms. Maybe not ever again. And you dare suggest a repeat performance?"

He looked shocked; his expression somewhat reminiscent of a man whose faithful old dog had just bitten him. "You're serious?"

"Of course, I'm serious. I feel like you've ignored my every word since the wedding That you've dismissed everything I said as nonsense..." She stopped speaking when something in his eyes gave her pause. "Oh, my God, I'm right, aren't I? You been *managing* me. Treating me like one of your business deals. I know how you and Gramps have operated over the years. If somebody doesn't see things from your point of view, you wear them down, until they come to realize that *your* way is the only way."

She got up, unconcerned with her nudity—it was too late for modesty now anyway—and fled for the bathroom but he was hot on her heels, and caught her wrist to spin her around and face him before she even reached the door.

"Let me go," she demanded furiously, yanking her arm out of his tight grip.

"Lilah, come on, be reasonable," he said, using his most rational voice, which infuriated her even further. "You know that you'll put on this attention-seeking display of wanting a divorce and make meaningless noises about how this marriage isn't quite what you wanted it to be. But once you're done being an entitled brat, you'll recognize that you knew exactly what the fuck you were getting when you agreed to marry me. You've known me for more than half of your life, you *knew* I didn't do commitments, and love, and all the other shite... but your massive ego can't handle the fact that you couldn't change me. So you have to put on a show of indignation, right? Before you settle down and we can get on with our lives. So I'm giving you the space to do that."

"You're humoring me, you mean?" Her voice was thick with bitterness and grief

"If you want to put it that way," he said, lifting his shoulders in an easy shrug. "Personally, I see it as pandering to your ego."

This man didn't know her at all. He thought he did, but the woman—the *brat*—he thought she was didn't exist. She'd never existed. But it seemed that Ben hadn't really bothered to get to know Lilah or understand her after their first meeting, when—yes—she *had* been an entitled, spoilt brat, possessive over her grandfather who'd suddenly brought a stranger into their midst. But she'd very quickly gotten over the hurt at suddenly having to share her grandfather's affections with that moody, orphaned boy. Because she'd felt empathy toward Ben, had wanted him to feel welcomed, accepted, and a part of the family.

And all the while, Ben had only ever seen her as that sulky, bitchy little rich girl who'd been less than welcoming to him on their very first meeting. And he'd allowed that to color his perception of her for all these years.

How his resentment must have grown when he'd become her de facto babysitter over the years. All those times they'd spent together in his office, while she'd been studying and he working… Lilah had thought they were bonding, that he enjoyed having her around. While Ben had likely seen it as yet another duty to perform to keep Cyrus's bratty granddaughter happy.

His last words hung heavily between them, and she stared at him, her wounded heart in her eyes as she absently rubbed the ache away from the wrist he'd grabbed. She saw the dawning regret in his beautiful eyes, and shook her head against the apology she could see forming in them. She did not want his apology, not for words he'd clearly meant.

"Lilah, I'm—"

"*Don't.* You meant what you said, no point apologizing for it."

"But—"

"I'm going to grab a shower. Why don't you try to reach the doctor again?"

He was still standing outside the door, uncharacteristically hesitant, when she stepped into the bathroom and shut it in his face a moment later.

She stood with her back to the door for a long time and silently wept.

SEVENTEEN
This horribly empty moment

"Lilah."

The sound of her name startled Lilah out of her restless sleep and she opened her eyes in bleary confusion, not quite sure where she was right now. Traveling often left her disoriented and the last twenty-four hours had been a confused blur of places and faces all underscored by a horrendous sense of dread and impending disaster.

"What's happening? Is it Gramps? Is he okay?" she asked, her voice thick and slurred. She was laying stretched out on a sofa in a private waiting room at the hospital, she now recalled, as she sat up slowly and smoothed her hair down. She tugged at her blouse and flattened her pleated skirt down in an attempt to neaten herself up a bit. She knew that she probably looked a mess, but that was to be expected since she'd insisted they come directly to the hospital after leaving the airport. It had been too late to speak with the doctor, but they had been allowed to see Gramps, who'd been heartbreakingly unresponsive and unaware of their presence.

Her eyes were trained on Ben's somber face. He sat on a big chair close to the sofa. He didn't look like he'd slept at all, his face was dark with stubble, hair mussed and his shirt sleeves were rolled up to his elbows with the hem trailing out of the waistband of his charcoal chinos

"The doctor wants to speak with us."

"What's the time?" she asked, getting up and doing more futile smoothing of her hair and clothes.

"It's just gone eight in the morning." He got up as well, tucking his shirt in and rolling his sleeves back down. He ran his fingers through his hair and immediately looked almost immaculate again. If not for the stubble, she wouldn't have guessed that he'd spent fifteen of the last twenty-four hours traveling. "He wants to see us in his office."

"Any word on Gramps?"

"No change. You ready?"

"Hold on." She scrounged around her shoulder bag for a breath mint and popped it, offering him one as well. He took it without comment, before holding out his hand to her.

For a second she stared at the proffered hand in confusion, until she understood that he was waiting for her to take it.

Oh.

She wavered for a second, before busying herself with the clasp of her bag. She kept her head ducked as she brushed past him—ignoring his hand—on her way to the door. She was aware of him standing there for a second, and felt his eyes boring into the back of her head, but refused to look at him. He sighed, impatience and annoyance riding on the long exhalation of air, and moved to catch up with her. He dropped a hand to the small of her back and steered her to the left when she turned right at the exit.

"It's this way."

She said nothing, merely adjusted her course and walked beside him in silence.

"MR. AND MRS. TEMPLETON, good morning. I trust you had an uneventful journey back?" the doctor greeted somberly, running a hand through his luxurious salt-and-pepper mane, causing it to stick up in tufts. He was a distinguished looking man in his mid-forties, sporting black rimmed glasses and a neatly trimmed beard. He looked like he hadn't slept in weeks. He offered Lilah a small smile. "I'm Dr. Jason Mendelssohn. I'm so sorry I haven't been available to talk before now but I've had back-to-back surgeries."

He directed them toward a couple of uncomfortable chairs before sitting down behind his desk across from them.

"How's my grandfather?" Lilah asked after sitting down, dispensing with the formalities and keen to get to the heart of the matter as soon as possible.

The doctor sighed and tugged at his short beard.

"He's stable, but his prognosis isn't good."

Lilah's stomach dropped and she swallowed before framing her next question. "What's wrong with him?"

"I'm afraid there's no easy way to put this, Mrs. Templeton... but your grandfather has end stage pancreatic cancer. At this point there's little we can do but keep him comfortable."

Lilah stared at the man uncomprehendingly, not sure if she'd heard him correctly.

"What?" She was dimly aware of Ben's hand creeping over her cold, clammy one where it tightly clutched the arm of the chair, and she latched onto him desperately, squeezing his fingers so hard it actually hurt *her*. "That can't be right."

"Lilah…"

"No Ben, that's not right," she insisted, her voice gaining strength as her outrage grew traction. "He's only been treating Gramps for a few hours. He can't just say that! With all due respect, Dr. Mendelssohn, you haven't had enough time to run the proper tests. We can't simply take you at your word about something like this. Tell him, Ben."

"Mrs. Templeton," the doctor said, his voice patient and gentle. "I've been your grandfather's oncologist for the last year, trust me when I say we've done all the tests and we've tried all the treatments."

"I don't trust you. How can I trust you when I don't even know you?"

"What's important is that your grandfather trusts me," Dr. Mendelssohn said calmly. "And he has done so for the better part of a year."

"I don't…" She turned to Ben, her eyes wide, her vision blurry with tears. She couldn't quite see his face but he was pale, he looked grief-stricken. Her fingers tightened around his. "I don't know you. *We* don't know you and I think it's only right that we seek a second opinion in this matter."

The doctor gave Ben a slightly confused glance, before clearing his throat and putting his hands on his desk to steeple his fingers.

"I recognize that this news has come as a shock to you and I completely understand your desire to seek other opinions, but your grandfather has fought long and hard, he's exhausted, and about six months ago he eschewed all form of chemotherapy in favor of palliative treatment. He's made his decision and understands what comes next."

Lilah shook her head in denial.

"No. I refuse to believe that. Gramps is a fighter; he wouldn't simply give up. And he would have told us. He would never have kept this from us." Her voice shook with emotion and she covered her mouth in an attempt to stifle the imminent tears. "I think I want a second opinion."

"Of course," the man said amenably. "But while your grandfather is in this unresponsive state, the decision for any further testing falls to his medical proxy."

"Bring me whatever papers need to be signed and—"

"Mrs. Templeton," the doctor interrupted her gently. "You aren't his medical proxy."

Lilah blinked at him in astonishment. "Of course I am. I'm his only living relative."

"When he was first diagnosed, your grandfather specifically stated that he wanted Mr. Templeton as his medical proxy and legally appointed him as such."

Lilah turned to look at Ben, who met her eyes without an ounce of guilt or remorse in his expression. "But why would he do that?"

"Lilah," Ben murmured, leaning over to stroke her back gently. His palm came up to massage her nape beneath her fall of hair and she unconsciously leaned into his comforting touch.

The doctor cleared his throat awkwardly and got up, a squeaky wheel on his chair protesting the sudden movement and startling Lilah into looking at the man whom she'd already decided she hated and didn't trust at all.

"I have to do my rounds. Unless you have further questions, I'll leave you in privacy to discuss this matter. The rest of my day is open, barring emergencies, so please feel free to contact me anytime."

Lilah watched, not bothering to disguise her dislike, as the man donned a fresh white coat, pocketed a stethoscope, and vacated the office.

"I don't trust him. He could have been filling Gramps's head with lies and misinformation this last year."

"To what end?" Ben asked reasonably.

"I don't know. Greed? People often find creative ways to take advantage of Gramps."

"Your grandfather is not a fool, Lilah," Ben reminded her, his reasonable voice now laced with exasperation. "Do you think he would have accepted a prognosis like that without getting second, third, even *fourth*, opinions?"

"But why wouldn't he tell us?" she asked, her voice high and squeaky with tears. "He was so sick and he allowed us leave him to deal with this alone."

"Cyrus is a proud and stubborn man. He loves being your strong, protective hero, someone who can move mountains for you. Maybe he didn't want you to see him fighting a losing battle."

"It's not a losing battle," Lilah denied hotly. "It's *not*! We don't know that it is… he tried to fight it without us in his corner. Maybe with additional emotional support, knowing how much we love him, he'll have more reason to fight. We have to talk to Gramps, convince him to consider alternative treatment plans… mayb—"

"*That!*" Ben seethed, dropping his hand from her neck to jab a finger in her direction, his face darkening. "That *right* there is why

I think you're a selfish brat. And probably why Cyrus wanted *me* to be his medical proxy. For fuck's sake, Lilah. He's dying. Sorry to put it so bluntly but he is. And maybe he didn't tell you because he wants to go out on his own terms. He doesn't want to be forced into trying *alternative treatment plans* that'll make him feel sicker to gain only a few days or weeks more. But he would do them if you insist, Lilah, because he would do anything for you. And you would force him to bow to your will because Lilah wants whatever the hell she wants."

"Well, I need to hear that from him, Ben, not you," she said with as much dignity as she could muster, while she blinked back even more tears.

"Would you listen?" he asked skeptically.

Stung, she could do nothing but stare at him through huge, wounded eyes.

"Well, you've already decided that I wouldn't, so what I say right now won't carry much weight, will it?"

He sighed again and this time the sound was weighted down with sadness.

"I shouldn't have lost my temper. This news has obviously come as a great shock to you and, as they say, denial is the first stage of grief, so obviously you'll want to consider all the alternatives before you accept such a bleak prognosis."

"Don't you want that too? He just told us Gramps is dying, Ben. And I know you love him too, so surely you agree that we should explore any and all avenues here."

There was a long, odd moment of silence before he replied, and when he spoke he seemed like he was carefully considering each word before saying it. "Of course I love Cyrus, and I want what's best for him... and I believe what's best for him is what makes *him* happy. We should respect his wishes on this, Lilah.

Would you want him to suffer just to keep him with you a little longer?"

She stared into his deep blue eyes mutely, her lips trembling and tears slowly flowing down her cheeks.

"Did you know?"

There was a spark of something in those beautiful eyes of his and he swallowed before asking in a hoarse voice, "Did I know what?"

"That he'd made you his medical proxy?"

There was a slight tic in his jaw, before he shook his head. "No. But honestly? It doesn't surprise me. He trusts me to make rational decisions, and you're not always rational, Lilah."

"Does that mean you won't sign off on a second opinion?"

He sighed tiredly and rubbed his nape before tilting his head up to glare at the ceiling for a moment.

"Would that make you feel better about his decision to accept only palliative care?"

"His decision to die, you mean? Nothing would make me feel better about that."

"Regardless, it's his decision. Can you even comprehend how much pain he must have been in to make a decision like that?"

"I want to see him."

He nodded and stood up, before—once more—offering his hand to her. She ignored it again and got up under her own steam.

"GRAMPS?" Lilah whispered, sitting beside the frail old man's bed, listening to the various machines he was hooked up to bleep and buzz and whoosh.

Nothing, not even a flicker of an eyelid.

Lilah fought back her tears as she reached for skeletally thin hand, the blue-veined skin paper thin. His palm was ice cold and clammy and entirely limp.

His stillness terrified her. She'd noticed how much weight he'd lost at the wedding, but he'd dropped even more body mass in the few short days since then.

"Gramps, it's Lilah," she said, keeping her voice cheerful and optimistic. "Ben and I are *both* here. We love you… please, *please* Gramps. Wake up."

She stifled a sob, but wasn't as successful at keeping the overflowing tears at bay. She lifted the back of his hand to her cheek and wept soundlessly, not sure what else to say or do. He looked truly frighteningly ill and for the first time Lilah privately acknowledged that the doctor had probably been telling the truth, which meant that her grandfather had kept this from her for a year.

He hadn't trusted her to support him through this. Or to make unselfish decisions on his behalf. Maybe this was his twisted way of trying to protect her but all Lilah could think of was how little time she'd spent with him over the last twelve months. First, nearly working herself to death by overbooking her business and spreading herself too thin, then her foolish vacation to Paris—the worst way to spend a medically advised break—and, after returning home, being distracted by Ben, rethinking her business model, and then the wedding plans. And this week, with the honeymoon—this time she was unable to prevent the despairing sob from escaping—he'd been on the brink of *this* while she'd been away on a fake honeymoon.

"We should have been here," she lamented softly. "We should *never* have left."

"Lilah," Ben's voice was a whisper and his hand landed heavily on her narrow shoulder, reminding her that he was sitting in the chair beside hers. "You can't think like that."

"If I'd known I would have stayed."

"You must know that Cyrus was aware of that fact. And that's why he didn't tell you."

She shot him a fulminating, resentful glare through the sheen of tears, and was satisfied when he appeared to flinch.

"If he kept it from us, it's because he didn't want to destroy our so-called happiness. He wanted us to enjoy our honeymoon because he believed in the lie *you* created."

"It's best not to have that discussion in front of Cyrus," he reminded her, frost crystallizing on his every word and Lilah's eyes dropped to her grandfather's drawn face in remorse. He was right, she shouldn't have brought it up in front of Gramps.

Her lips thinned and she returned her focus to her grandfather. She continued to talk to him, just nonsense, telling him about the Maldives, their hotel room, the bioluminescence she'd seen on her last night, things she knew he would have asked her about if he could.

Ben sat stoically by her side, ignoring his constantly chiming and chirping phone, and staring straight ahead with very little expression on his face. But—while she would never admit it out loud—it comforted her to have him there.

Nursing staff entered and exited the room so quietly, Lilah barely registered their presence—they merely checked his vitals and monitored his IV drip, which someone had told her contained only fluids and nutrients. He was on a morphine drip as well, and Lilah suspected that was the reason Gramps was so quiet and unresponsive. She considered asking them to lessen the dosage, to see if he would be able to speak with them, but after hours of sitting by his side, staring into his beloved, emaciated face, she'd privately acknowledged that for him to have deteriorated so quickly, he must have been in immense pain, and she couldn't subject him to that... not even to speak to him and ask him why he had chosen to leave her out of this crucial part of his life.

Not even to say goodbye.

"The end of a life is equally as important as the beginning... maybe more so," she whispered after hours of silence. Ben had tried to coax her into eating about two hours ago, but she'd refused to leave her grandfather's side. Terrified that Gramps would slip away while she was gone.

Ben started at the sound of her voice and Lilah wondered if he'd fallen asleep, but didn't shift her eyes from Gramps's face to check.

"What?" His voice was even raspier than usual after so many hours of not being used.

"At the beginning of our lives we're strangers to everyone, nobody knows who we'll be or how much they'll love or hate us. We're shiny and new, and undiscovered. But at the end..." Her voice broke slightly, and she was aware of him staring at her fixedly, but couldn't meet his eyes. It was too painful to look at the man from whom she needed comfort the most right now, but who felt like a complete stranger to her in this horribly empty moment. "At the end, we have people we love, and who love us. Not being able to say goodbye, is the worst kind of pain imaginable. I wish..."

She finally turned to him, the never-ending tears once again overflowing, as she finally acknowledged that she may never speak to her grandfather again. Never experience his comforting hugs, never hear his rumbling belly laughter, never again see the spark of love and pride in his eyes when looked at her.

"I wish he'd told us, Ben. I wish he'd allowed us the share this very important step of his journey with him. All of these months, I could have been spending time with him, collecting even more memories of him to add to my treasured collection. And I'm so *angry* with him for depriving us of that."

She wiped at her face and nose with an already sodden tissue, only to have it gently removed from her grasp, and replaced with a fresh one.

Ben smoothed her disheveled hair from her damp face and stared into her eyes. Always so damned intense.

"Maybe he didn't want you to have memories of him in pain and sick and weak from chemo or radiation, Lilah," he told her quietly. "Maybe he wanted your memories of him to remain untainted by this disease. Maybe he considered it a gift to you."

"I understand that, but death is a part of life, sometimes it comes like a thief in the night, as it did with your parents. It took them from you suddenly. Violently. Sometimes it's slower, gentler. And yes, sometimes, that slowness isn't gentle, it's lingering and cruel... but with your parents there was no opportunity to undo hurts, make apologies, say final I love yous. With Gramps, there was. There were still opportunities to create new, happy memories despite the malevolently lurking specter of death. But this right now is as sudden and as brutal as an accident. Why would he do that to us? To *you* especially, after everything you've already been through?"

"He thought it was the right thing to do," Ben whispered hoarsely, looking haunted and she reached over to cup his by-now bearded jaw in the palm of her hand. It was the first time she'd voluntarily touched him since that last night in the Maldives.

Her response was quiet and unequivocal. "It wasn't. It's cruel. But I love him and I *do* understand. Gramps needs to control everything. I know that. Yet even though I understand, I find it hard to forgive him for this and it hurts so much, Ben. *So* much. I don't want to feel this way."

He made a gruff, distressed sound in the back of his throat and gathered her into his arms as the dam finally broke and Lilah gave in to the torrent of tears that had been threatening since the doctor had first told her exactly what they were dealing with. She buried her face in his chest, allowing him to drag her over into his lap and hold her close, while she cried and cried.

When the storm finally abated, she lifted her head and stared at him through swollen eyes. He looked awful, his face was grey with exhaustion and strain, his eyes were red-rimmed and bloodshot.

"I ruined your shirt," she said in a thick voice, and he gave her a grimace of a smile.

"It was pretty fucked up already. Wrinkled, travel and sweat stained, quite gross really… so your snot and tears probably left a clean spot on the fabric."

She smiled at his weak attempt at levity and her eyes once again drifted over to Gramps.

"He's a fighter. Maybe he'll get through this," she said, her voice small and lacking in conviction.

His arms tightened around her and he kissed the top of her head.

"Maybe."

She laughed, a soft despairing sound. "I thought you didn't do that."

"Do what?"

"Waste time on empty platitudes."

He shifted slightly and adjusted his hold around her body. She felt the weight of his cheek come to rest at the top of her head, his beard catching some of the messy strands of her uncombed hair.

"Well, I need a few comforting platitudes myself right now," he said on a sigh. "Cyrus is strong, Lilah. A fighter. *Maybe* he'll pull through this."

She sighed shakily. "You're such a liar. But... thank you."

CYRUS BECKETT SLIPPED AWAY QUIETLY and peacefully that same night. Lilah and Ben were right by his side when he took his last halting breath and passed from this world into the next.

At first, Lilah was panicked and confused by the lack of urgency and activity when the cardiac monitor flatlined and went off into that sustained monotonous beep that signaled the cessation of a heartbeat.

"No," she gasped in horror when she realized what the noise meant. "*No.*"

Dr. Mendelssohn stepped into the room, accompanied by a nurse—Calvin—who'd been nothing but kind and considerate to Lilah and Ben through the interminable night.

The doctor stepped over to the bed and stopped the horrible noise, before checking her grandfather's vitals. His mouth was drawn into a tight line and he slanted Lilah and Ben a quick sympathetic look before taking notes on her grandfather's chart and checking his watch before murmuring to Calvin, "Time of death: three forty-four a.m."

Calvin checked his watch as well and nodded. "Confirming time of death at three forty-four a.m."

"No," Lilah moaned. She pushed to her feet and was peripherally aware of Ben coming to his more slowly. "Why aren't you doing something? Bring him back. Please, *please* bring him back."

"Mrs. Templeton, you grandfather signed a DNR—uh, that's Do Not Resuscitate—order. Do you understand what that means?" She nodded automatically in response to the gentle question. "I'm so sorry for your loss. Cyrus was…" Dr. Mendelssohn shook his head with a small sad smile. "He was a great man. And he'll be missed."

Somehow this DNR thing felt like the final betrayal and her legs gave way. She felt Ben's strong arms closing around her, saving her from falling, and was aware of him asking her if she was okay. But she could barely hear him beyond the angry buzzing in her ears.

Gramps was gone.

He was really, really gone.

He'd been her only family, her rock, the one person who had truly loved her above all others in this world and now he was gone.

And all she was left with was a fake marriage and husband who borderline despised her.

She heard the high keening cry of grief and was embarrassed to know that it came from her, but there was absolutely nothing she could do to stop the wail of pain and loss. Ben turned her in his arms and held her tight and knowing that he felt this loss as keenly as she did, Lilah accepted the solace of his embrace and tried her best to offer some modicum of that same comfort in return.

She squeezed him tightly and wept inconsolably in his arms and she could only hope that Ben let go of his rigid self-control long enough shed a few tears as well.

EIGHTEEN
Not a sustainable situation

"Blake's here." Ben's voice was muted but firm. "I think you should see her. She's worried about you. We all are. C'mon, cupcake, you haven't gotten out of bed since the funeral. And that was three days ago in case you've lost track of time."

"I don't want to see anyone," Lilah said. "What are you *doing*?"

The indignant exclamation came when Ben unceremoniously yanked the thick, warm comforter off the bed, leaving her curled up in a defenseless fuzzy pajama clad little ball in the middle of the denuded bed.

"You're getting up and heading into that bathroom to brush your teeth and take a shower. For your sake as well as mine. I can't keep sleeping next to your increasingly rank body."

"You're welcome to sleep elsewhere," she told him with a petulant glare, sitting up, her slowness screaming her reluctance to him.

"It's *my* bed."

"Fine!" she said, getting up and acknowledging privately that maybe she *had* been in bed for too long when the room rotated drunkenly around her. "I'll move to the spare room."

Of course, she could always move out completely, but the mere *thought* of that right now was too emotionally taxing.

His flat, unimpressed stare told her exactly how he felt about her response.

"You sleep with me."

"Me man! You woman! Woman do what Man say!" she said in a deep voice, mocking him. She thumped her chest for good measure and felt alive for the first time since Gramps's death ten days ago.

His lips twitched, but he kept his expression schooled to absolute neutrality.

"*Now* you're getting it," he said with a satisfied nod and she rolled her eyes, trying hard not to be amused by him.

"Arrogant butthole," she complained and stalked toward the massive en-suite.

After the horrible night Gramps had died, they'd come directly to Ben's luxurious penthouse apartment in Clifton. Her things—which had been sent over before the wedding—had been neatly unpacked and arranged in the lavish walk-in closet that she now shared with her husband. The apartment had three bedrooms and one had been converted into an office space for Ben. She absently wondered where she could set up her own temporary workspace, but immediately shoved the thought back down. That felt too much like moving on... and it felt like a betrayal to even think of the future so soon after Gramps's death. Even though, logically, she knew he would want her to.

She stepped into the massive shower with its white and navy-blue subway tiling and dual rainforest shower heads, and once she had the streams set to massage, she sighed in absolute bliss.

She hated to admit it—she reflected as she toweled herself off—but Ben was right, she'd really needed this shower, in more ways than one. She felt refreshed, revitalized, and ready to face the world. At least for a little while. At the back of her mind and at the center of her bruised heart, was a niggling ache, like a gnawing toothache, constant and threatening to flare up into overwhelming pain at any given moment.

But for now it was tolerable.

She padded into the massive walk-in closet and for the first time appreciated the work the anonymous staff member had done in here. It would take some tweaking to conform it completely to her preference, but not much. Her eyes trailed over to Ben's side of the closet. So many suits. She trailed a finger along the uniform jacket sleeves in varying muted tones of navy blues, charcoals, blacks, and dark grays. The man had great taste in designer wear, but no sense of adventure in his style. But this was Ben, whose picture showed up in the dictionary next to the word *staid*. Then again, he also appeared—shirtless—in the urban dictionary under the words *smokin' hot*.

It was unsettling to see their clothes in such intimate proximity. It brought home to Lilah how real this was becoming. She'd resolved not to live with him after they returned from the honeymoon, but that resolution had gotten lost beneath the massive weight of grief and somehow, she'd never verbalized her intention to live on her own. It had been too easy to stay here with Ben, to take solace in his closeness, and in their shared grief.

Now, a week-and-a-half after their return, she recognized that while she'd been buried beneath her grief, this had become their normal. And she wasn't sure how, or when, to broach the subject of leaving. She feared she was becoming entrenched in his home, and, worse, she felt no inclination to leave just yet. Or anytime soon.

And that apathy alarmed her. She shouldn't get too comfortable here, this wasn't her home. It couldn't be.

So what if Ben had held her close every night while she cried herself to sleep? Who cared if he'd taken time, he could ill afford to lose, away from the office to grieve with her? What did it matter if he made excuses to touch her any chance he got? Not in any sexual way mind you. Intimate little pats and strokes, sometimes meant to comfort, often just touching for the sake of it.

She reflected on these things that she'd taken for granted over the last ten days. Ben might even think that she was too grief-stricken to notice the growing intimacy between them, but she'd noticed those quiet moments of closeness, and she had appreciated them.

She shimmied into a pair of faded denim shorts, and a plain white camisole top. On impulse she dragged one of Ben's crisp white button-up shirts on over the cami. It was miles too big, but she liked the look of it. She rolled the way-too-long sleeves to her elbows, fastening it to just below the curve of her breasts. She tucked the hem of the over-long garment into the front of her shorts, leaving the tail to hang over her butt and halfway down her thighs. She checked her reflection in the mirror, wondering how Ben would react to her wearing one of his pricey Tom Ford shirts. He was always so fussy and particular about his stuff. She remembered his reaction when she'd slept in his t-shirt. But then flushed when she recalled that he hadn't been too particular about wearing it on their long flight to the Maldives.

Her hair—which she'd washed and towel dried—was tousled and messy, honey-colored highlights streaked throughout the mass courtesy of the Maldivian sun. Her miserable honeymoon seemed years ago, considering everything that had happened since, but what had occurred between her and Ben on their last night there remained shiny and bright in her memory. Something to take out and marvel at amidst all the misery.

Lilah wondered if her fear and uncertainty—combined with her relative lack of experience—had served to heighten her reaction to his every caress. It was a pretty bit of self-deception, allowing herself to believe such nonsense, but it saved both her pride and her conscience. Because she'd certainly felt guilt about enjoying what had been a transcendent life-affirming act even while her grandfather lay dying thousands of miles away.

She and Ben hadn't discussed it since, and she hoped they never would. She knew she'd implied they might repeat the act if he wore protection, but the whole thing had left her feeling vulnerable and raw and it was better if they never slept together again.

She checked her reflection one more time, this time noticing her puffy, red-rimmed eyes and her wan paleness beneath her healthy tan. But that couldn't be helped and she threw back her shoulders and left the room to find her best friend.

BLAKE'S ASTUTE gaze missed nothing as Ben dithered around Lilah for a few endless moments.

"I forgot to tell housekeeping to stock those chocolate digestive biscuits you like," he told Lilah, a frown flirting with the furrow between his brows. "And we're out of your favorite tea."

Unsurprising, Lilah thought wryly, considering the many cups she'd consumed over the last ten days.

"Trudy"—his housekeeper—"assures me it will be restocked by the end of the day. Meanwhile, if you need anything, just uh—well… I'll be in my study—so knock, I suppose." He was hovering like an over-protective granny and it was both unsettling and endearing.

"We're fine," Lilah told him firmly, and he took a hesitant step back, appearing reluctant to just turn away and leave. "Ben, I'm okay. Honestly."

His brow settled into the heavy frown that had been threatening moments ago and he shoved his hands into his trouser pockets, still hesitant.

"Okay. Good." Another probing stare into her face, before he made a sound in the back of his throat, pivoted on his heel, and left.

"Wow, that was… Who even *was* that?" Blake asked with an amused snort and Lilah, staring at the space Ben had just occupied, found herself wondering the same thing.

What on earth was that about?

"He's been concerned," she found herself explaining to Blake, while not even certain herself what was going on with Ben.

"I know," Blake said with a nod. "He said as much when he asked me to come around."

"Ben *asked* you to come?"

Blake grimaced and got up, coming over to enfold Lilah in a warm hug, which Lilah returned gratefully, the ever-lurking tears once again surging into her eyes and scalding a path down her cheeks. She'd needed this, she hadn't even realized how much until this very moment.

"I'm glad he did," Blake said. "I've been meaning to come, but

I wasn't sure if you were ready for visitors yet. I guess I was waiting for you to call. But I should have known better. I know you; you're always trying to put on a brave face, trying to disguise your pain."

"And you're not a visitor," Lilah chastised, tears thickening her voice. "You're family, you never need an invitation to see me."

Still, she was grateful that Ben had contacted her friend. It showed a level of sensitivity and care for Lilah's emotional needs that she hadn't believed him capable of.

Blake dragged her to the sofa and they sat down next to each other, Blake holding onto her hands as she turned to face her. She searched Lilah's face, those inquisitive, alert eyes not missing a thing.

"You haven't been sleeping," she said.

"Not much," Lilah admitted.

"Ben told me you haven't been eating much either." She ran a worried glance over Lilah's slender frame and her hands tightened around Lilah's.

"Lile, you have to eat."

"I know. But I haven't had much of an appetite since he died, Blake. I've tried but I can't. I just keep thinking about how Gramps will n-never e-enjoy another m-meal again and—"

"You can't think like that," Blake told her sternly. "And Uncle Cyrus of all people would hate to see you make yourself ill. You know that."

"I know that," Lilah acknowledged with a grimace. "I do. But I miss him so much. I used to call him every day, at three, like clockwork and we'd have a catch up."

Oh, God, here came the tears again. She tried to stifle them but they were unavoidable.

"I'm sorry." Her voice was muffled behind her handkerchief and Blake made a tsking sound.

"You cry if you need to, sweetie," Blake said, her hand stroking Lilah's back. "I'm right here."

It was something of a relief to spend a few vulnerable moments in Blake's undemanding and unjudgmental presence. Her friend held her while she wept, making soothing little noises as she ran a hand up and down Lilah's back.

"Better?" Blake asked a few minutes later, when the immediate storm had passed and Lilah nodded, wiping her eyes self-consciously.

"A bit."

"Want to raid the kitchen for snacks? I've been dying to nose my way around Ben's lair. Where does he hide the corpses of his countless discarded minions?"

The gleeful words—in reference to Ben's many failed personal assistants—startled an irreverent giggle out of Lilah, who immediately covered her mouth in horror.

Blake squeezed her forearm in reassurance, "It's okay to laugh, Lilah. Uncle Cyrus always loved your laugh."

Lilah gave her friend a watery smile and waved her arms expansively. "This place is your basic bachelor pad, really. Three rooms upstairs, one spare converted into an office and the other stuffed to the gills with gym equipment. Kitchen, scullery, living area down here. Private infinity pool on the terrace, with panoramic ocean and mountain views from just about everywhere. And best of all, a roof garden."

"Ooh, right up your alley. You going to have your *hoes* over to overhaul said garden?"

Lilah's smile faded like mist on a summer's morning and she wondered if she'd be here long enough to start a garden project here. She would love to. It was all very basic up there, a service-able, succulent garden with zero pizzazz. If she had her way, she'd turn it into a lush, but water-wise, wonderland.

"I don't know," she said, recognizing the wistful note in her voice. "Maybe."

Blake didn't push her, instead hooking her arm through Lilah's and smiling at her. "Show me around and tell me about the Maldives."

"Only if you tell me what the hell happened between you and Rhys at our wedding."

Blake laughed, the sound warm and genuinely amused.

"We were both nicely buzzed after the toasts, had a hot and heavy snog through a couple of slow songs, and happily went our separate ways soon after you and Ben disappeared on us."

"That's all?" Lilah couldn't conceal her disappointment and Blake chuckled again.

"That's it, sorry it's not quite the juicy gossip you were hoping for. I mean, the man is hot, but he's carrying *waaaay* too much baggage, even for a one-night stand."

"Oh no, I really hoped he was finally moving on," Lilah said with a sympathetic wince and Blake lifted a shoulder nonchalantly.

"Yeah, all that brooding is hot from a distance, but the whole *still in love with his dead girlfriend* thing doesn't work for me at all." Even though her voice was light, her eyes were somber.

"That's understandable," Lilah said. Rhys's long-time girl-friend had died nearly a year-and-a-half before and, honestly, Lilah hadn't seen him with any other woman aside from Blake since then.

"And how was the honeymoon?"

Lilah's silence was so heavy and loaded after that breezy question, that Blake's gaze immediately sharpened on her face.

"What's wrong? What happened?"

"Nothing."

"Lile..."

"I mean it, Blake. Nothing's wrong, I was just constantly worried about Gramps, because he wasn't returning my texts, I should have known then that something was wrong and insisted we come home early." Not quite a lie, yet not entirely the truth either.

"You can't know what people keep from you, Lilah. You just can't. You're not a mind-reader and you're not responsible for anyone else's decisions."

"He left me a letter, you know," she confessed on a whisper and Blake stared at her for a long moment.

"Your grandfather?"

"Yes." They'd wandered into the kitchen and Lilah moved away from her friend to take a bottle of apple juice from the fridge. Anything to keep her face averted from her friend's probing stare. She grabbed two glasses and busied herself pouring the juice into the tall glasses.

"When?" Blake asked, taking the proffered drink from Lilah.

"His attorney gave it to me," Lilah said, placing the bottle back in the fridge with more care than it needed. "After reading the will."

The will had been read the day before the funeral. And while Lilah hadn't really been interested in attending—knowing that her grandfather's will would hold little surprises—Ben had still dragged her out to the attorney—Mr. Newcombe's—office for the reading.

It had all gone pretty much as expected, with Lilah inheriting the bulk of his estate, and a few generous settlements for long-standing staff including Gretchen and Lucille. Ben had been the beneficiary of a few *very* generous insurance policies, several holiday properties, as well as Cyrus's extensive fleet of exotic sportscars, and the old man's much-loved luxury yacht. And Ben and Lilah now shared ownership of the house in Bantry Bay. The letter had been for Lilah alone, and she had sensed Ben's concern and curiosity when Mr. Newcombe had drawn her aside to hand it over.

"What did it say?" Blake asked.

"I haven't read it yet."

"Why not?"

"It's the last words I'll ever read from him. And I'm not quite ready for that final farewell yet."

Blake gave her another sympathetic smile, her eyes reflecting her understanding.

But Lilah hadn't been entirely honest with her friend. While it was true that she was delaying that sense of finality reading Gramps's letter would give her, she was also not ready to be confronted by whatever his reasoning had been in keeping his disease from her. She suspected he would attempt to explain it in his letter and part of her feared understanding and even agreeing with him, while an even larger part was terrified that she wouldn't get it and the hurt and betrayal she still felt would never quite go away.

She continued to reflect on the dilemma while she gave Blake her requested tour of the apartment. She knew her friend was aware of her distraction but was grateful when Blake tactfully refrained from questioning her any further.

And as they moved from room to room in an apartment that she hadn't visited at all before her engagement to Ben—and even after that she'd only been here once—her distraction gradually gave way to curiosity. She'd had zero interest in truly getting to know the space since moving in. Too preoccupied with her grief and her vague belief that she'd move out at some point. But now she was finally appreciating the airy beauty of the luxurious space.

"He's got pretty good taste," Blake said a while later, unconsciously repeating Lilah's exact thought, after they'd completed their tour of the spacious penthouse—they'd respected Ben's privacy and stayed away from his office though—and found themselves sitting on a couple of patio chairs in the middle of the bland roof garden. In fact, this garden was the only space in the place that didn't reflect any of Ben's personal taste.

The interior of the penthouse was decorated in vibrant shades of blues and greens, and littered with beautiful artwork by little known—or unknown—artists. A lot of his decorative items appeared to be random pieces picked up from flea shops or markets in various parts of the world. Everything reflected a personality that was anything but staid, and it once again brought home to Lilah how little she knew the man she'd once believed herself in love with. How much of himself he'd kept back from her over the years.

Now she and Blake sat up on the roof, in front of the frameless glass railings and, from their vantage point on the mountainside, stared down at white sands and turquoise waters of Clifton's 3rd beach. The sand was dotted with umbrellas, and tiny distant people, lounging, swimming or playing.

It felt a whole world away.

"I never understood why people like these beaches," Lilah murmured, tilting her jaw toward the pristine beach down below.

"I mean... look at it," Blake said. "It's perfect."

"But the water is so cold and unwelcoming. Frigid. Why do we do that? We know that it's not going to be a pleasant experience, but we still go back time and time again to torture ourselves. Surely no amount of beauty is worth that pain? When we have so many other beautiful beaches with much warmer water to enjoy, why keep coming back here?"

Her voice wobbled on the last word and she sensed Blake's head turning toward her, while she kept her own gaze forward.

"Lilah, what's going on? This isn't just about your grandfather, I sensed—during our few short communications while you were on honeymoon—that something wasn't right. Hell, I sensed it at the wedding."

Lilah's face crumpled and she buried her face in her hands.

"Oh no," Blake whispered, scooting her chair closer and wrapping her arms around Lilah. "Oh sweetie, please talk to me."

"He doesn't love me," Lilah confessed in a raw voice. "He doesn't love me, Blake. He never did. I'm not sure he even likes me."

"I don't..." Blake's bafflement was clear as her words stumbled to a halt. "*Ben*? You're talking about Ben?"

"You warned me, I know you did. And like an idiot I didn't listen. I should have listened."

"No, I thought he'd be too cold and distant for a warm, emotionally generous woman like you, but I never dreamed he didn't... Why do you say he doesn't love you? What makes you think that?"

Lilah laughed bitterly and met her friend's confused and concerned gaze through a sheen of angry tears.

Oh but the anger felt good after all the pain and she clung to it, desperate to hold it close and keep the numbness at bay.

"He *told* me," Lilah said, swiping at her tears with the backs of her hands. "On our wedding night. No, on our wedding day, in the frikkin' car after we left the church. He told me he didn't love me and he'd believed that I was compliant in some crazy scheme to marry him for convenience. And he was *happy* about that compliance, he thought it would suit us to have some kind of love-less marriage arrangement. Have kids, live together and feel *nothing* for each other."

"Oh, my *God*. What the fuck? Who does that?"

"Ben does that. Because Ben doesn't believe in love, but—*get this*—even though he was uncomfortable with the thought of me thinking *he* was in love with me... he has now *oh-so-generously* decided that maybe it would be okay if I believed myself in love with him. Since that would make things easier for me."

"Jesus, what the fuck kind of sociopath is he? Lilah, you can't stay in this. It's nuts!"

"I know that. I told him so. He married me because it was what would be best for the precious company, and because it would make Gramps happy... and he thought I married him for the same reasons."

"Your grandfather wouldn't have wanted a loveless marriage for either of you."

"I tried telling him that but..." She shrugged. It felt so good to finally get all of this off her chest. To tell someone who loved Lilah and who would be one hundred percent on her side. "I was so humiliated, Blake. So embarrassed to tell you. And before all of this with Gramps, my sole focus was to end this farce as soon as possible—without upsetting Gramps of course. I initially told Ben I'd stick it out for only a year."

She went on to explain the rest of her decision to Blake but ended on, "But then we got the call about Gramps and we were both so upset and we slept together. And it—God help me—it was *amazing.*" She told Blake about what had happened afterwards, the condom, the argument, the humiliating realization that he hadn't taken a single word from her seriously. That he'd dismissed her anger and threats to leave as some kind of tantrum not to be believed.

"I don't know why I'm here," she confessed. "After Gramps died, I fell to pieces. But I feel like Ben did a little too. I feel like we need each other right now. And I'm not sure what my next step should be."

"You fucking *leave* him, Lilah," Blake said, pretty much confirming what Lilah had already known in her heart of hearts. "Your mutual grief aside, this is *not* a sustainable situation. You'll fall into a routine, you'll get too comfortable, you'll start to think that maybe this isn't so bad."

"It's *bad*," Lilah said, her voice hoarse with stress. "I know it's bad. I know I should leave. And I will. I don't want this. And with Gramps gone"—she choked up a little, it was still so hard to say that out loud—"there's no reason to drag it out. But part of me feels like leaving so soon after his death would be a betrayal to Gramps, like we—*I*—should at least respect his memory enough to stick it out for just a few months longer."

"He wouldn't want you to be unhappy."

"I know that. But if he were here, I'd want to make *him* happy. And me with Ben… that has always been his dream."

"No, Lilah," Blake's voice was quiet and desperate. "You can't stay with him because of—"

"Oh, I'm *going* to leave him. But not right now. I'll stay a while. Not for a year as had been my original intention. Merely for a couple of months. Until the dust settles." It was a decision she'd literally made while talking it through with Blake but it sat well with her.

She was suddenly certain that this was the correct course of action. And having a definite deadline settled that uneasy pit in her stomach. She felt better, steadier.

Purposeful.

"And you're determined to do this?" Blake asked, resignation in her voice. She knew how stubborn Lilah could be. "Promise me you won't let him talk you around to his way of thinking. Promise me you'll *never* settle for less than you deserve."

"I promise," Lilah said with a small smile.

"I'm going to hound you so much about this. Constant emotional welfare checks."

"I'd appreciate that, because I'm quite certain I'm going to need them."

"Are you going to tell him about your plan?"

"I'll give him the heads up, I suppose, but it seems pointless. He won't believe me anyway. In the end, the only thing he'll believe is his own eyes when I walk out that front door."

"And I'll be here, supporting you every step of the way," Blake promised, her voice and eyes resolute.

Lilah smiled, relieved to finally have someone to talk to about this. Happy to no longer feel so alone.

NINETEEN

This small token of comfort

That night, when Ben crawled into bed beside her, Lilah —who was getting much too used to his presence in her bed—turned toward him and peered into his expressionless face on the pillow beside hers. He was watching her intently, mouth drawn into a tense line.

"You look tired," she observed and he nodded.

"We've been losing contracts," he surprised her by confiding. "Long-standing, massive contracts."

"Because of Gramps?"

The deep cracked sound of agreement that rumbled from his throat grated over her nerve endings and brought her clit and nipples to hard points. God, would she ever not be turned on by that sexy voice?

"The timing is unfortunate; a lot of these contracts are coming up for renewal over the next few months and they've given us notice of their intention not to renew. I have to get back to the office soon." He sounded apologetic, as if he were letting *her* down somehow. "Do damage control. Convince them the quality of our service hasn't dropped. Our share price tumbled in the days after his death and the board is panicking about that as well. We've more or less regained our previous standing on the market but I think everyone will just feel better if I was there to show them that it's business as usual."

"Of course," Lilah murmured, not sure why he felt the need to explain this to her.

There was a long pause, during which he simply stared at her. "Will you be okay?"

"What do you mean?" She was genuinely baffled by his question and she heard him swallow before he brought his hand to her face and stroked her cheek with the backs of his fingers.

"Without me?"

His question startled an incredulous laugh from her. His hand stilled and, for a fleeting moment, she could swear he looked hurt. The expression faded so quickly; she dismissed it as a trick of the light.

"I'll be fine." Her voice was dry and she barely managed to keep the sarcasm at bay. "In fact, I think I'll go back to work too. I may have to set up a work space in the living room for now though."

She'd had to give up her studio rental space after deciding to take her mental health break. She hadn't been sure when she'd return to full time work and it made no sense to keep paying for a space she wasn't using. Now, it felt a bit like a starting over, even though she'd already had so many queries from past and future clients about when she was returning that she knew she'd be inundated once she started taking bookings again. She didn't want to make the same mistakes, and had to place restrictions on how many clients she would see per day and per week.

"That won't be necessary."

"What do you mean? Of *course*, it's necessary. I'm not going to sit around here all day doing nothing, Ben! I know you think my work is little more than a glorified hobby. But I'm damned good at it, and it makes people happy. And—"

"Jesus," he muttered with a sigh, his long-suffering tone of voice halting her in mid-tirade. "I *meant* it won't be necessary because I've already had a space set up for you."

She gaped at him in surprise.

"You have?"

"In my office. Yes." The words were curt and she could tell he was—well she wasn't sure what he was. Irritated, maybe. Impatient, perhaps... Yet her brain kept circling back to *hurt*. He seemed hurt again.

"Thank you?" She truly wasn't sure how she felt about sharing an office with him again. They hadn't done so since her college days, back when she was a foolish young girl with a massive crush on an unattainable guy.

"Fuck," he muttered beneath his breath, the exasperated word heavily tinged with exhaustion. "Just go to sleep. I'm knackered."

Lilah sighed and turned away from him, tucking her hand under her head to stare at the wall. He moved around for a bit before switching off the dim bedside light and settling down as well. He usually slept with his front to her back and during the night she often woke to find him spooning her, his knees cozily tucked into the crooks of hers. So often over the last week she'd woken up crying in the night, and Ben would drape an arm over her, tug her against his warm chest and hold her while she wept. He would make gentle soothing, shushing sounds and kiss her hair and temple. They never spoke of it in the mornings that followed but Lilah had come to rely on his solid strength and for the first time, now that she wasn't as laden down by her own grief, she considered his.

Did he cry when she cried? Or did he stifle those emotions? Did he need her to hold him as well?

She was ashamed that it had never occurred to her on any of those long, desperately sad nights, to turn in his arms and reciprocate his comforting embrace.

Ben's reserve made him seem so self-contained and impervious to the frailties of human emotion. She knew if she brought it up now, he would clam up. And freeze her out. She wasn't willing to risk that rejection. Not when she'd decided to leave in just a couple of months' time.

She sighed again and he seemed to mistake the sound for sadness and hooked an arm around her waist. She froze for a moment, before relaxing into his warmth. She placed her hand over his where it rested on her abdomen and stroked his skin soothingly. Able to offer him at least *this* small token of comfort.

"Did you enjoy spending time with Blake today?" he asked after a moment's silence.

Lilah hesitated before replying. This was new, Ben never indulged in small talk, never asked her how she felt, or how her day was.

"Yes. Thank you for inviting her over."

The gentle stroking of his hand on her abdomen paused before continuing.

"No problem."

Curiosity prompted her to ask, "Why did you do it?"

"You have to process your grief, Lilah. And I thought having someone you trusted to talk to about it would help."

"Have *you* processed your grief?" Another pause in his soothing stroking.

"I'm dealing."

"How?"

"In my own way."

She gritted her teeth in frustration, it was like talking to a stone sometimes. She turned in his arms, and could barely make out his features in the dark.

"*How?*"

"Don't worry about it," he dismissed. "I'm fine."

"You wouldn't tell me even if you weren't, would you?"

No reply, but the truth was there, lurking in his stubborn silence.

"I think about that night." His words were abrupt, bitten off, clearly reluctantly conceded and she stared into his face, not seeing much more than the gleam of his eyes.

"That night?"

"I think about how it was between us. How you felt against me, your lips on mine... on *me*. I think about it all the fucking time. At the most inappropriate times. And I want to do it again."

She swallowed thickly, as the memory of that night came back to her. The fear and the grief, followed by his intoxicating kisses and lingering touches. How he'd taken that fear from her and replaced it with wonder, excitement, and pleasure. She'd thought about it often too... wishing he would do that for her again.

Wanting him to.

But knowing that it could never be repeated.

"I don't want that." Her words were firm and her voice resolute.

"I bought condoms," he told her. His tone was almost triumphant, as if he truly believed that was the only thing holding her back.

"You wasted your money."

"Lilah, I really want this to work between us. I think we could—"

"Ben, I'm leaving," she interrupted him, not wanting to rehash this same futile conversation again.

"No, you're not," he said with a scornful little laugh.

"I am. In June."

Two months from now.

"What happened to one year?"

"You know I only stipulated that time frame for Gramps's sake. With him gone, there's no reason for us to put up any appearances."

"There's still the board."

"You don't care what they think."

"Maybe I do." She felt him shrug, his unconcern palpable. "And why this arbitrary two-month time frame? Why not right now, if you're so damned determined to leave?"

"Because, I think it would be disrespectful to Gramps's memory."

"You're making no sense. The year is off the table because he's gone, but somehow not leaving right now is disrespectful to him? Make up your fucking mind."

"I can't explain it. I feel—"

"I can," he interrupted rudely. "You want to stay and you'd use any excuse to do so. I'm guessing that come June, you'll find another reason to linger. Stop playing these damned games. I think you've punished me enough for not loving you, don't you? So why don't we just call it even and start our married life together?"

"You think I'm *punishing* you?" Lilah scoffed. She sat up and switched on the bedside lamp to flood the room with warm light. He sat up too and glared at her, his irritation plain to see. "Ben, I don't want to punish you. That would require too much damned emotion and energy. I just want to cut my losses and move on with my life. You're right, staying for two months is a stupid idea. Gramps would want us to be happy, and neither of us currently are."

"I'm fine. Don't presume to know what the hell I'm thinking and feeling, Lilah. I'm just *fine*. I'm content. I want our marriage to work. I want us to be together. But that's not good enough for Lilah Iris Beckett, is it? You want some impossible — Where are you going?"

She climbed out of bed and grabbed her pillow.

"I'm going to sleep on the sofa," she said, her movements angry as she whipped a comforter from the blanket storage box at the foot of the bed.

"Don't be ridiculous, Lilah, c'mon, get back into bed."

"I'm being perfectly reasonable. I refuse to sleep next to your condescending ass for another night. I'm moving out tomorrow."

"I don't want that."

"I don't care what you want."

He got out of bed too and loomed over her, a big, hulking man wearing only a pair of black boxer briefs, his expression menacing.

"Get back into bed."

"No."

"Don't make me carry you back."

"You lay *one* hand on me and I swear I'll scream the place down," she threatened from between clenched teeth, not really concerned that he would force her to do anything she didn't want to.

He glared at her, before taking a deliberate step back. "God, you're such a fucking brat!"

"And *you're* a prick."

She sailed out of the room and slammed the door behind her with a satisfying bang.

LILAH WOKE to the sounds of pots and pans rattling in the kitchen. She blinked up into the brightness, a little disoriented. Why was she in the living room, staring out at the bleak sky visible through the floor-to-ceiling sliding doors that led out to the terrace and infinity pool? She rubbed the sleep from her eyes and sat up on the massive sofa where she'd slept buried beneath a marshmallowy comforter which currently puffed up around her waist.

"Morning." The low raspy growl came from the kitchen behind her and she turned to face Ben, who stood behind the massive butcher block island. He wasn't wearing a shirt and his hair was mussed, as if he, too, had just woken up.

"Morning." She returned his greeting a little self-consciously as their argument of the night before came back to her.

"Eggs or pancakes?" he asked, and she was taken aback by the inane question.

"You're cooking?" she asked in surprise while stifling a yawn. She couldn't recall ever seeing him cook before. He heated up and ordered in.

"Trudy has the weekend off, remember?"

She did *not* remember that at all. The last week-and-a-half had been a blur and she hadn't noticed much of anything. It took her a second to even remember that today was Sunday.

"Uh... pancakes, I suppose." His lips quirked at the corners, and his eyes smiled at her. The expression was warm and unexpected and Lilah wasn't sure what to make of it.

"You've always been a complete sucker for pancakes," he said. His tone fond and reminiscent.

"It was the only thing Gramps could make," she said with a nostalgic smile. "Which is why I always asked for it whenever he got the urge to cook. Breakfast, lunch, dinner... if Gramps was cooking, I'd request pancakes. It saved his ego. And of course, I really *do* love pancakes and he made great ones."

"I didn't know..." His voice husked up and he cleared his throat with an awkward cough. "I didn't know Cyrus couldn't cook. I thought you always asked for pancakes because—"

"Because I'm an entitled brat who never considers anyone else's preferences?" she completed for him and a frown flitted across his brow before he shrugged. She refused to be distracted by the play of muscles in those broad, powerful shoulders and shifted her eyes to his face...

Not better.

"You did a great job of saving his pride, Lilah, because I never had a clue."

"I had twelve years with him before you showed up, Ben," she said, keeping her voice gentle, not wanting him to feel that it was in any way a slight. "I knew him very well. I don't think he even realized why I kept asking him for pancakes. I learned early on that there was one thing he cooked very well and it swiftly became my favorite meal." She laughed fondly at the memory. "I don't think his vanity allowed him to acknowledge what a truly terrible cook he was."

"I wouldn't be so sure," Ben said sounding thoughtful. "I used to feel petty as fuck, because I kind of resented that he never asked me what I wanted. Now I'm guessing he only asked you because he knew what you would want. And he knew he could deliver."

Lilah smiled, liking Ben's take, enjoying the notion that Gramps had known she'd had his back like that.

"I thought you were being selfish," Ben said, his rasp several decibels lower than usual and her eyes searched his face for some clue as to why he sounded so melancholy. As usual, his beautiful features told her nothing... but his clear blue eyes screamed his emotions louder than any words could. In them she saw shame, regret, and sadness. A depth of sadness that took her breath away.

"Because you never asked Cyrus or me what we wanted, never considered that maybe we'd want something else for a change. It never once occurred to me that..." His voice petered off, as if he wasn't sure how to end that sentence. The uncertainty was new in Ben. He was always so sure of exactly what he wanted to do and say. Lilah let him flounder... choosing not to make this any easier for him.

Ben watched her for a long moment, the sadness now replaced with mute apology. He exhaled softly and lifted his shoulders in an odd, uncertain, almost helpless way.

He released her eyes and busied himself in the kitchen. Lilah watched him for a few minutes and then shook herself. She should probably shower and start packing. She could move back into the house she'd shared with Gramps in Constantia. Gretchen was there, they could keep each other company while Lilah figured out her next steps. There was also the house in Bantry Bay... everything in her balked at the thought.

No. Too many memories there and she wasn't quite prepared to face them yet.

There was always Blake, but her friend enjoyed living alone.

She came from a large family where she'd had to share a bedroom with three sisters. She liked not sharing her space now and, though she knew Blake would welcome her with open arms, Lilah was reluctant to ask her to, even for a short while.

She wasn't ready to tell any of her *hoes* about her marriage, and so couldn't approach any of them.

She knew it was a little ridiculous having this problem. She was one of the wealthiest women in the country right now. She could live anywhere her heart desired. But she wanted to be with people she loved. In places that felt familiar. That felt like home.

She was deep in thought—considering all angles to her problem—and gnawing on her thumb cuticle when a coffee mug appeared in her field of vision. She gratefully latched onto it with both hands.

"Thank you," she told Ben after taking a deeply satisfying sip of the hot, aromatic brew and nearly scalding her tongue in the process.

He nodded and slid a plate heaped full of pancakes—drizzled with butter and honey, just how she liked it—and crispy bacon onto the coffee table in front of her. He left and returned with some cutlery, two empty plates and a second mug of coffee.

"Help yourself," he invited, handing one of the empty plates and a knife and fork to her. Before loading his own plate with some steaming pancakes and a couple of strips of bacon. He balanced his plate on his lap and dug straight in. Not bothering with a knife, using the side of his fork to cut into pancakes.

Lilah lowered her feet from the couch to the floor and reached for her own plate and a smaller helping of pancakes and butter. She took a cautious nibble and was surprised by how ravenous she was. Days of barely touching your food would do that. She was relieved to feel her appetite reviving and she scarfed down the modest first helping in no time, and soon found herself reaching for more.

They ate in silence. It wasn't a particularly comfortable silence, but—considering their fight the night before—it wasn't too terrible either. His pancakes were great, buttery and delicious.

"These could almost rival Gramps's," she said, and he grinned in genuine warmth.

"Well, I learned from the best," he said. "I watched him make them often enough. I never get the amount of sugar quite right though. He didn't measure it."

It *was* a little heavy on the sugar, but it was still pretty tasty.

She sopped up some honey and butter from her plate with the last bite of her pancake and finished it with a satisfied sigh. "That was really good, Ben. Thank you."

He nodded and took a sip from his cup, watching her over the rim.

"I don't want you to leave." The words were abrupt, unexpected, and startled Lilah into looking up.

"Ben…"

"I think you *should* stay those two months. I'd appreciate it. Just until we get everything sorted with Cyrus's estate, and the market settles. It'll also give you time to figure out what your next step would be. And to get back into the flow of things with your business. I know you've taken some time off to plan for the wedding. And before that there was your vacation to Paris. I feel like your business has been on the back burner since then. It'll take time getting it back on track."

Ben didn't know the specifics of why she'd taken that time off, she hadn't told him or Gramps about her health issues. She knew Ben had disapproved of her decision to close up shop for so long.

It had probably reinforced his belief that she was capricious and spoiled. That her business had been a whim.

But he was wrong about her not being able to pick up where she'd left off. Because she was highly sought after in her field, she had new and old clients waiting in the wings for her return. But she needed to rethink her social media strategy and her scheduling. Starting up professional collaborations like the one she had with Blake, partnerships, sponsorships would be a little harder. So Ben *was* right about Lilah needing time and stability to get her business organized in a way that suited her new vision.

He pushed to his feet, coffee mug still in one hand, and Lilah was momentarily diverted by his long, naked legs, with their muscular calves, and beautifully muscled, runner's thighs... She refused to dwell on the way those boxer briefs cupped his thick bulge and firm butt, and instead stared at the strong, beautifully veined tanned hand he held out to her.

"I have something to show you," he said, when she continued to merely stare at his hand without reaching for it. *"Please*, Lilah."

The soft desperation in those two words was novel enough to prompt her into action. She took his hand and allowed him to tug her up. She was wearing a white cropped cami top, a white, butt hugging pair of boy shorts, and a pair of ankle socks. She refused to be self-conscious about her near-nudity when he didn't seem to care about his. And she *absolutely* refused to acknowledge the gleam of desire she saw in his eyes when he gave her body a quick, appreciative once over.

He squeezed her hand and took off toward his office, tugging her behind him. He pushed the door open, let go of her hand, and stood aside for her to enter.

She gave him a quizzical look, before passing him and entering what she'd considered his private domain.

It was nice in there, as huge and bright and airy as the rest of the place, with the same breezy mismatched decorative style that was present throughout his home. Lots of blues, greens and whites, a massive glass desk facing the huge wall of windows that overlooked the Atlantic ocean. She didn't know why anyone would want to work anywhere else when they could be in here.

"I wanted you to see this before you made your decision," he said, the desperation from before creeping back into his voice. She couldn't make sense of why it was there.

She was on the brink of telling him that she'd already made her decision to leave when she finally understood what it was that he wanted her to see.

Her hand came up to cover her mouth and stifle the betraying gasp of delight when she spotted the smaller version of his glass desk against the left wall, directly in front of the window. From Ben's desk all you could see was sky and ocean, but from that smaller one—she walked closer to investigate and smiled—you could see the street, the beach, people. It was a people watcher's wet dream.

Across from the desk, tucked beside a bookshelf filled with financial almanacs, boring economic handbooks, and various tomes on marketing, was a different work space altogether. One set up with a shoot through umbrella, several studio lights, and some of the props she'd stored at the Constantia house after terminating the lease agreement for her previous studio.

"You could bring your clients here," he told her, sitting in his office chair and leaning back to watch her carefully. "Once I'm back at work, I'll only use this office in the evenings. So you'd have the office space mostly to yourself. We may have to share at times, but I'll let you know ahead of time. And you and I are used to sharing a work space anyway."

The last was said with a tiny smile, one that invited her to share in his nostalgia. But she couldn't enjoy the memories of them sharing his various offices anymore. She'd once treasured them, now all she could think of was that Ben had felt coerced into sharing his office with her. Had considered it part of his babysitting duties.

She simply couldn't smile about that any longer. Not when he'd likely felt stifled by her presence and imprisoned in his own space.

She dragged the chair from the smaller desk closer and sat down across from him, watching him as intently as he was watching her. Trying—and failing—to read his expression.

She chose not to respond to his last comment and diverted the topic back to the present. "Ben, you *do* realize that my clients are dogs, right? Dogs and their people."

"Of course, I do. Think of the amazing shoots you could on the terrace, up on the roof. In here. With the ocean as your back-drop. The dogs—and their people—would love it."

"And you'd be okay with a bunch of strangers traipsing through your home on a daily basis?"

It was admirable really, how manfully he managed to keep that cringe in check.

"Right now, it's *our* home. And I want you to feel comfortable here."

"I don't know," she said, betraying her nerves by chewing on her cuticle again. She folded her thumb into her palm when she realized what she was doing. "I don't think it'll be a good idea for me to stay here, Ben."

"Why not?" She could hear the frustration edging into his voice.

"Because you only have one bed."

"I could fix that. It's not a problem."

She gave him a long, searching stare, but could see no deception in that blue gaze. And not a trace of manipulation on his handsome face. Then again, an expert manipulator would be good at hiding his true intentions from others.

She felt like a complete sucker, even considering this suggestion, but—she glanced over at that desk again—she was so tempted.

"Why don't you give it a week or two?" he suggested in a hushed voice as if she were a wild deer he was afraid of startling. "See how you like it."

"I have other options," she whispered, and his throat moved before he nodded.

"I know you do."

"If I do this it's because it's convenient and nothing more."

"Okay."

"How will you solve the bed problem?"

"I'll take the sofa tonight. And have the king replaced with two queens tomorrow."

The room was massive enough to allow for that.

"It seems like a terrible inconvenience."

"It's not." His tone brooked no argument.

"You're not just doing this out of some misplaced sense of responsibility, are you? Because you don't have to do that. You don't owe Gramps anything."

"I owe him *everything*," he corrected fiercely, sounding affronted.

"You don't have to pay that debt for the rest of your life, Ben. Gramps wouldn't have wanted, or expected, that from you. You're taking care of his company. That's enough."

"It's not enough," he said with a brief shake of his head. "But that's beside the point. My reasons for doing this, for wanting you close, are complicated. For now, why don't you forget about my motivations and put your own needs first? You want a reliable base from where to restart your business. I can provide that for you."

"I could go home." His mouth thinned at her words and she was startled to recognize that he did *not* like it at all when she referred to any other place but here as her home.

"Back to *Beckett's Retreat*, you mean?" Ben was the only one who ever called the house in Constantia by that name. Her grandfather had named it such way back in the seventies. He'd named all his properties. It had been a *thing* back then. Lilah had always found it ridiculously pretentious and thankfully Gramps had fallen out of the habit of using those names. But Ben had called it that since his very first day with them.

"Yes. *Home*," she replied and that set off the tic in his jaw.

"You could," he said. "But do you *want* to?"

Sometimes he was too astute for his own good. She worried her upper lip with her teeth before shaking her head.

"No. Not right now. It's too soon."

His face softened. "I agree. Gretchen has been asking me when we intended to come around and supervise the packing up of his personal belongings and I'm not..." His face contorted with grief and he shook his head. "I don't think either of us are ready for that yet."

"No."

They had a moment of mutual, silent reflection, before Lilah exhaled gustily.

"Okay, I'll stay." She wasn't caving in. She *wasn't*. She was merely going back to her original plan. That was all. "But only because it's convenient, and because I don't want people prying into our personal business so soon after Gramps's death. I'd rather be left alone than forced to answer interminable, nosy questions about our marriage when this time should be about remembering Gramps."

"Agreed."

TWENTY

You're playing with fire, cupcake

The following Monday, Lilah was sitting at her desk, staring out at the gloomy sky, elbow on her desk and chin propped in her palm. It was a week since she and Ben had made this living and working arrangement, and it was actually going surprisingly well. Ben had returned to work the previous Tuesday and she rarely shared this office space with him. The first time they'd actually worked together in this room had been the Saturday past.

Lilah and her assistant Kirby—who currently worked remotely—had been updating her social media accounts and Ben had brought some paperwork home from the office. They'd spent a surprisingly companionable few hours absorbed in their tasks. Each getting the other a drink or snack whenever they left the office for the refreshments.

Their sleeping situation wasn't too bad either. It was kind of like having a very hot, platonic roommate. One who occasionally crawled into bed with you to hold you and comfort you when you cried in your sleep.

That had happened three times over the course of the week. Which was an improvement on the first week after Gramps's death when she couldn't go a few hours without dissolving into tears at night. It was creating a disturbing intimacy between them. Every time he got into bed with her, they fell asleep wrapped in each other's arms, and she woke up in the mornings pressed up against him, butt nestled against his insistent hard-on. Neither of them ever acknowledged that morning erection, but it was hard to resist grinding up against it. Especially when she awoke—as she had this morning—with his huge palm cupped over one of her small breasts and her stone hard nipple scorching a hole through the fabric of her silky cami top.

Her phone pinged and she glanced down at the screen and then smiled.

Her *Horti Hoes* chat group.

> OLIVE
> @LilahB how're you doing, hon? We miss you and we're thinking of you 🩶 🩶

Lilah's eyes misted as she stared at the text and contemplated her response.

> **ME**
> Hi, ladies! I miss you guys too. I'm okay, I suppose. It's rough at times, but getting there 🙏 🤍

> **KES**
> You up for some drinks with your emotional support hoes?

Lilah gnawed on her lower lip. She needed to get out. She hadn't seen anyone but Ben and Trudy in the last week. Blake was out of town, but they spoke regularly.

Staring out at the gunmetal gray clouds, which threatened heavy rain soon, Lilah found herself suddenly quite keen to see her friends. To discuss future gardening projects with them—there was one in particular that had been flirting at the edges of her mind since Gramps's death. She would love to pick their brains about it.

> **ME**
> I think that's a fantastic idea. When? Where?

There were a few back and forth suggestions. Until they finally settled on Wednesday night at a popular eatery in Observatory.

> **ME**
> I can't wait to see you all. And I'll bring pics of Ben's rooftop garden. It needs a makeover, suggestions and volunteers welcome 😊 😷 . And I have another project I want to discuss with you guys.

> **IVY**
> 🍃 OMG! Can't wait. I've been dying to get started on a new project, so I'm in, no matter what.

Lilah and her gardening club had been responsible for several community urban gardens in impoverished areas, all of which were flourishing now. They'd helped a few primary schools start vegetable gardens... and, of course—on a smaller scale—often spent time helping out in one another's gardens. They'd all met years ago in college and despite coming from completely disparate backgrounds and having vastly different interests—apart from gardening, of course—they'd hit it off and had all been fast friends since.

They chatted for a while longer and exchanged a few hilarious memes before the conversation petered out as everybody drifted back to work.

Lilah was reorganizing her digital portfolio when a quiet voice disturbed her concentration a couple of hours later.

She looked up to find Ben standing beside his desk watching her.

"Forgive the disturbance," he said.

"How long have you been standing there?"

"A couple of minutes, I called your name at least four times, but you were engrossed in your work."

"What are you doing here?"

"I live here," he said, deadpan, and Lilah gave him a flat, unimpressed stare, which seemed to amuse him if the wry twist of his lips was any indication. "I needed my tablet." He held up his hand to show her the device he held. "I forgot it."

That wasn't like him. Ben was ultra-efficient, and had the memory of an elephant. He didn't forget, or misplace, items.

"Okay." She wasn't entirely sure what else to say in response to his words and he hesitated.

"I don't have to rush back," he said, tugging his shirt and jacket sleeve back to glance at the Patek Phillippe watch that Gramps had given him for his twenty-first birthday. He'd rarely worn the watch before, saving it for special occasions, but Lilah had noticed that he'd been wearing it almost daily since Gramps's death. "It's nearly lunch time, you want to grab a bite somewhere?"

"I was just going to have a sandwich," she said, and he straightened the knot of his already straight tie. An unnecessary gesture that—on anyone else—Lilah would have considered nervous.

"A change of scenery would be good for you. You haven't ventured out since…" His didn't complete the sentence, but obviously she didn't need him to.

"I'm going out with my *hoes* on Wednesday," she said, and he shoved his hands into his pockets, his eyes boring into her face intently.

"Oh. Well, that's good. It's great. I'm happy to hear that." And yet he looked disappointed.

"But I think lunch would nice too. A low-stress way to ease my way back into the world."

His eyes lit up and she stared at him in wonder, fascinated by his uncharacteristic animation.

"Do you need some time to finish up what you were busy with?" he asked and Lilah shook her head, and pushed her chair away from her desk.

She was wearing an oversized ivory colored off-the-shoulder knit pullover top, with charcoal grey drawstring yoga pants. It was a chilly day in mid-April, and even though the apartment was climate controlled, and kept at a perfectly comfortable twenty-two degrees Celsius all year round, Lilah liked to dress for the season.

She had fluffy socks on her feet, which tended to make her slip and slide all over his heated marble floors. She saw him eyeing the socks askance, and—knowing what was coming—resisted the urge to roll her eyes.

She saw him battling the impulse to say something, but Mr. Know-It-All was incapable of curbing his tongue when it came to imparting his "wisdom" upon others.

"You're going to fall on your arse if you persist on wearing those damned socks around the flat, Lilah."

"So you've said before," she reminded him with an irreverent grin. "But they're so awesome for floor surfing. Look…"

Without warning, she took a few running steps and launched herself at him. She whooped like a kid and flailed her arms for balance when she skidded across the floor at ridiculous speed directly toward him. In the few seconds it took to get from point A to point B, she wondered if she should have given him more notice, because she was in serious danger of body slamming him.

But she should never have doubted him. He stepped aside at the last second and hooked an arm around her waist in an attempt to bring her to a stop. But her momentum took him in a complete circle, and his arms wrapped securely around her, while he swung her around with him. Her arms instinctively wound around his neck for balance and by the time he staggered to a standstill, she was laughing in wild exhilaration. Her laughter eventually faded and she grinned broadly up into his glaring face.

"You could have hurt yourself," he admonished in a stern voice, but she could tell his heart wasn't in it. His eyes were warm as they scanned her face.

"Nah," she denied, and nonchalantly waved his concern aside. "I knew you'd catch me."

"One day I might not." There was a somber note in his voice and it struck a chord with her.

She uncurled an arm from around his neck and—as if driven by instinct—palmed one lean cheek.

"But you did today," she murmured, an embarrassing throatiness in her voice. "And I'm grateful for that."

She was standing on her toes, chest flush against his, one arm still wound around his neck, her mouth a hair's breadth from his, while her eyes peered into his strangely vulnerable blue gaze intently. She was the one who should have been out of breath, after her mad dash across the room, but instead, it was Ben whose breath was coming in uneven pants. She felt his heart racing against her chest and marveled at it.

"Sometimes, I forget you have a heart," she whispered.

His eyes flickered and his mouth thinned. "It's a muscle, like any other. It serves a purpose."

Of course, it did.

Lilah smiled sadly, and exhaled—a slow, controlled release of breath—not sure what other answer she'd expected from her pragmatic temporary husband. But she was grateful for the very *Ben* response. It reminded her how mismatched they were.

She dropped her hands to his chest and exerted gentle pressure—enough for him to know she was ready to be released. But instead of loosening his hold, his arms tightened. His eyes flashed in, what looked like, disappointment but remained laser focused on her lips.

For a second she was certain he was going to kiss her but he screwed his eyes shut and stepped away from her with what seemed to be a colossal amount of willpower.

"I'll grab my shoes and a jacket and we can head out," she said, and turned and fled before he could say anything else.

LUNCH WAS PLEASANT ENOUGH. Ben seemed genuinely interested in how she was spending her days. She watched him closely, looking for boredom or disdain. In the past he'd barely refrained from using air quotes whenever he'd referred to her work, but right now he listened attentively, asked questions and even offered suggested on how to get new clientele.

"Have you ever considered broadening your client base?" he asked, while neatly quartering his hamburger. He'd manfully striven to disguise his grimace when she'd suggested a popular burger place in the area, and had then surprised and delighted her by ordering the biggest, messiest burger on the menu, complete with fries and a chocolate shake. But dividing the burger into four, easily managed slices was such a quintessentially Ben solution to a messy problem, that it delighted Lilah even more than his order had.

"Broadening how?" she asked, sucking some mushroom sauce off her thumb. Lilah had zero qualms about getting her hands dirty and her face smeared with grease. Hands-on was the only way she could possibly enjoy a burger.

Ben didn't immediately answer and she lifted her eyes to find his gaze transfixed on her mouth, where she was still licking mushroom sauce off her fingers. Feeling unquestionably wicked, she deliberately swiped her index finger through the thick, creamy white sauce and smeared it over her lower lip, before swirling her tongue around the tip of her finger, licking it clean, and then sucking it knuckle deep into her mouth.

His eyes were feverish and he licked his lips and swallowed thickly, his fork frozen mid-air halfway to his mouth. She watched beads of sweat pop on his forehead and he shifted uncomfortably in his seat. That heated gaze lifted to hers and when he realized she was watching him, his eyes narrowed.

"You're playing with fire, cupcake," he warned, and she gave him her most guileless smile.

"Sometimes, when I look at you... I think maybe it wouldn't be so bad to get a little scorched," she confessed, and was delighted when she startled a rare laugh from him.

"And sometimes when I look at you... I think maybe God put

you on this earth to drive me stark, raving bonkers," he said, voice low and gruff.

That made her laugh. Her first genuine laugh in weeks and this time he was the one who looked delighted.

They exchanged a looked of shared amusement and after taking a sip from her colorful unicorn milkshake, she wriggled forward in her seat—elbows on table— and rested her cheeks in her palms.

"So what did you mean about broadening my client base?"

"Exactly what I said, why pets only? Why not babies? And older kids? Family portraits? Even weddings? Diversify."

"Ben, you don't know this, because I doubt you've ever looked me up or anything, but I'm kind of a big deal in pet photography," Lilah confessed. "I know you think I lack focus and that this is just some kind of hobby to me. But my brand is currently associated with exclusivity and high demand."

She stared into her milkshake before deciding to finally disclose her reason for going on hiatus.

"I spent *years* creating this brand, Ben. And cultivating a reputation of perfection and uniqueness in an over-saturated market. And my client base grew and grew to the point where it became unmanageable. Last year, I suffered a series of stress-related asthma attacks, and my doctor was concerned that I would have to be upgraded from mild persistent to moderate persistent asthma. He insisted I take a break and reduce my stress levels. I love what I do, I never thought it was particularly stressful, until one day I recognized that it was. I was so concerned about not disappointing anyone, I rarely said no to a booking. I worked twelve-hour days, and then worked six hours more in post-processing after I got home. Eighteen-hour days, five-and-a-half days a week. It was a lot. It was at that point that I understood I was this in demand because I'm *that* good. My reputation is strong enough that I could take a break, come back after a year or so, and be able to pick and choose my projects. My clients would still be there, even if they have to wait months for an opening in my shooting schedule."

"Why didn't you tell me about your health scare? Or Cyrus?" he asked, his face pale and his voice shaky.

"Excuse me, but have you met yourself and Gramps? You two would have collectively lost your shit and smothered me with your overprotective alpha maleness. I was trying to breathe, not suffocate! I figured it out by myself. Y'know, like an adult? I'm healthier and I'm trying to make better choices as far as my career goes. I'm easing my way back into business."

"I-I underestimated you, Lilah. I didn't comprehend how fucking brilliant you were at your job. I was a condescending arsehole."

"You were," she agreed without heat. "But look at you now, admitting to your failings. Well done, Ben."

"I wouldn't exactly call them failings," he corrected with a glower. "Just a misapprehension of the facts."

She chuckled. "You were doing so well for a second there."

He had the grace to look chagrined and shifted his shoulders uncomfortably.

"I'm trying to say," he continued doggedly, "that you handled the whole thing admirably and I should have been less of an arsehole about the whole thing."

She shook her head, still laughing. "And I think you've handled your avoidance of actually saying the words *I'm sorry*, pretty damned admirably too. Well done."

He avoided her eyes and that made her laugh even harder.

"Anyway, I've always yearned to carve my own little niche in this world," she said, stirring her thick milkshake with the thick stainless-steel straw. "I know it seems impractical, considering... well, my name, I suppose. Which is my business is called *Petography by Lile*. I didn't want anyone immediately associating my business with the '*Beckett Heiress*'." Her lips thinned when she used air quotes for the despised moniker the press had given her after Gramps's death.

She suddenly gave him a self-effacing grin and rolled her eyes, inviting him to share in her humor. "Although, having my studio in a swanky penthouse in Clifton would likely be a dead giveaway."

"Is that why you haven't had any photoshoots at the apartment yet?" He looked troubled instead of amused.

"God, no!" she scoffed. "I have so many people excited to see me back on social media and I've been receiving an overwhelming amount of enquiries. So I decided to wait for Blake to return from Durban instead."

He frowned in confusion. "What does that have to do with anything?"

"A lot of her clients are interested in my services too. I thought a good way to ease my way back into work was to have a quick competition, a lottery of sorts, for Blake's clientele. Five winners and we could use some of the pictures from their photoshoots as promotional material just before I start taking bookings again."

His face cleared and he speared another piece of hamburger with his fork. "Of course, Blake runs that doggy day care thing?"

"Pet grooming business."

"Right." His face was expressionless and she just *wondered* if he thought she and Blake were a couple of spoiled rich girls playing at being grown up.

Well, if that's what he thought, she needed to disabuse him of that notion immediately. He could denigrate *Lilah* in his mind as much as he wanted to, but her friends were off-limits.

"Yep, that's right. Her *nationwide* pet grooming business, with over a hundred employees, fifteen mobile parlors, and five brick-and-mortar stores. She has a client list that includes celebrities, politicians, athletes, and influencers. And the business earns an annual revenue of over three million rand."

"She still washes dogs for a living though," he said, his face completely devoid of expression, but something about the rigidly straight line of his mouth told her he was messing with her. She narrowed her eyes at him, and her suspicion was confirmed when he refused to meet her gaze.

She plucked a blue mini marshmallow off the top of her obnoxiously pink milkshake with its multicolor sprinkles, and tossed it at him. It landed on his cheek and kind of stuck there for a second before sliding wetly down the craggy planes of his face.

He reached up and removed the marshmallow from his cheek, bringing it around to stare distastefully at the bright blue, gooey confectionary. The blue was coming off on his fingertips.

He quirked a brow at her and—maintaining eye contact all the while—popped the sticky treat into his mouth.

"That milkshake looks revolting by the way," he pointed out, and Lilah wondered if she should tell him that his teeth were blue. "What the fuck is the thought process behind it? Was the unicorn supposed to have been blended into it? Because if that's the case, it's grim as hell."

She blinked at him, having never really considered that angle before.

"Uh..." She snort giggled as she contemplated his words.

"Maybe it's meant to be something unicorns consume? Like unicorn nectar or something?"

Another skeptical brow quirk.

"What's it taste of?"

"Wanna sip?" she asked, holding the glass toward him and his face actually contorted in revulsion which made her giggle even harder.

"God *no*. I just told you it looks repulsive."

She stirred the confection again and held it up for him to see the swirled together blues, pinks and purples.

"It looks awesome," she disagreed.

"Looks like unicorn barf." His disgruntled words had her chortling, and it truly felt wonderful to just laugh at silly shit again. It was especially gratifying when her laughter coaxed another one of Ben's rare smiles from him. Seriously, the man was entirely too selfish when it came to those beauties.

She took an experimental sip from her milkshake, smacked her lips and lifted her eyes to his. "Yep... that's it. That's the flavor. Unicorn barf. And it's *delicious*."

He palmed his face and his shoulders shook helplessly, while he strove to hide his laughter from her.

When he finally dropped his hand, the laughter had faded, but it still shone in his eyes.

"I always found it absurd how you could be fascinated and amused by the simplest things," he said. "I remember you once stopped dead in your tracks to watch a squirrel drag a couple of nuts up a tree. It annoyed the hell out of me, I had important business to discuss with Cyrus and you kept him there for nearly half-an-hour making the most ridiculous off-color comments."

Lilah recalled that day, she'd been nearly sixteen and had been possessive of her time with her grandfather. When Ben had approached them on their daily walk around the gardens, she'd seen the purposeful look on his face and had been desperate to keep Gramps with her a little longer. Of course, it didn't hurt that Ben lingered as well, she'd truly had the most embarrassingly obvious crush on him.

"Oh yes, I remember that squirrel. He kept dropping both nuts, but refused to leave one behind."

"I never realized how many dirty testicle related puns you knew before that day," Ben said. "I probably would have been impressed if I weren't so irritated."

"Students at all girls' schools have to keep themselves occupied in some way," she said with a laugh. "Blake was the worst when it came to dirty jokes, she picked them up from her older brothers."

"The thing is," he said, his voice reflective. "I can't for the life of me remember what the urgent business was I needed to discuss with him… but I clearly remember how happily Cyrus laughed at every one of your stupid puns."

"What are you getting at, Ben?" she asked softly, and he lifted his shoulders awkwardly.

"I don't know… I guess maybe that you're like sunshine, Lilah. You brightened up Cyrus's life and, lately, I've found myself appreciating the light you bring to my life and my home as well."

Lilah wasn't sure what to make of that. How to respond to it. Why he was saying it. Was it some kind of ploy? Another way of trying to convince her to stay in this marriage with him?

But he looked painfully embarrassed, red creeping up from his collar and into his face and she could tell that it had been an honest, spur-of-the-moment comment. And that Ben himself wasn't sure how to react to the confession.

"I just thought you should know that," he said, his cracked voice much raspier than usual.

"I appreciate that. I cherished my moments with Gramps. I *do* desperately wish there had been more of them."

"He cherished those moments too. He cleared his schedule, switched off all his devices and forbade his staff from contacting him when he had anything planned with you."

Lilah smiled and swiped at a sneaky tear that had crept its way onto her cheek. Ben looked alarmed and regretful at the sight of the tear.

"I didn't mean to make you cry, sweetheart, I just thought you should know how much you meant to him. And how I'm starting to get it. I'm understanding that he loved you not just because he had to, not only because you were his granddaughter, but because of the person you are. Because you brought laughter and light into his life. Because spending time with you, was time well spent."

"Please don't say these things," she whispered. "I don't know why you'd say this. I can't—*won't*—change my mind about us. About this marriage. It's not real. I deserve more than this. More than *you*. And I don't think Gramps would have wanted this for me if he knew… if he knew what I knew."

"What is it that you think you know, Lilah?" Why did he have to sound so damned patient and understanding? She hated it. Hated that it put her on the back foot and made her feel like *she* was the one who was wrong about this.

"I know that you don't love me."

"I care about you. And I find that I quite like you. A lot actually. More and more each day."

She gave him a mute, frustrated glare, and shook her head in anger.

"Ben, stop playing these stupid mind games, please," she begged, digging her thumbs into her temples. "Just stop. You *know* what I mean. We were having a good day. We were enjoying each other's company. Why did you have to…"

Her thick voice faded as she found herself physically incapable of speaking.

"You're right, I shouldn't have brought this up right now."

"No, you shouldn't bring this up ever. There's no point."

"I disagree."

"*Ben.*"

"I disagree," he repeated staunchly.

"Well, then… I suppose that's your prerogative. But *I* have nothing left to say on this matter."

THREE WEEKS LATER, on a chilly, but clear Saturday afternoon, Lilah was up in the roof garden with her *hoes*. They were all dressed in their finest gardening ensembles—t-shirts, sweatpants and sunhats or bandannas—and had each been assigned a particular section of the rooftop. They weren't talking much, but had plans to follow up the day's Big Plant with ice cold cocktails and snacks.

"Afternoon ladies," Ben's deep voice called from the door. "I thought you could all do with some refreshments. You've been at it for hours."

Lilah, who'd spent most of the morning kneeling while planting wild rosemary and lavender bushes in massive wood pallet planter boxes, stood upright and winced when her back protested the sudden movement. She put her hands into the dip below her spine and stretched, trying to relieve the kinks.

Ben—looking sinfully hot in faded thigh-hugging jeans and an open-necked black dress shirt—stepped into the garden, clutching a tray of tall, icy drinks. Whatever they were, he must have made them himself since he—*they*—didn't have any live-in staff and Trudy had weekends off.

"Oh, my God, Benjamin Templeton, you're always such a frikkin' lifesaver," Kes crowed from the colorful, mixed salvia corner she was working on. The other women chorused their agreement and all flocked over to the man bearing drinks. Everyone except Lilah, who stood watching him warily.

They'd barely spoken since their lunch three weeks ago. He no longer came home unexpectedly during the day and, because he was still doing damage control after Gramps's death, he'd spent most of the last couple of weeks traveling both in country and abroad. In fact, just yesterday, he'd returned from a trip to Copenhagen to speak to one of their biggest shipping container partners about the future of their relationship with BME. According to what he'd told her last night, just before falling into an exhausted slumber, the meeting had been a complete success, and the news of the continuing partnership had settled a lot of investor and shareholder nerves. It seem as though the company was stable again; Ben's leadership was assured and Gramps's legacy would remain intact.

Despite her lack of interest in the inner workings of Gramps's company, Lilah had been relieved to hear that. For Ben's sake more than her grandfather's. God knew, Ben didn't know how to fail and a lesser outcome would simply never have occurred to him, but Lilah was relieved nonetheless.

With one hand still pressed against the niggling ache in the small of her back, she watched him excuse himself from the circle of animatedly chatting women, one drink still balanced on the tray.

"You okay?" he asked once he'd reached her, his eyes on the hand massaging her back.

"Stiff back from bending over all day."

"It's looking great up here," he said, his eyes skimming over the rooftop, taking in the amount of work they'd done in just one morning.

"It's a two-day job, minimum. It was a logistical nightmare getting enough soil and compost up here, but luckily my favorite garden center came through with the delivery. The ladies'll be back next Saturday for the finishing touches." He handed her the glass and placed the empty tray on a nearby bench.

She took a cautious sip of the pink concoction.

"*Whooo* boy," she gasped, fanning at her mouth face, eyes streaming. "You sure you put enough gin in this drink?"

His eyes widened and he took the glass from her to take a sip.

"Jesus... *fuck*, that's pretty damned strong," he agreed, his eyes going to the group of women still merrily laughing and chatting where he'd left them. "None of them breathed a word about how strong it is. And it all came from the same pink gin and tonic mix that I'd whipped up."

"There's tonic in this?" she asked incredulously and took another sip. *Nope*, no tonic. At least not that she could taste. "*Lies*! You're a lying liar who lies!"

"Look at them," he breathed, staring at her friends, and sounding almost awed. "They're tossing it back like it's water for fuck's sake."

"Oh they know how to hold a drink, those girls. We may look

like nerdy plant-loving snowflakes, but we were the rowdiest bunch of party girls at college."

"I know. I have firsthand knowledge of exactly *how* rowdy, remember?" His voice was dark. Somber. And Lilah's eyes flew to his in horror as that night, eight years ago, came flooding back. The night Ben had rushed her to hospital, absolutely certain she was dying. She'd been so scared—barely conscious—but could still vividly recalled the look of stark, desperate terror on Ben's face as he'd carried her into the emergency room, pleading for somebody, *anybody* to help her.

"Well, *I've* never really been one for strong alcohol," she said, injecting lightness into her voice as she set the glass down in the tray on the bench.

He still looked pale and dazed and she tried to shake him out of it by grabbing hold of his hand and dragging him to her corner of aromatic lavender and rosemary.

"I've been working on the herb garden," she told him. "The fragrance will permeate throughout the garden. When they mature, the bushes will be about waist high—your waist, not mine—and they'll attract bees, butterflies, birds. It's going to be beautiful."

"It's already beautiful."

She beamed up at him, happy that he liked it. This was her gift to him. A peaceful place for him to retreat to, away from the frenetic pace of his world.

"The ladies were talking about another special project you were working on," he said, watching her closely.

"It's nothing," she said, her cheeks going rosy. Not sure how much she wanted him to know about that.

"They said it was about Cyrus?"

"Oh, God, who said that? Darbi? It was Darbi wasn't it? She's such a blabbermouth."

"Uh… quite honestly," he admitted gruffly. "I've always had a little trouble telling them apart."

That startled a laugh out of Lilah. She looked over at her very disparate group of friends in amusement. They were tall, short, curvy, slim, black, Asian, brown and white. None of them looked or behaved remotely alike. Ben had just never cared to pay attention to them long enough to work out who was whom.

"So what's this project?" he asked and Lilah hesitated.

"You're going to think it's stupid," she said, reluctant to share it with him.

"Or maybe I won't."

Or maybe he wouldn't.

"I'm planning a commemorative public garden or park for Gramps. But more than that, I'm thinking of establishing a charitable foundation in his name. Gramps loved green spaces, he loved gardens and forests and, well, I don't have to tell you. You know this already. It's all still quite tenuous, but I wanted this foundation to provide grants to worthy community-based projects to build parks, play areas, and green spaces in impoverished areas with significant urban decay. And once I have all the kinks ironed out, I was thinking it would be wonderful if the opening of the garden coincided with the announcement of the foundation."

She was chattering nervously, she could hear the pitch of her voice increase while each word fell faster than the last, until they were almost colliding into one another. She took a breath, peering closely into his face. He was staring at her as if he'd never seen her before and she wasn't entirely sure what to make of that odd, bemused expression.

"I know what you're thinking," she ventured, her voice hesitant because—honestly—she had no real clue what the hell he was thinking. But she'd take a stab at it nonetheless. "A foundation, am I right? Such a useless spoiled rich bitch thing to do."

"That's not what I was thinking, at *all*." The denial was soft, almost gentle.

"Then what's up with that face?"

"What face?" He touched his jaw as if to check that all was well with his face.

"That stoic, *I'm Hiding What I'm Feeling Because What I'm Feeling Isn't Good* face."

"What I'm feeling is pride, Lilah." His voice was shaky with emotion and the fact that he chose not to hide that from her, touched and shocked the hell of Lilah in equal measures. "I'm so fucking proud of you. Cyrus would have loved this idea so much. It's goddamn perfect."

"Do you think so?" She hated that her voice had that wavering, little girl quality to it. As if she was seeking validation, when she didn't need his validation or approval.

"Do you really want to know what I think right now, Lilah?" he asked, stepping toward her and broaching her personal space without a care. He cupped her face in his palms and loomed over her, his shoulders hunched in an attempt to close the distance between them.

TWENTY-ONE
Just a kiss

"Well?" he prompted. "*Do* you?"

She nodded, helplessly ensnared by his feverish gaze. "Tell me."

"I'm thinking I would fucking *die* if I go another second without my lips on yours."

He didn't wait for her response, instead doing exactly what he'd so eloquently claimed to be yearning for. He took her mouth in a hot, voracious, no holds barred, oxygen and energy sapping kiss.

None of the kisses they'd shared before now even remotely compared to this one. It burned as hot as fire and robbed her of her breath as it scorched through the oxygen around them. She whimpered—helpless beneath the onslaught—and her arms crept around his waist for support, as well as to pull him closer. His hands were still on her face, tilting her head to the side, in order to have better control over this *amazing*, brain-sizzling, limb-melting, life-altering kiss.

He used his tongue only sparingly, and to wonderful effect; subtle flicks, strokes and licks designed to make her crazy.

He ended the kiss slowly, easing them both out of it with soft sighs, and delicate nibbles. He lifted his lips from hers, and she opened her eyes to see that *his* eyes were still shut. His lips were parted, and as she watched, the tip of his tongue slid over his full lower lip as if he was savoring her taste.

She and Ben simultaneously became aware of the whoops and applause coming from her group of raucous friends, and Ben's eyes opened to stare into hers, a mix of guilt and amusement flitting over his face.

"Wow," she breathed, and he grinned boyishly.

"You okay?"

"*So* okay," she said, matching his grin. "Where did *that* come from?"

"I think it's always just been lurking away somewhere inside of me."

"You mean you don't kiss all the girls like that?"

She was only half joking, but he was serious as a heart attack when he replied, "Only one girl, Lilah. Only you."

"Phew, guys, I mean we know you're newlyweds, but *dayuuu-uuum*," Kes said, as the other women came over to join them.

"But yeah, thanks for the show. It was so hot it should have come with a parental advisory," Ivy joked, her eyes sparkling.

"Who even knew you had that in you, Benji?" Darbi asked, holding her hands to her impressive chest. "That there was some inspired oral communication skills, my man."

A dull flush crept up Ben's cheeks and he hastily mumbled something about "getting back to work" and fled. They watched him go before all dissolving into hysterical laughter. Well, all of them except Lilah, *she* was still giddy and shell-shocked.

"*Sies*, Darbs, you embarrassed the poor man," Olive joked, and they all laughed again.

"Oh, any man who kisses like that has *nothing* to be embarrassed about," Kes said, fanning herself. "I mean, I could have spontaneously combusted just from watching."

She reached over and pressed a hand to Lilah's forehead. "How you feeling, girl? You look a little flushed. You *must* have a fever after that shit!"

More ribald laughter from her irreverent *hoes*, and Lilah finally snapped out of her daze to duck away from Kes's hand.

"C'mon guys, you're being ridiculous. It was just a kiss."

"*Just* a kiss, she says," Darbi hooted. "And Jason Momoa is *just* a man."

"The Mona Lisa is *just* a painting," Olive chimed in.

"*Bohemian Rhapsody* is *just* a song," Kes piped up.

"Newton's Universal Law of Gravitation is *just* math," Ivy inserted eagerly and everybody groaned and glared at her.

"Seriously, Ivy? You couldn't come up with something sexier than that?"

"What? It's sexy! We wouldn't have space travel without it." More hard staring. "Or... Netflix?"

"If you have to defend it this hard, it's just not worth it," Darbi muttered, tossing her waist-length fire red braids disdainfully.

"Okay, fine... uhm — the Coliseum is just —"

"Forget about it, girl," Kes told her with a sympathetic pat on her back. "The moment has passed."

"Anyway, our *point* is —"

"Oh, you mean you actually *have* one?" Lilah asked sarcastically.

Olive gave her quelling look before continuing, "Our point is that we all really like Ben, Lilah. A lot. How could we not after what he did for us back in college? But I don't think we've ever seen him that—I don't know—so...so..."

"So fucking passionate," Kes said in her usual blunt way, running a hand through her short, sleek blue-black bob.

"So absolutely *gone* for you." Ivy's smoky voice was quiet, her hazel eyes—so striking against her perfect brown skin—intent. "We knew he had to love you. Of course he does, he's known you for years, he married you. But I don't think we've ever seen it until today. Until that kiss."

"God, that kiss," Olive said, looking a little swoony. "It was so romantic."

"Could we stop talking about this now and get back to work?" Lilah asked, uncomfortable with the discussion, not sure she wanted to hear all of this.

It was everything she would have loved to hear before her marriage to Ben. She would've eaten it up with a spoon. Now all she could think of was how her husband didn't love her, how his kisses may mean that he desired her, but that he *wasn't* gone for her, as Ivy had put it. He was merely hot for her.

"Daaaaw, she's all shy about her sexy husband loving the hell out of her," Darbi squealed. The other ladies put their hands to their cheeks and all *aaaaw*-ed simultaneously.

Lilah laughed at their ridiculousness and turned back to her lavender and rosemary. Experience told her that if she ignored them, they would lose interest.

Sure enough, after a few more chuckles and silly comments, they all drifted back to their respective corners, and conversation went back to the occasional stupid, dirty joke.

The ladies stayed for dinner — ORDERING pizzas — and eating it out on the terrace by the pool. The tolerably chilly temperature dropped straight into cold once the sun went down, and they gathered around the fire pit with lap blankets, plates balanced on their knees and wine glasses clutched in hand.

"Ben!" Darbi suddenly squealed, spotting him in the kitchen through the massive windows. He froze at the sound of Darbi's shrill voice, his hand on the fridge door. He turned, his reluctance evident in the slowness of the movement, to face them.

"Come and have some pizza," Kes called, waving him over. The other women all chorused their agreement, but Ben didn't move, his questioning eyes on Lilah. She grimaced apologetically and nodded.

Ben squared his shoulders and walked slowly toward the doors, looking very much like a man walking toward a firing squad.

"Thanks for the invitation, ladies, but I don't want to intrude," he told them with an urbane smoothness, offering a regretful smile. "It's your ladies' night and I have some work to catch up on."

"You have to eat, don't you?" Olive asked with uncharacteristic brazenness.

Ben gave Lilah another look and she scooted over on the wood and stone bench which encircled the fire pit and lifted her lap blanket, inviting him in.

He didn't need a second invitation, climbing over the bench and sitting down beside her, immediately warming up the left side of her body with his delicious heat. She lifted her plate silently, offering him a slice, and he took it with a smile.

He remained quiet while the women continued their conversation about their asshole bosses and colleagues.

"How often does it happen?" Ivy asked Olive who was—ironically—picking the olives off her pizza. The woman shrugged miserably.

"*All* the time," she mumbled. "His wife calls and I'm supposed to blatantly lie to her. Tell her he's in a meeting, when he's full on snogging the HR rep in his office. The frikkin' *HR* rep, for fuck's sake! His wife once called me from an emergency room, desperately trying to reach him after an accident, but he had an afternoon *meeting* with—let's call her Suzie—from HR and told me to please go to the ER and sit with his wife. Oh, and to take her flowers. God, she was so damned grateful for those stupid flowers!"

"Ugh, that's awful. Poor woman!" Kes said.

"She should leave his deadbeat ass," Darbi said, waving a hand. "Why stay with such a piece of shit?"

"She doesn't have a clue anything's wrong. Because I'm covering for him, and she likes and trusts me... so I feel like *I'm* the one who's cheating, if that makes sense."

Sympathetic murmurs from everyone else.

Darbi told everybody about her creepy colleague, who kept clipping his toenails right at his desk, in the laboratory they shared—Darbi was a lab technician at a pharmaceutical company.

Ivy—the owner of an upmarket clothing boutique in Constantia—regaled them with stories of some of her most insufferable, entitled clientele.

Everybody had a story, or several, to tell. Lilah contributed with tales of some of her over-protective helicopter pet parents.

"What about you, Ben?" Ivy asked the man who'd been sitting silently in their midst. He'd been listening intently, eating his pizza and taking proffered sips of red wine from Lilah's glass. Occasionally smiling at some of the more outlandish anecdotes.

"Please, he had the best boss, Mr. Beckett was a saint," Darbi dismissed.

And Lilah turned to face Ben, who was staring thoughtfully into the fire pit. "Was he?"

Her voice was quietly curious. She knew Gramps had tasked him with the impossible, tedious, and likely frustrating job of keeping an eye on Lilah. And she knew it wasn't at all what Ben would have wanted to be doing.

"Cyrus? A saint he was not," Ben said, his eyes lighting up. "He once made me fly to Durban to pick up a chicken korma from his favorite Indian restaurant."

"*No*," Lilah gasped, both horrified and amused. "He didn't! Did he?"

"I was about twenty at the time, just an intern. And so damned eager to please my mentor."

"Tell us you at least got to use that swanky company jet," Kes said with a giggle.

"I did. The man had a craving, I needed to get his food to him fast." He cast a sidelong glance at Lilah after that admission. "He swore me to secrecy afterwards, because he didn't want you to find out about it, Lilah. He wanted to avoid a lecture on carbon emissions and being environmentally conscious."

"He would have gotten one too," Lilah said, her voice grim even though she couldn't keep the laughter from her eyes. "It was ridiculously wasteful."

"He anonymously donated a substantial amount of money to your favorite tree planting organization the very next day though," Ben said, squeezing Lilah's thigh reassuringly under cover of the blanket and she shared a smile with him. That was

Gramps in a nutshell, he could be outlandishly exorbitant but also incredibly generous and conscientious.

The evening ended shortly after that, the ladies departed in a flurry of goodbyes, all lightly buzzed, and took a ride-sharing service home.

"Tired?" Ben asked after locking up behind Kes, who was the last one out.

"Yes. It was an exhausting day. But it's a good tired. I had fun."

"They're a nice bunch," he said, putting his hands into his back pockets and staring at her. She was sitting on the large sofa, fingers of one hand curled around the stem of a half-full glass of red wine. "I think I finally have a handle on who's who now."

Lilah snorted, "It only took you eight years."

Ben sighed, poured the last bit of red wine into an empty glass and sat on the opposite end of the sofa. That left about two meters of space between them. He gazed out at the blackness beyond the terrace doors, one arm stretched out on the back of the sofa toward her. He took—what looked like—a fortifying drink of the glass that he held clutched in his other hand.

"I always thought they were a bad influence. Because of that night."

"What happened wasn't our fault."

"No. It wasn't. I knew that. I had Jackson"—one of the personal security team that worked for Gramps—"go back to that house and track down as many of those guys as he could. We didn't have enough for an arrest... but he and a few of his colleagues put the fear of God in them. He let it be known that we would be watching them and if anything like that happened again, we would know and we would take action."

"You did that?" she asked, touched, and surprised by the revelation. She'd always believed that the men involved in the incident had gotten off without any real consequences, as men too often tended to. Leaving five young women—girls really—too scared to trust boys for a long time after that. To now learn that Ben had taken such decisive action was heartwarming and—once she told them—would only cement his image as a hero to the others.

"I did. But that night shook me and I was irrational. And I allowed it to color everything to do with your friends—and *you*—for a long time."

"How long?"

"Until very recently."

"Until today, you mean?"

"Lilah." Her name drifted toward her on a gentle sigh. "You nearly died. I didn't... I couldn't..."

He stumbled to a halt and she watched him, waiting patiently while he gathered himself.

"It scared me. And I don't like being scared. Or feeling vulnerable. I don't like not knowing what to do in a situation. And I resented you—*and* them—for putting me in that position."

"For what it's worth," she said, "they always liked you. Saw you as some kind of knight in shining armor."

He made a tortured sound that *could* possibly have been a laugh.

"How could they not? I'm a fucking prince, don't you know?" The self-deprecation in his voice was a revelation.

"*They* certainly think you are," she said, and he pinned her with his piercing gaze.

"What about you? Did *you* think I was some prince? Some mythical knight?"

"No. I never once thought that."

"Not even when you were in *love* with me?"

"No, not even then."

He was itching to ask her, she could see it, but in the end, he dropped his gaze to his glass, staring down into the ruby red depths of his wine as if he expected it to yield the answer to the question he'd chosen not to ask.

"Don't you want to know what I *did* think?" she asked, keeping her eyes glued on that handsome averted profile.

He swallowed and his jaw clenched before he shook his head mutely.

"Why not?"

"Because no matter what you thought about me, it was bound to have been a lie designed to make yourself believe in this image of us that only existed in your mind."

She refused to let it hurt her. Especially since she knew he hadn't said it to hurt her. He was merely stating what he thought was a fact.

She nodded.

"Fair enough."

Her equable response seemed to surprise him and his head jerked up as if to verify with his eyes what he'd just heard.

"I want to be honest with you, Lilah. I don't want to ever mislead you about anything again. I want to put the past behind us. Start fresh, from a place of honesty. And see where that takes us."

She finished her wine and set the glass aside before asking, "Where would you like it to take us?"

He said nothing but his eyes spoke volumes and she sighed and rubbed her palms over her face, exhaustion weighing down her movements.

Her favorite playlist had been on shuffle in the background, and there was a brief silence as one song faded to an end, followed moments later by the achingly familiar introduction of Etta James's *At Last*. Their gazes met as the violins throbbed poignantly in the background and Ben drained his glass, before pushing to his feet and holding a hand out to her.

Lilah stared at the big hand in blank astonishment, before his quiet voice asked, "May I have this dance, Lilah?"

She stared up at him, her eyes welling and she swallowed past the lump in her throat as she remembered how gut-wrenchingly painful their last dance to this song had been.

"*Please.*" The shake in his voice, combined with the slight tremor in his hand, was what prompted her to place her palm in his. His hand closed around hers and he tugged her into his arms, just as Etta's incomparable voice crooned the eponymous opening line of her classic song.

Ben folded her close, one hand flattened against her back and the other held hers in a relaxed grip, close to their bodies. Lilah's free hand crept up over his broad shoulder and around his neck, and she lay her head on his shoulder.

He slowly guided her around the room—his scent and heat enveloped her—and they swayed in time with the gentle, romantic strains of the beautiful song, feet barely moving.

His lips hovered close to hers and their breath mingled. Lilah's eyes drifted shut as she found herself suspended in this moment with this man, who was creeping his way back beneath her defenses.

He let go of her hand to cup her cheek. Her now free hand slid beneath his shirt and came to rest on the silky, hot flesh of his chest, right above his racing heart.

"Lilah, *mo chridhe*," he whispered, his lips brushing against hers. She'd never heard that phrase before and wondered what it meant. She was about to ask him, when his lips sipped at hers and her legs turned to butter. No person should have this amount of power over another human being. Yet Ben did over Lilah. All it took to fell her was the delicate, searching touch of his mouth on hers and she became a desperate wreck of a woman.

He lifted his head to stare at her, and his eyes said it all, roaming over her face with a hunger than bordered on starvation. The stark desire she saw in his expression robbed Lilah of her breath and suddenly all she could think of was that kiss they'd shared earlier.

The last note of the song lingered in the air like a benediction and even after the song ended and a new one began, they continued to sway together.

"Lilah." Again that soft, prayerlike whisper, followed by another kiss. A little less restrained than the one they had shared earlier on the roof.

This was a fraught meeting of tongues and teeth and lips.

Lilah wasn't sure how it happened, but when she came up for breath, he was sprawled on the couch and she was straddling his lap, riding the hard ridge of his cock. His hands were spread over her ass cheeks, head thrown back, eyes closed, lips red and swollen from their near violent kiss. He looked undone... and Lilah loved it. Loved having this much control over her usually implacable husband.

She kissed him again. A gentler, sweeter caress, and after one last grind against his hardness, regretfully lifted her weight off him.

His eyes opened and found hers. That usually astute gaze was bewildered, and lost.

She ran a lingering hand over his cheek and gave him a regretful smile.

"Goodnight, Ben."

"Lilah…"

She ignored the pleading in his voice and clambered off his lap to stand in front of him on unsteady legs with weak knees.

She stared down at him, noting his messy hair, his unbuttoned shirt, his ragged breathing, that *massive* erection straining at the fly of his trousers and felt an immense sense of satisfaction that *she* was responsible for his hot disheveled mess of a state. She couldn't affect him emotionally, but she damned well had an undeniable physical affect on him.

She felt almost bad leaving him in such a state, but she knew that sleeping with him would be the absolute worst thing she could do for her own emotional well-being.

She tried to walk away but as she passed the couch, she stopped directly behind him and stroked both hands through his hair before tilting his head back. She bent and gave him a soft and sweet upside-down kiss, regret and apology in the gentle caress.

"I'm sorry. But we can't do this again. It hurts too much."

She pressed a lingering kiss on his furrowed brow and this time walked away without looking back.

TWENTY-TWO
Breathe with me

Despite her earlier exhaustion, Lilah felt energized after her shower. By the time she returned to the room, Ben hadn't come to bed yet, and she stared at his empty bed for a long, pensive moment, before crawling beneath the covers.

She wasn't remotely sleepy and after tossing and turning for half-an-hour, she sat up abruptly. The rest of the apartment was eerily quiet, but Lilah wasn't foolish enough to seek out her husband right now. If she did, she would probably wind up in bed with him, negating pretty much everything she'd said and done earlier. That would be pretty damned terrible, no matter how tempting it was to throw caution to the wind.

She considered his words about needing a fresh start. It was a wise sentiment and one that resonated with her, but not for the reasons Ben would have hoped. She was terrified to read Gramps's letter, frightened of the disappointment she would feel if she couldn't understand the reasoning behind his decision making.

But that fear was holding her back. It was keeping her tethered to the past and poisoning her memories of her beloved Gramps. Lilah needed to read his letter and move on with her life. What shape her future would take remained uncertain, but Gramps was gone, and clinging to his unread letter like it was some kind of talisman to ward off that painful reality, was foolish.

And childish.

She got out of bed and padded to her dresser, where she'd kept the letter stored in her jewelry box.

She took it back to bed and sat on top of the covers staring down at her name in the familiar bold slash of his handwriting. She ran trembling fingers over the lettering, lifted the envelope to her nose, futilely hoping for a whiff of his favorite aftershave. Her eyes misted when she smelled nothing at all.

She carefully ran her finger under the wax seal he liked to use when he was being particularly fussy, and smiled fondly at the sight of it. He loved putting the family crest on everything. His Scottish roots coming to the fore.

She removed the two sheets of neatly folded paper and sucked in a deep breath and—no longer able to delay the inevitable—bent her head to read.

My Dearest Lilah,

You have always been the light of my life. Everything I've achieved in this world has been for you. I know that the news of my cancer and of my death, has left you confused and hurt. Keeping my illness from you was a difficult decision. When I was first diagnosed, I railed against the gods, the devil, science, everything and everybody I could think of. I saw all the best specialists. They all had the same prognosis. A year at the most. My first thought was of you. And Ben. And all the things I've yet left undone. I focused on Ben first. He was easier. He needed to succeed me and I fought tooth and nail to make that happen. He was the best choice, really... and the board knew it. You, my dear heart, all I ever wanted was your happiness. And I hated the thought of you worrying about me and fussing over me and watching me deteriorate and fearing the inevitable end. I didn't want that sadness to overshadow everything we still had left to do together. Seeing you happy made me happy. I opted out of my chemotherapy 6 months ago, just before you returned from Paris. I know that Ben feels in some way responsible for you. And perhaps I fostered that belief in him. He always tried so hard to please me. But I've always believed, in my heart of hearts, that you two are right for each other... not because —as Ben mistakenly imagines —you need to be taken care of, but because he does.

Without you, Ben is isolated, an island a million miles from the rest of the world. Lonely, buffeted by storms and weathered by strong winds. He needs your sunshine to keep him flourishing. He doesn't know that, he thinks this is about you. But it's also about him. You're strong, loyal, loving, and you love him. You're good for him, sweet pea. You're good for each other. Ben needs someone loving and warm in his life. And you, my Lilah, need someone who will always place

*you above all else. Watching the two of you grow closer
these last several months has been a great source of joy
for me.*

You were each the best gift I could give the other.

*I hope you haven't been too hard on him for keeping the
news of my disease from you. It hasn't been easy on
him either. He's struggled with this secret, and seeing
his concern, his need to make everything better for me ,
has merely validated my decision to withhold this
knowledge from you. Because if it impacted our unflap-
pable Ben in such a way, it would surely have been an
intolerable burden for you to bear.*

*I know you will think this is unfair. That you'll be angry
with me for a time, but I do hope that someday you will
understand that protecting you has always been my
number one priority. And you'll recognize that all of
my decisions have come from a place of love.*

*Live and love and be happy, sweet pea. That's all I've ever
wanted for you. I'm sorry I won't be there to see the
beautiful life you and Ben will have together. But the
certainty of it brings a smile to this old man's face and
happiness to his heart.*

Love you to the moon and back. Forever and Forever.

Gramps

LILAH READ and re-read the words several times over but
couldn't wrap her head around the enormity of what they
revealed. She just… *couldn't.*

Gramps's handwriting blurred and she felt a wrenching sob
tear up through her chest. It emerged with a dull rumble of
desolation.

"Oh, *God*. Oh, my *God*." She put the letter aside and wrapped her arms around her torso, rocking herself back and forth as she tried to contain the swell of agony that threatened to envelope her and smother her.

She felt sick. She *was* sick… she stumbled from bed and lurched to the en-suite where she only narrowly made it to the commode and emptied the contents of her stomach.

How was she supposed to deal with this? Gramps, Ben… all the lies? How could Gramps think any of this was okay?

How?

"Lilah? Jesus, what's wrong?" Ben's alarmed voice jerked her out of shocky daze. She pushed shakily to her feet, flushing the toilet, and staggering to the sink where she rinsed her tear-drenched face with cold water and gargled some mouthwash.

When she felt a little more able to face him, she turned to stare at him. His eyes were concerned. His face pale.

"You knew." Her voice was reedy when it emerged from her ice-cold lips and his gaze wavered.

"What?"

"You knew Gramps was sick," she said, happy to hear a bit of volume creeping into her voice, as the shock began to recede to be replaced by a tidal wave of sheer rage.

"Lilah."

"You knew. You fucking *knew*! Yet you still insisted we leave on that joke of a honeymoon. When he was here dying. And you *knew*."

"I swear to God, Lilah, I thought we had more time. I would never have insisted we go if I knew his time was so short. He told me he was fine. He said the doctor assured him… *Fuck*, Lilah, you have to believe me."

"I don't have to believe a damn thing you say, Ben! I have no reason to. You've lied to me time and time again. You have zero respect for me and I'm done with you.

"I don't care what Gramps said… I only care that he said it to *you*, and you kept it to yourself. Selfishly hoarded information about *my* grandfather like I had no right to know. I knew you were jealous of me, but I didn't know to what extent. Did you enjoy having his ear, keeping important secrets from me like you were the grandchild and I was just some random stranger who didn't deserve the truth?"

"No! Christ. *No*, that's not how it was. I wanted to tell you."

"You *didn't*."

"He wouldn't let me."

"Fuck you, Ben! Since when do you let anyone dictate what you should or shouldn't do?"

"I let Cyrus. I respected him and loved him. He asked me to keep his secret and God help me, I did. But I urged him to tell you. You had a right to know. I told him that."

"And when we got the news of his collapse? You couldn't tell me then? You left me in agony all night, using my vulnerability as an excuse to fuck me instead."

He flinched and stared at her in horror. "*No*, you mustn't think that. It wasn't at all—"

She cut him off again, having no interest in his excuses. "And after *that*, at the hospital when I was telling the doctor we needed another opinion, you'd met him before hadn't you? You knew him? And you let me sit there like a fool, questioning him, doubting him, when you had all the information already, and could have shared it with me at any time, but—yet again, even at such a crucial time—chose not to."

God, the more time she had to process it, the more massive and unforgivable his lie became.

"Lilah, I know how this looks but Cyrus, he begged me not to tell you."

"How long have you known, Ben? Since the beginning?"

"He told me just after he stopped chemo."

Lilah's hand flew to her mouth as her nausea resurfaced.

"Oh, God. And right after that you started 'dating' me. That's the *real* reason you married me, isn't it? Granting a dying man his wish."

"He never explicitly asked me to marry you." That wasn't a denial.

"Why did you do it? To secure your place in the will? In the company?"

"You know that's not true," he growled, now starting to look pissed off as well. *Good,* because Lilah was spoiling for a fight. "I don't know what the fuck would have happened to me after my parents died, if not for Cyrus. I told you before; I owed him everything. Marrying *you* seemed a small price to pay."

The phrasing was designed to hurt her, she could see it in his eyes. He was angry too and wanted to land his own barbs. But Lilah's anger shielded her from the worst of it, even though she knew she would feel the bruises later.

"*God*, I must have seemed like such a gullible idiot to you. Falling for lie after lie after lie."

"I have many faults, cupcake, but I never lied to you!"

"What the hell would you call this then? If not a great, big, staggering lie of omission? And all that other so-called honesty? That was just subterfuge, you might not have lied to me Ben, but you've been deceiving me, Every step of the way."

"You're being so fucking irrational. You can't blame me for —"

"Then who the *hell* am I supposed to blame?" She practically roared the question at him, so furious by now that she was unable to contain it anymore. She wanted to be loud, aggressive, she wanted to break things and throw things.

She wanted to *punish* him.

"Am I supposed to blame Gramps? In case it's escaped your notice, Ben, Gramps isn't here! All I have left is you. You, who could—*should*—have told me about my sick grandfather. He would have understood and forgiven you for that. Me? I don't understand and I will *never* forgive you.

"And then tonight," she shook her head wildly. "All that absolute *crap* about starting fresh from a place of honesty? Are you *shitting* me? A place of honesty, when you've been keeping this huge secret from me? If Gramps hadn't mentioned it in his letter, would you ever have told me?"

The swiftly concealed guilt in his expression answered the question before he even spoke. "With Cyrus already gone there was no point in telling you. I knew it would only upset and hurt you. And I was right."

The last emerged on a grim tone of validation and defensiveness and it merely served to infuriate Lilah even more.

She chose not to respond to that and pushed past him rudely, exiting the en-suite and heading straight into the walk-in closet.

"What are you doing?" he asked when she dragged a small duffel bag from the top shelf of her side of the closet.

"I'm leaving."

"Don't be ridiculous, it's after midnight."

"One of the security guys can escort me back home."

"Fuck it, Lilah, *this* is your home."

"No it's not. And you continually repeating it won't make it so." She started dragging clothes into the bag, shoving in silk tops and cashmere sweaters with equal amounts of indifference.

"I'm not letting you leave in this state."

"You can't stop me. I c-can't even express—" She paused, breathing so hard it made her cough until her eyes watered. But she managed to get the rest of what she wanted to say out, in a small tight voice. "I can't express how m-much I truly hate you right now."

He reeled, paling, looking like someone had just punched him in the gut.

"You don't mean that."

"But I do," she sobbed, still fighting for each breath, knowing that she needed to calm down, but was unable to do so. Not with him standing right there, with his highly punchable, beautiful face so temptingly within reach. "I fucking do. I hate you. I loathe you. I *despise* you. I never want to see you again."

He shook his head in denial, still looking dazed.

"Lilah, please, just try and slow down your respiratory rate, okay?" he said, his voice quiet and shaky. "You're practically hyperventilating."

She detested his rational tone of voice, hated when he *managed* her. It set her teeth on edge and made her feel about ten. She glared at him, bag still clutched in her hand, her clothes spewing out over the top of it.

But he was right. That was the worst of it, Ben was *always* right! She was struggling now. Fighting to catch her breath while her chest closed up. It felt like someone had their fists wrapped around her lungs and was painfully squeezing every drop of air from her body. She heard the betraying high-pitched wheeze that warned of an imminent attack creeping into each shallow exhalation.

She reached for her inhaler and but she was in her night clothes and the inhaler was on her bed table.

Ben stepped toward her, but she shied away from him with a

glare. He held an inhaler up, clutched between his thumb and forefinger and she grabbed it and sucked in the metered dose gratefully.

She waited for the bronchodilator to do its job, but nothing happened, and she panicked, taking in a second dose.

"Lilah?" Ben's voice was sharp and alarmed. "Shit. Come on, sit down, baby. You *have* to calm down, okay?"

He wrapped an arm around her hunched shoulders and he led her to the chair by her vanity, where he sank to his haunches in front of her, taking her hands in his. His concerned eyes sharpened on her face and the dark pupils, so striking in the middle of the ocean blue of his irises, dilated to the point where only a sliver of blue remained. He swore shakily.

"Your lips are going purple. I'm taking you to the hospital."

Lilah — incapable of speech by now — shook her head and held up the inhaler.

"Alright, a few more puffs, *leannan*," he acquiesced. "But first try and breathe with me. Nice, deep breaths."

She tried, but it felt like she was breathing through a straw… It didn't help that the source of her stress, the trigger for this attack was sitting there calmly telling her to breathe like it was the fucking easiest thing in the world.

"L-lea…" The word wouldn't emerge, but she could tell by the way he flinched, that he knew exactly what she wanted to say. That she wanted him to leave her alone. But she knew he wouldn't.

He would never let her go through this alone. And perversely, that helped calm her somewhat. Despite her anger, her hurt, and her resentment, she knew that Ben would move heaven and earth to keep her safe. It was his curse, this disproportionate sense of responsibility he felt toward her.

Tears seeped down her cheeks as she weakly lifted her inhaler and took another dose, while Ben squeezed her free hand reassuringly and kept talking to her. Calmly, gently, guiding her through it. It took several more doses before she could breathe freely again and sensing that the crisis had reached a turning point, Ben led her to the room and to her bed.

"No. I'm leaving," she said, exhaustion dragging at every word.

"Tomorrow, okay? Tonight, I need you to rest. Please, Lilah."

Feeling as wrung out as a dishcloth, she accepted defeat for now and crawled beneath the covers.

She was asleep in seconds.

TWENTY-THREE

Eight Years Ago

"**B**en?" The voice on the other end of the line was an urgent whisper and Ben—who'd left a meeting to take the call —frowned in alarm.

"Lilah? What's wrong?"

"The girls and I are in some trouble. We were tricked into believing we were invited to this big varsity party. But when we showed up it was to find only second and third year boys here. We wanted to leave but they won't let us out. I told them I needed to pee and came to the bathroom to call you. We're scared, Ben, we don't know what to do."

"Where's Sheena?" Ben asked, trying to tamp down his impatience. How was this *his* problem? Lilah had a female guard— young—chosen for her ability blend in with the students.

"You're going to be angry."

Ben sighed and pinched the bridge of his nose. Lilah's management fell under his unofficial purview. Cyrus had never specifically said it was Ben's job to keep an eye on her, but Ben had taken it upon himself to be something of a big brother to the little pest. He'd hoped that it would get easier the older she got, yet here they were—nineteen-year-old Lilah getting herself into shit as always.

"What did you do?" he asked in weary resignation.

"I ditched her back at campus, snuck out of the library bathroom window."

"Fuck me," Ben groaned, squeezing his nape. He already had a headache building. "What's the address? I'll call Sheena and tell her where to pick you up."

"I, uh, I kind of took her phone. I didn't want her to call anybody until I had a chance to get away cleanly. I hate having a bodyguard. I know she's supposed to be inconspicuous, but she's not. For once I just wanted to be like everybody else here."

Ben scraped a hand over his face and stared back at the budget meeting longingly. As a rule he fucking hated budget meetings—especially ones that ran late on a Friday evening—but it was so much more preferable than dealing with this Lilah shit.

She just wanted to be like everybody else? When her grandfather was one of the wealthiest men in the country? The kid was fucking deluded.

"Give me the address," he demanded. She whispered the address of a house somewhere in Newlands. Ben jotted it down on a post-it note, phone pinched between his ear and shoulder. "How many boys are there?"

"I don't know," she sounded pretty panicked, and she was starting to wheeze a little. Ben knew she had asthma and had seen her handle a few mild attacks, so he wasn't particularly concerned. "I think maybe ten? There are only five of us first year girls."

"Stay in the bathroom if you can," he commanded her, waving

his assistant over, and muffling the phone against his chest as he explained to her that he was stepping out for a while. He instructed her to have his occasional close protection officer—Jackson—meet him round front in one of the company cars.

"I'll try but my bag is in the other room, one of the guys took it from me and said I wouldn't need it if I was just going to pee. Luckily, my phone was in my jeans pocket. But Ben... my inhaler is in the bag and I don't feel so great."

Ben was becoming more and more alarmed.

"Try not to panic, okay? Jackson and I are on our way. We'll be there in under ten minutes."

He heard loud knocking and a muffled male voice and Lilah's quavering response: "Yes. I-I'll be right out. Ben... please hurry."

She hung up before he could tell her not to and his stomach knotted in anxiety as he climbed into the car and succinctly explained the situation to a grim-faced Jackson.

He'd promised her under ten minutes, but traffic turned it into nearly twenty. He tried calling her, but it went straight to voice mail and Ben felt utterly helpless—picturing every worst-case scenario under the sun.

What he found—when he and Jackson slammed into the large house in an affluent neighborhood—was so much worse than anything he could have imagined. The four girls—Lilah's friends, he vaguely recognized them from the few times she'd invited them around to family events—huddled around an unresponsive Lilah.

Twelve big bruisers—rugby players by the looks of them—towered over the women intimidatingly. Their body language was aggressive, threatening, and the girls looked absolutely terrified.

But Ben had eyes only for Lilah, who was on the floor, looking tiny and broken.

A few of the guys tried to block his progress as he made his way toward them, but he barely paid them any heed, punching and shoving any bastard who got in his way, while Jackson deftly dispensed with any others who tried to interfere. The rest—wisely—chose to disappear.

"What happened?"

"She had an asthma attack—well, she's having one still, I think," the cute, curvy dark-skinned girl with her hair in short bouncy twists told him tearfully. "Her inhaler didn't help. She lost consciousness just a minute before you arrived. We begged them to call for an ambulance... but..."

"Is she breathing?" Ben could barely get the question out, going to his knees beside the too-still Lilah.

"Only barely," one of the other girls—the intense Asian one maybe, he couldn't be bothered to look, afraid to take his eyes off Lilah.

"We're so sorry. We thought this was a real party," another girl said, tears in her voice. "It was going to be our first big campus party but they were the only ones here. I don't know how this happened. They were awful, Lilah was fighting for every breath, it was so scary and they wouldn't let us help her at first. They thought she was faking it."

Ben clenched his teeth and bit back a growl, wanting to pummel those fuckers all over again, but Lilah needed him, he couldn't do that.

"I've called an ambulance," Jackson said. "But the closest hospital is just five minutes away. It may be faster to just drive her. You take the car and I'll stay with them and make sure they all get home safely."

Ben nodded, scooping Lilah up into his arms and ignoring the heated protests from the other young women, who all demanded to be taken to the hospital as well, so that they could be there for

Lilah. Jackson could sort that out, Lilah was his priority. Lilah, who was drifting in and out of consciousness, whose chest was barely moving, whose lips were turning blue. Jesus, she looked dead and that petrified him.

It was hard to focus on driving when he wanted to pull over every five seconds to check her breathing, but the logical part of his brain told him that getting her to the hospital as fast as possible was her only chance of surviving this.

It was tough letting her go when the trauma team took over. He had to be physically "encouraged" by two men — security officers who were much smaller than he — to step aside and let the doctors work. They escorted him to a waiting room, where he found a beleaguered Jackson waiting with Lilah's friends.

"They were adamant about being by her side," the big guy told him, looking decidedly harassed.

Well, Ben could hardly argue with that, not after his own reluctance to leave her in the care of strangers.

Cyrus was in Australia and Ben decided to wait until he had real news before calling the man. He slumped in his seat and buried his face in his hands. Cyrus had trusted Ben to look out for Lilah and she had nearly *died* — could still die — under his care.

He could never let anything like this happen again.

PRESENT DAY

Ben watched Lilah sleep; she was always so exhausted after an attack. And this had been the worst one in eight years. She lay curled up on her side with a hand tucked under her cheek. She looked pale and vulnerable. For a disorienting moment, he imagined himself back there, in that hospital room with her eight years ago. Waiting for her to wake up, not sure when—or if—she would.

He sucked in a shuddering breath at the traumatic memory of her hooked up to machines—tiny and fragile in that huge hospital bed—a tube shoved down her throat because she'd been incapable of doing something as fundamental as breathing.

That was the first time he'd understood just how dangerous asthma could be. Before then he didn't think he'd even considered it a real illness. Just more attention seeking behavior from Lilah. A couple of puffs from that damned blue inhaler during her teens had always been enough to distract Cyrus, who'd immediately drop everything to focus on Lilah. It had been infuriating and Ben had never truly understood Cyrus's concern until he'd seen firsthand how bad it could get. And comprehended how much worse it could have been.

After that night he'd sworn to himself that he would ensure that nothing like that would ever happen to her again.

And he'd failed at that self-appointed task. First at their wedding, which had luckily been a relatively minor event, and now *this*.

Fuck.

This was his fault. He hadn't once considered that Cyrus would mention Ben's complicity in the old man's decision to keep his disease from Lilah. He'd assumed that particular secret had died with his beloved mentor. He should have softened the blow somehow, told her beforehand. He wasn't sure why he hadn't. After Cyrus's death he'd been under no obligation to keep it from her any longer.

Only... he'd known she would react badly and he was enjoying the growing intimacy between them. The way she'd let him hold her those first few nights, he'd needed that comfort too and he'd been reluctant to lose it.

Now she was threatening to leave again. She was *always* threatening to leave him. And his chest tightened at the thought. He wasn't sure he had anything left in his arsenal to convince her to stay. Not for this. This was indefensible.

And the thought of her leaving...

He shook his head in denial. They were family. All the other one had. It made no sense to give up on that.

She shifted slightly and he sat up—immediately alert— watching her face intently for any sign of discomfort. But she was just adjusting in her sleep.

The faint sound of crinkling paper caught his attention and his gaze sharpened, as he searched the bed looking for the source of that noise.

He finally found it, the letter, tangled up in the bedclothes. He gently tugged it free, not wanting to disturb her, and attempted to smooth the hopelessly wrinkled paper. She was angry now, but these were Cyrus's last words to her. And even if the contents infuriated her, she'd want to keep it.

He tried not to read it—it was a private communication and reading it would be an invasion of privacy—but he caught a glimpse of his name, and it snagged his attention.

Ben needs someone loving and warm in his life. You were each the best gift I could give the other.

Was that truly what Cyrus had believed? That Ben and Lilah were a gift to each other? Or, indeed, that Ben was worthy of such a gift?

Cyrus had valued Lilah above all else. She'd been his most priceless treasure and he'd wanted only the best for her. Ben had always sincerely believed that Cyrus had only wanted him to marry Lilah because she needed protection, care, but he'd never considered how much value Cyrus must have placed on Ben himself to entrust his beloved Lilah into his care.

Cyrus would have expected Ben to love her, cherish her, and all Ben had done was hurt her. And humiliate her by mocking her love and throwing it back in her face.

He didn't read any further, respecting Cyrus and Lilah's privacy. He folded the letter with great care and placed it on the bedside table where she would see it when she woke up.

Ben had called Lilah's allergist after she'd fallen asleep and the man had been satisfied after hearing Ben's account of what had happened, and believed that she was through the worst of it. He'd agreed to stop by in the morning if Lilah and Ben felt it necessary.

None of that was going to stop Ben from remaining right here, by her bedside, all night just to watch her breathe.

LILAH CAME TO AWARENESS SLOWLY. She felt completely limp and drained and just... *exhausted*. She recognized the signs; knew that it was because she'd just suffered a major asthma attack. It usually left her feeling wrung out for several days.

She frowned, eyes still shut, something wasn't right. And she couldn't quite place her finger on what it was. She inhaled slowly, drawing in the breath as deeply as she could, and smiled when she could do so without any impediment at all. It was always such a relief to be able breathe normally after an attack. The sheer, claustrophobic terror and panic of being unable to draw in enough oxygen was very hard to recover from emotionally and mentally. And that initial pure breath upon waking up the morning after an attack was—for Lilah—an important first step toward recuperation.

Who knew air could feel like such a decadent treat?

Well, Lilah did, and it was something nobody else in her life would ever understand.

She opened her eyes—ready to face the world again—and then immediately wished she hadn't when the first thing she saw was Ben uncomfortably slumped in the narrow wingback chair that usually sat—unused—in the corner of his room. He'd pulled the chair right up to the side of her bed, close enough to touch her if he wanted to. He was asleep, still wearing last night's clothes, hair mussed, beard coming in dark and thick.

The memories of last night rushed back in an agonizing flood and stole the breath right out of her lungs again.

No.

Lilah absolutely was not ready to face him this morning. Or at all, ever again.

She had to get out of here. She didn't even have to pack. She just needed to grab her purse. She had more than enough clothing still at the house in Constantia.

She sat up and swung her legs over the side of the bed—opposite to where Ben sat sleeping—and fended off a bout of dizziness as she dragged herself up. It said a lot about Ben's exhaustion that the usually light sleeper remained dead to the world when she stumbled and hit the night stand, sending the lamp wobbling.

His breathing didn't even change.

She crept to the walk-in closet and winced when she saw the bag with her clothes spilled all over the floor. She quickly stepped over it on her way to the en-suite, feeling too drained to even consider finishing the frenetic packing she'd started last night. Instead, she focused on the most immediate and basic of concerns, brushing her teeth and emptying her bladder. After that, she sent a quick text message to Jackson—telling him she needed a car ASAP.

She looked respectable enough in her shell-pink fleecy pajamas, and wasn't going to bother changing right now. Not when time was of the essence.

She slipped her feet into her favorite pair of pink UGG boots, picked up her handbag, and walked to the front door, battling exhaustion and dizziness all the way. She could rest when she got home, for now it was important to get out of here. Away from the liar who seemed to be under the delusion that he was the world's best husband.

She would wait for Jackson downstairs. She paused after unlocking the door and stared down at her left hand.

Well... that wouldn't do at all. She tugged her wedding ring and engagement rings off her finger, they resisted over the knuckle, but in the end slid off quite easily. She left the rings in the empty fruit bowl, on the kitchen counter, next to Ben's keys and wallet.

She took one last look around the apartment, and then left without another backward glance.

BEN AWOKE with a start when his phone buzzed in his shirt breast pocket. Disoriented, he darted a panicked glance around the room, then frowned at the empty, unmade bed.

"Lilah?" He sat up running a hand through his hair, and cast another look around the room, hoping it would yield some clue as to where she was. He checked his watch; it was nearly noon. He never slept this late but he'd only drifted off at around six that morning, every hitch in Lilah's breathing sending him into a minor panic and keeping him from sleep. In the end exhaustion had won out and it would probably be more accurate to say that he'd passed out, rather than fell asleep.

He tilted his head, listening for any movement that would tell him where Lilah was in the apartment but he heard nothing.

"Lilah?" He added volume to his voice, and heard the note of concern creeping into his tone.

No answer.

Shit. What if she'd passed out? She was so stubborn, even weak as a kitten, she'd be out there trying to do shit she wasn't supposed to do right now. And—pissed off as she was with him at the moment—she wouldn't ask him for help.

He leaped to his feet and dashed to the en-suite but found it empty. There were signs that she'd been in here though, she'd left the toothpaste uncapped again—he hated when she did that—the basin was wet and a hand towel lay discarded on the vanity beside it. She wasn't great at putting things back in place, something Ben was learning to live with.

He was learning to live with a lot of things.

Having her around every day—for one—her cozy clutter encroaching on his sterile space. The fresh scent of her favorite perfume lingering in the office, on the furniture, in their bedroom. Hearing her in the other room as she left excitable voice notes to her friends. Holding her close at night when she cried, her irresistible soft warmth a source of solace to him as well.

Where the fuck was *she?*

He'd gone through the entire apartment twice, top to bottom, roof and terrace included, before accepting that she wasn't here.

He dashed back to the en-suite, the bag she'd stuffed full of random shit last night was still laying in the middle of the floor, but she was nowhere to be found.

She really was gone.

His stomach sank as he tried to process that information. He wandered into the living room, his mind racing. All her things were still here... at least there was that. She'd be back. She had to.

He fumbled for his phone, still in his pocket, remembering that it had buzzed earlier. Maybe it was a message from Lilah. But when he checked it wasn't—it was an early alert for a meeting tomorrow morning.

He checked his messages, none from Lilah. He stared at her name at the top of the screen for a moment. Their last text exchange had been about her friends coming over yesterday to work on the roof garden. Lilah had asked him if it was okay, as if she didn't have every right to have her friends over in her own home.

He tapped a quick message to her:

> **ME**
>
> Hey, where did you go? You shouldn't be out so soon. You'll wear yourself out.

The message was immediately verified as read. But there was no indication that she was typing a reply. He stared at the screen for a few minutes, waiting for some sign that she would reply but nothing.

He waited a while longer, then tried calling.

Straight to voice mail.

He clenched his teeth and tried again.

Same result.

This time he left a message: "Lilah, what the fuck is going on? Answer the damned phone!"

By now he was pacing restlessly from the bedroom, into the living room, and round the kitchen counter. It was on his second pass through the kitchen that he spotted her rings gleaming in the fruit bowl next to his wallet.

He stopped dead, forgetting about the second irate message he'd been about to leave and disconnecting the call instead. His arm dropped limply to his side as he stared at the rings for a long, blank, confused instant.

No.

That was the only word bouncing through his brain in that moment.

No...

She'd been threatening this very course of action since their wedding day but he'd always been confident in his ability to change her mind and make her see his point of view. He'd honestly never expected her to simply walk out.

He sank down onto one of the bar stools and stared blankly at the fridge door for a few long beats.

He gradually came to realize that he was practicing the same deep breathing exercises he usually employed to keep Lilah calm when she was on the verge of an asthma attack. He only now recognized that the technique could be quite effective in warding off panic attacks as well.

Not that he was panicking. Not at all. This was a manageable problem. *Lilah* was a manageable problem.

He ignored the niggling voice at the back of his mind warning him that this was the type of thinking that had led to this dilemma in the first place. She was hurt right now, feeling betrayed by both Ben and Cyrus and — he sighed deeply — he didn't fucking blame her one bit.

It *had* been a betrayal. Cyrus should have told her. Ben had urged the old man to do so, but Lilah came by her stubbornness honestly. Because once Cyrus had made up his mind to do something it had been damned near impossible to change it.

And if he was being entirely honest with himself, Ben knew that the moment he'd discovered that Cyrus hadn't told Lilah, *he* should have done so.

She'd said she hated him. That she would never forgive him.

The pit in his stomach expanded and he swallowed down a surge of nausea at the memory.

What if she meant it? What would her hate feel like? What shape would it take? She'd never hated him. Resented him for a short time, back when she was twelve, but after that...

Ben was honest enough with himself to admit that—while he eschewed the very notion of romantic love—he'd started to enjoy the idea of Lilah possibly feeling something like that for him. Had told himself he'd be kind about it, and graciously accepting of it. And that he'd make her happy.

But the thought of Lilah hating him left him feeling hollow and panicked. He didn't want that at all.

He'd fucked up. He knew he had. But he could fix it. He was confident of that. She just needed to understand that...

His shoulders sank and the wind left his sails as he comprehended that he didn't know what she needed to understand. He didn't *know* what would make her happy. All he knew was that he hadn't been succeeding at the job.

He used to think Lilah was such a simple creature. Easy enough to please with sporadically doled out portions of affection and attention. But she was... complex. Interesting. Sweet. Stubborn. So fucking sexy.

But deserving of more.

And Ben didn't know what that more should be.

For the first time in his life Ben felt real fear that he wasn't up to the task at hand.

That he may have lost his wife for good.

"IT'S FOR YOU, *LIEBCHEN*." Gretchen entered Lilah's room after only a perfunctory knock and held a smart phone out to the younger woman.

Lilah stared at the broken screen with a bleary frown, having just woken up from a sound sleep.

"For me?" she repeated, confused. Who could be calling her on Gretchen's phone?

"*Ja*," Gretchen said in her no-nonsense way.

Lilah sat up and pushed her hair out of her face.

"Is it Gramps?" she winced as soon as she asked the question and Gretchen's face softened in sympathy.

"Sorry, habit," Lilah muttered, and took the outreached phone from the other woman's grasp. Gretchen retreated instantly and when Lilah saw the name on the screen she sighed in annoyance.

"What do you want, Ben?"

"What the fuck are you playing at, Lilah?"

"I told you I was leaving." She stifled a genuine yawn while she was speaking, but was happy with how nonchalant it made her sound. The seething silence at the other end of the line spoke volumes.

"You didn't have to."

"Oh, but I did," she disagreed, happy with the blithe note that she managed to inject into her voice.

"I know you're upset, but let's be reasonable about this, okay?"

Lilah inhaled sharply, refusing to dignify that condescending comment with any sort of response. The silence stretched between them, while she waited for some acknowledgment of her right to feel this way.

She heard his soft, even breathing on the other end of the line as he seemed to wait for *her* to break the silence, but she wasn't going to bend. Not this time.

Finally, her patience was rewarded with an exasperated sigh and a muttered curse word.

"Come on, Lilah, you're being silly."

"Well then," she breathed, fighting to maintain an even tone, when all she truly wanted to do was reach through this damned phone and strangle the dumb man. "Aren't you lucky to no longer be saddled with my unreasonable silliness any longer?"

"Lilah, I shouldn't—" She disconnected the call before he could complete whatever annoying thing he was going to say next and glowered at the cracked screen for a moment longer, before laying back down and burying herself under the thick comforter, covering her head and huddling in her warm cocoon hoping to keep the world at bay for a little while longer.

TWENTY-FOUR
You hate losing. Period

"You can't keep ignoring my texts and calls."

Lilah froze at the sound of Ben's voice coming from over her left shoulder. She was walking through Gramps's favorite part of his extensive gardens. He'd been so proud of these king proteas, and they were on the verge of blooming. Walking through his prized protea section, Lilah felt had felt that sharp pang of loss knowing he wouldn't be able to enjoy them this year.

She screwed her eyes shut for a moment, after hearing that voice, and gathered her composure. She'd known that this confrontation was inevitable and had been expecting Ben to show up at some point. She just hadn't known when. Frankly she didn't think it would take a week, but here he was, exactly seven days after she'd walked out. Countless text messages and voice notes later.

"None of your texts or voice mails had anything new or interesting to say," she said with a lift of her shoulder. His mouth tightened but he didn't rise to her bait.

"So you listened to the voice mails? Because you damned well haven't been reading my texts. Which is why I'm a little baffled when you say they have nothing new or interesting to say. How would you know when you haven't read them?"

"Maybe because I know you?"

"Do you?" he challenged, and she gave him her most insincere smile.

"Let me take a stab at guessing what those texts said... *Lilah, you're being silly. Lilah don't be ridiculous. Lilah, get your arse home. Lilah, we can make this work.* How am I doing so far? Or maybe you brought out the big guns? *Lilah —*"

"Stop," he snapped, holding up a hand. But—judging by the expression in his face—she hadn't been too far off with her guesses.

"Not one *Lilah, I'm sorry. I was wrong. I should have told you. Please forgive me*? Right?"

"Maybe I was saving the *I'm sorry's* for a face-to-face conversation."

"It wouldn't matter. Your apologies are inconsequential and I wouldn't believe them anyway." She was amazed to see him flinch in response to that.

"Then what do you want from me?" his voice was hoarse, the question almost despairing.

"A divorce. Now. Not in six months or a year. But right now. So that I can move on with a clean slate."

"I don't want that."

"I don't care what you want, Ben. You married me to please a dying man. Since that man is no longer with us, you no longer need to keep him happy. So please consider your debt to him repaid in full."

"I told you I can never—"

"Oh, my *God*," she interrupted him, impatience simmering away beneath the exclamation. "I don't care if you think you can never repay him, I'm done being your fucking penance, or punishment, or whatever the hell twisted reasoning you had for marrying me."

"We're a family." His choked statement shocked her and she gaped at him. Not sure how the hell to respond to that. "*You're* my family. You're all I have in this world. I refuse to give up on that so easily. I refuse to lose you."

"Come on, Ben, let's not pretend I'm yours. I've never been yours and you've never been mine. It was all just a massive con designed give an old man his dying wish. Only I was conned too, because I didn't know he was dying and I naively believed what was happening between us was real."

It was the first time Lilah had admitted as much. She'd clung to her false pride by professing to have married him for business reasons. Fooling absolutely no-one. But this marriage was over and there was no longer any reason to keep up the needless pretense.

"This is my life too," she continued in a low, but determined, voice. "And I want you out of it. I'm filing for a divorce next week."

He staggered back—that was the only word she could think of to accurately describe the lurching movement—eyes feverish in his too pale face as he stared at her in disbelief. Lilah would have laughed if it weren't so damned tragic, he looked like a man whose pet Pomeranian had just bitten him.

"Lilah…"

"I have nothing more to say to you, Ben. And, like I told you before, I don't think you have anything new to say to me. It's best if you go."

She didn't wait for him to respond, instead she turned on her heel and walked away without looking back.

LILAH WAS as good as her word, Ben was served divorce papers late Thursday afternoon by a very young, very nervous officer of the court. The man looked both awed, and terrified to be in Ben's massive 30th floor office, which overlooked Cape Town harbor.

Ben impatiently ushered the gawking man out of his office and immediately went through the documents. Their prenup protected both of them from any "unreasonable" divorce settlement demands, but right now Ben wasn't feeling reasonable. He would have loved for her to make impossible demands, something he could fight, rail against, use as an excuse to delay these proceedings. But she was being perfectly civil. She wanted nothing from him. Just a divorce. And Ben hated that they hadn't made any purchases together, didn't own a pet, and possessed nothing to say "this is ours we should split it". Something that would prove to her that this marriage was real. A shared experience, rather than just a sad chapter in her life that needed to end.

But they didn't have any normal couple stuff. Nothing they'd seen together and simply *had* to have for their home. No assets to split, no fond keepsakes to cling to and fight over.

When this marriage was over it would be as if it had never happened. And—without Cyrus to act as a link between them—

she would fade from his life. Ben glowered at the papers in his hands, before slowly crumpling them in his fists.

He refused to lose her.

Despite her many protestations to the contrary, Lilah was *his*. And he was keeping her.

WINTER WAS PROPERLY SETTING into the Mother City now. Lilah loved the crisp, cold, often wet days of a Cape Town winter. The brusque ocean air, the chill on her skin. She loved how green and vibrant everything got during the rainy season. The season had put a halt to most of her outdoor gardening activities and she and the *Horti Hoes* spent most of their weekly gatherings gossiping, drinking, ostensibly planning their spring planting projects.

One of the projects that had been gaining momentum was the foundation Lilah wanted to set up in her grandfather's name, as well as the public green space that she intended to create in his memory. She had narrowed down three possible locations for the public garden. But site was subject to municipal approval, and needed to get the nod from the board of trustees she was setting up to oversee the foundation.

She was keeping herself busy and, in the six weeks since she'd filed for divorce, had tried her utmost to forget that she had a soon-to-be ex-husband lurking in the woodwork.

It would be a lot easier to do if he wasn't constantly trying to contact her. She'd put his texts on mute and had stopped torturing herself by listening to his voice mails. But that didn't stop him. He sent gifts, which she returned unopened, and had tried to contact her through Jackson and Gretchen, and various other household staff members—until she'd prohibited them from even approaching her with a phone in hand.

And—worst of all—the divorce proceedings had stalled. The man point blank refused to sign the papers.

She knew why he'd done so... he wanted to irritate her into confronting him about it. Which would be playing directly into his hands. He wanted to see her. That much was clear. He'd come to the house several times demanding to speak with her in person while Gretchen, who refused to be cowed, stonewalled him at the door.

He'd been suspiciously quiet over the last three days and Lilah was trying not to think about what that meant. Hopefully it meant that he'd given up, and if that was true, Lilah should definitely *not* be feeling this curl of disappointment in her gut. It would be good if he gave up, then they could both move on with their lives.

She walked into the bright studio space, in Green Point, that she was renting for her business.

"Morning, Kirby," she greeted her assistant/receptionist with a wide grin and placed a latte on the reception desk for the young woman. "How's our day looking?"

"Morning, Lilah," Kirby said with a smile, and lifted her latte, tilting it toward Lilah in appreciation. "Thanks for this. I need it, traffic was hell today."

Lilah offered her a small sympathetic smile, and took a thirsty gulp of her own—too hot—cappuccino. She couldn't really relate, Jackson had arranged for a driver to take her where ever she needed to be. Lilah rarely drove herself anywhere. She had a driver's license but she doubted she'd ever have the guts to drive in real traffic after all these years of being chauffeured everywhere. Besides, it had been drilled into her that she never go anywhere without some kind of security, and after the incident at college, she'd never tried to ditch her security people again.

"We have a pretty full day ahead of us," Kirby was saying, staring at her computer monitor, which reflected back onto her trendy prescription glasses. "We're wrangling six-week-old golden retriever puppies in our first session. An action shoot with a Belgian Malinois and her skateboarding owner after that, a few standard mommy-and-me shoots for the rest of the day, ending with a senior and his human family."

"I ever tell you how much I love my job, Kirby?" Lilah said with a grin and Kirby smiled widely back at her.

"Only every damned day, boss!"

"What time is our first session?"

"Not till ten."

"Fantastic, gives me time to catch up on some admin."

Kirby saluted her and Lilah laughed. She picked up a stack of waiting messages and mail from Kirby's desk and, still sipping her cappuccino, made her way to her own desk. She went through her emails methodically replying as needed. When that was done, she leaned back in her chair, put her feet on the desk and flipped through the post. It felt like every second envelope was junk mail and she tossed it in her little wastepaper basket without thought. She'd formed a nice rhythm and had nearly worked her way through the stack, when a smaller envelope caught her eye.

She picked it up and stared at the bold, instantly recognizable handwriting for a long moment, wondering if she should just chuck it like the other junk, but in the end her curiosity won out.

Why would he send her a letter? Was it just to say all the same things he'd been trying to say in his texts and voice mails?

She carefully unsealed the envelope and extracted a single sheet of paper from it.

At first glance there didn't seem to be too much written on it. She plucked her lower lip between the thumb and forefinger, still wondering if it would be wise to read this. But in the end decided she might as well, since she'd already opened the damned envelope.

Lilah,

I think about what you said to me the night before you left all the time. First thing in the morning and last thing at night. I hear you telling me how much you hate, loathe, despise me. Those words have haunted me for weeks. And I can't stand the unrelenting, agonizing memory of them because I don't want you to hate me, leannan. Even though I know you have every reason to do so. Please don't hate me, Lilah. The very notion of it is abhorrent to me.

Ben

LILAH READ and re-read the short letter—note, really—a dozen times, then read it again. She flipped it over to see if she'd missed anything, but the other side of the page was blank.

What a weird little letter. She didn't know what to make of it. She *should* toss it out with the trash, instead she read it again. His words felt so honest, so *raw*... so unlike Ben and she didn't want to throw it out. Not yet. She needed to let it simmer for a bit, settle. Then she'd decide what to do about it.

She folded it carefully and placed it in her desk drawer, but every time she had a break during the long day, she would take it out to read it again.

By the end of the day, she still hadn't decided what to do about it, and transferred it into her handbag to take home with her.

She'd moved into the house in Bantry Bay about a month ago, preferring it to the massive, extravagant mansion in Constantia. It was also a lot closer to her studio.

This house, while large, had a cozy beach house appeal to it. And even though it stirred up too many memories of Gramps, they were largely good memories and she managed to keep her feelings of betrayal and resentment at bay. She'd had parts of the place redecorated before moving in—her room, the living room, and kitchen—areas where she would spend the most time. She'd fashioned it in a way that made it feel more like her home than Gramps's holiday bolthole. And she was settling in nicely.

Once at home, she kicked off her shoes, poured a glass of shiraz and padded, barefoot, to the living room where she sank onto the massive sofa, with her legs tucked under her. Glass in one hand and Ben's letter in the other.

She read it again, even though she knew it by heart now. She didn't know why she was so fascinated by this confusing and pathetic little letter.

She just... *was*.

She finished her glass and got up to fetch the bottle for a refill. While she was up, she found a pen and some note paper as well. She sat down with her refilled glass of wine and after taking another fortifying sip, began to write.

BEN HATED GOING HOME these days. He worked longer hours just to avoid it. Got up before dawn in the mornings and returned home after midnight. The business had never been in better shape, but Ben couldn't say the same about himself.

He couldn't stand the echoing silence when he walked through the door at night. The place felt like a fucking tomb, devoid of life and joy. He tossed his wallet and keys into the empty fruit bowl on the kitchen counter and tried not to think about the morning he'd found Lilah's rings in that bowl. The morning his life had taken a nosedive down the toilet.

Today's post had been neatly placed on the counter beside the bowl, Trudy was always so damned old school conscientious about doing that, even though the entire pile would likely consist of junk. He picked it up and lifted his arm to yeet it into the trash can when the small, pink envelope right at the top of the pile caught his attention.

His breath snagged and he dumped the rest of the pile onto the counter, while grabbing up the envelope with shaky, eager hands. He was *very* familiar with that small, neat handwriting. He'd seen it often enough over the years when helping Lilah with her math homework, or her college assignments. She'd never actually asked for his help, but he told himself it was to stop her vocal moping around his office, whenever she encountered a problem she had difficulty with.

He tore the envelope open, and only afterwards regretted not taking more care with it, hating that he'd torn through her pretty, but practical—kind of like the woman herself—hand-writing.

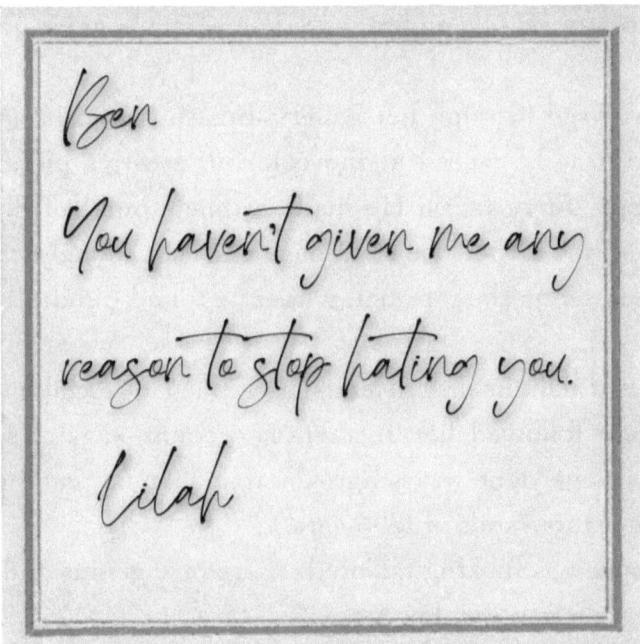

Ben

You haven't given me any

reason to stop hating you.

Lilah

That was it, three lines, in response to the letter he hadn't even been sure she would receive. Or look at if she *did* receive it. The letter he'd written impulsively after a—lonely—tequila shot too many. The contents of which he couldn't quite recall, but knew had to be somewhat maudlin if they accurately reflected his constant state of being these days.

His lips tilted at the corners as he stared at her curt response.

If she wanted reasons to stop hating him, he would damned well give them to her…

He would just have to figure out what those reasons were.

But this was communication. It was better than the weeks of silence that had come before it.

Ben picked up his phone and opened up the browser. He stared at the screen for a moment before doing something he knew he should've done weeks—no years—ago, he typed Lilah's name into the search engine and immediately navigated to her website.

He browsed through her gallery, breath stuttering in and out of his lungs as he stared at the colorful, creative pictures of all those happy, furry faces. He made a quiet sound of disappointment when he reached the last image and immediately called up a broader search on the internet, where he found hundreds of other pictures.

Images Lilah or her friends had put on social media. He immediately followed her Instagram account—again, something he should have done years ago—noting that he was but one of hundreds of thousands of followers.

God, she was fucking talented. A creative genius and Ben had spent years denigrating her art.

He was ashamed and disgusted by his own arrogance. All those times he'd dismissed what she did as nothing but a frivolous hobby. The immensity of her talent humbled him and he wanted her to know exactly how fucking proud he was of everything she'd achieved despite his lack of support and encouragement.

He'd be damned if he went another six weeks without seeing her or talking to her.

"YOUR THREE O'CLOCK IS HERE," Kirby announced two weeks later, dragging Lilah's attention from yet another confusing and peculiar letter from Ben.

Lilah,

Everything around me reminds me of you, the scent of your perfume lingers everywhere, your toothbrush remains in the bathroom, your clothing still occupies more than half of my closet space and I find that I don't mind that at all. Because I find myself desperately clinging to these reminders that you once lived here with me. I spend hours in the beautiful garden you created on the roof. I was disappointed when your friends arrived to complete the job without you. I finished planting your rosemary and lavender, by the way. Don't worry... I was under Darbi's strict supervision and I promise, I didn't fuck it up. Not with Darbi watching. She's quite the tyrant. The garden is looking beautiful. I sent pictures, but I doubt you saw them. I hope your friends shared their photos with you. I hope you cared enough to look at them. Take care of yourself.

Yours, Ben

PS. I'm working on the whole giving you reasons not to hate me thing

B

GOD, the man was infuriating. What the hell was he up to? And would she foolishly reply again, like she did last time? She wouldn't. She knew she wouldn't, she had no reason to. Best to nip whatever madness this was in the bud right now. She refolded the letter and shoved it into her desk drawer. Her movements sharp and decisive.

She even dusted her hands off afterward. It could stay there, collecting dust, until she forgot all about it.

"Lilah?" Right. Her three o'clock was here.

"Yes, Kirby, buzz them in and show them to the studio. Offer the usual tea or coffee with biscuits for the owner, doggy treats for the client. I just need to pop into the ladies' room for a spell." Fortunately the bathroom was in the studio. Some of the other rentals in this building didn't have indoor plumbing and their tenants had to use the public restrooms.

It was as she was washing her hands that it occurred to her that her period was late. She froze and stared at her reflection blankly, hands still under the stream, while she frantically tried to recall when last she'd had her period. In all the chaos and confusion following Gramps's death and then leaving Ben, she honestly wasn't certain if she'd had one last month.

It was nearly two months since she and Ben had slept together, and even though she'd been relatively certain pregnancy was not a concern, she now had major doubts. She drew in a shuddering breath, not sure how she felt about the possibility of having a baby. Being a single mother.

Feeling the panic set in, she took a few deep, slow breaths, fighting for calm. She was putting the cart before the horse here, no need to panic or worry right now. It was one—maybe two— missed periods. She'd had a topsy turvy few months, it was quite possibly just a stress response.

She rinsed her face and patted away the excess moisture with some paper napkins, still practicing her deep breathing. She took a moment to center herself and—relatively calm again—stepped out of the bathroom. Only to slam right into a solid brick wall that hadn't been there only moments ago. She reeled for a disorienting moment, and a hand came up to her arm to steady her.

"Whoa, easy there, *leannan*. Are you okay?"

Oh, *God*, this was the last thing she needed right now.

"Ben?" She hated how flustered she sounded and inserted a bit more authority into her voice. "What are you doing here? You can't be here! I'm working."

"I know."

"I have a client coming soon."

"Yes. That's us."

Us?

Lilah's eyes tracked to his feet, where a tiny, shivering dog hid behind Ben's legs, just one teary black eye and a perky ear showing as the little animal stared up at her fearfully.

"Ben, please tell me you didn't obtain this poor creature just to have a valid reason for worming your way into my studio?"

"I could have wormed my way in here *sans* dog, Lilah," he said, his deep voice chastising.

Damn it, she'd missed the sound of that sexy voice. She'd missed that half smile and those striking blue eyes, and just the sheer *presence* of him. And she didn't even know how much, until this very moment.

She refused to show him how his presence was affecting her, and hated that he'd caught her at such a vulnerable moment. The possibility of pregnancy still loomed fresh in her mind and now here *he* was. She was terrified of simply blurting out her concerns to him, but she knew Ben well enough to recognize that he would try to use the news to his advantage. He would attempt to convince her to come back and give their marriage a chance if there was a baby on the way. And Lilah knew, baby or not, she was not going back to that cynical excuse of a marriage.

She also knew that if she *was* pregnant, Ben had the right to know. And she *would* tell him… eventually, and then only after she was absolutely certain.

"Do I even want to know what's going on in that complicated brain of yours?" Ben mused, and she glowered at him.

"You should take this poor dog back to his owner, Ben," she said. "I have real work to do."

Ben bent at the waist to pick the trembling dog up and tuck it close to his chest, with its compact body draped over his forearm. It was a black and white short haired Chihuahua, and it was wearing a pink sweater with a pink, sparkly collar.

"This is Fifi. She's a two-year-old rescue." The tiny dog's tongue was hanging out the side of her mouth and she appeared to be wall-eyed. Typical Chihuahua, really. Obnoxiously cute. "I confess, I'd planned to adopt something a little more robust, but Fifi had just been surrendered to the shelter a few days before. Her previous person died and she was bounced around from family member to family member for a few months before they gave her up. She looked so fucking out of place there. She was wearing little legwarmers and a fluffy blue sweater. I don't know how the hell it happened, but three days later she was mine. And she came with all these accessories. I figured she was used to her creature comforts, and her designer wear, and far be it from me to deprive her of them."

"You're serious?" Lilah asked, unable to resist scratching behind Fifi's adorable pointy ears.

"Yes. I've had her for nearly two weeks."

"Who takes care of her when you're at work?" His cheeks went ruddy and he shifted his shoulders uncomfortably.

"Uh, she's been coming to the office with me. Just until we can figure out a more permanent solution. She's a good dog, very obedient, sleeps under my desk most of the day, quiet as a mouse."

Lilah had no idea how to respond to this development and stared at him in confused consternation. The thought of Ben doing his high-powered alpha executive thing, with a tiny dog snoozing under his desk, was a little incongruous to say the least.

And also charming as hell.

"What made you decide to get a dog?" she asked on a despairing whisper and he swallowed, his hold on the dog tightening slightly. "And why come here?"

"I came here to commemorate Fifi's adoption with a photo-shoot..." he said and then swallowed, before adding, "And because I miss you."

"There are other really good pet photographers you can try," she said, ignoring the last. "I could give you their details."

"I don't want anyone else, Lilah. I've Googled you. I've seen what you can do and I'm so fucking ashamed I never bothered looking you up before. Because your work is fantastic and you're the only one want."

"I'm afraid you can't have me," she whispered, and he flinched, his face paling.

"Lilah, I know I've made mistakes, and I understand why you're angry with me..."

"Ben, I don't think you understand a damned thing. If you did, you would *never* have come here today. Seeing you... being around you hurts so damned much. And that's not something that can be changed or fixed. You're the worst thing that's ever happened to me, the biggest mistake I ever made, and I want to stay as far away from that mistake as possible."

She immediately wished back the angry, hurtful words when she saw how they impacted him. He took it like a massive body blow, actually sucked in a pained breath at the shock of it, his face leeched of all color, his lips tightened, but his eyes, which had been hopeful and pleading just moments ago flared and she saw the pain bloom in them for a few brief, revealing seconds, before he iced her out. A frigid shutter coming down to conceal his emotions from her.

"I never meant to hurt you, Lilah. I genuinely thought that you could be happy with me."

"How could you think that when you were keeping such a massive secret from me?" She shouldn't have asked that question, she didn't want to engage him any further on this topic, but her pain demanded explanations. Even when she knew those explanations would only further exacerbate that pain.

"You're not going to believe me, but those six months before our wedding? I actually thought you knew about Cyrus's illness. I assumed you agreed to marry me because of that. I thought we had an understanding; we were marrying because it would make Cyrus happy."

She laughed; the sound high-pitched and hysterical. She clamped a hand over her mouth to stifle the wild sound and stared at him in wide-eyed horror and disbelief.

"You thought I knew?" she asked, the question muffled behind her hand. "I don't believe that. How could you have thought that? If I'd known, I would have spent more time with him, I would have wanted to spend my every waking moment with him. Instead I spent most of them with *you* in a series of joyless dates, fooling myself into believing you were falling in love with me. How could you believe such a thing, when I never once talked about my *dying* grandfather to you in all that time? How could you assume I would prefer spending all those hours in your stilted, forced company instead of with him?"

He was petting Fifi's ears, but the movement seemed agitated, almost desperate, as if he were trying to soothe himself, rather than the dog.

"You don't have the best track record when it comes to confronting pain, Lilah," he pointed out.

"What the hell makes you say *that*?"

"Because I watched you break up with several boyfriends over the course of the years and you bottled it up and refused to talk about it. I thought you were following the same pattern with Cyrus. And I wasn't going to force you to talk about it unless you brought it up first."

"*I* don't have the best track record when it comes to confronting pain?" she repeated incredulously. "Are you joking right now? You never once talked about your parents after coming to live with us. And have you even cried for Gramps? Properly cried? I'm not the one who has a difficult time dealing with challenging emotional situations, Ben. *You* are, and the only reason you never talked about it was because *you* weren't comfortable bringing it up. If you had, if you ever made any attempt to have a real conversation with me, you would have recognized that I had no idea Gramps was sick.

"Instead, you made up this fiction that I was in some lala imaginary land refusing to face up to my grandfather's imminent death? You've spent years underestimating me... thinking the absolute worst of me, and for some reason you believe that I'm up for years more of the same treatment in the future? I think not. *If* what you say is true, and you really thought I knew about

Gramps—and I have my doubts about that—then it's yet another example of how little you know me. Truthfully though? I think this is just your way of retconning the immediate past to suit your own needs, and paint yourself in a more sympathetic light.

"I'm done. *We* are done. When are you going to get that through your thick, stubborn skull? I'm not playing games. I don't need time to cool down. I just need to move on with my life."

For the first time, she saw her words finally penetrate that aforementioned thick skull…

"Jesus." His voice was a thready, stunned whisper. "Lilah, please, I can't lose you."

"Ben, you don't give a damn about losing *me*… you hate losing. Period. And you hate that I'm not falling meekly in line like your many minions at the office. You'll get over it, and realize that we're both better off out of this toxic situation."

Fifi—sensing the tension between them—whined unhappily and Ben instinctively cuddled her close to his chest as if to comfort her. It was a sweet, uncharacteristic gesture that that touched Lilah. God, she was such a sucker sometimes.

"We'll leave," he told Lilah in a gruff voice and she gave him a regretful half smile and nodded.

"I think that would be best," she said. "I'll text you the contact details of a few great pet photographers in the area if you're still interested."

"Yes… uh… I think…" He floundered for a moment before nodding. "Yes, please. I should go."

He turned to go and then hesitated for a moment, before turning his head to look at her, his eyes dark and turbulent.

"I truly regret everything that has happened, Lilah."

"So do I." She hesitated before adding, "And Ben? Please

don't let Fifi be yet another female you promised to love but were only using to further your own needs. She doesn't deserve it. Please give her the love and care you were unable to give me."

His lips thinned and he hesitated—looking like he was about to speak—but he frowned darkly and left without another word.

She watched him walk to the front door, that confident, long-legged stride eating up the short distance in just a few steps. The bell on the door tinkled and he was gone.

"Are you okay?" Kirby asked, the gentle concern in her voice dragging Lilah back to her current reality. "That looked really intense."

"Uh, yes... Fine. I'm sorry. We're, uhm... in the process of getting divorced."

Saying it out loud made it feel more real. Then this heartbreak would be behind her and she could finally move forward with her life.

"Oh, God, Lilah, I'm so sorry, I had no idea. I would've given you a head's up but he called and pretty much begged me to slot him in if we had any cancellations. I told him you rarely had any cancellations and that we had a waiting list, but he said he wanted to surprise you with the dog—an early birthday present. So, when we had a slot freed up for today, I didn't think anything of giving it to him."

Lilah nodded. "It's okay, Kirby. It's not your fault. I know firsthand how persuasive"—*manipulative*—"he can be. We needed to have a conversation anyway. Do I have any other appointments today?"

"Not until four-thirty."

"Right." Lilah pushed a shaky hand through her heavy fall of hair. "I just need to dash out for a bit. I'll be back in time for the next shoot."

"Of course," Kirby agreed, unable to disguise the curiosity in her eyes.

Lilah grabbed her bag and coat and left without another word.

Before she could move forward, she needed one crucial question answered first. And that required an urgent trip to the pharmacy.

TWENTY-FIVE

Nine Months Ago

Ben stared at Cyrus, not wanting to believe what the man had just told him.

"Are you sure?" he asked hoarsely, unable to think of anything else to say.

"Yes."

"Cyrus, there are other doctors. Other treatments, experimental drugs... medical trials. It's not like you to simply accept a prognosis like this."

"Of course I didn't just *accept* this, Ben!" Cyrus all-but-shouted. It was so uncharacteristic for the gentle old man to raise his voice that Ben actually jerked in shock. Seeing his startled reaction, Cyrus softened his tone and continued. "I've been poked and prodded dozens of times over the last six months, and every doctor I've seen has come to the same conclusion. Inoperable. End stage. No longer than a year to live—well, six months now, I suppose. I'm dying, son. And I've already endured months of intensive chemo and radiation. And I can't face the prospect of more of the same."

"I never even noticed," Ben whispered, horrified. His eyes tracked over his mentor's lined face, only now seeing how much weight he'd lost, how pale and shaky he was. Cyrus had already been balding, so the hair loss from his treatment hadn't been obvious. "How could you keep this from me? I could have helped; I would have taken up more of the slack."

"Ben, you've been the de-facto chief for nearly a year as it stands. You do everything already. I'm past ready for retirement, we just need to make things official. Nobody will be surprised when I nominate you for CEO."

"Lilah," Ben suddenly remembered. "Jesus. Have you told Lilah?"

"Not yet. I'm not sure I will."

"Cyrus, you can't leave her in the dark. She deserves to know." Ben felt a little resentful that he had to bear the burden of this knowledge alone, while the precious little princess was sheltered from all the ugliness in life as usual.

"Not yet. But soon. Maybe," Cyrus said, exhaustion in his voice. He sank back in his massive, black leather desk chair wearily. Cyrus had always commanded attention in this room—his lavish home office. He'd sat on that chair like it was a throne and everybody on the other side of the desk mere peasants. Now the chair seemed to swallow him. He looked like the tired, sick old man he was, and Ben felt a lump form in his throat, while his chest constricted as he finally registered that his mentor, the man who'd been as a grandfather to him for so many years, would be gone soon.

"Tell me what I can do to make this easier, Cyrus?"

"Just promise me you'll take care of Lilah. I worry about her;

she's been quiet since her return from Paris. She's always getting involved with the wrong men. I do wish she'd find someone solid, dependable. Someone like you..." His voice faded and he coughed, a full body spasm that rattled deep in his chest. "Once, long ago, I'd hoped you and Lilah would—" He shook his head and laughed tiredly. "Of course, that was just a foolish dream. You two soon made it clear that you're not compatible at all. But an old man can wish. It would just set my mind at ease if Lilah could find someone like you. But I doubt I'll live to see it."

Ben stared at his mentor, his friend, his adopted grandfather, seeing the concern etched on his face. Lilah was the only one who could make the old man fret like this. Flighty, carefree Lilah, who'd always been spoiled to within an inch of her life. Ben didn't want Cyrus to spend his last months worrying about what would happen to Lilah after he was gone. He would have to find a way to lessen that concern.

A plan began to form in the back of his mind. A crazy, dumb plan that would only work if Lilah was fully on board with it. Which meant Cyrus had to tell her as soon as possible.

"When will you tell Lilah, Cyrus?"

Cyrus made a vague gesture with his hand and shrugged, before saying, "Later. Soon. I worry it'll upset her. And stress can trigger an asthma attack."

The thought of Lilah suffering another severe asthma attack sent a shudder of pure dread down Ben's spine. That was a complication he hadn't considered.

"Sometimes, the best way for Lilah to deal with bad news is to pretend everything is just fine. I like to humor her... especially if it means keeping the stress reaction at bay."

That wasn't fucking healthy at all, but Ben understood Cyrus's reasoning, having seen firsthand how bad her asthma could be.

"So when I *do* tell her, don't be surprised—and don't judge her—if she just carries on as usual. It's her way of coping."

Ben frowned, something niggling at his brain. He was starting to feel a little manipulated here. Cyrus coughed again, this time it wracked his body completely until he was hunched over, and in pain.

Panicked, Ben leaped to his feet and rounded the desk—all thoughts of Lilah, and Cyrus's possible conniving, fleeing in the face of the man's very real distress.

"Tell me what you need," he demanded urgently. Cyrus pointed toward the glass of water on the desk and Ben handed it to him. The old man grabbed it with both hands and chugged down the water.

"I need you to be a rock, Ben," Cyrus whispered, after catching his breath again. "For me and for Lilah. Can you do that?"

Ben squeezed the old man's bony shoulder reassuringly, a surge of love and affection swelling in his chest. He would do anything for this man.

"Yes, Cyrus, I can do that."

BEN WOKE WITH A GASP, he gazed into the darkness for a moment and automatically reached across the bed, searching for the small, warm body that had been such a source of solace and comfort to him these last few weeks.

He found her curled up into a tiny ball in the empty space beside him, and tugged her over for a snuggle. She snuffled and snorted as she awoke, and gave his stroking hand a delicate lick, before settling down to sleep again.

His ground rules upon bringing her home was that she "absolutely stay off the bed" ... which she'd done like the good girl she is. But by the second day, he hadn't seen the harm in letting her up for a cuddle; by the fourth, she was taking short naps on the bed while Ben attempted to read—he had a hard time focusing on much since Lilah had left—and by the end of the week, she was sleeping behind him, curled up against his back.

Now, as he cuddled his dog, he continued to stare into the darkness, thinking of Lilah, wondering how she was, if she missed him, or thought about him as often as he thought about her.

It was infuriating, this longing. This need to know what she was doing, where she was, *how* she was...

Where had it come from? How had it come into being? This was more than just the promise he'd made to Cyrus. He could take care of her even if he was no longer a part of her life.

But he didn't want that. He wanted so much more than that...

"So, are you ready to talk about whatever the hell's been going on with you lately?" Rhys asked Ben the following morning when the men were getting changed after a highly competitive tennis match. Ben had won. Only because Ben had desperately needed an outlet for his frustration, grief, and turmoil and he'd taken it out on his hapless friend, mercilessly sending him sprinting to and fro across the tennis court.

"Other than my mentor dying and my wife leaving me you

mean?" Ben asked acerbically, as he fastened his watch around his wrist.

"I know how close you were with Cyrus and I understand how hard that must have been for you, but you didn't want to marry Lilah. I figured her leaving you would have been the best outcome to a bad situation."

"I made a commitment when I married her," Ben told his friend. "A commitment I fully intended to honor."

"A commitment to Lilah or to Cyrus? Because quite frankly, if it was to Cyrus, then you and Lilah are probably both better off out of it, bru."

Ben stared at his friend for a moment, considering the question.

"To Lilah… of *course*, to Lilah."

"Does *she* know that?" Rhys asked, towel drying his wet hair vigorously.

"What the hell kind of question is that? Of course she knows…" But he didn't sound very convincing, not even to his own ears. How could she know that? First, he'd inferred it was for business reasons, and then—after Cyrus's letter—he'd all but admitted that he'd married her to make a dying man happy.

He tried not to wince when he thought about their wedding album which had been delivered to his apartment a few weeks ago. The photographer had also uploaded it to a file sharing website, for them to distribute as they saw fit.

He'd glanced through the album but had stalled only a few pages in, his attention snagged by an image of Lilah in the church, smiling up at him after Cyrus had lifted her veil. That broad, happy grin of hers, amber eyes sparkling—as if she were on the verge of laughing just for the sheer joy of it—nose wrinkled like she was about to share a joke with him. Just so *Lilah*. A Lilah who had disappeared mere minutes later, and who hadn't—as far as Ben knew—smiled like that since.

He'd chased that beautiful smile from her lips. And now he found himself wanting it back.

"My commitment was—*is*—to Lilah. But I fucked up," Ben admitted to Rhys, whose brow raised at the confession. Ben didn't often admit to culpability, mostly because he was usually right. "I let her think it was to everyone *but* her. And I intend to fix that."

Rhys laughed, the sound filled with genuine warmth and amusement.

"The one thing you've always told me about Lilah is that she's stubborn as all hell. So I'll wish you luck with that, brother. I'm pretty sure you're going to need it."

Ben sighed and hoped his despair wasn't too evident in the forlorn sound.

"I don't know what I'll do if she won't forgive me, Rhys. If she refuses to take me back. I've had a taste of life without Lilah and I can't imagine spending the rest of my days without her by my side."

"Why is that, Ben? What's changed? You? Her?"

Ben considered his friend's quiet question, not sure how to reply. The easy answer would be that Lilah had changed, but that would be a cowardly fucking lie. Lilah hadn't changed. She'd always been a little spoiled, sure, but she was also sweet, cheerful, and unselfish with her warmth and affection.

No, Lilah was the same person she'd always been. It was Ben's perception of her that had changed. He was finally able to see Lilah for who she was. And it shamed him deeply to know how badly he'd misjudged her.

He was desperate for another chance with her, but he feared

that his warm and generous Lilah was all out of charity when it came to Ben.

SATURDAYS WERE Lilah's favorite day of the week. She slept in, lounged around in her PJs all morning, and liked to treat herself to a decadent brunch. The Saturday following Ben's unexpected invasion of her work space was different. Yes, she was still in her PJs by the time midday rolled round, but it was as a result of moping rather than decadent lounging.

She'd spent the morning throwing up and feeling quite sorry for herself.

She was almost certainly pregnant. And she wasn't entirely sure how she felt about that. Yes, the plan had been to start having children almost immediately, but with her marriage being a non-starter, naturally Lilah hadn't anticipated becoming a mother anytime soon.

But after a positive home test, pregnancy was becoming a certainty more than a distant probability. She had an appointment with her gynie next week, which would likely confirm her suspicion.

She groaned, and buried her face in her knees. She'd always wanted to be a mother, but she never thought she'd be doing the parenting alone. Well, she knew Ben would co-parent, but she'd hoped to evict him from her life entirely. Hard to do when they were sharing a child.

She was staring miserably out at the magnificent ocean view, happy that the day was as gloomy and gray as her mood, when she heard the bleep of the alarm deactivating. She sat up, head tilted, as she listened again. Her part-time housekeeper had the code to the alarm system, but the woman wasn't due in today. Lilah was supposed to be alone and she was happy to wallow in her solitary misery.

She heard an unfamiliar scrabbling sound on the tiled flooring and then froze when she heard Ben's voice chuckle and say, "Easy now... don't run."

She sat up, swung her legs over the edge of the sofa, and pushed to her feet.

A tiny—*familiar*—dog darted into the living room, saw Lilah and ran yapping at her, clearly seeing her as an intruder in her own home. Lilah stared down at the furiously barking little terror, not entirely certain what was going on here.

Ben entered the room, a couple of bags slung over his shoulders. His eyes widened when he saw Lilah and he immediately commanded, "*Shit*, Fifi, no! Stop that."

To her credit, Fifi immediately obeyed, sitting down on her haunches and glaring up at Lilah with curled lips.

"What are you doing here?" Both Lilah and Ben asked simultaneously, then stared at each other sheepishly. Ben gestured for Lilah to reply.

"I moved in a few weeks ago. I prefer it here. You?"

"I need a change of scenery, and there's not much green space for Fifi to run around in at the apartment. She loves your rooftop garden, but I thought she'd enjoy the open spaces here more."

"But... *I'm* staying here," Lilah pointed out.

"This place belongs to both of us," Ben reminded her.

"Can't we work out some kind of schedule?"

"It seems to me that you've moved in, right? So how would a schedule work if you're living here full time?"

"If you gave me advance warning of when you want to be here, I could stay in Constantia during those times?"

"*Or* we could share," Ben was using that infuriating reasonable voice of his. The one he tended to use when he was managing her.

"I'm not sure that would work for me," she said, and he frowned, dropping the heavy looking bags on the floor. The resultant thuds made her jump.

"This place has seven bedrooms, an entertainment lounge, a cinema room; we could quite easily share without getting in each other's way."

"I don't want that."

"You want me to go? Or do you want to leave?" His calm voice made her feel unreasonable and bitchy and she chewed on the inside on her lip, before shrugging.

"How long do you intend to stay?"

"I haven't decided yet. A few days."

Lilah stared down at the dog, who at least had stopped snarling at her and was now just glaring. She couldn't believe he'd actually kept this cute little bundle of aggression and nerves. But there she stood, smaller than life, her body language hostile.

Ben was a notorious workaholic, he spent long hours at the office. If he stayed on his side of the house, and she stayed on hers, they could easily avoid each other. Especially if he followed his usual work patterns.

She gave a brusque nod.

"Okay, we can share, but you take the mountain-facing room at the end of the hall. And stay out of the blue bedroom, I've converted it into a work space. I'm sleeping in my usual room."

He said nothing, merely nodded meekly.

"And call your vicious guard dog off. I probably won't murder you in your sleep... *probably*. So she can relax."

He full on smiled at that, and Lilah averted her eyes, not wanting to be charmed by that smile. She felt like hell, undoubtedly looked worse, she didn't need this perfect man in her space, making her feel inadequate with his otherworldly damned good looks. Ugh, and now she would have to hide her constant nausea from him too. Why hadn't she considered that before her easy acquiescence?

It was too late now, he picked up the bags again and called Fifi to heel. The little dog obeyed smartly and she watched the unlikely duo vacate the room.

This was not ideal. She hadn't once considered that fact that they now co-owned the Bantry Bay house. It had simply never occurred to her that he may occasionally want to stay here as well.

She wrapped her arms around her torso and sank onto the sofa again, her eyes back on the gray horizon.

When Ben returned less than five minutes later, he was carrying a bright pink fluffy cushion, which he tossed onto the floor next to the currently dead fireplace.

"Lie down," he told Fifi, who happily trotted over to the cushion—well, dog bed—and curled up. The dog was out of her ultra-suede pale pink harness and leash ensemble and was now wearing a pink coat with faux ermine trim. Her liquid black eyes tracked Ben's every move, as he strolled into the open plan kitchen and started opening and closing cabinet doors.

"I'm going to make lunch, you want some?"

Not sure who he was talking to, Lilah stared at him in confusion and he smiled again, she marveled at how easily he was smiling and wondered why he appeared to be in such good spirits.

"You talking to me or the dog?" she asked, and he actually laughed.

"*Lilah*, would you like lunch?"

"This isn't exactly staying out of my way, Ben," she felt compelled to point out.

"Surely we can discuss the parameters of our arrangement over this one shared meal?"

"I'm not really hungry," she said, not wanting him to witness her jumping up and dashing for the bathroom if the food made her nauseous. He actually looked disappointed by her reply.

"I'm making your favorite," he cajoled, and she narrowed her eyes.

"What's my favorite?" she asked, and he gave her another one of those easy grins.

"Chicken parmigiana with mashed potatoes," he replied, acing her test.

"Get *out*, you don't know how to make chicken parmigiana," she said, forgetting herself for an instant. He actually laughed at her reaction, his eyes sparking with humor.

"You're right, I don't. My cooking skills are a bit more basic than that... but I can order in."

"What were you really going to make?"

"Ham and cheese toasted sandwiches." His sheepish reply startled a laugh out of her and he looked oddly pleased by her response.

"Sure. I'll have a toastie," she said, and he smiled again. Why did he look so happy just because she was having a sandwich with him? What the hell was going on with him today?

She looked at him, really gave him a thorough once-over, when he passed her and sank to his haunches to give his dog a biscuit to munch on. He was wearing a pair of faded almost to gray jeans and a navy-blue button-down shirt. He'd lost weight. She could see it in his face. And in the loose fit of his jeans and shirt. His dark hair was longer and scruffier than he usually wore it, and his strong jaw was dark with stubble.

"You look like hell," she said, always honest to a fault. He looked up from where he'd been fussing over Fifi and gave Lilah a wry once-over.

"You're one to talk."

"Rude."

"I'm not the one still in my fleecy pajamas at twelve-thirty in the afternoon."

"It's Saturday, and it's raining, so I'm the sane one here. This is the only way to spend a wet weekend. Besides, I wasn't expecting company."

"Don't you usually see your friends on a Saturday?"

"Friends?" she asked with a quizzical tilt of her head. "What friends?"

"Don't make me say it," he said, grimacing.

She continued to stare at him in wide-eyed innocence.

"Say what?" She shouldn't be enjoying this exchange so much.

She was angry with him. She hated him. And yet… she'd missed cranky, straitlaced Ben so damned much. Turned out it wasn't very easy to oust someone who'd been a part of your life for the better part of fifteen years.

"Your… your *hoes*, okay?" he relented, and she chuckled.

"We cancelled today," she told him. "Some of the other girls weren't feeling too well. Seasonal colds and flus maybe."

That was a lie… the others *were* meeting today, but Lilah had cried off. Pleading exhaustion. Which was technically true. Exhaustion and nausea.

"So, you kept the dog," she said, eager to change the subject. His eyes tracked to his dog, who was still delicately chewing her biscuit.

"Of course I did. I made a commitment. She's mine now." Something in that simple possessive *mine* sent Lilah's nerve endings tingling, and she swallowed in an effort to lubricate her suddenly dry throat.

"And you—uh—" she coughed, stumbling over her tongue. What the hell was wrong with her? "You like having a dog?"

"I've never had a pet before and I lucked out with Fifi"—the dog's head lifted at the sound of her name and Ben grinned affectionately—"she's an extremely clever girl. She knows all the basic commands, doesn't mess in the house, is eager to learn and to please."

"The perfect woman," Lilah quipped, unable to keep the note of cynicism out of her voice.

"Not quite," he said, his voice dropping to a low rasp. "The perfect woman is five-ten, with honey-streaked brown hair, amber eyes, a killer smile, and a generous heart."

She stared at him mutely, unsure what to say in response to that... he didn't seem to need a response. He gave Fifi one last pat on the head and jumped up agilely. He passed Lilah on his way to the kitchen and his subtle woodsy aftershave left a scent trail that nearly grabbed her by the nostrils and dragged her behind him like lovesick puppy. She actually dug her fingers into the couch's armrest to stop herself from getting up and following behind him.

God, sharing this house with him was going to be damned near impossible if this was her reaction after just half an hour in his company. She needed time to gather herself, to strengthen her resolve and reconcile herself to the idea that he was going to be around for the next few days.

"I'm going to grab a quick shower and get dressed," she muttered, getting to her feet and setting off Fifi's warning growls again. Although, Lilah noticed, the dog couldn't be bothered to drop her biscuit while issuing said warnings.

"I can't take you seriously when you growl at me with a snack in your mouth," she told the dog, who side-eyed her, and growled even louder at the words.

"You don't have to bother on my account," Ben said, rummaging through cabinets again, finding utensils and cookware.

"Oh, you don't have to worry about that, Ben. I would *never*," she said in her sweetest voice and he glanced up to level that damned devastating grin on her.

"That's good then. I wouldn't want to inconvenience you in any way."

She rolled her eyes and left without another word.

BEN WATCHED LILAH LEAVE, a small smile lingering on his lips. It was so damned good to see her again. To talk with her, tease her. He'd missed her. Of course, he knew that he'd missed her. But until he saw her again, he hadn't known how *much*. It felt like he'd been reunited with an essential part of him that had been missing for too long. Like he'd been half-alive until that reunion.

He had to come clean. He had to tell her he'd known she was here all along. She hadn't forgiven him for the last untruth… he couldn't add another to the massive pile of lies already smoldering between them. If he wanted her eventual forgiveness, he had to start the unsavory task of digging into that reeking pile of crap, with the end goal of reducing it to nothing.

And he had to start soon. Now… *today*. With this one small lie.

He busied himself with lunch, dumping some precut frozen

fries into the air fryer, and preparing a simple green salad. He started the toasties only when he heard her soft tread on the stairs. He glanced up when she stepped back into the living room and the quick *welcome back* he'd been about to utter froze on his lips... she was wearing a pair of tight high rise jeans, and a short, long-sleeved, cable knit pink crop top that left a sliver of her toned tummy on display. Her drying hair fell to her shoulders in a tousled mass, and he could smell her shampoo and shower gel all the way into the kitchen. Vanilla and something citrusy. Fucking *mouthwatering*.

She hesitated in the doorway for a moment, before making her way to the kitchen. Fifi stood up in her bed, and growled, hackles raised. Ben growled his own low warning at the dog, who gave him a pissed off look before sitting down again and watching Lilah with her distrusting beady eyes.

"Your dog does *not* like me," Lilah said as she slid onto one of the bar stools. She propped her chin on her hands, resting her elbows on the kitchen counter.

"She's not great with strangers, but she'll get used to you and then realize that you're another person with opposable thumbs who can access her treat jar. She's very food driven, as soon as she sees you as a potential provider of snacks, she'll be your best friend."

Lilah slanted the dog an amused glance and chuckled when she saw that Fifi was still staring at her like she thought Lilah was Satan's handmaiden.

"This is more than I expected. Or asked for," Lilah said uncertainly when Ben slid her plate with two toasties, some fries and a portion of salad, across the counter toward her.

"I won't be offended if you don't finish it all," he said, and fixed his own plate. He chose to remain standing across the counter from her, so that they could talk to each other while eating.

She delicately picked at one sandwich, while he scarfed down half of his in a few quick bites.

"I lied to you," he admitted, deciding that it was best to bite the bullet and confront this issue head on.

She froze, hand suspended in mid-air where it had been in act of transporting a black olive to her mouth.

"Lied about what?"

"I knew you were staying here. I was, however, surprised to find you home when we arrived. I thought you'd be out. I regret the lie but I needed a breather." Not a lie. "And Fifi *does* need some more green space." Also not a lie. "And I wanted to see you." Well, wasn't *he* just on a truth-speaking streak right now?

"Why did you want to see me?" she asked.

Ben considered his reply, looking at it from all possible angles, before saying, "Because I missed you and I was concerned about you."

"You should get out of the habit of being concerned about me, Ben," she said, popping the olive into her mouth and chewing slowly. "Maybe if you'd even once seen me as an equal instead of this broken doll in need of care and fixing, we could've had something. But when our entire relationship is based on what you think you can do for me and not how we can take care of each other, it becomes unsustainable. You've seen me as a burden, to be coddled and lied to. Although you probably saw that as *protecting me from the truth*, instead of lying to me. Right?"

"I'm sorry."

She looked so utterly astonished by the apology, Ben actually found himself flipping through his memories of their entire history together… looking for any former apologies he might have made to her.

There were none. Well, none where he specifically used the words, *I'm sorry*. And yet he could vividly recall her quite liberally and nonchalantly peppering those two words throughout their entire relationship history…

Starting with that heartfelt *I'm sorry about your mom and dad* back when they'd first met.

I'm sorry I dropped your stupid phone in the toilet.

Ooh, I'm so sorry I slayed you at Scrabble, Ben. Maybe pick up a dictionary once in a while.

So easy for her. While *he* had hoarded his apologies like they were gold.

It was time to change that. He cleared his throat, feeling awkward as hell, and said it again, "I'm *so* sorry, Lilah. You deserved better from me. From Cyrus. We weren't fair."

She looked confused, as if she weren't entirely sure what to make of his words.

"Why are you saying this now?"

"Because it needs to be said."

"Do you want something from me?"

Oh, *God*, that small, uncertain voice killed him. He hated that she had zero confidence in his sincerity, that she always believed him to be working some angle.

"No, *mo chridhe*, you can do with that what you will. But I want you to know that I mean it."

She tore a corner of her sandwich off and listlessly nibbled on it.

"Okay." Then asked, "what does that mean?"

The question confused him.

"What does what mean?"

"*Mo chridhe*, what does it mean?" She'd mangled the pronunciation but the meaning was clear.

"I said that?" he asked, stunned. He must have dropped it into the conversation without realizing it. His Gaelic was just about non-existent apart from a couple of words here and there, but his mother had used the endearment *all* the time, when he was a boy. As far as Ben could recall, he had never said it aloud before.

"You did. It's not the first time, you said it the night we danced as well. Is it the same as the other one? *Leannan*? Sweetheart?"

"Something like that," he hedged, still stunned that he'd dredged up the endearment from some distant, long-forgotten part of himself and not sure he was ready to delve into his reasons for using it now. His own appetite lost, Ben stared down at his toasted sandwich without enthusiasm.

"I see." She sounded unconvinced, but mercifully didn't seem too interested in pursuing the subject.

"You still hate me, cupcake?" Ben asked, desperate for her assurance that she did not. Even though he knew the likelihood of that assurance was less than zero.

"I have to, Ben," she whispered. She met his eyes, her own gaze filled with anguish and determination. "It's easier than loving you."

She pushed her sandwich aside, looking a little pasty as she stood up. She swayed and he jumped up in alarm but she found her balance almost immediately.

"Thanks for the sandwich, but I find that I'm not quite hungry right now. I have some reading to do. I'll see you later."

She walked away and left him crushed in her wake.

TWENTY-SIX

Doomed from the start

"**O**h. Good morning," Lilah greeted Ben the next morning, when she wandered into the living room and found him flat on his back on the couch, play-wrestling with Fifi. The dog instantly stopped play-ing, sat possessively on Ben's chest, and snarled at Lilah as she walked toward the kitchen.

Lilah snarled back, startling a deep laugh out of Ben. He sat up, scooping Fifi off his chest in one smooth movement and put her on the floor. The dog trotted over to her water bowl for a drink, before nosing her way around the kitchen, dining, and living room.

Ben joined Lilah in the kitchen and she tried to hide the fact that she was checking him out. He was wearing only a pair of charcoal boxer briefs, with a white t-shirt. Despite the weight he'd lost, he looked mouthwatering, and Lilah actually swallowed to prevent herself from slobbering all over him.

A squeak sounded from the floor and they both jumped in

fright and then laughed simultaneously when they realized it was Fifi, playing with one of her toys. The dog was in a pink and blue onesie with the words *My Daddy Wuffs Me* embroidered on the back.

"What the hell is she wearing?" Lilah asked in amusement.

"Her pajamas," Ben said, padding to the kitchen on bare feet, yawning as he walked. "You want coffee? Espresso? Cappuccino?"

"Uh, nothing, thanks..." The thought of coffee made her feel sick to her stomach. He slanted her a surprised glance.

"Seriously? You're barely functional first thing in the morning without a hit of caffeine."

"Maybe later, my stomach is a bit unsettled this morning."

He still looked troubled, but helped himself to a double shot espresso and walked to the breakfast bar with his cup, leaning both elbows on the counter and staring at her for a minute. She waited and, after a moment, he took a sip from his espresso mug, without saying a word.

Lilah knew how hard he must have bitten his tongue not to ask if she was okay. And appreciated the effort he was making to respect her privacy.

She poured herself a glass of orange juice and sat down at the breakfast bar and watched him through narrowed eyes.

"What?" he finally asked.

She nibbled at her lower lip before speaking. "I know Fifi came with her own wardrobe but I would never have expected you to actually take the time to dress her in these finicky little jackets and things."

He ducked his head and took another sip from his cup.

Oh, what was *that*? He was avoiding her eyes!

"Ben?"

He muttered something and her eyes widened, she wasn't sure if she'd heard him properly. "What did you say?"

"I said *I* bought her the onesie," he repeated, before adding almost defensively, "She seemed cold at night, even under the covers. And she looks so comfortable in her little pajamas."

"What else did you buy her?"

He shrugged, and sounded surly when he itemized, "A couple of jackets, some sweaters and t-shirts. A new collar and ID tag, because her old tag was outdated. Toys. A couple of dog beds. A car seat and safety harness. All the stuff a responsible pet owner would get."

"Ben... most of her things are *pink*. You've never liked pink," she pointed out, trying very hard to disguise her growing smile. She'd also noticed that Fifi's sparkly pink tag read *Daddy's Princess* on the one side.

"And?" he asked in response to her statement. "She looks great in pink. And I don't mind pink. I just never had an opinion on it before. I still don't really, I just think it suits Fifi."

"Okay," she said with a small smile and he took another quick sip from his cup.

"You want breakfast?" he asked, and she shook her head.

"Not yet."

"Fifi and I are going for a walk later... if you want to join us?"

She hesitated, tempted, before thinking better of it and shaking her head. "I don't think so, I'll stay in and read."

He looked disappointed but nodded, accepting her excuse without argument.

They sat quietly for the next few moments, both of them staring out at the still rainy and gray view, only Fifi's squeaky toy breaking the oddly companionable silence between them.

"Did you get the link to the wedding album?" He finally asked, and Lilah tensed.

"I did." She twirled her glass round and round on the marble surface of the counter. "Gramps looked really happy, didn't he?"

"Yes."

"I'm glad." She hesitated a moment, not sure if she wanted to ask the next question. Not at all certain she wanted to know the answer. "You once said he didn't know about your reasons for marrying me. But that was when I believed you'd married me because of the business. Did he know... it was because of his illness? Did he ask you to?"

Ben held her gaze, his eyes intense and sincere. "No. He didn't ask me to do that, Lilah. Not once. He kind of implied that it was something he'd always dreamed of and maybe he manipulated me into it. Maybe I *allowed* myself to be manipulated but he never asked. I never offered. The idea was mine alone. And I found myself more than willing to implement it."

"Why?" The question was a helpless whisper.

"Because I wanted to make him happy. I just never considered how selfish it was. How unfair I was being to you. I married you fully intending for it to be a permanent arrangement but never once considered *your* long-term happiness. I thought if I was willing to make such a sacrifice for Cyrus, surely you would be too. And that was the premise I worked from."

She worried her thumbnail cuticle with her teeth as she stared at him assessingly.

"Did you really think I knew about Gramps's illness?"

"Yes. Cyrus led me to believe he would tell you. And then he went on to say that your way of coping with grief was to ignore it and pretend everything was fine. I thought it was unhealthy as fuck but..."

"But you were so used to believing the worst of me, you didn't even question it," she completed for him and he grimaced.

"I'd seen you do it with break-ups. I thought you were immature. I based that opinion on the reckless girl I thought I knew eight years ago...and never once took the time to get to the know the woman you'd become since then. That asthma attack when you were in college terrified me. It was easier to just base everything I thought I knew about you on that one horrifying incident —and take it upon myself to insure it never happened again— than it was to recognize that in the fifteen years I'd known you, that was the worst I'd ever seen it. And that it had been as a result of forces completely out of your control. I was unfair. And I'm so fucking sorry."

She stopped worrying her cuticle and instead started plucking at her lower lip with her thumb and forefinger as she pondered his words.

"I've had a couple of bad scares since our marriage," she pointed out.

"And both of those times were because of me. I was responsible for causing the one thing I'd done my utmost to prevent for the last eight years. I always carry an inhaler in the pocket of whatever jacket I'm wearing in case of emergencies."

Well, that was an unexpected and touching revelation. And explained why he had an inhaler on hand at the wedding and the night she'd read Gramps's letter.

She cleared her throat, moved by the unexpected confession, but she still had to set him straight. "That's really sweet, Ben, but it's not up to you to manage my disease. You can't control when these things will happen."

"I was the stressor..."

"Again, *my* disease, doesn't matter who or what the stressor is… you're not responsible for my asthma. You can't swaddle me in bubble wrap, or prevent me from making stupid mistakes, you can't protect me from life's ugliness. I *never* wanted that from you. All I ever wanted was a lover, and a husband. Someone who was *in* love with me as a person and who loved me as an equal. Someone who wanted to spend as much of their waking moments with me as possible, who wanted to laugh and cry with me. Play with me. Just *be* with me. Someone to hold my hand when I'm scared, and breathe with me when I can't physically manage it on my own.

"And I wanted to be that person for him as well. A friend and lover. A companion to share his pain. It's the simplest thing in the world. But it's not something I can have with you. I know that now."

"I shouldn't have kept it from you," he blurted out. "I should have told you immediately when I realized that you didn't know about Cyrus. But I only discovered how little you knew on our wedding day. After your vows I felt blindsided. And then in the limo you clearly had no clue…"

Lilah inhaled sharply as the awful events of that day came flooding back. Well, that explained so much. Ben had been in shock too. Explained, but didn't excuse.

"I didn't handle it well and I couldn't tell you the truth right at that moment. We had a venue full of guests waiting for us, wedding pictures to get through, and Cyrus was so happy. I was pissed off as hell with him, but I wanted him to enjoy that happiness for a little longer. I understand that it was at the expense of *your* happiness, and I *hate* that. But I had to make a judgment call and it was the wrong one."

"No," Lilah said with a tired little sigh. "At that moment it was the right one. Gramps had put us both in a terrible position. He thought he was doing the right thing, but he should have known his pack of lies and half-truths could come tumbling down at any second. It's really a miracle you didn't figure it out before the wedding."

"I *would* have if I'd made any kind of effort to be more present, Lilah. I thought you were being so fucking delusional, with your happy wedding plans, and what I thought of as your refusal to even talk about Cyrus's illness. I thought it was just Lilah being her usual eccentric self, unable to cope with the reality of the situation. I was so fucking eager to believe the worst of the woman with whom I intended to spend the rest of my life …"

He shook his head, self-disgust evident in his eyes and on his face. "It was absolutely inexcusable. On our wedding day, your asthma attack merely served to lend credence to Cyrus's belief that you couldn't handle the truth and I just kept it to myself. I took us off on that fucking honeymoon and you didn't even have the chance to say a proper goodbye to your grandfather and I truly hate myself for that. I spoke with him a few nights before he died. It was the last time I heard his voice, and I was so angry with him for not telling you. I made him swear he would as soon as we got home. And when he died, part of me unfairly blamed you for the fact that the last words I spoke to him were recriminations."

His eyes gleamed with moisture and for the first time, Lilah caught a glimpse of how much pain Gramps's death had caused him. And that was only because he was finally allowing her to see that pain.

She reached over and gently brushed a hand over his stubbled jaw. He helplessly leaned into her touch, dislodging the tears that had welled in his eyes. One tracked down his cheek and pooled beneath her index finger.

"We were pretty much doomed from the start, huh?" she said on a whisper, and he made a soft sound of denial, his eyes blazing fiercely into hers.

"You do believe me, don't you?" he asked, an edge of desperation in his voice.

"Yes." His face went slack with relief. "Gramps put you in an impossible situation. I'm sorry for that."

"Lilah, I was always going to ask you to marry me. I believed it was inevitable."

"Ben... if none of this had happened, if Gramps hadn't been ill, if you'd come to me at some point in the future, when you finally decided I was mature enough or not flaky enough to qualify as your wife, how would you have proposed this marriage to me?"

He hesitated and she smiled, no bitterness in her expression, or in her voice when she said, "Exactly... your offer wouldn't have been what I was looking for. And I would have said no."

She leaned toward him and kissed him softly on the lips.

"Thank you for telling me all of this. I forgive you, Ben."

She picked up her glass of juice and left him sitting there, a hollow look in his eyes and pain etched on his face. She was grateful they'd had this talk. Forgiving him would go a long way towards healing her own broken and battered heart. Even the thought of co-parenting a child with him no longer seemed untenable. They could have an amicable, emotionless relationship without the specter of his lies about Cyrus coming between them.

And that relieved her.

BEN GROANED as he watched her retreat from the room. She'd forgiven him and yet she felt further away from him than ever before. This was not what he'd wanted. This was the opposite of what he'd hoped for.

Her hatred had flayed him... but her indifference? That would fucking kill him.

A tiny whimper dragged him out of his funk and he stared down at Fifi, who had her front paws endearingly perched on one of his feet as she stared up at him, a quizzical tilt to her head.

He smiled and bent to pick her up and cradle her in the crook of his arm.

"You must be hungry." Her head tilted again, at the sound of one of her favorite words; *hungry*. "Let's get your breakfast and then we can get changed and take that walk."

A head tilt in the other direction when he said "walk". She was so fucking adorable. He kissed her round little head and put her down again where she danced around his feet, eager for her food.

He got her fed and had some toast and marmalade while she ate, even though he wasn't really hungry. He kept hoping Lilah would come back downstairs but he didn't hear a peep from her for the rest of the morning. By the time he was dressed in a cargo pants, hiking boots, flannel shirt and bomber jacket, she still hadn't come down.

He hoped she didn't feel trapped in her room because of his presence, and by the time he had Fifi in her pink and black houndstooth harness coat, he hoped that she'd come out and eat something while they were gone. He hated the thought of her feeling confined to quarters because of him. If that was the case, it would probably be best if he left.

He sighed as he and Fifi traversed the steep path down to street level. It was starting to drizzle, but the shitty weather suited his mood. Fifi didn't seem to mind it either, trotting along smartly at the end of her leash, attracting stares, and smiles where ever they went. By the time they reached the steep path back up toward the house, she'd had enough and the little princess demanded to be picked up and carried the rest of the way.

Ben was a slave to her every command and tucked her under his jacket—since the rain was coming down harder now—and made his way back up to the house.

It was quiet when he let himself back into the house. They'd been gone for nearly an hour and a quick glance at the kitchen revealed no extra dishes in the sink. Only his breakfast things. He frowned, it wasn't like Lilah to skip breakfast... but he was making a concerted effort not micromanage her life or be hyper critical of the way she managed her health and well-being. That would be taking a step back from the progress he liked to think they'd made.

"Since when have you been such an eternal optimist, Ben?" he asked himself under his breath, shaking his head, laughing at his own foolishness.

Optimism was fading fast though. After their last exchange, he wasn't sure at all if there was any hope left here anymore. She'd forgiven him. She didn't seem to hate him anymore.

Those were all wins.

So why did he feel like a massive loser right now. Like he'd gambled everything in a high stakes poker game and lost.

He had nothing left to sweeten the pot. It was time for him to admit defeat and give her that divorce she wanted.

Ben and Fifi changed into more comfortable lounging clothes, him into gray sweatpants and hoodie, Fifi into a warm pink sweater. He grabbed a snack bar from the pantry, and a tough chewable treat for Fifi and they both settled down on the big living room sofa to watch some TV. Ben laying with his head on the armrest and his legs stretched out on the sofa, and crossed at the ankles.

He rarely watched television. It wasn't a favorite activity of his. He preferred to stay in motion when he was bored, or read when he was looking for entertainment. But today he was happy to just eat his snack bar and watch some horrific zombie movie.

Fifi grew tired of her snack and crept onto his chest to snooze. Ben absently played with her silky ears and felt his mind drifting, while he watched the outlandishly gruesome scenes unfold onscreen.

LILAH AWOKE from her nap feeling even more exhausted than she'd been when she'd crept under the covers a couple of hours earlier. When she got up, she was happy to discover her stomach had settled a bit and she was ravenous. Which was a good thing, since it was nearly six in the evening and she hadn't really eaten anything all day except a couple of crackers.

She yawned, donned her favorite slippers and left her room. A bloodcurdling scream made her pause halfway down the stairs. She didn't know what the hell Ben was watching but it sounded terrible. More screams and some stilted dialogues were followed by a flurry of gunfire.

Curious now, she hastened down the rest of the steps and found Ben sprawled on the sofa, fast asleep. Fifi was curled up on his chest, her head up, ears alert as she stared at Lilah, with a curled lip.

She was a nasty piece of work, but looked so damned cute in her little sweater, Lilah had to grin. Poor thing, she was trying so hard to be a badass while dressed up like the canine version of a Barbie doll.

Lilah's eyes tracked to Ben's face and her smile faded. He looked like an exhausted little boy, with his habitual frown smoothed away, jaw slack, a soft snore soughing out on every third or fourth exhalation. His lips looked soft, kissable, and she longed to run her fingers through the rumpled mess of hair and over his dark, bristled jawline.

Her fingers curled into her palms and she straightened her shoulders determinedly. This constant need to touch him was a lingering after effect of the feelings she'd once had—*still* had, really—for him. It would pass. She just had to retrain her brain. And that would take time.

She moved toward the kitchen and checked the pantry. Happy to discover she had all the ingredients for a quick *pasta aglio e olio* and salad.

She quietly went about cooking the dish, and she was soon joined by Fifi who jumped off the sofa and sat on the floor a couple of meters away, probably hoping that scraps of whatever Lilah was cooking would find its way to the floor.

Lilah lured her over with the occasional dog treat, which Fifi took with unflattering wariness, before darting away to consume it a safe distance away from Lilah. She always made her way back though, her inherent gluttony winning out over her caution.

"That smells great," Ben's voice, sleep roughened and sexy came from the direction of the slightly sunken living room, where he'd sat up on the sofa without her noticing.

"It'll be ready in five minutes, if you want to join me?"

He yawned and stretched extravagantly before getting up. He looked lithe and athletic in those gray sweatpants and Lilah's throat went dry with lust.

Yes, she found him sexy. She was going to have to give herself some slack over that. The man was hotness personified. Didn't mean she was going to act on her attraction to him… ever again. But she could admire the way those pants clung to his taut butt.

He came over to join her in the kitchen, watching her from the other side of the island, while Fifi danced around his feet, shamelessly flirting for his attention. He gave her an affectionate smile and a quiet "good girl, Feef. You're a great dancer, aren't you?". And then refocused on Lilah.

"You need me to do anything?"

"Where do you want to eat?" she asked, and he shrugged.

"The covered terrace? It's turned into a nice enough evening now that the rain has stopped and the furniture out there is likely still dry since it's not windy."

She nodded. "Want to set a couple of places on the table out there?"

He grabbed a couple of placemats, plates and utensils and immediately got to work. Lilah transferred the pasta into a serving dish, took the garlic bread from the oven and the fresh salad she'd prepared out of the fridge, putting them all on the counter for him to transport next. She carried a decanter of cold water and a couple of glasses out onto the terrace and joined him a minute later.

He was waiting for her and pulled out one of the wrought iron chairs from beneath the glass topped round table and took her hand to seat her. Lilah, accustomed to these little considerations from him, thought nothing of it, until her hand settled in his and the contact sent a buzz of adrenalin and electricity sizzling through her body. She snatched her hand back immediately and sat down self-consciously, hoping he hadn't noticed her reaction.

He said nothing, but sat down across from her. Fifi settled

beneath the table, staring up at them with sad, hungry eyes, through the glass.

"Ignore her," Ben told Lilah. "She's a little con artist. I swear, she'd do anything for a snack."

"Oh, I definitely noticed that. She even pretended to be my friend just to wheedle a couple of treats from me."

Ben smiled fondly down at the dog, before bringing his eyes back up to hers.

"You were right when you implied that I may have gotten her as an excuse to see you again."

Lilah scoffed at his words. "I didn't imply anything, Ben. I full on said it."

His lips twitched and he nodded, conceding the point. "Well, you were right. I did do that... and I didn't give any consideration to what I would do with the dog afterward. I can be selfish when it comes to shit like that in my personal life. I never consider the bigger picture. I'm always more focused on what it would take to achieve my goal right now. In business I think months ahead, *years* ahead. But I don't apply that same ethic and patience to my personal relationships."

Lilah stared at him, not saying a word.

"You know that," he breathed. "Of course you know that. You were victim to it. Fifi nearly was too... I wouldn't have allowed her to creep into my affections the way I have. She would probably have lived a life of splendid luxury and emotional neglect. But what you said really resonated with me."

"What did I say?" Lilah tried to think back to that day but drew a blank on what he could be referring to.

"The thing about not letting her become another female I promised to love only to let down in the end."

Lilah looked down at the dog again. Fifi definitely wasn't

living a life of emotional neglect. Lilah couldn't recall the last time she'd seen a dog more spoiled and loved.

"That's good." She really couldn't think of anything else to say. Lucky Fifi, at least Ben was capable of loving a dog. That boded well for the next woman who ventured into his life. Maybe he'd level up his emotional commitment and take a shot at loving a female of the human variety.

He was still staring at Lilah intently and she smoothed her hair uncomfortably, not sure why he was looking at her like that.

"Let's eat before it gets cold," she whispered, hoping to change the subject. Or at least shift his focus.

Thankfully, it worked, and his gaze dropped to his plate.

"This looks amazing," he said.

"I do know a trick or two in the kitchen," she said with a smile and he offered her a tentative smile in return.

"Tastes great," he offered when he came up for air after practically inhaling a few mouthfuls of pasta.

"I'm glad you like it," she said, eating her own meal with a great deal more caution. She was happy when it didn't threaten to come back up, but kept her own portion size small, not wanting to push her luck.

"Do you remember your parents?" he asked unexpectedly after they'd eaten mostly in silence.

"Not really. They died when I was only three. Gramps is the only parent I truly knew. He told me about my mom and dad, but they always seemed like a fairytale to me, you know? The handsome prince and princess who met and fell in love and had a little girl whom they loved to the moon and back.

"I know that I have my father's hair and smile and my mother's build and eyes. I know that they both used to sing *Sweet Child O' Mine* to me when I couldn't sleep. And I only know that because Gramps took over that duty after they died." She smiled fondly at the memory of her grandfather singing the song to her even into her teens, whenever she was sick, or had had an asthma attack. It had never failed to comfort her.

Ben took a drink of water as he considered her words, a small, fond smile on his lips as he listened to her talk.

"Sounds like Cyrus did a great job of keeping them alive for you."

"Yes, but like I said, they never seemed real to me. Gramps was my family. And later…" She hesitated, a quick spasm of pain tightening her chest, and probably reflecting in her face. "Later there was you. You were part of my family too. I cared about you. I hero worshiped you. Followed you around like a lost puppy. And eventually I had that stupid crush on you… but through it all, I only wanted the best of everything for you."

"*Why?*" He sounded genuinely baffled and almost angry. "I was a stranger. Somebody your grandfather initially dragged kicking and screaming into your home. Why the fuck were you so accepting of someone who was a rival for your grandfather's attention and affections?"

"Because, I knew Gramps loved me and just because he cared for you wouldn't make him love me less. I *was* jealous at first, I wouldn't have been human if I wasn't. But you seemed so adrift, so sad, and so angry that I quickly empathized with you. You'd lost your parents. Same as me. But while I had Gramps, you had nobody. And I thought, '*well, he doesn't have nobody. He also has Gramps and he has me. We'll be his family*'. But I was a child. I now know that it was hard for you to see us as your family, why would you? I was a pesky kid and Gramps was a stranger who'd uprooted you from everything you knew. You'd had a whole life and suddenly it was gone."

"I quickly came to appreciate what Cyrus had done for me. I was realistic enough to know that without him, I would have wound up in foster homes or more likely, on the streets. I was left with nothing. Nobody. There was no money to inherit, no life insurance policies, or fixed and liquid assets. My parents lived from pay check to pay check. They owned no property and had no savings. They loved me. I loved them. They were good people and I still miss them. But they were miserable together. They rarely spoke, not even to argue. I was the only thing they had in common. It's hard to believe in true love when you're the child of such a cold and sterile union."

He swallowed down another gulp of water and watched Fifi who—having given up on scoring any scraps from the table—was now sniffing her way around the lush garden. The entire front of the property was surrounded by frameless glass fencing to preserve the magnificent views, so Fifi was quite safe to have a wander around. Even the pool was fenced off.

"I understand," Lilah said. And she really did. Even though she had long ago reconciled herself to the idea that Ben didn't— couldn't, or wouldn't—love her, she still appreciated the insight as to why that was so. Appreciated that it wasn't something in *her* that he found inherently unlovable.

"I don't think you do, Lilah. I'm trying to tell you that—"

"I think I'm pregnant."

Her words brought whatever he'd been about to say to an abrupt halt and he stared at her in absolute shock and no small amount of horror.

Well, that was flattering.

"Shut your mouth, Ben… you're catching flies."

"Uh, but… how?"

"Really? You're asking me how? *You*? After that massive wet spot you left on the bed in the Maldives?" He went bright red at her answer and squirmed in his seat.

"I thought you said it was impossible at that stage of your cycle."

"I'm pretty sure my exact word was 'unlikely'. Nothing is ever impossible."

"So, what… how sure…?"

"I've missed a couple of periods, been nauseous, had a positive home pregnancy test result. I'm going to the gynie tomorrow to find out for sure."

"But you think it's…"

"A distinct possibility, yes," she concluded for him. He looked pale and sweaty and Lilah wasn't entirely sure what to make of his reaction. Then again, she wasn't sure how she felt about this either.

"So what happens if you are?" he asked, his eyes dropping to her stomach and she swore she could see something close to longing in that gaze.

"We co-parent?"

"Co-parent?"

"You know…? Shared custody, two homes, that kind of thing."

"That's not ideal."

"It's all we have. Millions of couples do it."

"We could live together."

"Ben, that's not a good idea."

"Why not? We could live right here. We could raise her together; we could sing *Sweet Child O' Mine* to her if she's cranky or can't sleep. We could both be there to pick her up when she falls, and praise her when she succeeds."

"And what? Be like your parents? Trapped in a cold and

sterile marriage? Together only for the sake of our child? Why would you wish that on your own child when you know how it affected you?"

"Or we could be like *your* parents."

"I don't know how my parents were. I have only stories, told to me by someone who wanted me to have the happiest memories of them. I want us to figure this out, Ben. In a way that will be best for our baby."

"Us. Together. That would be best."

"*No*, it won't. And you of all people should know that. Look, I *get* it. I understand why you don't believe in love. But I do *not* want my child raised in the same environment that you were, and I do not want him going out into the world with that same belief that romantic love doesn't exist, just because *we* set a piss poor example for him. And you shouldn't want that either. It's better if he grows up with two loving parents who are better apart than together. Parents who back each other up, and respect each other."

He shoved his way back from the table and stood up to glower down at her.

"I feel like you're fucking taking what I told you completely out of context and using it against me to back up this shitty decision about *our* kid that you already seem to have made!"

"No, that's not what I'm doing. I'm sorry if you think that. But even before you told me about them, I'd already decided that co-parenting in separate homes would be best for all of us."

"*You've* decided? I should get a damned say in this as well."

"Ben, be reasonable."

"What if I told you I love you?" he threw the question at her wildly, almost desperately and this time, Lilah was the one who gaped at him.

"Seriously? You're playing the *what if* game with me again? Why? Because naïve, stupid Lilah fell for it once before, maybe you can get away with the exact same hypothetical again? And fool me into thinking it's some kind of declaration of love?"

"Fuck." He ran a shaky hand through his hair and shook his head. "That's not what I'm doing. I *do* love you."

"Yes, I know," she said, sarcasm adding a sting to her voice. "But you're not *in* love with me. We've had this conversation before, Ben."

"No, damn it. Lilah, I *am* in love with you."

She laughed, the sound wild and hysterical, and she finally surged to her feet too, absolutely furious with him.

"Oh, my *God*, you really do think I'm an idiot, don't you? You'd say anything to get your own way. You'd even lie about something you know is deeply important to me. That's despicable, Ben. Let's continue this conversation when you find your integrity again. Because right now, you've stooped so damned low, even a snake in the grass would stand taller than you."

She tossed down her napkin and stormed off the terrace, fury lending wings to her feet.

TWENTY-SEVEN

Messy and crazy and complicated

T here were flowers in front of Lilah's bedroom door the following morning. Freshly picked, likely from the garden, they were wrapped in newspaper and propped up against the doorframe. A note was placed in between the dew dampened petals.

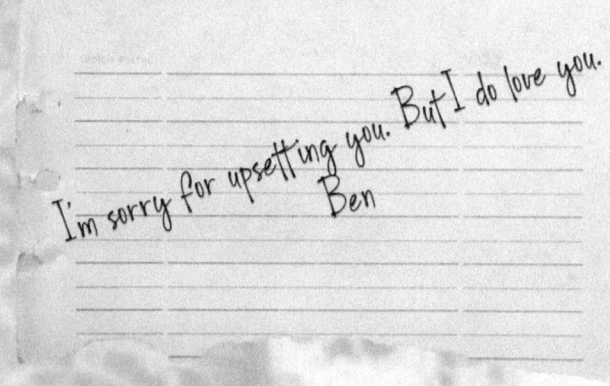

I'm sorry for upsetting you. But I do love you.
Ben

She sucked in an impatient breath. Of course, he'd be doubling down now. The foolish, stubborn man.

She crumpled up the note, and shoved it into her robe pocket and carried the flowers downstairs. The house was quiet, and she guessed he—and Fifi—must have gone to the office already. The aroma of coffee, mingled with his aftershave, lingered in the air, and she inhaled deeply, ashamed of how addictive she found the smell of him.

She found a vase for the flowers and left it on the counter.

She made herself a pot of green tea, happy that the nausea seemed to be at bay this morning. A white envelope on the kitchen counter caught her eye and she carried her mug over to the couch and sat down on one of the bar stools to stare at it. It was her letter from Gramps. On the envelope, in pencil—written in Ben's hand—was the note:

You left this at the apartment and I thought you might want it back. I didn't read it.
B

Lilah poured a cup of tea, and lifted the envelope, staring at Ben's words. He was right, she *had* regretted leaving it behind. She was happy he'd been considerate enough to save it for her. The envelope was creased and tear-stained. Lilah ran the flat of her palm over it in a futile attempt to smooth out the creases.

"Oh, Gramps," she sighed.

She took a sip of her tea and removed the letter from the envelope again and re-read it. She smiled through a haze of tears when she read:

Without you, Ben is isolated, an island a million miles from the rest of the world. Lonely, buffeted by storms and weathered by strong winds. He needs your sunshine to keep him flourishing. He doesn't know it; he thinks this is about you. But it's also about him. You're strong, loyal, loving, and you love him. You're good for him, sweet pea. You're good for each other. Ben needs someone loving and warm in his life. And you, my Lilah, need someone who will always place you above all else.

Gramps had always been such a—usually successful—schemer. So how the hell could he have been so wrong about Ben and Lilah?

They're weren't good for each other; all they did was snap and snarl and hurt each other. But God help her, she *did* love the fool man and that was her failing. Her curse. This foolish, futile love for a man who *liked* being an isolated island. And anyone who drifted too close would be smashed to pieces on the jagged rocks he'd put up to shield himself from any intruders.

But he did have a tender side, the side he kept hidden from the rest of the world. She'd seen it in the way he respected and cared for Gramps, the way he always tried to look out for her, the way he could talk her through an asthma attack. She'd seen the little considerations, like bringing drinks for her friends, ensuring his pantry and fridge were stocked with her favorite food and drinks. *Knowing* her favorite snacks and beverages when even Lilah wasn't aware that she had such clear preferences.

She thought back to his caginess when she'd asked him about the new phrase he'd used the other day. It had been an endearment; she knew that much, but she didn't think he'd been honest about the meaning

She wasn't sure of the spelling but did a quick voice search. It took three attempts before the search engine finally recognized her pronunciation as the Scottish endearment *mo chridhe* meaning *my heart.*

Her hand covered her mouth in an attempt to stifle a sob. He'd appeared shocked when she'd asked him about it, seeming not to have realized that he'd used it.

Why would he—

Her phone dinged, thankfully dragging her from her confusing thoughts, and she swiped at the screen to check the message.

> **BEN**
> What time is your appointment today?

> **ME**
> 10:30

> **BEN**
> Do you want me to come with you?

> **ME**
> No. Thanks.

He was typing and typing and typing… after nearly a minute his response floated onto the screen.

> **BEN**
> Okay

Judging from the amount of typing he'd done, and the amount of time it had taken for him to respond, Lilah guessed that there was a lot left unsaid in that one, mild *okay*.

She considered her response.

> **ME**
> I'll let you know what she says as soon as I'm done.

> **BEN**
> Thanks

Lilah didn't reply. Instead, she firmly put both text and that confusing, sweet endearment from her mind while she finished her tea.

She'd carved out half of the day for this appointment, instructing Kirby to rearrange her schedule to accommodate the shoots she had to postpone today. She'd go in to the studio to do some admin later, but she wasn't sure she'd be up to people'ing regardless of the outcome of her gynecologist appointment.

THE TEDDY BEAR was too much. Ben stared down doubtfully down at the medium-sized plush brown and gold bear he held tightly clutched in both hands and considered tossing it into the car boot. But it was too late to do that, the car was parked further down the road—it was murder finding parking in the city—and the glass door leading out to the street of the gynecologist's office swung open to reveal Lilah. She stepped out onto the sidewalk and didn't immediately notice him when the wind grabbed at her skirt and lifted her hair. She battled to keep both in check, her startled half-shriek, half-laugh snatched away by the same rude wind.

God, she was lovely. So damned beautiful… he couldn't quite believe he'd ever thought her anything less than perfect before. Her cheeks were rosy from the frigid wind blowing in off the ocean. She looked adorable in a short plaid skirt, black leggings, knee length brown leather boots, a caramel-colored ribbed crop pullover top that exposed the tight body-hugging white top she was wearing beneath it. She also wore a cute beret—that matched her skirt—tucked over her long, loose hair, and a waist length, sheepskin lined brown leather jacket.

She looked up and froze when she saw him standing there. Fifi on a leash at his feet, bear in hand. Her lips parted in surprise, but he couldn't get an accurate read on her emotions because she was wearing huge, round sunglasses.

"Ben? How did you know where to find me?"

"I asked Jackson." Her mouth thinned and her head whipped around as she looked for her driver, but Ben had dismissed the man, informing him that he—Ben—would be taking his wife home.

"Do you want to go somewhere for lunch?" he asked, and she shook her head.

"I want to go home," she told him in a not-quite-steady voice.

"Okay." He tucked the stupid bear under the same arm that held Fifi's leash and gently took hold of her elbow, gratified when she didn't flinch away from his touch. "The car's this way."

He led his unprotesting wife to the sleek, dark blue S-class Mercedes Benz he preferred to use for work. His driver Cabot—one of Jackson's men—solicitously opened doors for them. Once they were seated, Ben plonked the bear between them and propped Fifi onto his lap. She shed a lot and Ben's previously pristine five-hundred-dollar suits were often salted with short white hairs. He brushed her daily to keep her shedding to a minimum, and made liberal use of a lint roller on his suits as required, but not picking her up was never an option.

Lilah said nothing, staring out of the window for the duration of the short drive from Green Point to Bantry Bay. And Ben didn't ask, not wanting to pressure her into talking until she was ready.

The thought of a child with Lilah... the very notion stole the breath from his body. And he found himself wanting it so fucking *desperately*.

When they arrived home, she was the one who picked up the bear as she got out of the car. She went straight to the living room and sat down on one of the huge chairs, still holding the toy.

Ben removed Fifi's harness and leash and let her out, before joining Lilah in the living room on the sectional across from her. She was inspecting the bear closely.

He waited.

"It's cute," she said of the bear, the tremor in her voice now an uneven wobble. She dragged her sunglasses off and set them on a side table. When she met his eyes, Ben sucked in an anguished breath. She looked distraught and he wasn't sure what to make of that.

She tucked the bear close to her chest—as if for comfort—and shrugged.

"So it was a false alarm. No baby. The doctor thinks the missed periods are a result of stress, the nausea because of a mild tummy bug and the—uhm—the test was a false positive. I'm not pregnant."

Ben tightly entwined his fingers and let his folded hands dangle between his spread knees, his elbows on his thighs, as he fought to keep his breathing even and the debilitating agony of disappointment at bay.

"I see."

"So you're off the hook," she said, injecting forced cheer into her voice. "We both are."

"Only... I *really* wanted that baby," Ben confessed on a hoarse note. "In the last twelve hours she became so fucking real to me."

"It's probably for the best," Lilah said, and Ben could hear a disappointment that rivaled his behind the forced pragmatism. "We couldn't even figure out how we would make it work."

"We would have," he said with heartfelt confidence.

"I'm sorry, Ben. I shouldn't have told you anything until I knew for certain."

"I'm glad you told me; this isn't something you should go through alone."

"It's nothing really... not even a loss. You can't mourn something that never existed."

"You can mourn the idea of it," he said, and her face crumpled. "Oh, cupcake, come here."

He held his arms open to her and she didn't even hesitate, she got up and crossed the short distance between them, leaving the bear on the chair behind her. She crept into his lap and he held her close while she curled up against his chest and wept. He buried his face in her silky, scented hair and allowed himself to enjoy her soft, comforting warmth in his arms, sharing the pain of loss with her, wishing that their relationship was on a different trajectory. That he could start over, do things differently, and give them a real chance of success.

His admission of love last night had clearly caught her off guard and he couldn't blame her for that. Not after everything he'd put her through. It was what he deserved, really. Losing her, just as he was ready to admit the depth of his feelings for her. He'd left it too late, clinging to his stubborn pride and ignorance for no damned good reason. When he had so much to fucking lose.

"Why do you call me cupcake?" she asked in a thick voice once the storm had passed, and he'd handed her his handkerchief to help her mop up.

"I'm pretty sure you're going to hate the answer to that question," he confessed with a wry grin.

"Oh?" She lifted her head from his chest and glared him though red-rimmed eyes. Her nose was pink, her cheeks flushed and her eyes swollen. She wasn't a pretty crier, but she was still hands-down the most beautiful woman he'd ever seem. "Now you've *got* to tell me."

"Your wedding dress. It was lovely and all but it was also really damned big, sweetheart. I thought you resembled a sugary confection in it. A mouthwatering cupcake. I think it was the—uh—shape of it? Of the skirt?"

She eyed him askance, her lips pressed into a thin, unimpressed line.

"That was a bespoke Vera Wang gown, you philistine," she huffed, and he offered her an apologetic smile.

"It really *was* pretty," he appeased.

"I wanted to look like a Disney princess," she admitted. "It was a bit childish, I know. I felt like an idiot afterward, when—well—you know?"

Her voice faded miserably and he sighed—the sound weighed down with his own misery.

"I'm sorry I made you feel that way."

"I understand. It was a shock. Your fake wife suddenly blathering on about love and forever afters."

"I never once thought of you as a fake wife, Lilah. Quite the opposite."

A quiet little whine alerted them to the fact that Fifi was sitting on the couch next to them and watching them with a tilted head. Neither of them knew how long she'd been sitting there.

They both laughed, the tension broken and Lilah shifted from his lap to the couch next to him. Leaving Ben with empty arms and a bereft heart.

Fifi shocked them both by crawling into Lilah's lap and curling up for a snooze.

"Oh…" She stared at Ben with wide eyes and whispered, "What do I do?"

"Pet the brat, that's what she's after." Lilah's hands dropped to Fifi's ruff and she ran her fingers through the lush fur to be found there with a happy sigh.

Ben watched them for a moment.

"Lilah?"

"Hmm?" She looked up at him with guileless eyes and his tongue tangled in his mouth as he stared at her.

"I've been a fucking fool."

She stared, her mouth dropping open in shock. Ben, deciding that it was all or nothing right now, slid from the couch and knelt in front of her, his hands on either side of her hips. Fifi kept sleeping, even though Lilah's entire body seemed to have turned to stone.

Turned out Ben had one last thing to gamble, after all. His heart. He might as well add it to the pot, because if he lost her, she'd be taking the fucking useless thing along with her anyway.

"I wasn't able to identify the obvious truth that was staring me in the face for years. Everything I've always felt for you; fascination, attraction, impatience, confusion, anger, lust, fondness, annoyance, tenderness… it all adds up to one thing. Something I think maybe Cyrus saw, but that I didn't recognize because it was beyond the scope of my previous experience."

"What's that?"

"Love, *leannan*."

"Ben… you don't have to…"

"I've been pretty adamant that I don't want a divorce, right? That I wanted us to stay together and live the life I'd planned for us. But that gradually changed. I found myself recognizing that my vision wasn't enough. It was too limited in its scope. And I came to appreciate that what I really wanted, Lilah, was the life *you'd* envisioned for us. Not some cold, cynical arrangement but something warm and alive and vibrant and messy. Because loving you is messy and crazy and complicated."

Tears were beading her long, luscious lashes now and overflowed down her cheeks. He wiped them away clumsily, not sure what they meant. His heart was throbbing in his throat. What the fuck was going on with the damned thing? Previously so dependable, an efficient muscle doing a damned fine job, it had become unpredictable, dictating emotions and decisions.

"Last night, I made a mess of it. I know it was bad timing and I don't blame you for thinking it was because of the baby. But I *do* love you, sweetheart. Beyond all reason. You're the beat of my heart, the breath in my lungs, the blood in my veins.

"I've made so many mistakes, Lilah. I've said stupid, untrue things, deliberately designed to hurt you. You were never a disappointment to Cyrus. He was so proud of you and I couldn't understand it. I didn't know how he could be so supportive of your photography when I believed it was a waste of time and energy. I thought it was just another way of spoiling and indulging you. I'm so sorry I ever made you think, even for a second, that Cyrus wasn't proud of you.

"Then that night, after you read his letter, when I said marrying you was a small price to pay for Cyrus's happiness, I wanted to hurt you because you were threatening to leave me. I didn't want you to leave and instead of telling you that, I said the shittiest thing I could think of. All these years of accusing you of immaturity and I was the one who reverted to a sulky, cruel child when I couldn't get my way. I knew I'd hurt you and I hated myself for doing so, and yet, I couldn't fucking shut up and just tell you that I didn't want to lose you. That I loved you. That I needed you. I should have apologized right then, but I didn't. I was such a fucking spineless prick. I'm so so sorry for everything I've ever said and done to hurt you, mo chridhe. You didn't deserve it. And I know I don't deserve another chance with you.

"Especially since my mistakes aren't limited to just our marriage, they're littered throughout our relationship since the moment we met. I misjudged you. I mistreated you. I failed you.

And I honestly couldn't fault you for finally walking out on my ass, but, Lilah I truly fucking adore you. And if you leave me, you'll take the sun with you. If you'd just give me a chance…" His breath was coming in sobs now, his eyes blurred, he couldn't tell if she was reacting to his words. He feared she wasn't. That this was too little too late. And his desperation added an embarrassing tremor to his voice. "I know that right now you hate me, but I'm fucking begging you to give me another chance, *mo chridhe*. I swear to God, I would move heaven and earth to make you happy and make you love me again."

LILAH STARED up into Ben's starkly handsome face, his eyes were brimming with tears, his expression stark with fear and—yes—something that looked like love. He had no reason to lie to her about this. Not with the baby out of the picture. He had nothing to gain from saying these things, by humbling himself like this. Not even *Ben* liked winning enough to literally go onto his knees and beg. And no doubt about it, that was what he was doing. He was begging for his—*their*—marriage. For a second chance.

For her love.

For his happiness.

"Ben, I never hated you. Not really. You hurt me. You kept massive secrets from me and treated me like a child." He winced, averting his eyes, but she caught his jaw in her hand and turned his head until he was looking at her again. "I hated how you belittled me and my love for you on our wedding day. And I hated how that, combined with your deception about Gramps, made me feel. So small, stupid, and insignificant. Like a sacrificial pawn on a gameboard that only you could see. And yes, that love I thought I had for you dimmed, and lost its sheen. It couldn't flourish, Ben. Not in such a hostile environment."

"An arctic tundra," he murmured, taking her back to her ridiculous talk of love being like a plant. She was surprised he remembered that. His hands moved, before they'd merely been resting on the sofa beside her hips, but now they moved up to cup her waist. Nothing more than that. But it was contact and it burned through the layers of her clothing.

"Lilah, my *heart* was that arctic tundra," he said, his voice a low, self-conscious rumble. "It was a frozen wasteland. But you were wrong about nothing growing on a tundra, sweetheart. My love for you grew there. At first a tiny, ugly, insignificant thing. Barely breaking through the frozen surface. It was scarcely visible to the naked eye, but it was there. All it needed was your sunshine to flourish and grow, wild and beautiful and untamed. It cracked through the surface and filled all the emptiness that was there before. It bloomed into this magnificent, incredible force of nature."

"Way to turn my metaphor against me, Ben," she said, breathless, excited... starting to believe what she could see in his eyes. Wanting to believe it. Terrified of disappointment.

He sucked in a deep breath and asked, "Do you still hate me, Lilah?"

"It would be easier than loving you," she admitted with a resigned sigh. "But what I was trying to say before you schooled me on the whole arctic tundra thing, was that I never truly hated you. But I never truly loved you either. Not the way I should have. I was still on the whole fairytale princess true love's kiss thing. It was unrealistic. What I feel for you now — by comparison — is grittier, it's real, it has thorns, but it also has the most magnificent perfect blooms to counteract those thorns. There's no such thing as a perfect love, Ben. Not really... but there's the one who holds you when you're crying, the person who breathes with you when you can't breathe on your own. The crazy bastard who adopts a dog just as an excuse to see you again. There's the misguided guy who sends sad, bizarre letters when he can't reach you by email, text, or phone. The man who fucks up by marrying you for all the wrong reasons, with the very best of intentions. I love you, Ben. I've always loved you... But I've only recently learned how it feels to be *in* love with you."

He sobbed, his face contorting.

"You do? Lilah? You're sure?"

"I'm willing to take a chance on your love, if you're willing to take a chance on mine."

"Then, do you think you'd be willing to wear these again?" He fished a leather cord out of from the neck of his shirt and dangling at the bottom of the cord were her rings. She inhaled deeply and her eyes flooded.

"Oh, Ben," she whispered, choking back her tears.

"I've worn them around my neck since you left. In the hopes that one day I could convince you to wear them again." He dragged the cord up over his head and unknotted it.

Lilah held up her trembling left hand and he slipped the rings back onto her finger.

"Lilah Iris Beckett Templeton, you're the owner of my heart, the keeper of my soul, and the source of my joy and laughter. Without you, I cannot exist. With these rings, I vow to love and cherish you for the rest of my life," he promised in a voice that shook with the force of his emotions. Lilah's tears overflowed and he made a distressed sound, wiping away the moisture with gentle fingers.

"Those are some excellent vows, Ben," she said, a huge smile on her face. "Do you think we can seal them with a kiss?"

"Fuck, yes." He kissed her quickly, spontaneously, and then with more intent.

Fifi gave a startled yelped when she got squashed in the middle of the clinch and they both jumped apart guiltily, laughing when the dog gave them both an indignant glare and stalked away haughtily to her bed.

They grinned at each other, breathless, giddy, happy... and kissed again. A long, hard, hungry embrace. He was still kneeling between her now spread thighs when they came up for air and she had her arms wrapped around his neck and her fingers curled into the hair at the back of his head.

"I want to make love with you," Ben told her, after another long kiss. "Slowly, fucking thoroughly, I want to kiss every inch of you, stroke you, pet you, suck you and lick you. I want to bury my cock so deeply inside of you that you won't know where I end and you begin."

"Well, stop talking about it," she commanded him on a breathless whisper. "And do it."

He chuckled. "Jesus, you were always such a bossy little thing."

"Not bossy, I just know what I want. And right now, I want you..." Her hand skirted down his torso to find the hard ridge in his trousers. She squeezed and he made a dark, deep, sexy sound in the back of his throat. He pushed to his feet and she yelped when he hooked an arm around her waist and took her with him.

"Wrap your legs around my waist."

"Yes, boss," she responded tartly, and he slapped her on the ass, before cupping his palms over her round butt. Supporting her, while she did as he'd commanded and hooked her ankles over each other to stay in place. Her arms were still around his neck for balance. The position placed her spread pussy right on top of his groin and they both enjoyed the sensation of him rubbing up against her, as Ben easily carried her up the stairs and into her room.

He deposited her on the bed, and her arms fell away from his neck but her legs remained clamped around his waist, keeping her lower body hoisted above the mattress as he stood beside the bed. She shamelessly ground herself against him, and he braced a hand against one of her wooden bedposts to retain his balance as he thrust himself helplessly against her.

"Sweetheart, we keep this up and I'll cream in my pants."

"Hmm." The sound was throaty and her smile more than a little smug. "I don't mind that. Like a randy schoolboy coming in his pants, because he can't control himself."

"*Fuck.*" He groaned when she added a shimmy to her grind. She watched his face as he fought against his building climax and she reached up to drag her pullover and t-shirt off. It wasn't easy but she silently gave thanks to her hot yoga core exercises for giving her the strength to maintain this position. Ben was lost in sensation, his eyes shut, his forehead furrowed, mouth thin and tight as he fought to maintain control.

"Ben," she whispered, and he opened his eyes immediately, his pupils dilated when he saw her naked breasts. She smiled wickedly and toyed with her nipples.

"You're not playing fair." His voice was a broken rasp and it made her nipples harden even more.

"You could make me come with just that voice," she told him honestly, and he shuddered.

He finally brought his hands to her ankles, still locked around his waist, and managed to unhook them. Lilah pouted as her hips lowered to the mattress, thighs splayed, there was a damp spot at the crotch of his trousers and she realized that it had come from her.

"Oops, looks like I owe you a new pair of pants, Ben," she said without any real regret in her voice.

He didn't reply, but pinned her with a hot, wicked look, before unzipping her boots and tossing them aside. Next, he peeled her leggings and panties off in one motion, they were as ruined as his pants.

"You're so fucking gorgeous," he said—staring down between her spread legs in reverence. He grinned when her pussy spasmed at the sound of his voice. "Poor little pussy looks thirsty for my cock."

God, she loved how filthy her straitlaced husband was in the bedroom. It turned her on so much.

He peeled his pants down over his lean hips and then stopped.

"I'm going to use a condom, okay?" he said, surprising her. "I think we should discuss when we want to start our family later. But right now, I just want to love you."

"Okay," she whispered. "Thank you."

He bent to kiss her, and removed a condom from his *wallet* of all places.

"You kept a condom in your wallet? That was optimistic of you."

He chuckled, tossed the wallet aside, and donned the condom efficiently. "Sweetheart, I lived in hope every day for fucking months."

He planted a hand next to her head, with the other fisted around his cock, as he positioned himself for entry.

"Next time," she said in breathless wonder as he gently

pushed his way into her. "I want to kiss you and touch you and pet you."

"Fuck, yes. Anytime, *mo chridhe*. My body is yours to command."

They didn't speak much after that. Just gentle encouragements, moans, and pleas as their lovemaking started slow and soft, despite the raunchy start, and built in intensity, with Lilah reaching multiple orgasms, each peak higher than the one that came before it. By the fifth, she was exhausted and Ben, by now on his back, with her drooped over his chest, surged up into her one final time with a pained, choked groan as he came for what seemed like an eternity.

When his body finally went limp, he lay shuddering beneath her, his strong arms wrapped around her back as he held her tightly for a moment, before lifting her and depositing her next to him. He deftly removed the condom, set it aside to be discarded later, and gathered her close. Lilah gradually became aware of the fact that her skirt was still hiked up around her waist. She made a muffled sound and attempted to wriggle out of it but could barely move. Sensing her discomfort, Ben helped her shimmy it up over her breasts and head, and tossed it aside, before hugging her close again, his body heat keeping her warm.

"I love you, Lilah," he whispered into her hair, and Lilah, barely awake, smiled against his chest.

"I love you too, Ben."

"I may forget to say it sometimes," he warned, fingers trailing up and down her spine.

"M'kay."

"I never want you to think I'm not saying it because I don't love you, I'm just not used to it. It's hasn't been a part of my lexicon and I just have to practice until I get good at it."

Lilah sighed. Seriously? She wanted to slip into a sex coma and this man was over there using words like *lexicon* and wanting to have a serious discussion and shit? After the most amazing sex in the history of the world?

Seriously?

"Lilah? Did you hear me?"

So it looked like they were doing this after all. She pressed her palm onto his chest and propped her chin onto her hand to stare up at him. He smiled and smoothed her hair out of her face.

"You don't have to say it all the time, Ben. As long as I know you feel it. Never let it become a habit, something you say by rote like *fine, thanks* in response to *how are you?* Say it when you feel like you absolutely can't let another second pass without letting me know you love me."

He smiled and kissed the tip of her nose.

"I love you, Lilah. *So* fucking much." He was irresistible when he was being cute. She kissed his chest to show him her appreciation.

"And since you want to have serious discussions instead of enjoying the post-coital glow," she said. "What was all that about the condom?"

"I think we should wait before having kids."

Her eyes widened.

"Really? You were all for the whole baby thing when we got married."

"But that was when I thought I could make you happy by giving you babies to keep you occupied and content."

"Are you shitting me?" she asked, raising her head as she glared at him indignantly.

"I was an arsehole and a moron," he said with a placating pat on her back.

"And sexist as hell."

"Yes," he agreed. "But if you concur, I think we should wait. Spend time with each other, enjoy one another. And when we're both ready to share our lives, and our love, with someone other than a spoiled Chihuahua, we should have a baby. What do you think?"

He was right and honestly, after the whole maybe-pregnancy scare, she wasn't sure she was ready to be a mother yet. She would have loved that baby, and given him everything he needed, but a part of her had regretted possibly having to take another hiatus from her business, just when she had it up and running again, and she'd felt too young and unprepared for motherhood.

"I agree." She settled down on her chest again. "I don't deserve you, you know? I'm the one getting the better end of the deal here. I hope to hell one day you don't look at me and wonder why the fuck you're married to such an undeserving prick."

Lilah sighed and shook her head.

"Not gonna happen. You're a farewell present to me from Gramps and vice versa. And not one I'm thinking of ever re-gifting."

"What?" He sounded baffled and, remembering that he hadn't read Gramps's letter, Lilah climbed on top of him, and straddled his broad chest—ignoring the spark of desire in his eyes—to lean over and open her side table drawer, where she kept Gramps's letter.

"I think you should read this," she said, after curling up next to him again. He stared at the envelope for a long moment, before —with clear reluctance—tugging it from her hand.

"Are you sure?" he asked, his voice quiet and hesitant.

"Yes."

His throat moved as he swallowed and she held the envelope for him as he tugged the letter free.

She didn't watch him as he read it, keeping her head on his chest, but she could hear his uneven breathing, the unsteady beat of his heart, and eventually the quiet rustling of the paper when he refolded the letter.

"Jesus. I don't—" The choked words died in his throat and she finally lifted her head to look at him. "I don't know what I did to deserve that man in my life. To deserve either of you. But I'm so damned grateful for the both of you."

His face was wet with tears, his expression somewhere between awed and devastated.

"He knew all along." His voice was reverent and shaky and Lilah smiled.

"Gramps was a wily old guy."

"He was right, about me needing your sunshine—I've often thought it myself—I don't think I'm able to function without you anymore, Lilah. You've fucking ruined me."

"Nah, I've improved you."

He chuckled, the sound rusty and joyful.

"Can't argue with that. You have improved me. And Cyrus knew you would."

"You've improved me too, Ben."

"I doubt that, cupcake, it's hard to improve upon perfection."

She laughed outright at that. "You're on a love and sex high right now, Ben. Be careful what you say, because my ego won't let you forget any of it. Now, for the love of God, Benjamin, can we please have a nap? You've worn me out."

"Yes, but Lilah?"

She sighed dramatically and lifted her head again. "*Whaaat?*"

"I really fucking love you."

Epilogue

ONE YEAR AND SIX MONTHS LATER

"I'm *really* nervous," Lilah told Ben, smoothing her damp palms down her skirt as she surveyed the gathered crowd of people milling just below the elevated podium.

"You've got this, cupcake. Everybody is having a good time; they're excited to be here. One short speech and you can have that glass of champagne you've been dying for, kick off your shoes and join your friends for whatever unruly shit you girls get up to when I'm not looking."

"Join *who*?" she asked with a confused tilt of her head and he glared at her.

"No."

"I don't know what you're talking about." She blinked at him in wide-eyed confusion. "What girls?"

"Oh, for fuck's sake, you're such a child sometimes. Join your *hoes*, okay?"

She chuckled and went onto her toes to kiss him.

"But you're so cute when you get all disgruntled, Ben." He pressed his palm into the small of her back and dragged her closer to give her a proper kiss. Somewhere in the distance, her *hoes* howled in delight.

"Stop that," she whispered, scandalized. "That would be okay with just our friends around, but there are all kinds of stuffy suits here today too. And I want to impress them."

"They'll be impressed with you, Lilah. They won't be able to help themselves, you're an impressive woman. A fucking force of nature. Just *look* at what you've done." He waved his arm over the gathered crowd, and further than that. The sprawling, three-mile-long park, complete with jogging trail, dog-friendly facilities, several man-made ponds and water features. They—and a few hundred workers—had planted thousands of indigenous shrubs, fully-matured trees and endangered fynbos. It was her—and the *hoes'*—pride and joy. A year-long project drenched in their blood, sweat, and tears.

The *Cyrus Beckett Nature Park*, situated in the southern suburbs at the foot of the mountain, easily accessible to people from all walks of life, was opening today. In the middle of November, on a perfect mid-spring day. Her opening speech—during which she would announce the foundation she'd started in Gramps's name— would be followed by an open-air concert. They had food trucks, face painting, activities for kids and dogs. Everyone was welcome and there were already thousands of people in attendance.

Ben squeezed her hand and gave her another kiss, before giving her a gentle push toward the microphone at the center of the stage.

"Good afternoon, everyone, my name is Lilah Beckett-Templeton and I'd like to thank everyone for coming today. As some of you may know, this park is dedicated to the memory of my grandfather, a wonderful humanitarian, a great lover of nature, and just one of the kindest souls to ever walk the face of the planet. He would have loved this place, and every corner of it was designed with him in mind." She spoke for a few more minutes about Gramps, and joked about some of the failed nature walks he'd taken her on. The crowd was friendly, cheering in the right places, nodding sympathetically in others, and she was relaxed and happy by the time she announced the foundation.

"So I'd like to think of this park as the first project of many. We have plans to create green spaces all over the Cape. We would like to involve schools, communities, families... our gardens will be for everyone to enjoy. It will educate children and elders alike. I hope it will serve in some small way to heal fractured communities. These may sound like big dreams, but I believe that we can build some amazing spaces, and take back some of the places crime and poverty and desperation have stolen from so many people. I thank you for listening. Have an amazing evening. And enjoy the concert."

She was so breathless and relieved to be done that she barely heard the cheers and applause as she blindly stepped back from the mic.

Ben hooked an arm around her shoulders and steered her back to the stage, where people were still clapping and stomping their feet.

"Soak it up for a second," he murmured into her ear. "All of this is possible because of your vision. And Cyrus's foundation is going to be a massive success with you at the helm. I'm proud of you. He would be too."

She smiled shyly and waved at the crowd, before giving Ben's waist a squeeze, mutely pleading to be released from the spotlight. He chuckled and led her away, stealing another kiss backstage.

He hugged her close, kissing the top of her head.

"You look so pretty today, I could eat you up with a spoon," he muttered, and she laughed and placed her hand in the middle of his chest to give him a little push. She was wearing a simple, pink slip dress, with a denim jacket and ankle boots.

"You look pretty hot too," she said, and admired the snug fit of his blue jeans and white t-shirt.

"C'mon, let's get you that promised glass of champagne and rescue Blake from my little diva princess."

Fifi had become a million times more insufferably entitled in the eighteen months since Ben had adopted her. She and Lilah at least got along now, but Ben was still her preferred person. She merely tolerated the *hoes*, Blake, and Rhys. And full on despised anyone else outside of their small intimate circle of friends.

"I'm going to have to take a rain check on that champagne," Lilah said as she hooked her arm through his and he led her through the milling crowd. Smiling every so often and accepting congratulations as they walked along.

"Hmm? Why? You're not ready to celebrate yet? You can allow yourself to relax, *mo chridhe*. The park is a success. The foundation has been launched. You can give yourself a little break. You've been running yourself ragged these last few months."

"I'm ready to celebrate… with some alcohol-free beverage."

He stopped dead and turned to face her, his eyes boring into hers.

"What are you saying? Exactly? Spell it out for your not-too-bright husband."

She went up onto her toes, wrapped her arms around his neck and whispered it into his ear.

He froze and stared at her in shock.

"What?"

"You heard me."

"Already? We only just decided a couple of months ago."

"Already," she said. "My gynecologist confirmed it this morning. Just over five weeks along. So I don't want to tell anyone yet. But yes, we're pregnant."

"We're pr—" He bent double and propped his hands on his knees.

"Are you okay?" she asked with a slight laugh, placing her palm on his back and patting soothingly.

"Fine. Just having a difficult time, uh… breathing is all."

"Okay, babe…" she murmured. "You're okay, breathe with me. That's right. In. Out. Nice deep breaths. Better?"

"Fuck me," he whispered, staring up at her in awe. "We're pregnant."

"Yes."

"*Fuuuck* me."

"I already have, Ben. That's what got us into this situation in the first place." He laughed sounding a little hysterical.

"Oh. She's got jokes," he quipped weakly, standing upright again, and engulfing her into a huge hug, lifting her off her feet in the process. "This is fantastic news, Lilah. You're amazing and I love you so fucking much."

"You okay now?"

"I will be, as long as you just breathe with me."

The End